BELLE

—————

UNBOWED NOVELS, #1

LIZ MELDON

ACKNOWLEDGMENTS

Thank you to my fantastic beta reader Amanda for all your love, support, and passion. You always let me know if I'm on the right track. I'd be lost without you. Shout-out to my phenomenal proofreader Phoenix, for catching my errors with poise and tact, and offering a point of view that always makes me stop and think.

Much love to my author besties group, my sun and stars, and my parents for being incredibly supportive of this journey. A huge shout-out to the amazing #bookstagram community for all your love and support! Last, and certainly not least, a great many thanks to my readers. Without you, there's nothing but me and my imagination.

Cover art courtesy of the amazing Daqri at Covers by Combs.

FEBRUARY

BELLE: PART 1

Belle

I'm terrified.

I've never done this before—two months on a private island, isolated from the rest of the world, just me and my new client.

A client who wants my unwavering submission.

What if I'm a horrible submissive? What if I fail?

Worst of all—what if I fall for the man I know I can't have?

Protect your heart, Belle, I tell myself. Protect it when he smiles at you, kisses you, binds you. Don't let Dean Donahue have it, as tempted as you are to surrender it.

Because escorts don't get fairy tale endings. We get paid.

Dean

I've wanted her from the first moment I saw her.

Belle Bennet, escort. Darling Belle, sweet girl, on her

knees, bound and gagged, writhing in pleasure—or pain. The choice is mine.

She is mine. Perfect in her naivety, she's the submissive I've been waiting my whole life to claim.

And for the next two months, I intend to have her—mind, body, and soul—any damn way I see fit.

The Unbowed series is made up of duet standalone romances featuring escorts and the rich, alpha men who love them. It contains steamy content, including consensual kink, and may not be suitable for all readers.

1

BELLE

"*H*ow would you like me to fuck you, baby?"

Oh god. I pressed my lips together, trying not to smile incredulously; it took everything I had in me not to snort in this very drunk, very sweaty gentleman's face. Candace had a whole mountain of rules for her associates to follow—and not laughing was one of them. Demure chuckles and a bad case of the giggles could be absolutely fine, depending on the situation.

But you didn't laugh *at* Elysium's patrons—ever.

The whole purpose of this underground kink haven was that our clients and their guests could feel comfortable in their sexuality. Let their freak flag fly—all that. To be laughed at... Well, it kind of killed the mood, and was very much an affront to the club's ethos.

Still, this guy had no chance of getting anywhere near me. Not tonight, two minutes out from closing time, and not ever, if I had my way.

Always the professional, I slapped on a charmed

hundred-watt smile and tipped my head to the side, making sure to flip my blonde curls. The art of distraction—most of us knew how to employ it effectively. His glazed-over stare tracked the curls. Both of us leaned against the top-floor bar, the one at the back usually only frequented by employees in need of a drink. I had a water pending; many went for something harder to get them through a shift.

Thankfully, I'd never needed alcohol to survive a night at Elysium.

Unlike many in the sex industry, I actually enjoyed my job.

Though I enjoyed it a little less with this guy's rank breath huffing in my face.

"Water for the lady."

Cue my knight in shining armor: Dan—twenty-six, part-time bartender, full-time law student at NYU—appeared right when I needed him. He set my enormous glass of water on the bartop, a straw bobbing between the dozen ice cubes, and then offered my gentleman caller a similar hundred-watt smile. To his credit, Dan's smile seemed just as distracting as my hair flip, and I couldn't blame the guy for taking notice. Dan Hill was model material; he'd done that part-time before Candace's recruiting team scouted him. When he realized he could make triple what most minimum wagers earned in a week by working a few nights at Elysium, he'd signed his soul away on the dotted line, just like all the rest of us.

Children of Hades.

It was what the associates went by, keeping on theme with Elysium's Greek mythology paradise schtick. Live out your wildest fantasies. Enter a judgement-free zone, where *you* are lord and master of all you survey. Let the children of the darkness cater to your every whim.

You know—standard marketing stuff.

Children of Hades, while ridiculous, sounded a lot better than *escorts*—or, more specifically, *fetish* escorts, which was what we all were.

"Victor, my man," Dan said, leaning over the bar and clapping the drunk on the shoulder. "Can I call you a cab? We're thirty seconds away from closing shop."

Victor, in his rumpled suit that likely cost more than my rent, pointed at me. "But I—"

"Belle's spoken for," Dan insisted as I discreetly grabbed my drink and backed away while he had Victor's full attention. "But I know a fetching creature named Jade who'd be happy to wait with you until your car arrives."

I wrapped my lips around the straw and sucked, guzzling down nearly half the glass of freezing water as Dan sold Victor on Jade—Jade, whose sole job was to wait with patrons for cabs. She wasn't just happy to do it—that was literally what she did all night, from open to close.

Better than bathroom duty.

Or cleanup duty, I guess.

When Dan's gaze met mine over Victor's shoulder, I mouthed my thanks, cheeks warming when the bartender shot me a wink before refocusing on getting Victor out. By now, he'd probably forgotten all about me, especially when there was someone ready, willing, and able to put up with what was bound to be some very sloppy groping—until the car showed up, anyway.

Mind you, Jade was known for occasionally hopping in the last car of the night, bumping up her earnings a few hundred dollars by spending the rest of the morning with a lucky patron. It wasn't unheard of for the Children of Hades —guh, that *name* always got me—to go home with the men, women, and couples who frequented our fetish club, an underground den of sin beneath owner Candace's Fifth Avenue fashion boutique, but that wasn't for me. I didn't do meet-ups either; I liked seeing all my faithful clients *here*, in the safety of the club, where there were rules, regulations, fines, and beefy bouncers.

Well, I *hadn't* done meet-ups—until six months ago.

When I'd agreed to go away with a new client. Out of the country. Couriered by private jet to his private island for two whole months.

Just him and me and the Caribbean Sea.

Anxiety skittered through me, leaving my hands cold and my mouth dry, and I took another much-needed gulp of ice water, hating the way my heartbeat spiked just thinking about it. I'd had six months to prepare for this. I'd gone out with the client in question—Dean Donahue: thirty, Dominant, one-third owner of the Donahue real estate and hotel empire, billionaire in his own right—twice a month for coffee dates since all this had started. Candace called it a trial period, a courtship; she didn't like sending any of her associates away with clients unless both parties were one hundred percent comfortable. It was the same for every escort who accepted a job outside of the city. The courtship differed from couple to couple, but the purpose was clear: to get to know the person you'd be spending a ridiculous amount of time with—for money.

And I liked Dean. Given his wealth, status, and panty-melting good looks, I had gone into all this expecting the guy to be a snobby jerk. He wasn't. He seemed like a genuinely nice guy. Dominant personality, sure, but that came with the territory.

Still, our plane left tomorrow—oh, *today*, technically, at noon. My suitcases had been sitting by the front door of my studio apartment since yesterday—and the nerves had plagued me since last week. I couldn't shake them, no matter how many pep talks I gave myself in the mirror, or how many times I smiled and nodded when coworkers told me how *lucky* I was.

I just...

It was scary. I wasn't too proud to admit it. I was scared. Two months as a near stranger's submissive?

Scary.

I let out a soft breath as the lights around Elysium turned up, switching from their dimmed setting to something much brighter. 3 AM—we were officially closed. When I had first started working here a year ago, I'd hated this time of night. Nothing said *sleazy sex dungeon* like lifting the mood light to reveal every seedy nook and cranny.

In time, however, I had started to look forward to the place brightening up. No longer sleazy, no longer seedy, Elysium had become my home. I liked seeing her after a long night, standing strong as ever, memories of the full booths, the occupied playrooms, and the illuminated center stage on the lower level making me feel—whole.

It was ridiculous—I knew that. Feeling whole and complete, like a well-rounded person, even though I worked six nights a week in a fetish club.

But I loved it. The people, my escort family. The clients, the joy they got out of what we provided. The atmosphere. The costumes. The excitement. The thrill of each new night, of limitless possibilities.

The judgement-free kink.

3 AM. The curtain closed. The lights came up. The actors could become themselves again.

Stabbing my straw into the big chunks of ice in my cup, I scanned the second floor for a familiar face. The cleanup crew had already begun to make their rounds, wiping down the red-leather half-moon booths that lined the walls up here. More lights flickered on, bright, giving the corridors that branched off from the main socializing arena a sterile look. Beyond, down the hallways, I knew the playrooms would be getting a thorough once-over, every surface, every toy, sanitized within an inch of its life and put back, ready for tomorrow's performance.

While I was free to go, I couldn't bring myself to leave. Although—I crouched down to undo the straps of my six-inch stilettos, stepping out of each shoe with a moan. Another thing I loved about the lights coming up: I could finally take off my shoes. When I had first started here, I'd been doing strictly foot-fetish work in the playrooms, and I hadn't needed to wear heels. Sure, some clients requested them, but that was for a *maximum* of two hours per client. The rest of the time, I usually swanned around Elysium either barefoot or in pillowy slippers, and then got to spoil myself with weekly spa treatments on the company dime.

However, once I'd started dabbling in the Dom-sub scene, officially both a foot girl behind closed doors *and* a submissive performer on the grand stage, heels came with the territory. They were no less comfortable now than they'd been when I first shoved my pampered feet into them seven months ago.

Drink in one hand, shoes in the other, I drifted toward the employee lounge with a sigh. Behind the black door with *Children of Hades Only* embossed across it in gold lettering, next to Dan's bar, we had a huge locker room equipped with showers and washer-dryers. I shuffled along slowly, slurping the last of my water, not wanting to go in there—not wanting to put my everyday clothes back on, not wanting to go home.

Not wanting tomorrow to come just yet, even though it already had.

Mercifully, a familiar face *finally* caught my attention. What was supposed to be one last quick glance over my shoulder showed me Penny—twenty-eight, full-time kink escort, Elysium Domme—leaning against the railing near one of the booths, her heavy-lidded gaze cast down to the level below, a tumbler of scotch in hand. The upper floor had a giant cut-out in the center, opening to reveal the lower-level stage, cage, and dance area, permitting voyeurs to take in the shows.

After leaving my spiky shoes next to the bar, I padded over to Penny and sidled right up beside her, nudging her voluptuous hips with my own, all the while pointedly ignoring the steep drop between this floor and the one below. The bump seemed to jolt her out of whatever thought had forced those crimson lips into a frown, and she straightened, her entire being seeming to lift when she looked up at me.

"Hey, babydoll." She smoothed a hand over her raven locks, not a single hair out of place, and gave me the customary Penny once-over. "How's that ass?"

My cheeks burned at the thought, and I swatted her away when she leaned over to check.

"It's *fine*," I assured her, though it did suddenly smart a little, as if startled to be back in the presence of the woman who had beat on it mercilessly three hours earlier. Penny lingered, nonplussed by my attempts to squirm away, and pulled at the lace fringe of my little lingerie boyshorts.

Three nights a week, I did a public scene with one of the professional Doms at Elysium. As per our request, Candace usually scheduled Penny and me together—and it worked out for us just fine. Not only were we best friends, but we paired well together for the patrons. Yin and yang. Angel and demon. Teacher and student. Dominant and submissive. Penny was the exotic counterpart to my innocent girl-next-door look. While I had to spend an hour before each shift curling my long, thick blonde hair, she could slick her black waves up in a high pony and call it a day. My makeup was light: pinks, creams, taupe—a lot of blush and concealer. Penny always rocked a wicked cat-eye and a bold lip.

We were a dynamic duo. When I'd first made the tentative step into the submissive arena at Elysium, curious about exploring the lifestyle that had been a secret guilty pleasure of mine since I read my first spanking scene in an old romance paperback, *and* keen for a pay raise, Penny was the only one I trusted to guide me. Teach me. Train me—at least enough to please a crowd. Pleasing an individual Dom was different, she had always insisted, but playing it up for an audience was easy. Do as you're told. Squeal. *Be* your character.

Tonight had been the old angel and demon routine—and the demon was doing the punishing. Dressed in identical corset and lingerie getups, Penny had been the demon in black, I'd been the angel in white. *Woe is me*: I'd been captured by a terrible Mistress, and my stubborn self-righteousness had gotten me in trouble for the last time!

Honestly, the crap the production guys come up with.

I'd had to crawl around the stage, ball gag and all, while she flogged me—gentler than she would have with anyone else—for the eager crowd. We then finished our performance with a light paddling over a lucky patron's knee. My screams had been for show at first, but eventually it'd started to sting a little—and then my noises had been one hundred percent authentic.

"Huh." Penny went back to leaning against the railing, her scotch jostling around inside her glass. "Maybe I shouldn't have marked you up before your big debut."

"It's fine," I told her with a grin. "I've got lotion at home. Is it...bad?"

"Bit red," Penny checked one last time, "but it'll be gone by the time Dean sees it."

Speaking of red; my cheeks burned bright at the implication, and I forced myself to take a breath, fiddling with my straw. In my peripheral, I noticed Penny swirl her drink, head tipped to the side as she studied me.

"So, big day today," she said softly. "How are you feeling?"

Terrified. I bit the inside of my cheek, staring at the ice in my glass like it was the most fascinating thing I'd ever seen. Penny sighed, then downed the entirety of her scotch in a single gulp. Setting the crystal tumbler aside on the flat, dark wood railing, she ducked down to take off her shoes— the same pair as mine, only in black and red instead of white and pink. Seconds later we were the same height again.

"Belle?"

"Pen, do you think I'm making a mistake?" I winced. The question had tumbled out before I could stop it.

"Belle." She angled herself toward me, leaning an elbow on the railing, and played with one of my curls. "You are about to earn more in two months than what a lot of people, no, the *majority* of the people in this country make in a year."

Two hundred fifty thousand dollars, excluding Candace's cut.

Two months of being Dean Donahue's submissive, six days a week, twenty-four hours a day—and my bank account would increase by almost 250K. I should have been bouncing off the walls. Twenty-three-year-olds everywhere could only *dream* of that kind of paycheck.

I had balked at the number initially, back at the first liaison between me, Candace, Dean, and both of their lawyers. When the company lawyer said the number out loud during our first meeting, I had cackled—straight up crazy-witch *cackled*. It had been mortifying, but after Candace broke down how much work I'd be putting in, the hours, the physicality of it all, I could swallow it better.

Even now, t-minus nine hours before kickoff time, I was still working on accepting it—the money, the sheer magnitude of what I was about to do.

Sure, going to an island paradise with a hot guy for two months sounded great in theory—but I wouldn't belong to myself, except on Sundays. The rest of the time, I belonged to Dean Donahue, hence my steep, carefully negotiated price tag.

"I know," I managed, hating that I sounded so weak, so unsure, so—*young*, "but—"

"It's okay to be nervous," Penny insisted. "This is kind of a hardcore thing—and you're not really hardcore yet. Which is *fine*," she added hastily. "I mean, I was surprised, at first, that Candace even okayed all this, but then I learned it was with Donahue."

"Yeah?"

"Honey, I would have said something if it was anyone else." She stopped fiddling with my curl, her hand moving to her heavily cinched-in waist. God, her boobs looked great in that corset. Despite my interest in the conversation, I briefly looked down at *my* cleavage, wondering if it looked as great as hers, then shook my head and refocused as she carried on. "Dean's a good Dom. He's been coming to

Elysium for the last, what, five years whenever he's in New York. I've played with him in scenes before. He was fantastic with every sub, even the ones who sucked ass. And not literally sucked ass, but just *sucked*. Like. Awful enough as a submissive that I had Candace move her back to shot girl."

When her ruthless smile surfaced, the smile that everyone else balked at but I found endearing, I forced a laugh. Ha-ha—*awful* submissive. *Ha*. Never mind that one of my biggest concerns was failing miserably as Dean's sub. I'd only been a stage submissive for about three weeks before he put in this crazy request for a two-month getaway, and while I'd learned a lot from Penny in the six months that followed, I wasn't great. Passable. I could follow instructions—but what if I too sucked ass? After all these months of coffee dates and meetings with the lawyers and back-and-forth conversations about our limits... What if I just sucked as his submissive?

What if I ruined everything? What if, in the end, I wasn't really what he wanted?

"I mean, you already went over all your hard and soft limits," Penny said, seeming not to notice that my mind had gone elsewhere as she examined her manicured black French tips, perfectly plucked brows slightly furrowed. "You have a rundown of most of the big play sessions, which, personally, I think kind of takes some of the fun out of it— knowing exactly what he wants to do."

I bit the insides of both cheeks this time to hide the burn. Yup, I knew exactly what Dean Donahue wanted to do to me—and knowing hadn't taken the pressure off in the slightest.

Nor did it turn me on any less, no matter how many times I read over the dossier his and Candace's legal team had put together.

"You've got the contract," Penny sighed, still fussing over her nails, "and you have your daily check-ins with the office, and you have safety procedures in place. I'm not really sure what else there is to worry about."

"Yeah," I said weakly. "Right. I don't know what I'm freaking out about."

Not only was it stipulated in my contract that I needed to call the home office daily at a specific time to confirm that Dean hadn't murdered me, but Candace would have a two-man team stationed on Saint Thomas just in case I needed to get out of there in a hurry. Sure, they'd still have to take a boat to reach Dean's island, but it *did* make me breathe a little easier knowing I had people in the region.

"Hey." One of those French-manicured fingers lifted my chin, forcing me to meet Penny's gaze. "It's okay to be nervous."

"You said that already."

"I think it's worth repeating," she told me with a grin. Then, in a very un-Penny-like fashion, she pulled me into a hug, our hiked-up boobs crushed against one another beneath our rigid corsets. "You're going to be fine, Belle," she whispered in my ear, and I squeezed her just a little tighter, my eyes prickling with tears. "Seriously. I'm a phone call away if you need to talk."

We broke apart at the sound of other associates meandering toward the employee lounge door, and I wiped under my eyes with a sniffle, refusing to let a single tear fall. Still, I couldn't help but feel touched: Penny didn't Mama Bear anyone here but me. In fact, her reputation around Elysium was that she had been here forever and suffered no fools. I had been, and still was, a fool when it came to our job, but she had been ceaselessly patient with me—right from the moment I'd sat down next to her at a human sexuality seminar my final year at NYU.

Fat load of good my honors specialization in psychology was doing me now, but it was thanks to Penny, the dominatrix extraordinaire who had lured me into the darkness, that my student loans had been paid in full just one year later. Being debt-free courtesy of kink was pretty awesome, and, given I had exactly zero idea of what I wanted to do as a Real Adult, I figured another year or two at Elysium would give me *more* than enough financial cushion while I eventually figured it out.

"Okay, well…" I trailed off at the point-and-whispers of the others as they breezed by Pen and me. By now, I ought to be used to it. A lot of the more experienced associates in the bondage and discipline arena would have *killed* to be Dean Donahue's girl for the next two months. They'd been talking about me ever since negotiations first started.

Penny stared a few down for me, her glare withering enough to send the peanut gallery scampering.

"I should change and probably try to get some sleep before…everything," I finished lamely. Honestly, I *was* looking forward to the adventure, to the prospect of a tropical paradise in the middle of this awful east coast winter. Why did I feel so petrified—and just how obvious did it read on my face?

"I'll come with," Penny said without missing a beat. She linked our arms together and pulled me away from the edge of the balcony. "We can undo each other's corsets."

My wry grin bloomed into a full-blown smile, paired with outraged laughter, when she smacked my butt.

Only at Elysium.

HOUSE RULE #4

Belle will refer to Dean Donahue as Sir at all times.

2

DEAN

*W*as there anyone else on the fucking planet more pathetic than me right now?

There I was, sitting in a six-thousand-dollar suit, in the back of a stretch limo. Engine running. Heat on. *Inside*, while bundled-up pedestrians shuffled by on a bitterly cold February morning in Manhattan. Bathed in Lady Fortune's good graces, waiting for the most stunning creature on this whole damn island to join me, with two blissful months of clear blue waters, unfettered sunshine, idyllic solitude, and daily games of dominance and submission ahead of us— and I couldn't stop thinking about plane crash statistics.

How many there had been this year already.

How many there had been *last* year.

The year before that.

How many survivors.

How many fatalities.

How many died on impact—how many died hours later in the water. Hypothermia. Sharks. Exhaustion. *Drowning*.

Once, eons ago, a therapist had told me to face my fears: research the actual statistics. Immersion therapy. Drown myself in *numbers*. Well, all that quack had managed to do was feed the beast. Now, every time I prepared to board my private jet, I had facts and stats racing through my head. No matter how long the flight. No matter where I was headed.

How many died. How many survived. How often. Causes, risk factors—pilot error.

Really. What a fucking nightmare.

I could have popped open one of the champagne bottles in the cooler, maybe even dipped into the whiskey, but I'd learned many nuggets of information these last few months on our coffee dates—and Belle wasn't much of a drinker. Not unless she *had* to for a private function, and even then, she nursed a single glass of champagne all night. I didn't want to make her uncomfortable, nor did the thought of our first real interaction as Dominant and submissive being tainted by the scent of booze sit well with me. So, the limo's little bar remained untouched. Bottles unopened—though tempting.

My doctor had prescribed me exceptional knockout pills for some of my longer flights. The nonstop flight from New York to Saint Thomas would only take us four hours, maybe a touch over, depending on wind speed. I had no intention of being a groggy, incoherent twat for the duration of that either—not when I had something special planned for Belle midflight.

I was just going to have to get over this. Someday. Terrified of flying; I was the family joke come vacation season and had been since childhood.

Taking a deep breath, I sat up straighter, locking my phone and slipping it in the pocket of my suit jacket. *You are Dean fucking Donahue.* I had built a name for myself outside of my family's reputation—I could get on my own private jet with my submissive, for fuck's sake.

A quick check of my Breguet wristwatch told me she ought to be strolling along—now. In the corner of my eye, the door to her building swung open, and my driver hopped out, hurrying around the front of the car, sliding a little on the icy pavement, to deal with her luggage. I smoothed a hand over my hair, checking my teeth in the tinted window's reflection, then scooted along the back bench of the limo to the door.

"Thank you," I heard her saying as both my driver and the building's doorman struggled with her enormous pink suitcases. Door open, I sat there for a moment, only mildly intimidated at the thought of juggling those *and* my own bags after the flight; once we reached Saint Thomas, the hired help was gone. Beyond a weekly grocery delivery straight to my island and a biweekly house cleaning, I had no intention of sullying the vacation I had been lusting after —literally *drooling* over—for the last six months by spoiling the mood with outsiders.

With people who didn't understand what we were doing —what I wanted. Needed. *Craved*.

I got enough of that in my personal life.

And after six of the most miserable months of my professional career, I had a right to vacation *my* way.

"They aren't too heavy, are they?" Belle asked, still hovering by the doorway, her full mouth dipped in a concerned frown. Christ, those mammoth Chanel suitcases *looked* heavy as fuck—but I'd carry them like they were nothing when we were alone.

Because that was what a good Dom did. He carried the weight, the burden, the baggage of his submissive like it was nothing.

And he never complained—a notion utterly lost on wannabes. I honestly couldn't count the number of whiny, self-indulgent Neanderthals I'd met over the years desperate to become Doms just so they could take their emotional shit out on someone else. Pathetic.

The *gift* of submission...

Well, wannabes would never understand it.

"Not to worry, Belle," I insisted as I climbed out of the limo, pleased to find the sidewalk curb cleared of snow. "I'm sure they're just fine—right, boys?"

"Yes, sir, Mr. Donahue," my driver remarked. The suitcase thudded noisily as it clunked from curb to street, and I noticed him wince before looking to me. I lifted an eyebrow. *Don't damage anything. Oh, and good luck getting those in the trunk.*

As he and the doorman wrestled with the logistics of fitting all our baggage in one place, I smoothed a hand down my suit jacket. Belle stood fiddling with her fingers, brow still creased with worry as she watched her suitcases. Her distraction allowed me a moment to take her in, to peruse her figure from bottom to top in that lazy, possessive sort of way that always made her blush.

Brown leather boots clung to her slim yet firm legs, stopping at the knee. Beige stockings carried on from there, guiding my gaze up to the ballerina skirt, which stopped mid-thigh. I swallowed hard; I would very much like to see her twirl in that skirt.

While not suitable for a New York winter, her thin grey jacket would do her just fine until we reached the jet, though when I noticed her starting to shiver a little, I sprang into action.

"Belle," I said, striding toward her—noticing the way she flinched and immediately faced me. Her frown vanished, and by the time I swooped down to press a quick peck to her rosy cheek, she wore the smile that had first caught my eye on Candace Clemonte's extensive registry. Belle had such a beautiful smile. Warm. Natural. What I liked most was that it didn't try to sell me anything—it was so very *genuine*.

Logic that I realized was flawed. Escorts were never one hundred percent authentic with their clients. I wasn't foolish enough to think she put no effort into the way she looked at me, into the way we looked at each other. Still, I had a decent understanding of who she was as a person, beneath the pink gloss and warm smile. She was too new to the game to craft a convincing persona; it was one of the reasons, one of the many, why I'd chosen her.

Fought for her.

Candace hadn't wanted to let her go. The owner of Elysium and every escort working within it had wanted to take more time—*train* her better. I wanted her just as she was: perky, bubbly, sweet, authentic.

"Come along." I motioned toward the open back door of the limo. "Let's get you out of the cold."

She moved without hesitation, not shying away when my hand fell to the small of her back as I escorted her across the six feet of sidewalk. Her ponytail bounced with each step, and I imagined how it would move with my fist wrapped around its base. I inhaled sharply: she had tied a pink satin bow there. Belle seemed preferential to pink—to girly outfits and soft aesthetics. I had told her to dress herself accordingly, that I enjoyed the look on her.

Good. She was listening already. I noticed that she had gone light with the makeup too, following another one of my, well, *suggestions*. I wanted her to be comfortable, yes, but I much preferred my submissives barefaced and fresh. Few women in my experience were willing to go to such lengths, particularly women who did this sort of thing professionally, yet Belle had opted for nothing more than a coat of mascara on her upper lashes, and perhaps a hint of concealer elsewhere. The colour on her lip was neutral. Another plus. I so *despised* spending an eternity in the bathroom cleaning red lipstick off my lips, my cheek, my cock.

Much to my delight, she accepted my proffered hand to help her into the limo, still beaming up at me with that damn infectious smile. Even her eyes seemed to sparkle, despite the day's dreary overcast. Royal blue. They suited her. Women who favoured pink and femininity were easy to dismiss for some—yet the depth of her eyes gave Belle substance.

I so enjoyed a woman with substance.

It had been quite some time since I found myself in the company of one outside of my friends and family.

Quite some time.

As I helped her into the car, ensuring that she didn't stumble into the back seat, I realized that much of my anxiety had disappeared. Well, perhaps not *disappeared*. Ebbed. Temporarily. Slipping into my Dom shoes again, adopting a casual control over something as ordinary as crossing the sidewalk and getting into a car—it soothed me. Made me feel more myself.

A quick check round the back of the limo told me the boys were still wrestling with our suitcases, so I grazed a hand down my jacket, catching the buttons on the way, and climbed in after Belle. She shuffled over a little to make space for me, seating herself at the far corner of the back bench as I slammed the door. With her pink Chanel purse on her lap, Belle fiddled with the gold chain, her gorgeous blues jumping everywhere—except to me.

Perhaps I wasn't the only one with nerves today.

Still, I had fully prepared for her nerves. I accepted

them. As far as I understood it, Belle hadn't been escorting for long; she didn't see clients outside of Elysium, and she had only done *performances* as a submissive. I'd be the first Dom to have her.

A little shiver ran through me at the thought, just as it always did.

The thrill of molding a new submissive to my every whim—*electrifying*. And a monumental responsibility. I'd set the tone for all her future encounters. I had to do it right.

Starting now.

With a soft clearing of my throat, I climbed forward and resettled on the long leather bench that ran the length of the limo, then popped open the minibar.

"What would you like to drink, Belle?"

Not *would* she like *a* drink. What. You couldn't mince words as a Dominant, otherwise it was your own damn fault when your submissive inevitably fucked up.

And setting a submissive up for failure was just cruel.

"Water, please," she said. She paused for a beat, her soft inhale followed by a very quiet, very demure, "Sir."

I stiffened, a much more potent, much more *striking* shiver racing through my body.

My cock twitched.

Sir.

I hadn't heard that word in so *long*...

Not in the way I wanted to hear it, anyway.

Hand still hovering in front of the minibar, I glanced over my shoulder at her, expression hard—dark, even, if the brighter flush in her cheeks had anything to say about it. She ceased fidgeting with her purse, and my cock pulsed again when she wet her lips and swallowed hard. Hesitantly, she lifted her gaze to mine, and I held it unflinchingly—but not long enough to force her to retreat.

"Water it is." Breaking our little standoff first, I plucked a cold bottle of Evian and passed it to her. The faint quiver of her hand when she accepted did not go unnoticed.

"Thank you, sir."

This won't be the last time I'll have you saying those words.

If I had it my way, she'd be screaming them next time. I swallowed a groan, discreetly readjusting myself as I closed the minibar's door. "You're welcome, Belle."

At the sound of the trunk finally slamming shut, I tracked my driver's movements on the other side of the tinted windows, then resettled myself next to Belle. With an arm stretched out along the back of the seat, I fixed my rumpled jacket, the roll along the path of my dress shirt's buttons. Quiet descended over us, thick with meaning— with implications—even as the driver busied himself up front. I rolled up the partition, noting the way Belle's eyes followed the rising screen, and then cleared my throat again, louder this time.

She looked from me to her water, then hastily cracked it open and took a sip, as if remembering she ought to drink what I'd given her. Fighting the urge to play with her springy ponytail, I focused on the smell of her perfume, detecting notes of rose, pomegranate, and wisteria. An image came to mind—I'd bought her some perfume, actually, just this past weekend, and spent nearly two fucking hours sniffing my way through the samples. Her scent triggered the memory of a delicate blush-pink bottle with a white and gold bow around its neck.

Basically what I thought Belle would look like as a perfume.

I hadn't gone with it: I'd erred on the side of caution and chosen something from Gucci, something the sales ladies helping me wouldn't stop gushing over. Maybe I should have gone with my gut instead.

Just as I was about to ask, about to rumble my inquiry in the shell of her ear, we pulled away from the curb, merging into the midday traffic with some difficulty. I sat back when the limo's rear wheel hit a pothole, the jostle plunging me back to my mindset from before Belle had appeared. The fear. The crushing, smothering anxiety of being that much closer to the airport—back with a vengeance.

Damn it. Pathetic, really. Absolutely pathetic. My phone dinged from the depths of my jacket. Two hours to go before takeoff. Two hours to navigate Manhattan's horrific midday traffic. Two hours until I'd be climbing the steep steps of my private jet, Belle's cute little ass in my face, her skirt flouncing about.

Two hours and fifteen minutes until we were airborne.

I retracted my arm as a surge of lightheadedness and cold sweats plagued me, then pulled out my phone in an effort to look busy. Muscle memory had me in my email browser within seconds, and I scrolled through, pretending to read one of the dozens of emails I downright refused to open. Names of general managers, board members, and even lower-level department heads whizzed by, and I stared at the screen with a furrowed brow like it was all rather important.

Really, I was concentrating on my breathing.

On forgetting the memory of where it all started— Richard, the bastard, telling me on my very first private flight that the toilet would suck me outside the jet the moment I flushed. Four-year-old me refusing to use the bathroom, refusing to get out of my seat amidst stomach-churning turbulence, for *eight* hours, until I wet myself.

The disappointment on my parents' faces, Richard

sniggering in the background, when they realized what a mess I'd been come landing.

I concentrated on forgetting the fear that one stupid ordeal had created in me. Tried. Failed. Failed to dispel the roil of my gut or the clamminess of my palms.

But I tried. After all, I finally had a new submissive to tend to now; this was the *least* opportune time for the aftermath of my childhood trauma to rear its ugly head.

And, really, I understood it was absurd. Pampered rich kid has tough time on his family's luxury aircraft—scarred for life. Ridiculous.

I wasn't this man.

I pulled in a deep breath and tucked my phone back in my jacket.

I was a *Dom*.

I stretched my arm out along the back of the seat again, this time toying with the end of Belle's ponytail.

I could do this. For my submissive, I could do anything.

I didn't have a choice.

3

BELLE

*W*ho was this man sitting across from me?

Not the same man who'd sat across from me on all those coffee dates. The Dean Donahue who had effortlessly led conversation, ordered my favourite scones for all our meet-ups, and told me—and a room full of legal people—*exactly* what kind of kink he wanted to engage in on our two-month trip... He wasn't here.

Glimpses of him had slipped through since he'd picked me up. My heart fluttered every time I saw them, a stark reminder that I found him *wildly* attractive—and that I shouldn't. Sure, it was great to have physical chemistry with a client, but I genuinely *liked* Dean, which, as Penny reminded me constantly, was a recipe for disaster with escorts. It led to an inevitable downfall, some awful implosion. First and foremost, it led to heartache, something I intended to avoid. It also had you switching back to the lower-paying gigs at Elysium until Candace could trust you not to get *too* involved again, and that infringed on my plan to create a sizeable financial buffer that would carry me when I was ready to pursue my *real* passions in a year or two, whatever those might be.

As I crossed my legs, seated opposite him on a gorgeous private jet, I tried to find the real Dean—all the while fearing that this new Dean might be the actual Dean I'd get once we were alone. Always checking his phone. Always looking everywhere but me. Quiet, reserved, distracted, his smiles few and far between.

This wasn't him.

Infused with luxury and elegance, his plane dripped opulence, from the private shower to the ridiculously plush leather seats. Light grey and white carried throughout the interior, black and gold accents giving the décor a distinctly masculine feel. We had settled into a pair of cushy seats facing one another, the pullout table tucked away for takeoff. Beside me, an enormous white couch spanned half the length of the passenger area, and there were two more sets of seats facing one another next to the large oval windows.

And if I was being honest, none of it felt like Dean. He might have rocked a tailored black suit on every occasion we'd met in the past, but to me, Dean's spirit was jewel-toned. Venetian rose. Azalea. Indigo. Ocean blue. Jasper red. Rich and alluring, velvety and seductive. Warm, too. Comforting. In control yet reassuring.

So, who the heck was *this* guy?

The plane rattled as it evened out, our ascent into New York airspace complete. I adjusted the seatbelt digging into my waist; facing Dean, I had essentially taken off backwards, my body lurching against the climb, seatbelt death-gripping me in place. Now that the captain had announced we'd reached our cruising altitude, I had no qualms unbuckling myself. The plane shook again, harder this time, bopping through turbulence, and suddenly Dean's large hand snapped onto his armrest. With a deep breath, he closed his eyes, white-knuckling his way through until the plane settled again.

I frowned, studying him in silence.

The white knuckles. The clenched eyes. The deep breaths. The pale face. The clammy forehead.

He wasn't a different person.

Dean was scared of flying.

The realization hit me like a runaway freight train, and I let out a soft, relieved breath—all the while hating that I found relief in his suddenly very obvious, very real fear. Still, I preferred knowing that the Dean I'd been so taken with on the ground would probably reappear as soon as we stepped onto the tarmac.

Nibbling my lower lip, I watched him, waiting for him to relax. Another slight bump—a rise up, then a sharp drop— only made things worse.

Poor guy.

My heart broke for him. I could understand that fear. I felt it every time I was up somewhere high. The only reason I *didn't* freak out whenever I got on a plane was because I couldn't really see the ground. My fear of heights only kicked in when I could guesstimate just how many feet I'd fall before I slammed into the concrete.

In that moment, I knew I had to do something—because that awful *feeling*, like you're about to die, resonated deep within me. In that moment, Dean wasn't just my Dom, my client, my employer.

Dean Donahue was a human being.

And he was scared.

And it broke my big, overly emotional heart.

Just pretend not to notice, Penny's voice insisted at the back of my head. *He's probably embarrassed. You saw nothing.*

No. I saw it. I saw it plain as day, and I couldn't believe I had missed it. Couldn't believe I hadn't clued in, that I'd let him suffer by himself. Well, no more.

I hesitated briefly. Was this how an escort should respond—or was I already getting too emotionally involved? I'd been told to look out for this. I'd been told to engage, but protect myself, too.

Then again, escorts cared for their clients, right? They looked after them, saw to their comfort, their needs. This wasn't just me being me—it was me doing my *job*.

But as I sat there staring at Dean, at his gorgeously tanned complexion, the dash of freckles across his nose hinting that he spent most of his time hopping between family-owned luxury hotels in Malta, Italy, and Greece—I couldn't help but wonder what I ought to do to make this right. I knew his kinks, his interests. I knew he had an older brother and a younger sister, that his parents—English dad, American mom—were still married, and that he had a net worth of about eight billion dollars to his name as of this year. He preferred decaffeinated drinks on our coffee dates. His smile was like a homing beacon to all women within a one-mile radius.

And I knew that at some point in the next two months, he wanted to put a leash on me, march me like a dog around his island, and then tie me to a palm tree and have his way with me.

It was in our information packet, right after all the legal jargon.

But for all that, I didn't *know* him—not where it really mattered.

Still, there was one thing that could always distract a

man. My cheeks burned at the thought. It was bold—maybe too bold for a guy who seemed to really dig my girly-pink, wide-eyed innocence thing, a thing I hadn't even realized I *did* until I started working at Elysium.

Semi-sure I could go through with this, I smoothed the bumps and rolls out of my white cardigan, undoing one of the baby-pink heart-shaped buttons and opening the material a little. It didn't exactly highlight my cleavage or anything, but it suggested—*something*.

Without a word, I stood, taking a moment to steady myself when the plane rumbled. Now that we were just above the cloud cover, sunshine streamed in through the window between us, and I quickly reached over and closed the shutter. The vanishing light had Dean opening his eyes, eyes that darted to me as I crossed the space between us and climbed onto his lap.

"What are you—"

"You looked like you could use a distraction," I murmured as I situated myself, legs straddling his rock-hard thighs. Rock-hard *everything*. We'd hugged before, and I had a pair of eyes in my head, so I'd known I'd be in for a treat the second he took his shirt off—but feeling it, *him*, was another experience entirely.

Okay, don't be weird about it. Focus on the task at hand.

His whole body seemed to stiffen beneath me, his hand still white-knuckling the armrest, and I noticed him swallow hard when the plane bobbed again. I glanced over my shoulder at the closed cockpit door. Seriously. Weren't private jets supposed to be more luxurious in every way than commercial airliners? Shouldn't this be a more relaxing ride?

Tentatively, I pressed my hands flat to his chest, then smoothed them up the muscular dips and swells. Sage-green eyes. Kissable lips. Just a hint of scruff, sandy blond like his thick hair, perhaps a touch darker. It was hard *not* to let my mind run wild with a man like Dean.

No. Focus. I rolled my shoulders back, hands cupping his face, and then leaned down to kiss him. At first, it was nothing more than a tentative brush of my lips against his, yet as I inhaled, I breathed in his masculine scent—a scent that had me thinking of the outdoors, of sitting before a roaring fire at a lakeside cottage, bundled in thick blankets and wrapped in someone's arms.

Dean's arms.

Goosebumps erupted beneath my cardigan. His gaze dropped to my lips, tracking my tongue when it wet them. Gently, my thumb trailed across his lower lip, his minty breath warming me.

Just as I was about to go in for another easy, curious graze of my mouth, Dean responded. He surged up and claimed me with a much fiercer, much more demanding kiss, one that I felt shoot straight between my thighs. I moaned softly, molding myself against him, arching my back as his arm snapped around my waist. Beside us, I heard his hand peel off the leather armrest, and suddenly it was wrapped around the base of my ponytail.

He tugged, forcing my head back just sharply enough for my heart to quicken. I gasped, eyes widening, and Dean seized the opportunity to thrust his tongue between my lips.

If I thought I'd felt his kiss between my thighs, it was nothing compared to his tongue—each teasing lick, each purposeful caress, seemed to sweep across my sex, across my clit, desire pooling in my core. Heat flashed deep within me, and I fought the urge to unbutton the rest of my cardigan and just rip it off, desperate to feel more of him, skin-to-skin. This moment wasn't for me. It was for him.

Not that I didn't think he'd enjoy the show. As I bucked against him, pleasure unfurled with each brush of my clit against his hardening shaft. It would have been easy to get lost in the moment, in the fire of his kiss, in the way his eyes raked across my face—in the way he steered me, drove me, held my reins with a fist around my ponytail.

The pink satin bow had been for him. I'd chosen it deliberately.

Something told me he liked it.

The thought gave me courage, gave me the strength to drag myself away from his lips, from his tongue, from the hint of teeth, *sharpness*, danger in his kiss. Breathing harder than I should, I braced myself on his shoulders and pushed back. While the arm around my waist gave way, he only *just* loosened his grasp on my ponytail, holding it the whole way down, moving from base to middle as I unbuckled his seatbelt, then slid down his legs and settled between them.

Unable to hold his stare, so riddled with interest and curiosity and blatant *need*, I sat up on my parted knees and discovered damp heat pooled between my thighs.

A client had never made me wet before.

With slightly trembling fingers, I went for his belt. Dean sat forward a little, as if to accommodate me, saying nothing as I fumbled with the buckle and battled with the unyielding leather. Sections of the contract danced across my mind—about a belt around my neck like a leash; a belt around my waist so he had something to hold while he pounded into me from behind; a belt for punishment, cracking mercilessly across my bare ass.

I shuddered, forcing myself to take controlled breaths. This was supposed to be for *him*. Not me.

He had already tented his black trousers by the time I popped the button and slid down the zipper, and I wasted no time pulling his briefs out of the way. His hand tightened around my ponytail the moment I touched his cock. Perfectly groomed, the shaft hardened further in my hand, its size impressive but not horribly intimidating—thank goodness, because how was I supposed to have sex with some enormous, ten-inch cock for two months straight?—as I guided it out, briefs tucked under his balls.

Dean inhaled sharply when I leaned forward and flicked my tongue across the engorged head. Salty precum replaced the lingering taste of mint from our kiss, and I tipped my head to the side, offering a little half smile as I waited for his go-ahead. I might have taken charge initially, but Dean ran this show—not the other way around.

His hand drifted up my ponytail, wrapping around its base again, no doubt crushing my cute little bow, and a slight quirk of one brow was all I needed. Taking a deep breath, I wrapped my lips around the head of his cock, then sucked, my core tightening pleasurably at the way he groaned. Wanting to start slow, I trailed my tongue down each side of his shaft, top to bottom, before dragging my lips back up and taking him in.

Penny had warned me that the first time I was *this* intimate with a client, it would feel—strange. Unsettling, maybe. After all, my foot fetish clients usually touched themselves, or my feet, and all my bondage or discipline scenes had been with other associates at Elysium.

This was uncharted territory.

Sort of. As I gripped the base of his length, pumping my hand slowly, and worked the upper half with my mouth, I could acknowledge that I wasn't *that* innocent. Definitely not virginal. I'd given a blowjob before.

Yet somehow giving one to Dean felt more—intimate?

I swirled my tongue around the head, rather enjoying

the way his body jerked at the movement, and then plunged back down again, taking him as far as I could, until my mouth met my fist.

"*Fuck*, Belle," he hissed, and instinctively I shot up, worried I'd done something wrong, grazed him with my teeth, maybe? I bit my lower lip, brow creased with worry; I'd been trying so hard not to—

Without a word, our eyes locked, and Dean steered my head back to him, thrusting between my lips with a soft growl, his hand tightening around my ponytail. A little squeal escaped me as he filled my mouth, nudging the back of my throat before retreating.

"Hands behind your back," he ordered gruffly, and I scrambled to comply, grasping each wrist for good measure. Wet heat greeted me as soon as I drew my knees closer together, my slit swollen and sensitive. A blush blossomed across my cheeks, and, with Dean's cock in my mouth and his hand on my ponytail, I couldn't exactly turn away to hide it. Still, as his hand slid down and grasped my throat, lifting my chin just a little, something in the way he studied me said he liked the blush—a lot. "Good girl."

I exhaled sharply, shocked at how two insignificant words, words I'd heard time and time again in other scenes, could have such a profoundly arousing effect on me now. My pussy clenched at the thought, at the steely rumble of his voice, at the heat in his eyes as he started to thrust slowly in my mouth. I held my wrists tighter, trying to relax my jaw and take as much of him as I could—hoping this had done the trick, that he was no longer stuck in the pit of fear that I was all too familiar with.

He kept me like that for—god knows how long. On my knees, at his feet. Hands behind my back. Lazily fucking my face as he watched me with a dark, hooded look I'd see in my dreams tonight.

Finally, just as my knees started to scream, he raised me up by my ponytail, then guided me toward him with the hand on my throat. Then, rather than pumping his cock between my lips, he used my mouth instead, forcing my head up and down. I tried to just breathe through it, but the hand on my windpipe made that increasingly difficult, as did the pace. My eyes watered. I choked on him—more than once. My hands came loose behind my back, bracing myself on the leather seat, and I pretended not to hear his chastising tsk over the symphony of our racing, staggered breaths.

I *needed* to brace myself, prop myself up, or I might just—

Well, pull away. That was what I wanted to do. Pull back, catch my breath, wipe the tears out of my eyes.

Slip a hand between my thighs.

But Dean's grip was as merciless as his pace, his balls soon slapping against my chin as he thrust up to meet me, half out of the chair, until he finally spilled himself down my throat. I struggled to swallow the sudden influx of cum —struggled, but damn it, I *did* it. Not a drop slipped past my lips.

With a shaky breath, Dean settled back in his seat and released my ponytail. As I eased away, his cock falling from my mouth to his lap, still semi-erect, his hand slid up my throat and cupped my chin. Gently. Affectionately, maybe. I couldn't help but smile when his thumb stroked my jaw.

"Do you feel better?" I asked, my voice thick—wet, even. I swallowed again, the taste of him lingering, my body aching from the roughest, most enjoyable oral I'd ever given.

Dean grinned down at me, his gaze still dark and lusty, but satisfied, too.

"Yes, *much* better," he told me with a chuckle, then wiped a thumb under my eyes, brushing the dampness away.

Neither of us seemed to feel the need to bring up why he'd been so tense—why I'd dropped to my knees in the first place. Which was just fine by me. Dean wasn't any less of a Dominant in my eyes because flying made him a bit anxious; all I'd seen was that my Dom had needed a distraction.

He'd needed *me*.

"Thank you, Belle."

"You're welcome, sir." My eyes fluttered closed when he leaned down, hand tightening on my chin, and kissed my cheek. Surprisingly, I found myself leaning in to the touch, to the warmth of his lips against my skin—and then felt oddly bereft when it disappeared.

Bereft and wildly turned on, mind you. I clenched, my sex still wet and swollen, desperate for some release.

But this wasn't about me.

So, when Dean helped me up, gently grasping me by the elbows, I went without a fuss, without so much as a pout. He steadied me when the plane rocked, and this time his entire being didn't tense. Beyond the slight twitch in his cheek, he seemed perfectly fine with the shuddering around us. Pride swelled within me, but I shoved it back down.

You just gave him a blowjob. You aren't winning the Nobel Peace Prize here.

"Bathroom is at the back," he murmured, offering another dimpled smile before releasing me. "Left door. Right is the bedroom, if you need it."

I nodded, and, on wobbly legs, made my way through the luxury liner to the sprawling bathroom.

Only to collapse against the locked door once I was inside, my mind racing, my cheeks burning, and my heart suddenly thundering.

"Belle, put your book down."

I dog-eared the page I was on, my heart skipping a beat, and closed Mary Shelley's *Frankenstein*—a book that was kind of just *okay*, but I'd thought might make me look a little cultured when Dean saw the cover. My real passion—smutty romance—was currently tucked away in my purse on my e-reader, and I had every intention of plowing through the dozens of unread books awaiting me on my off days.

Setting the book on the extended table now pulled out between our seats, I watched as Dean approached from the rear of the jet. About two hours into the flight, his shift in demeanor was palpable. We hadn't seen the pilots since they first welcomed us aboard, and despite the fact that I had just given my first client blow job, the atmosphere in the cabin had been relaxed. Easy. Light—after I'd calmed down in the bathroom, of course, my senses on fire after that blowjob. Dean had been working on his laptop this whole time while I trudged through Shelley's classic. We'd munched on a bag of salty chips together, and I hoped we'd eat something proper once we landed; I'd been so nervous this morning that I barely got my breakfast down, lunch had been out of the question, and now, hours later, my stomach was *not* pleased with my decisions.

When I started to stand, Dean shook his head. So, back

down I went, watching, waiting, until he strolled right up to my chair and knelt beside it, a large velvet box in hand.

I frowned, trying not to stare, but I'd always been the curious sort. What kind of jewelry could fit in there? Too big for a ring. Too wide for a bracelet. Maybe a necklace and earrings set?

"As you might recall, I had something planned for the flight," Dean started, holding the box out to me.

"I...do," I managed when I realized he wanted a response. While some of our activities had been planned in intimate detail, not *everything* had been outlined so vividly.

And I still wasn't sure if that was a good or bad thing just yet.

"Now, this is a game where there are no losers," he told me, his tone firm yet friendly, "and I suppose no winners, either."

"How can it be a game then?" I asked, quickly adding "sir" when he arched a brow at me. Grinning, Dean popped the lid up.

"Well, because games are fun. I think *this* will be fun, too."

I swallowed thickly at the sight of the device inside.

"Do you know what this is, Belle?"

"It's..." *Damn it.* I really needed to get a handle on all this blushing. Honestly, what kind of escort got so rattled over a sex toy? Not a very good one, probably. "It looks like a... remote-controlled vibrator, maybe?"

"Good. Yes, that's precisely what it is." Dean set the box on my armrest, then removed the little triangular remote from its indent in the plush velvet fabric. "This controls the speed of the vibrator."

He then picked up the pink silicone oval and placed it in my hand. A simple click of the button had it vibrating; I jumped, then let out a slightly embarrassed giggle when I felt him eyeing me.

"There are three speeds," he explained, cycling through each one. The third had the vibrator whirring angrily as it danced around my palm. I made a face. Wow. Kind of an aggressive setting.

"Now, you'll wear that," Dean told me—informed me, ordered me, "and I'll have the remote."

"And what's the game?"

"The game is seeing how long you can go without coming," he purred, switching the vibrator off as I swallowed hard. His grin turned downright sinful as he added, "I estimate five minutes, but perhaps you'll prove me wrong."

Oh god. I had no idea how long I'd last, honestly. At home, there was a single vibrator in my arsenal of sex supplies—which, granted, was pretty sad for an escort—and I rarely ever used it. My fingers almost always did the trick; no need for anything fancy.

Still—five minutes? Maybe if I wasn't trying, but I fully intended to put effort into this, if only to surprise him.

"I see your five minutes, sir," I said, lifting my chin as my hand closed around the bullet vibrator, no longer or wider than Dean's thumb, "and raise you to eight."

"Betting's a dangerous game, Belle." He stood, smoothing a hand down the front of his suit. "I'm not sure you're ready for the consequences should you lose."

My core clenched deliciously at his thinly veiled threat.

"Maybe not, but I still think—eight minutes," I said with a determined nod.

"Very well then. Off you go. There's lubricant in the bathroom if you need it."

Yeah. Definitely wasn't going to need any additional

lubrication. As I stood, my pent-up arousal from earlier came flooding back, and I slipped by him with a murmured thanks. Halfway down the cabin, he added another stipulation.

"Leave your stockings in there," Dean remarked, a hand on the back of my chair as he watched me, all the gentle warmth gone from his expression, ramped up a thousand notches to granite and fire instead. "Panties will stay on."

I licked my lips, pulse thumping between my ears, then nodded hastily. "Yes, sir."

Sensing time was of the essence, I hurried to the bathroom at the back of the jet, locking myself in with a deep exhale. *So it begins.* The blowjob hadn't been planned, but I'd known he wanted to do *something* on the plane—and this was it. I stared at the small pink vibrator sitting innocently in my palm.

I could do this.

I'd signed up to do this.

I was getting paid a *lot* of money to do this.

Still, as I set the vibrator on the counter and got to work peeling off my boots and stockings, I couldn't help but think foot fetish clients were a lot less work.

Less fun, too.

As a tentative excitement coursed through me, I popped a foot up on the closed toilet and grabbed the vibrator. True to Dean's word, there was a little bottle of water-based lubricant waiting for me, still in its plastic wrapper. While I appreciated the gesture, his thought of my comfort in all this, I didn't need it. Not if the dampness of my panties had anything to say about it. Sure, most of it was from before, but as I slipped a finger between my folds, just to check, I found myself wet already.

Something about Dean Donahue—it was like turning

on a tap. Those gorgeous eyes, straddling the line between green and grey. That sinful mouth, ordering me about like he owned me. And that accent—American, but getting more English by the second. The more Dom he became, the brighter his accent shone.

Yum.

My pussy protested the intrusion, but in a pleasant sort of way, tightening around the vibrator, clinging to it, a little bolt of pleasure pulsing through me. Once I had it in, I pulled my panties back on, but was sure to leave the stockings and boots behind. Biting the insides of my cheeks, I wandered over to the spotless mirror, noting the rosy colour in my cheeks, the unkempt flyaways sticking out around my head. I'd fixed my ponytail and bow earlier, but I had a feeling they'd get ruined again before the day was over.

The thought had a chill racing down my spine.

How easy it would have been to slip a hand between my thighs *now* and take the edge off. Maybe then I'd be able to prove him wrong—last ten whole minutes instead of his measly five.

I pursed my lips and sighed. No. The house rules were very clear when it came to *my* pleasure: orgasms required permission, nor could I indulge in any solo time for the next two months either.

Besides, while I might have been new at this whole submissive thing, I was determined to follow the rules—to be a good sub.

You can do it. I gave my reflection a high five, careful not to leave a handprint on the mirror, then left the bathroom after washing my hands, pussy wet as ever, and tried to ignore the pleasurable tingles I felt with every awkward, slightly stilted step. While only slightly bigger than a large tampon, the vibrator wasn't exactly made of cottony fabric, was it? The silicon had some give to it, but not enough to make walking comfortable.

Dean's eyes stalked me as I half waddled back to my seat, and when I hesitated, he nodded down to it. Right. Down I went, settling into the cushy leather seat with some difficulty, my bare legs prickling as I smoothed my skirt to cover my butt.

"Back to reading," Dean said when I looked at him curiously, awaiting my next instruction. Swallowing hard, I grabbed Shelley's Frankenstein again and opened to my dog-eared page. How was I supposed to concentrate on this *now* when I was just sitting here, waiting for the storm to hit?

I tried. I really did. Brows knitted, I read every word, my adrenaline spiking each time Dean shifted across the table. At one point, he pulled out his laptop again and started clacking around, as if going back to work. Huffing, I flipped the page louder than necessary—apparently, I wasn't one for being teased. Who knew?

"Now, remember, Belle," Dean said, his voice cracking through my gathering brain-fog. "You don't need to ask permission to come. Not this time."

"Yes, sir." A startled little squeak flew out of me when the vibrations started. While it was clearly on the lowest setting, I sat up straighter, my cheeks burning all the same. It felt good. Too good. I bit my lower lip, then stared pointedly at the page I'd been on, not taking in a single word. The low vibrations shot straight to my clit, and I uncrossed my legs to lessen the tension, the pressure—only the new position shifted the little bullet inside me so that it rumbled contentedly against my G-spot now.

Oh, this—might be harder than I'd anticipated.

I glanced tentatively at Dean, hoping he hadn't noticed, hadn't read all the thoughts that no doubt had flashed openly across my face. While I should have schooled my features, played it cool, I couldn't. Not with him studying me through heavy-lidded eyes, jaw set, remote controller held loosely in his left hand, thumb on the button.

Okay. Okay. You can do this. Just concentrate on Frankenstein's monster—my, isn't he doing an awful lot of complaining about the human race—

"Ah!" I jolted upright again when Dean increased the vibrations, that *click* of the button deafening in the suddenly too-quiet cabin. My paperback's pages creased under my death grip, and I tried to lean nonchalantly to the side to get a look at Dean's watch, but I couldn't find the right angle. Letting out a shaky breath, I sat back in my seat. It must have been, what, four minutes by now? Nearly there. Just needed to hold out a little while longer—

"You're at two minutes, Belle," Dean said without looking up from his laptop, "*just.*"

Damn it. "Oh. Right. Well, good."

"How are you doing?"

"F-fine," I told him, wincing at my stutter. Gaze still fixed on his sleek, thin laptop, Dean smirked.

"Hmm. So I can see."

The clack of his fingers to light grey keys resumed seconds later, and I tipped my head back. Honestly, *trying* not to come somehow made all this worse. Actually, forcing myself to slog through this boring book didn't help either. If only I had my romances... I considered it for a moment, then shook my head. No. Romances would make this ten times harder; none of the books I read were exactly fit for public consumption. A bit risqué. A bit titillating.

Still, I had to *try*. Jaw clenched, I picked up my book

determinedly and flipped through the pages to find where I'd left off on. Only nothing looked familiar. I couldn't even remember what had been happening in the scene before Dean upped the speed of this terribly wonderful device inside me. Something about Victor...doing something... Ugh, high school me had never been very good at English class; all I'd wanted to read, even back then, were my romances.

I eventually settled on a page—but only ended up staring at it, the words bleeding together as the vibrations continued their relentless torture, my body fought the urge to break, to shatter into a million pleasurable pieces. I sang the alphabet, itemized all the things in my luggage, and even tried to break down how much I'd be earning over the next two months to the *second*.

Nothing helped.

An eternity later, when the pleasurable licks of my impending orgasm swept across my hands, my chest, my nipples pebbled beneath my bra and cardigan—Dean upped the speed. I cried out, unable to stop myself, and tossed that damn book on the floor. No point in pretending anymore. Eyes shut, I gripped the armrests, doing a little white-knuckling of my own as my hips started to shake. This was torture. Sheer, unadulterated *torture*.

I fought so hard, my entire body gritted with the effort.

Clenching only made things worse. It heightened each sensation—emphasized the restrictiveness of my clothing, the sensitivity of my skin. If I dared relax now, however, I'd be done for. I'd plummet over the edge, come undone right in front of him, and I couldn't do that. Not yet. I still had more fight in me.

"Belle." My eyes snapped open to a vacant seat across the table. Work abandoned, Dean now occupied the sprawling white couch to my right. He sat there, one arm stretched out across the back, his legs wide apart and his gaze stormy. "Come here."

Did he think I could *walk* like this? As soon as my tensed thighs brushed together with the first step, it would all be over. Even the caress of my thin cotton panties was too much.

"*Now.*"

Well. That tone didn't exactly broker room for argument. Grasping at the top of my seat, I hauled myself up and shuffled around the table, then tiptoed across the aisle to him. Dean sat up straighter, no longer stretched out, yet still somehow consuming the space, filling the room. He patted his knee, and I waddled over, hardly moving my legs, to perch there—until he grabbed my waist and dragged me back. I inhaled sharply, hands curled to tight fists as he arranged me on his lap, my body so small tucked against him, back to chest.

"You can let go now, Belle," he breathed in my ear, his interest in our little game rubbing hard against my ass. I shook my head, knowing I could hold out just a little while longer, knowing that I had the determination to succeed.

Until his knee popped up between mine, forcing my legs apart. Until his hand slid between them, cupping me, my soaked panties downright shameful—but they made him groan ever so softly. Barely audible. I'd have missed it had his mouth not settled so close to my ear. I draped over him, legs splayed and hands resting on his taut forearms.

"You did it," he murmured. "Well over five minutes. Let go, Belle."

I shook my head, flushed and panting. "No, I-I can go longer..."

My whole body spasmed when he started to rub me, to

massage me in slow, torturous circles. White-hot bolts of pleasure licked through me, burning, *scorching* through my veins as I descended into madness—right there on his lap. The very small bit of sanity left in me ordered that I hold on, take it just a few moments more.

But the pleasure won out. Dean swept his thumb across my clit, once, twice, three times, still cupping me with the rest of his hand—and I lost it. I broke. Back arched, head tossed over his shoulder, I came undone with a breathless cry. Fireworks burst behind my eyelids, a gorgeous array of blues, greens, yellows, purples, reds—the rainbow of Dean's spirit. Just how I'd imagined it. Not white and grey, black and gold, not the masculine utilitarianism of this aircraft, but jewel-toned *explosions*. I lost control of my body, which had devolved into a writhing, shuddering, arching creature of lust that I didn't recognize.

A creature that, judging from the way he roughly kneaded my breast through all those dreadful layers, the way his teeth raked my neck, Dean Donahue fervently approved of.

He dragged it out, not stopping the powerful vibrations of that damn third setting until I begged him, until I actually *sobbed* the plea, unable to take it a second longer. At last, the vibration ceased, but his thumb continued to stroke my clit through my panties, taking long, leisurely sweeps as I trembled in his arms.

It was only when he stopped that I realized, at some point, I'd grabbed his wrist. While my one hand had been here, there, and everywhere, running over my hair, clutching at the leather couch, at the skirt hitched up around my waist, that other hand had locked around his wrist.

I stared down at it, at the way I clung to him. It suggested familiarity—an intimacy that we didn't have. Not yet. Maybe not ever.

Blinking hard, I loosened my grip, no longer able to feel his pulse race beneath my fingertips, and then pulled my hand away completely. It wanted to go back. As Dean sat me up, arranging me on his knee again, I craved the comfort—the security of clinging to him as the storm settled.

"Very good, Belle," he murmured, his one hand rubbing up and down my back, the other resting on my bare thigh. "Seven and a half minutes. You proved me wrong."

I brightened at the praise, pushing back the weird feelings in favour of something less confusing. "Thank you, sir."

A few other phrases sat on the tip of my tongue.

I tried.

That was so much harder than I thought it would be.

I didn't think I'd make it.

I swallowed them all; they'd just ruin the moment—take away from my accomplishment.

"Now, off you go," he said lightly as he helped me up. My legs felt like jelly, and I leaned into his steadying hand on my hip. When I finally dared look back, the darkness had lifted from his eyes—lessened, sure, but it hadn't disappeared completely.

Not if the tent in his pants had anything to say about it.

I hesitated, wondering if I should do something—if it was technically my job to take care of *that*. However, a quick pat on my butt and a nod toward the bathroom answered that for me.

"I've a box of Swiss chocolates waiting for you when you come back," Dean told me, his smirk stretching into a pleased grin when I clapped my hands together.

Bit embarrassing—squeeing over a box of chocolate, but

I couldn't help myself. Chocolate was *everything*, and, despite my initial nerves, I'd done an admirable job today.

Chocolate was my reward.

I could definitely get used to this.

"*Swiss* chocolate?"

"Just for you," he said as he settled back into the couch, his arm extended across it once more. "I made a pit stop in Zurich on the way to New York to ensure I was fully stocked. Go on."

A flood of warmth rushed through me at the thought—at the idea of Dean purposefully detouring to another country to spoil me.

This man who didn't even know me.

This man who had bought me for the next two months.

In an instant, the warmth shattered, and I was left with a slightly queasy feeling, a feeling I couldn't explain—and certainly didn't want to. So, I smiled instead and toddled off to the bathroom like a good girl.

Hoping that once we reached his private island, the line between my true self and the escort he was paying me to be would become much, much clearer.

HOUSE SCHEDULE (MONDAY–SATURDAY)

Early Morning: Wake Up, Breakfast, Check-In Phone Call for Belle
Mid-Morning: Office Work for Sir, Taskwork for Belle
Noon: Lunch
Early Afternoon: Pool Time
Late Afternoon: Playtime or *Additional Rest Time*
Early Evening: Dinner
Late Evening / Night: Free Time

HOUSE RULE #7

No panties. Swimsuit bottoms are acceptable during
pool time.

4

DEAN

*T*he difference a change of scenery—and a fantastic blowjob—could make was unreal.

We'd only been on Ixora Isle for an hour and already much of my stress had faded away. Named after the family of flowers that had bewitched me the first time I went hopping around the Virgin Islands as a boy, my private island sat about ten minutes from Saint Thomas by boat. Virtually isolated, it was the perfect retreat; I had bought and named it after a single showing. I'd had a gorgeous estate built atop it. I'd arranged the landscaping to my exacting specifications, all the while leaving much of the island's natural beauty untouched. I'd had an infinity pool installed. I'd had all the living quarters furnished and decorated—seven years ago.

And I hadn't spent more than two fucking days at a time visiting.

The family dubbed me a workaholic, but if I didn't do it, who the fuck would? *Richard*?

Mother and Father's firstborn had taken the reins,

booted me from my position, for all of what, a month, and already things were...

Well, they were headed down the same path they had been when I stepped up seven bloody years ago.

My teeth gritted at the memory, at the thought of all those emails sitting in my inbox, waiting, *begging*, to be answered. But for the first time in far too long, I had no electronic devices on me. No phone. No smartwatch. No tablet. No— anything. Dressed in nothing more than a maroon cotton tee and a pair of mid-thigh black swim trunks, I was free.

And with each lap of the waves upon the shores of my own private paradise, with each gust of beautiful Caribbean wind, I became freer still.

Hands in my pockets, I watched the rolling ocean through a pair of dark aviators, waiting to be joined by my houseguest.

A houseguest who was rather good with her mouth.

And who climaxed like a fucking angel.

Clear waters swept up the shoreline, stopping within an inch of my bare feet. Behind me sat a pair of slip-on loafers; while I intended to leave the beach shortly, having promised Belle a tour of the island and the house—save the third floor —before dinner, I needed a few moments to wiggle my toes in the sand. Today had been such a whirlwind: the flight and the anxiety it wrought; the sordid events *on* said flight, which, all things considered, had improved my anxiety considerably; then the trek from Saint Thomas's quaint airport out to a café, then the harbor, all that luggage in tow, followed by a boat ride through choppy waters that'd had poor Belle's stomach turning.

But we'd made it.

We had survived the first leg of this journey. Fifty-nine

days to go, right through balmy, beautiful February and March. No more New York winter for my submissive—just sun, sand, and sea for miles around us.

I turned away from the breathtaking ocean views, catching my trusty old bowrider docked at the small pier. It had been wasting away in the marina for far too long; even though I'd paid to have it maintained all this time, it yearned to slice through waves once again. I could have purchased a flashier yacht; the entire family had sniggered about it when I showed photos.

I didn't *need* some ridiculous yacht, nor did I want the hassle of staffing it. I could handle the bowrider just fine on my own—and for the purpose of this vacation, that was all that mattered.

North of the sandy beach upon which I stood, palms swayed in the late afternoon breeze. A smattering of natural foliage separated me from Belle, though I trusted she would be able to find her way from the house to the well-maintained path through the trees, then down to the beach. Although I was seldom present, I had people out here twice a month, rain or shine, to keep the property clean and maintained. When I had decided I would be bringing a companion on my two-month jaunt, I'd had much of the furniture and kitchen appliances replaced or updated. Bougainvilleas now encircled the house's main entryway, their blooms pink and white, and blush oleanders blossomed in the garden beneath Belle's bedroom window.

So many months of preparation—all leading to this moment.

I ought to be a bundle of nerves.

But the island soothed me.

Belle soothed me, quite unexpectedly. While I liked her well enough as a person, I hadn't known what to expect from her as my temporary submissive. However, if her efforts on the plane were just a taste of her abilities, then I considered my doubts quashed.

A grin crossed my lips when I spotted her cresting the hill, appearing right where she should be on the trail that spilled out between two mature palms. Blonde waves free and caught on the wind, she was a vision in white as she hurried somewhat ungracefully down the sandy slope, mouth spread into a full smile as she waved her sandals at me. She'd been barefoot at first, padding along after me for our tour of the island—only to be told her feet would need some protection when we tackled the more rugged forest paths.

And while I didn't consider those slips of leather—gladiator sandals, maybe, which would weave up her legs—to be adequate hiking shoes, I only intended to show her the basics today. I had included proper running shoes on her list of essentials, and I trusted she'd brought them for future walks.

"Ready!" she announced as she skipped down the beach, her delicate feet sinking into the sand, a little breathless when she bounced to a stop before me. Her shapeless white dress would have been *wildly* inappropriate anywhere else: the damn thing was sheer enough to show off her pink nipples through the fabric, and with the light behind her, every inch of that gorgeous figure demanded my attention. Sleeveless, the dress stopped at her ankles, yet it billowed in the wind, lifting to show off toned calves.

She popped her sunglasses down from the top of her head, then pushed them up her nose. While she had also expressed some nerves earlier—not aloud, but in her body language—it seemed the island had worked its charm on her, too. That smile—the ancient Greeks would go to war for that smile.

"Where to first, sir?"

I held out my hand, the thrill of hearing her say *sir* in that sweet voice not lost on me yet.

"We'll walk along the beach," I told her as she slipped her hand into mine, our fingers threading together a little too naturally, "and then up to the stairs there. They'll take us to the upper trails. I have a few spots I'd like to show you."

Hand in hand, we ambled across the beach at a breezy pace, and I regaled her with stories of the initial purchase, the construction of the house, and the dozens of environmental impact reports I had insisted upon. This island was a piece of my heart, despite how infrequently I visited, and preserving its natural beauty was essential. I welcomed the iguanas, the insects, the birds. So long as they weren't clogging my pool drain or chowing through my pantry, let them do whatever they wanted.

We paused at the base of the wooden staircase I'd had installed years ago, each of us slipping on our shoes. As I'd predicted, Belle's sandals wrapped intricately around her calves, requiring more concentration than I thought necessary for island living, but the effort did nothing to dampen her enthusiasm.

The creaking, groaning stairs, on the other hand, had her clutching at the back of my shirt as we climbed, one hand fisted in the fabric as the other ghosted along the side of the rocky cliff the stairwell wound around. I reached back to steady her and noted that the railing could probably use some sprucing up. By the time we reached the top, her carefree smile had vanished, replaced with an anxious, forced expression instead. Taking her hand again, I brought her away from the edge of the cliff. It was only a ten, maybe twelve-foot drop here, but the trails would take us up to a good sixty-foot plunge into the cove below.

She blossomed like an azalea bloom in the morning sun once we diverted onto the forest trails, stopping here and there, asking me to name trees, flowers, and birds. I did my best to differentiate between the various palms. I pointed out the thin, spiny thorns of the possumwood trees, and we paused to admire the little blue flowers on the guaiacwoods. Papaya trees, agave clusters, and grapevine. While most of the birds scattered at the sound of our conversation, I still managed to show her a pair of conures and a flock of yellow warblers.

"All the trails are clearly marked," I told her, tapping at a swipe of white paint on a palm trunk. "A few may be more overgrown than this, but you can explore them on your off days, if you'd like. They all connect at some point in the path."

"It's not like I can get lost on an island of this size," she mused, sunglasses popped up on her head beneath the shady canopy. "If I reach the water, I'll know I've gone too far."

I grinned, grasping her hand again before leading on to the spot I'd been most excited to show her.

As we neared the island's edge, the density of the forest thinned, giving way to the stunning view beyond. Belle fell quiet as we stepped out of the tree line and headed toward the cliff.

"You can see nearly all the islands from here," I told her, acquiescing when she tugged her hand away. I slipped both of mine in my pockets instead, taking in the sprawling blue waters dotted with green landmasses. To the left, the American Virgin Islands, under which my island fell, and to the right, the British Virgin Islands. Given I had dual citizenship, I could have purchased a luxury vacation home on either. In true Donahue fashion, I'd built my own instead.

Just over the cliff's edge, a gorgeous little inlet housed the perfect swimming cove. Usually calmer than the open sea, it offered a safe haven for admiring the marine life below the surface. I intended to take Belle out there soon.

"The cove is quite nice for swimming in," I said, expecting her at my side—only to find her about ten feet back. She nodded enthusiastically when I faced her.

"I'd love to swim in the cove, sir."

My brows dipped at the palpable shift in her energy. "You all right, Belle?"

"Fine," she told me, arms crossed, her smile forced again. "I just... I'm a bit nervous with heights, that's all."

Oh. Well, had I known that, I wouldn't have dragged her up the side of a cliff face and marched her to the brink of a sixty-foot drop. My jaw clenched. Fear of heights hadn't been in her file—and as her Dom, I needed to know *all* her limits, not just sexually.

Offering what I hoped was a soothing smile, I steered her further back from the cliff, adding another ten feet of distance before I stopped. "Is that better?"

Belle tucked her hair behind her ears, the humidity already starting to work its magic. "Yes, sir."

"I only wanted you to see the view," I insisted. My fingers trailed down her arm, stopping at her elbow. "Not like I intended to make you dive off."

"The view is lovely," she told me, her skin prickling at my touch. "The island is stunning. I just don't do well when I can see how far I'd fall if I tripped."

"Fair enough." As a man with a ridiculous fear of flying, I could sympathize. Beyond that, I didn't want her to feel frightened here. Good Dominants could inject a little terror into their sessions, but at no point should Belle feel unsafe. I couldn't allow that. Not for a second.

Silence settled over us, allowing for the swell of the natural world. Palm fronds rustling in the wind. Birds twittering across the forest. The waves pounding into the cliff below. Her sunglasses weren't quite dark enough to hide the way her eyes drifted up my body, hitched at my lips, then flicked up to meet my gaze. Unable to ignore the beckoning of those deep blues, I moved closer, the heat between us rising, drowning out the heat around us.

I caught some of her blonde locks between my fingers, rubbing the ends together, another whiff of her faintly floral perfume wafting over me. By the end of this week, I intended to know every part of her—every inch of her skin. What made her gasp. What made her scream. I'd know it all and enjoy every second of the learning process; even now, standing before her, the thrill of the hunt had my heart beating just a little faster.

Much to my surprise, Belle made the first move. She pushed up on her toes, her mouth seeking out mine for a rather chaste little kiss. Close-lipped and gentle. Her hand pressed to the middle of my chest, the other hanging loose at her side, her eyes a breath away from closing.

I took a deep inhale, quieting the beast roaring to life within my chest—the beast who loved to inflict pain and pleasure in equal measures, who loved to dominate, to control, to master. How could she know what such an innocent gesture would do to me? How could she know it'd rile me up, a dozen sordid images whipping across my mind's eye? Pushing her up against a tree and fucking her as the bark shredded her flimsy dress. Nudging her to her knees so I could sample her mouth again—and this time she would keep her arms behind her back like she was told. Ravaging her right here and now, not a soul around to hear her cries.

I had a weakness for wide-eyed innocence—for perky submissives whom I could utterly ruin. I hadn't had one in my personal life for *years*, nor had I spent such an extended period of time with one who submitted for money. Still, this was my first true vacation in far too long, and I intended to enjoy every fucking second of it exactly the way I liked.

Yet before I unleashed a single fantasy on Belle, I pulled away. Not an easy feat, given how easily she excited me, but I didn't go far. With a hand gently grasping her throat, my skin warmed as her breath quickened.

"Belle," I whispered, loving the way her name tasted, "you have to tell me when you're faced with something that makes you uncomfortable. I want us to be able to discuss it so we can both decide if it's something worth pursuing. Do you understand?"

After all, some discomforts could be overcome—if guided by the right hand.

Beyond that, I didn't want her feeling like she *had* to cater to my every need because of our—situation. While it might take a few days to figure out how we would interact with one another, Belle had always seemed easy to get along with. What I didn't want was a doormat, a woman who thought she had to spring into action twenty-four seven because I was paying her. The idea might be counterintuitive to some, but I hadn't brought her here as some chained-up sex slave. I wanted her to enjoy herself, too. I wanted her to be as close to her authentic, curious self as she was comfortable with.

"I understand, sir," she murmured, her breath catching when my hand tightened just a hint around her neck. She stood up taller on her tiptoes, that kissable lower lip caught between her teeth. I gave her a beat longer—for her to use her voice, to tell me that all this traveling had made her tired, that perhaps we ought to go back.

Nothing.

She merely pulled off her sunglasses and tossed them aside, exposing herself, baring her vulnerabilities.

"Good." I dragged her in for a far rougher kiss, taking full advantage of her parted lips to claim her as my own. My arm snaked around her waist, and I lifted her up as she squealed, her mouth frantic to keep pace with mine. I let the beast free, allowed him to consume, to drink her in for just a few perfect moments as she dangled there in my arms. Her pulse raced beneath my palm, and she gripped my T-shirt again, the neckline protesting the stretch of her little fists.

As soon as I lowered her back down, my hand left her throat and shot down her figure, questing purposefully over every curve until I reached the two pert globes of her ass. Belle giggled, a sound I happily swallowed, when I kneaded each—then tugged them apart, imagining how exquisite they'd look, shuddering, quivering, when I eventually took her from behind.

While my stiffening cock longed to be buried inside her —in *any* of her available holes, for he was an equal opportunist sort of cock—I wanted to return the gift she'd bestowed upon me on the flight.

The gift of her mouth.

So, with some difficulty, I extricated myself—from her pretty little mouth that chased after me, from her swollen lips and her flushed cheeks. Holding up a finger, I strode back toward the cliff's edge, but not so close that she could see over. As I kicked the rocks and dirt aside, I decided I could kill two birds with one stone: return a favour *and* help her properly enjoy the view.

Without a word, I settled on the ground, stretching out on my back—hoping the ants had more interesting mountains to conquer in the forest.

"Come here, Belle," I said as I settled down, hands threaded together on my stomach. "I want you to straddle my face."

When I didn't hear the dulcet pitter-patter of her gladiators, I sat up on my elbows and offered my best watered-down Dom scowl. After all, this wasn't playtime, even if our house rules were still in effect. This was—just for fun. For her.

Belle hesitated, fiddling with the billowy fabric of her dress. I pulled my sunglasses off, folded their arms in, and set them out of harm's way.

"Belle." My tone left no room for argument—in theory. "I've wanted to taste that cunt of yours from the first moment we met. Come *here*."

She jolted forward as if shocked by some delicious cattle prod, taking short, curt steps to close the distance between us. Shyly, she climbed down on top of me, crawling up my body with less coordination than I was sure she wanted.

"How should I...? Uhm." Belle gestured to my head, her cheeks positively aflame. Honestly—I'd never met an escort who blushed this much. She was perfect.

"Kneel over me," I instructed, tapping one side of my head, then the other. "Knees here and here. My shoulders will be between your calves. I'll do the rest."

She brushed my cock in passing, the caress only serving to worsen the tightness in my shorts. Belle seemed not to notice; she was too preoccupied with wrangling all the dress up my body. After she had finally passed my shoulders, she shuffled about, arranging her legs properly—and all I had to do for now was sit back and enjoy the view.

Belle's perfectly trimmed cunt was a vision. Cute little lips. Neat. Orderly. In an instant, I knew where everything was—and how best to attack. Her folds glistened with the beginnings of arousal, and it took everything I had in me not to lunge up and spear her with my tongue.

Instead I waited, dutifully, until she found a comfortable position. Her dress had fallen over my head in the meantime, which, I had to admit, made the whole ordeal hotter than comfortable. With the Caribbean sun unrelenting in the cloudless sky above, it was stifling under here. Sure, I could have put her on her back and tasted her just as well. I could have dropped to my knees—a real tit for tat scenario—and propped her up on my shoulders. There were plenty of other possibilities, but as I wove my arms around her thighs, smothered by her heat, her exquisite scent, I wouldn't have it any other way.

Suddenly, her dress disappeared; she must have realized she'd let it fall. Belle gathered it all in one hand while the other braced against the rock beneath us.

"Are you...? Is this all right?" she asked in an adorably small voice. I peered out from the curve of her pussy, grinning.

"Yes, just fine, Belle."

Whatever she intended to say next was lost in her breathy moan when I latched onto her clit. I worked the little bundle of nerves gently at first, teasingly, noting what kind of pressure made her twitch and gasp, what kind made her squirm and moan. The latter got me harder.

The next week would be a trial period for both of us. While we had met before, talked, spent endless hours in the conference room two floors above Elysium with lawyers in tow, we weren't familiar with each other's bodies. All that would change, of course, and *very* soon, if I had my way. So, while I lapped at her cunt, arms wrapped around her quivering thighs, forcing her to stay open for me, I not only used the moment as a means to return her earlier generosity, but also a learning opportunity.

I categorized the sounds she made—when she made them, how often, at what volume. I took note of her breath —when it fell harder, when she held it. I did my best to listen to her body as I explored her with my tongue, wishing I could add a finger or three for good measure—and maybe something else to plug her pretty little asshole. For now, however, I stuck to the basics. Rhythm. Consistency. Movement. If her body seemed to deflate, the tension seeping out of her, I tried something new to bring her back up again.

My back ached and my cock strained—both in pain, both easily fixable with the right creativity. But I pushed through, because this wasn't about me.

Well, it was a little about me. Perhaps even *for* me. But from the sounds she made, her high-pitched squeaks and strangled moans, and the way she shook in my arms, Belle wasn't exactly suffering up there.

Far from it.

Because some time later, both of us coated in a thin layer of sweat, my jaw pleasantly sore but still *ravenous*, her entire body stiffened. Had I been inside her, perhaps I would have felt her clench around me. As it were, my attention had been on her clit—and had been for quite a while. She keened softly, her hips grinding against my mouth, until she fell forward, gasping, and her dress fluttered down over my head again.

Did she just...?

Had she just...?

If I wasn't mistaken, Belle had just broken her first rule. And I, in turn, was required to dole out her first punishment.

As if my cock could get any harder.

Blindly, I grabbed at her dress and yanked it off my head, tucking all that fabric under my chin and fighting the urge to drag in a much-needed lungful of fresh air. The urge to control, to dictate the situation, to right a very grave wrong, kicked back in, and that feeling was far more gratifying than any deep breath. I nudged her up by her hips, bringing her onto all fours over me.

"Belle," I said, softly, dangerously, my inner Dominant bursting to life, "did you just come?"

HOUSE RULE #1

Belle cannot orgasm without permission.

*O*h my god.

That was—amazing.

Oh my god.

Wait.

Oh my god.

As Dean's steely inquiry cut through my post-orgasm haze, I realized where I'd gone wrong.

Ever since we landed, it had been such a whirlwind getting out here. That horrendously bumpy boat ride. Settling into my second-floor room. Unpacking and organizing all the lingerie. Trying to get into the right frame of mind for being an *escort*, not *me*—even when *me* enjoyed Dean as, well, *me*. On our island tour, I'd been so wrapped up in my thoughts, in the effort to be the fun, easygoing submissive Dean was paying for—that I had kind of let things slip in the heat of the moment.

He was just so good at *that*. All that mental preparation I'd done to ready myself for the first time a client touched me intimately had gone out the window. Because it wasn't weird. It wasn't clinical. It was intimate and passionate and *ohmygod*.

And then I'd ruined it by forgetting the first of many house rules.

"Belle," Dean said as I hastily scrambled off him. He sat up, wiping at the corners of his mouth. "Did you just come without permission?"

I bit my lip. I could lie. I could pretend I had just been *really* getting into it, but the thought of doing so had my stomach twisting. Dean was my Dom. We were supposed to be honest with each other—honest enough, anyway—even if honesty meant I was in for a world of hurt.

"Uhm." I brushed my dusty hands on my dress, squirming under his unflinching stare.

"Yes or no, Belle," Dean said, voice cracking sharp as a whip. "*Uhm* is not an answer."

"Yes." Pleasure still thrummed through me, the lingering aftermath of that stunning climax clinging to every inch of my body for dear life. Still, the longer this dragged on, the darker his gaze became—like *flint*—and fear started to crack through the haze.

"Yes *what*?"

"Yes, sir?" I winced, knowing from my scenes with Penny that I shouldn't answer a question with a question.

"No." He took a deep breath as he reached for his sunglasses and slipped them back on. "Tell me what rule you've broken, Belle."

"Rule number one," I said without missing a beat, not wanting to make this worse. "I came without permission, sir."

"Good." He stood, looming over me. "You know that means I'll have to punish you."

"Yes, sir." Punishment didn't scare me. Most of my

performances at Elysium were just elaborate, drawn-out punishments to entertain the crowd. Disappointing Dean bothered me. As he helped me up, then brushed the dirt off my dress, I realized it bothered me more than I'd expected.

"Stay here," he ordered, then turned and marched stiffly into the forest. Nibbling my lower lip, fidgeting with my nails, I shuffled away from the edge of the cliff. While I still couldn't see the bottom, the wind had picked up, whipping my hair about, and I didn't like standing so close.

But—Dean had told me stay *here*. Maybe he meant literally. Glancing between the tree line and the spot where he'd left me, I hesitated, then padded back, my heart racing, adrenaline pumping.

Although it couldn't have been more than a few minutes, it felt like an eternity had passed by the time Dean emerged from the trees again. I straightened, sucking in a panicked breath at the sight of the stick in his hand—a stick that I worried, momentarily, might be from one of those awful trees with all the spikes on them.

It wasn't.

Thank goodness.

But it looked thick and sturdy all the same. Dean snapped off a few of the smaller twigs and shoots, then paused, completely ignoring me, and smacked it against his upturned palm. Once, twice, a little harder on the second round. Seeming satisfied, he looked up at me, expression unreadable behind his aviators. I gulped.

"Lean against *that* tree," he pointed the nearest one out to me, "lift up your dress, and present yourself for punishment."

I stumbled forward on stilt-stiff legs, the command making me blush. As I braced one arm against the smooth trunk, the palm fronds high overhead whispering in the wind, he carried on.

"You'll receive two counts of five," Dean told me as I raised my dress, gathering all the excess fabric and hugging it to my chest like a pillow.

"Yes, sir."

"Normally it would be *three* counts of five," he remarked sharply, "but since it's the first day, we'll go lighter."

"Thank you, sir." My responses came automatically, like my mouth knew exactly what it needed to say—like it had memorized all the lines in this script. Meanwhile, my mind raced, trying to remember all the tidbits Penny had told me about taking a punishment. How to stand. How to cry out. How best to accommodate your Dom. Swallowing hard, I shuffled down and out, arching my back hard like I usually did on stage. In that moment, I wished I'd rubbed my thighs down with my dress; the breeze tickled my skin, still slick from our previous activity.

The one that had landed me in all this trouble.

I bit my lip and sighed.

"You'll count each strike."

"Yes, sir." I braced for the first hit, one arm on the palm trunk, the other holding my dress up to my chest, my chin resting on its fist.

Whack.

"Oh!" I shot up on impact, pain blooming across my right butt cheek.

That was a lot harder than Penny's first strikes during our shows.

"Belle."

"Sorry," I muttered, dropping back down into position, my face burning—my entire *body* burning. The second hit landed on my left cheek, no less gently, and I yelped, shooting up again.

"Belle," he growled, and I pressed a trembling, sweaty hand back to the trunk. Dean's shoes crunched across the landscape as he moved closer. "You know, I start over when you don't count your strikes aloud."

I squeezed my eyes tight for a moment. Right. Counting. The pain had just been so startling that I'd forgotten.

"Sorry, sir," I said meekly. A quick glance over my shoulder showed him nodding, then rearing back to strike again.

Whack. Both cheeks this time. I inhaled sharply, the part of my brain that focused on self-preservation screaming for me to get away from the man wielding the switch. A much softer voice, a gentle whisper, told me to tough it out—that I had earned my punishment.

That thought had me tingling between my thighs.

Dean cleared his throat pointedly.

"Three?" I offered.

"No." He almost sounded like he was smiling. "Don't be a brat."

"One," I said miserably, shifting my stance for the sake of comfort—*not* arching my back so dramatically this time. Dean, however, missed nothing.

"No, no, *you* wanted to thrust that ass out for me," he said, tapping each cheek lightly. "You'll hold that position until we're done."

Are you serious?

Penny had told me that anytime *that* thought crossed my mind when it came to my Dominant, so long as he wasn't pushing a limit, I ought to assume that he was, in fact, very serious. Huffing, I pushed an arch into my back, basically serving myself up for a sharper punishment.

Whack. Straight across both cheeks again. The sharp sting of each hit had started to blend together, my skin warming almost pleasantly. My toes curled. "Two."

Strikes three through five had me breathless and squirming. I couldn't imagine there was a spot left back there that Dean had missed. He didn't come across as the kind of man to do anything half-assed.

Speaking of asses—mine could have used an ice pack right about now. Or some aloe, preferably with someone to massage it in. I winced as I switched hands on the tree trunk, my entire body sticky and uncomfortable under the afternoon sun, under the heat, under the lash of Dean's stick.

A stick that was suddenly between my thighs, ghosting up and down each one. This time, I managed to hold my position, even though the caress tickled a little.

"Widen your stance." He tapped my right inner thigh twice, harder this time, and I shuffled further down the palm, then opened my legs further. Exposed. Vulnerable. On display. Unable to face him, not even to get a read on his thoughts, I tucked my chin into my chest and waited for the next set of five.

"Are you ready?" he asked, and when I nodded mutely, he barked my name.

"Yes, sir." Not really, but I'd done the crime.

Dean's next five strikes varied, both in location and timing. The backs of my thighs were up for grabs this set, and by the end I was crying out with each hit, each snap of the switch against my sensitive skin, and bouncing back and forth on the balls of my feet.

"*Five*," I squealed on the last blow, which had been in the exact same spot as strikes three and four. My lips quivered, my lower half ablaze. The whole area had probably gone bright red, and I suspected each strike would stay with me until tomorrow. I dreaded sitting for dinner tonight.

"All right. Up we go." Out of nowhere, Dean's hands descended on me. One on my lower back, the other on my arm as he helped me upright. My vision blurred as I straightened, and fat, heavy tears rolled down my cheeks. I blinked in surprise, forcing more out, and then hastily wiped them away, shooting Dean a furtive glance, hoping he hadn't seen them. From his frown, he had.

Damn it.

I shouldn't have been crying. I wasn't *sad*.

In fact, I was oddly alive. Exuberant, even. Like I'd survived some trial, as ridiculous as that sounded.

"Belle, are you okay?" Dean pulled me toward him, the stick forgotten in the dust a few feet from us, and wiped the wet tracks away with his thumbs. I nodded and released a watery laugh.

"I am. Really. I don't know why I'm crying. I didn't even notice it...during."

"Probably just the shock of it," he murmured, his arm curving around my shoulders, the weight of it oddly reassuring. I burrowed into him, arms folded between us, and smiled when he kissed my temple.

"Probably."

"You did very well," he told me, his voice whispery and soft again, all that flint and steel gone. "You took your punishment like a good girl."

"Thank you, sir." And I meant it. After all, there was a good chance we were both thinking the same thing—that I *hadn't* been all that great about taking my punishment. I'd squealed and flinched and jumped out of reach, especially at the beginning, but next time I would do better. I'd *be* better.

Still, his praise soothed me. It quieted the internal dialogue, the self-criticism, the doubt. It gave me confidence. It suddenly had me thinking that, maybe, I could do this. With him, I could be both Belle, the escort, and Belle, the human being, and not worry as much about keeping the two so rigidly separate.

In fact, as I stood there, snuggled up to his side as Dean pushed my hair back and dried my cheeks one last time, I found myself utterly spent—and happy. I could have curled up in his lap right there and slept the day away.

"How about this," he said as I tipped my head back to look at him. "We'll postpone the tour until after dinner. We'll go back, put some lotion on you, and you can take a nap for the rest of the afternoon. How does that sound?"

"It sounds nice," I admitted. "Really nice."

"Good." Dean stepped away, but only to retrieve my sunglasses. In an effort to *play* the good submissive, I'd tossed the cat-eye sunnies aside earlier as if they hadn't cost me a small fortune. As Dean slipped them back onto my ears, careful not to get any hair caught under the metallic arms, I decided I'd stop trying to *play* at being submissive. I'd quiet Penny's must-dos—and just *do*. From the way he handled me now, Dean seemed to prefer when I wasn't trying too hard—but this was only day one. That could all change on day two.

"I *do* think we'll need to work on your," Dean paused for a moment, as if searching for the right word, and then grabbed my hand again, our fingers twining, "*stamina*. Would you like to play another round of the game we played on the plane?"

"Now?" I asked, eyebrows shooting up. He shook his head, pulling me toward the trail.

"After your nap. Maybe while I cook dinner."

"Okay," I said brightly, looking away when he smirked. Clearing my throat, I added a nonchalant: "Or, you know, whenever—is also fine, sir."

Sunlight dappled his handsome face as we crossed the tree line, the canopy rustling overhead, and Dean kissed the top of my hand with a chuckle. "All right, Belle. *Whenever it is...*"

6

DEAN

*O*kay.

Ahi tuna—seared and resting.

Coleslaw—in the fridge.

Toasted taco shells—awaiting their filling.

Lemon vinaigrette for drizzling—next to the coleslaw.

Chopped sides—avocados, radishes, cilantro—also in the fridge.

Hands on my hips, I surveyed the tidied prep space, the dishes drying on the rack, and then set the pan in the sink to soak. Grabbing the bowl of spicy mayo I'd whipped up at the last moment, I dug into my pocket for the vibrator's remote and clicked the little device up to its final setting. Belle let out a strangled moan behind me, and I smirked, then slipped the remote back in my pocket and added the mayo into the very full, recently stocked fridge.

I had ordered our first round of groceries to be delivered yesterday. While there was a little company on Saint Thomas that did it, I had a team of staff on call to do the actual arranging inside my kitchen. I was rather particular about it. In fact, I had pushed my particularities into our contract—that *I* would be doing all the cooking for the next two months.

Belle could help if she liked. After her nap, she had padded downstairs, all sleepy-eyed but refreshed, and offered to prep the sides for our dinner—ahi tuna tacos. I hadn't let her do anything beyond cut vegetables, however. My cooking for us was part of the deal.

I loved cooking.

Yet I seldom had the opportunity to do it, either for myself or for company. Back home I had a private chef, and the resorts had no problem plying me with delicious options from their kitchens. But—I'd always liked doing it myself. I especially liked doing it for a submissive. Feeding her. Nourishing her. Caring for her by fueling her body—I relished the *intimacy* of cooking.

I had a whole dossier on Belle, separate from the packet legal had drawn up for both of us, that listed all the things she liked. Most of them had been off-the-cuff remarks on our coffee dates, but I'd made note of every one.

From there, I'd built a menu plan for the next two months. I wanted to keep it healthy and nutritious, altering some of her favourites to comply. Three weeks ago, she had told some anecdote about a trip to California with her dad, and I'd noted the way her eyes lit up when she recalled the surf shack fish tacos. Well, seared ahi tuna was a step up from whatever those heathens had served her.

I intended to spoil my submissive—both in and out of the bedroom.

On the other side of the coin, I also had a list of foods she *detested*. Should I need to get creative with my punishments, I always had brussels sprouts, and she'd eat every last one I put on her plate.

Closing the fridge door gently, I straightened and

stretched side to side, my back cracking. Behind me, Belle's efforts were growing louder—even with the bit gag. As I washed my hands in the deep sink, lathering them up with hand soap, my back to her, I had to admire her perseverance. She'd been at it for—seven minutes and forty-five seconds. Fifteen seconds better than on the plane, but still not quite where I wanted her.

Some of the scenarios I'd outlined required Belle to keep from climaxing for lengthy periods of time. From what I had seen today, she needed a bit of training in that area. Most of all, she needed to remember to *ask* to come; at least then I would know she was close and could respond accordingly. Back off. Ease up. Force her to do a task that would cool her down before we returned to the main event. Something. But if she didn't say anything, we would keep having incidents like this afternoon's transgression.

Not that I minded punishing her. And today *was* only the first day. Eventually, however, I would expect her to follow the rules.

Her muffled cry had my cock stiffening. She had been harder to ignore over the last few minutes, and I tucked my shaft into the waistband of my shorts before facing her after nearly eight torturous minutes for *both* of us: her fighting her climax, me unable to watch her naked body writhe.

The first floor of my four-thousand-square-foot vacation estate had been designed to feel open and airy. Glass windows encased the entire level, offering spectacular panoramic views of the island—beach, water, forest, and, although it was man-made, the pool. Granite countertops flecked with grey, gold, and white sat atop the L-shaped configuration of my kitchen counters. Stainless steel appliances everywhere you looked. A farmhouse sink—all the rage these days, according to my interior decorator sister

—and a dishwasher. To my left, the white stone staircase, glossy and smooth, led you upstairs, sequestered in by a glass railing. Below the stairs, a seating area: white lounge chairs, a glass coffee table, a two-seater sofa.

I'd taken tones from the island itself to offset all the white: the paintings, the rug under the coffee table, and the kitchenware were all reflective of the landscape.

The only piece that wasn't made of glass or white stone was the twelve-person walnut dining table. Apparently, seven years ago I'd had grand aspirations of entertaining large groups. These days, I only wanted to share the space with one person—and at the moment, she was strapped to that enormous table.

Well, bent *over* it, more like, and tied in place.

I strolled forward, hands in my pockets and a smirk on my lips, as Belle continued to wriggle and moan. Her sounds had become more strangled, more desperate as time wore on. I couldn't imagine the position was all that comfortable, but comfort hadn't been the point when I tied her there. With her ankles lashed to each table leg, I'd left her splayed and vulnerable—totally naked, forced to stand up on her tiptoes. Silk satin restraints—pink, of course, like all the goodies I'd purchased for this trip—knotted around her ankles and wrists. Bent at the waist, her body stretched over the dining table, hands clutching the satin laced around each wrist.

I sauntered to the far end of the table, where I'd looped her wrist ties around the two legs there. My goodness— Belle was a vision. Sprawled out. Utterly immobile. Trapped. Helpless, with a vibrator buzzing in her pretty little cunt and a bit gag in her mouth.

After she had assisted with dinner prep, I had her put the vibrator in place—but I didn't turn it on. Instead, I'd had her pull out our plates and wine glasses for supper, organizing them on a thatched carry-out tray. Then, just before I tossed the tuna on the stove, I'd had her strip naked and bend over one end of the table. She had done so without hesitation. In fact, she had seemed a bit giddy about it—until I bound her, firmly, and stuck a gag in her mouth. Then she started to shift about nervously, testing her restraints, the tightness of her bit.

"How are we doing, Belle?" I crouched down to meet her eyeline. "Have you come yet?"

She looked up, her watery eyes wild and desperate. Drool dribbled from her lips, the gag forcing her mouth open. A delightful red flush had erupted across her body, from her cheeks down to her chest. It was a shame I had chosen to arrange her this way: I would have enjoyed toying with her nipples, testing her tolerance. Another time. For now, I could relish the view of her marked-up ass instead.

"Well? Have you come yet?" I arched an eyebrow, and she shook her head frantically, mouthing a strangled, muffled *no, sir*. The bit gag, about two inches around and made of squishy silicone, allowed for more speech than a ball gag, and I had both on hand, in varying sizes. Here, she could still *almost* utter her safeword—apricots—if need be, but there was the nonverbal cease and desist—snapping her fingers twice—available to her as well.

Her answer had me smiling. "Good girl."

How beautiful she looked—bound and gagged. A teary-eyed, dribbling, trembling, blushing mess of a submissive. Belle was a gorgeous girl; any idiot could see that. But to me, what made her so exquisite was her exertion. Her effort. If I touched her, I'd likely find her sticky and hot. Biting down on her gag, she looked like she was trying so *fucking* hard not to come—and she never looked more lovely than when she tried to please me.

I tugged at her left restraint, wondering how that pink silk would look wrapped around her throat. "Are you ready for your reward?"

She hesitated, staring at me as though I might take it back, and then finally nodded, the movement paired with a long, agonized moan. Excellent. I'd been wanting to reward her for a long time. The chocolates on the plane had been all well and good, but *this* reward—it was a moment to bond between Dom and sub. And I lived for these moments.

I checked her restraints quickly, ensuring the knots were still tight, that she wasn't going anywhere. First on the table legs, then at her wrists. As I passed by, I also saw to her gag, tightening it one more notch, just for fun. Her faintly freckled skin glowed with a thin layer of perspiration, and it erupted in little bumps when I trailed my finger down the length of her spine.

Tonight, her ass was her crowning glory—so prettily marked from this afternoon's punishment. While I had knocked off one set of five, I had purposefully gone hard on her for the remaining two. She needed a taste of what was to come, of what might be waiting should she misbehave. Should she break the rules. Naturally, I had more tricks up my sleeve than spanking, but I so adored the way a submissive's skin tinged rosy pink after a good spanking. Belle's skin held the color especially well, seven distinct marks left across her buttocks and thighs.

Still, I wasn't sure how easy she bruised, and while the occasional bruise was a stark reminder to toe the line, I didn't want her covered in them by any means, her pale skin painted black and blue and purple. If she bruised easily, then she might need more time to recuperate. Over this first

week, I'd determine how far I could go—within her limits—
to avoid lengthy recovery times. After all, two months might
seem like all the time in the world for two people alone on a
private island, but it could race by in the blink of an eye if I
wasn't careful.

Time really does fly when you're having fun.

Belle had been at it for nearly nine minutes when I
finally shut the vibrator off. Her entire body sagged in relief,
and perhaps disappointment, but she shot right back up
when I slipped two fingers into her wet opening and
retrieved the little rod. Her arousal dripped down her
thighs, leaving her positively soaked. While that was
difficult to tear myself away from, I did, leaning forward to
set the vibrator in front of her face. She moaned softly as my
hips, my rigid cock, pressed against her undoubtedly
sore ass.

Straightening up, I noted that the braid I had plaited
into her hair remained. Not for long. Not after I had my way
with her, the satin bow at its base unlikely to hold.

As I smoothed a hand over her cheeks, admiring the
marks, a thought occurred to me: she could be lying. She
could have come twice by now and only become more adept
at hiding it. I shook my head, running my finger between
her slick, swollen folds. She *could* be lying, sure, about a
great many things, but trust was so key in a Dom-sub
relationship. I had to trust her, even if she was a *paid*
submissive, just as she had to trust that I wouldn't hurt her,
abuse her—that everything I did was in her best interest.

So, for now, I would move forward under the
assumption that she had been honest with me.

That she was *dying* to climax.

Her body certainly suggested as much.

"Belle," I murmured, speaking low enough that she had

to crane her head back, ear toward me, to hear, "I'm going to fuck you now, and for your reward, you can come whenever you'd like—as many times as you like. How does that sound?"

She moaned and looked away, then pressed her forehead to the table and moaned again. I grinned, tracing abstract shapes across her skin as she shuddered.

"That's what I thought."

I could have dragged it out. Made her suffer.

Instead, I pulled a condom out of my pocket and ripped open the shiny packaging. Despite our numerous medical examinations, the fact that Belle was on the pill, and my general dislike for condoms, I had some on hand for situations like this—when I didn't want to worry about the cleanup after. With everything that had gone on today, I figured Belle would hate to waste another half hour showering before she dug into her tacos. Once we were finished here, she could have a few moments to herself, then it was straight to the lounge area next to the pool for dinner under the stars, on reclining chairs that offered more cushion than those at the dining table.

Button popped, zipper open, my shorts fell unceremoniously down my legs, and I kicked them aside for better mobility. My cock dropped heavily against Belle's ass, and she jumped at the contact, squeaking. I so loved the noises she made.

After rolling on the condom, I eased my cock between her folds, using her arousal as a lubricant. She shifted about beneath me, moaning, arching her back and thrusting herself up to meet me.

Brat. *You'll have what I give you, not what you try to take.*

I gave her two light smacks, one on each cheek, wearing a lazy smile as I stroked myself.

From the moment I met Belle, I'd wanted to fuck her. If I could, I would have bent her over Elysium's office reception desk and had my way with her right then and there. But what I'd wanted most of all was this—her, bound and desperate, dripping with need and utterly helpless to attain her own pleasure. I could walk away right now. Leave her there. Eat my dinner at the head of the table while she stayed put until I was finished—and that would be almost as enjoyable as having her.

Almost.

After such a long day, Belle had earned her reward.

So, I gave it to her.

Gripping her hip with one hand, I steered my cock into her with the other. As soon as her wet heat engulfed me, I thrust hard, sinking all the way in with a groan. Belle mewled and tugged at her restraints, body arching up to meet me.

Fuck. For a few seconds, my vision went black. Black, followed by swirling galaxies and stars. She was so tight, positively *soaking*, trembling beneath me as I doubled over and blanketed her body. I pushed deeper, bucked my hips, lifting her off the table as far as the restraints would allow while she squealed.

Fuck, this was going to be a good two months.

Teeth gritted, I traced my fingers down her sides, enjoying the way she twitched and squeaked. Ticklish little thing. *Good.* I played with the end of her braid and moved my hips in slow circles, grinding her into the table. A part of me would have liked to just reach under her, between her thighs, and work her clit through a climax. Instead, I dragged my tongue along her spine, thrilled with the way her skin prickled again, and straightened.

I gripped her hips with both hands this time and pulled

her back, as far as I could, to spare her the bite of the table's edge. Then, without any pomp and ceremony, without any word of warning, I took her—hard and fast. A ragged scream tore from her throat as I pounded into her, our bodies slamming together. A symphony of slapping skin, Belle's noises, and my groans soon swelled across the first floor, drowning out the rest of the world.

The rest of my problems, concerns, worries.

All that mattered was her—and her reward.

I angled myself on the next thrust, shifting about so I could hit the little sweet spot along her inner walls with each pump of my hips. Her noises became sharper, squeakier. I caught my reflection in the nearby glass wall just as a feral smile crossed my lips; I had her.

Belle came like a wild woman, trying to flail, to arch and bow her back, but unable to move beyond what I had allowed. Her cries turned breathless and her cunt convulsed around me. I fell forward with a hiss, catching myself on the table as her pussy massaged me, hugged me, threatened to drag me into the storm with her.

Not yet.

No, I was determined to prolong her pleasure first. Shoving her back up against the table, I ground my hips against her ass, circling them, bucking them—whatever I could do to lengthen her climax. I even managed to force another breathy shriek out of her when I latched onto her clit, massaging it between two fingers as she continued to ensnare my cock in a vise-grip.

When she finally started to settle, her breathing less erratic, her eyes closed, I grabbed her braid and wrapped it twice around my hand. A sharp tug wrenched her head back. Belle straightened with a moan—perhaps in protest, but I didn't care. I held her like that as I resumed thrusting, fucking her with hard, brisk strokes.

Both mindful of the strain on her neck and operating under the assumption that my poor submissive was both tired *and* hungry, I forced myself to finish faster than I would have liked. I could have gone on. I could have stopped, toyed with her some more, and then—but we had two months for that. So, with one final thrust, one that lifted her off the table again, I let go.

I came with a groan, releasing her braid as I fell forward, my forehead settling between her shoulder blades. Like a snowflake, every orgasm was unique. This one hit me like a tidal wave, a stunning release of power and fury. As I folded over her, catching my breath for what felt like the first time in years, the heat of our bodies curled between us, pleasure lapping at me like a wave surging up the shore. It pulsed, growing weaker with each beat, until finally I could stand up without losing my balance.

With a weary, satisfied sigh, I undid Belle's gag clasp. It hit the table with a wet *thud*. My thoroughly used sub dragged in a deep breath of her own, then settled onto her cheek, her eyes heavy.

"Are you all right, Belle?" I massaged the base of her neck, pleased with her sleepy smile as she nodded. "Good. Let's get you ready for dinner then." Straightening once more, I gave her ass a gentle smack, avoiding the marks. "I'm afraid you're *woefully* underdressed."

Her giggle made my heart happy, and without another word, I saw to her restraints, all the while thinking that day one of this vacation—had been a day well spent.

HOUSE RULE #13

Sundays are for Belle to do as she pleases.

7

BELLE

Sunday, February 3rd

*S*unday, Sunday, Sunday, *Sunday!*

I knew I shouldn't have been this excited for a day off. I'd only been here two days. One and a half, technically, if you counted our half-day on Friday. In the grand scheme of things, I was only on day three of fifty-nine. The thought of a free day shouldn't have had me bouncing around, giddy—but what the heck. It did. Living on a tropical island, with a whole twenty-four hours to myself? Luxury villa at my disposal? Pool? Sand? Sun? Beach? Cinema room?

Of course, I'd make the most of today.

Puttering around my new room, I tossed everything I'd need for a beach morning into my tote bag: towel, e-reader, sunscreen, goggles. The flippers I'd carry down there. Just like yesterday, the weather on Dean's Ixora Isle was utter perfection. After a particularly harsh New York winter, all this time in the tropics ought to boost my spirits to the moon and back.

If only I wasn't still so *in my head* about things.

With a sigh, I planted my hands on my hips, scanning the space for anything I might have missed. Hair plaited back in a braid? Check. Bright white new bikini that made my cleavage look awesome? Check. Sunglasses? I frowned, searching the all-white linens of my freshly made queen-sized bed—one of the house rules: keep my space tidy—then the little glass tables on either side. A flicker of panic gripped me, and then—oh. Sunglasses were on my head. I rolled my eyes, readjusting them for good measure.

While there were a number of guest bedrooms on the second floor, along with an outdoor seating area overlooking the pool below, Dean had given me the nicest one—in my humble opinion. Spacious and airy, much like the rest of the house, it was just big enough that when I closed the door, I didn't feel claustrophobic in a place that so clearly belonged to someone else. This was my domain, even if it was all white and minimalistic, accented here and there with blues, greens, and browns that harkened back to the gorgeous forestry outside.

Tote packed, I quickly zipped into the ensuite bathroom to brush my teeth. Not only was there a standing shower with a rainfall showerhead, but also a large claw-foot tub big enough for two. Dean had made it clear on our tour after—*ahem*—our second round of his "game" that this was my space. He wouldn't enter unless invited, or there was some sort of emergency. Nor should I feel obligated to extend an invitation. He'd insisted that this room was *mine*, which I appreciated.

After all, not much else on Ixora belonged to me; it was nice to have my own little plot of land inside Dean's kingdom.

Teeth brushed, flyaways smoothed, I bounced back to

the bedroom and grabbed my tote and flippers. While I'd swum in both the Pacific and the Atlantic before, I had never done the snorkeling thing. All my gear had been purchased last month in preparation for this trip—hopefully it was up to snuff.

I shied around the huge window overlooking the gardens below. Dean had pointed out all the flowers he'd had added recently—maybe for me, a thought that gave me a funny feeling inside, but, then again, maybe not. At the time, I'd humored him, nodding and smiling and pointing out the ones I thought the prettiest.

As soon as he left, however, I had closed the curtain and hadn't opened it since. I didn't even look out the window of my *own* apartment. Even though I was only on the second floor here, standing next to it, to a pane that could lift up if I wanted, made my heart plummet into my stomach and my palms turn cold and clammy. No thank you, heights. I didn't need anything else around here making me nervous.

Because Dean did enough of that already.

This *job* did enough of that already.

By day three, I had already emailed Penny about some, not all, of my concerns, and as I shut my bedroom door, I could almost hear her voice reading the words of her curt reply in my ear.

Belle, you are getting paid a shitload of money to vacation on a tropical island for two months while some hot guy dominates you. Can you just enjoy it already?

As I padded down the staircase to the first floor, glancing behind me briefly, careful not to look over the glass railing, I couldn't help but feel just a bit silly. Penny was right. I ought to be enjoying myself. What Dean did to me—I liked it. A lot. I found I liked the punishments *and* the rewards, reminiscent of teenage fantasies inspired by dark romances read behind closed doors. The feel of Dean's hands on my body, his words dancing across my skin. The flint of his Dom stare contrasted with the warmth of his aftercare. I liked all of it.

But I still couldn't get completely out of my head—because, *should* an escort *like* a client the way I liked Dean? Or was professional distance a requirement in all scenarios?

It didn't feel very professional to like him, or to enjoy what he did to me, as much as I did, to think about both as I was falling asleep, fighting the urge to slip a hand between my thighs...

Once on the bottom step, I hastily scanned the first floor, my cheeks on fire. No Dean in sight.

We'd had breakfast together an hour ago, which he had still cooked for me like it was any other day, but since then —nothing.

Which was good. Apparently, I needed the space—on day three.

I plopped my sunglasses onto my nose with a sigh as I slipped out the sliding-glass door near that enormous dining table he'd bent me over on our first night. My mind shouldn't be racing. I should be in the moment. I *should* enjoy myself, just like Penny's email had said—but I knew for a fact she didn't lose herself in her sessions with clients. She had the professional distance down pat.

I glanced back at the glass, lingering for a moment, pretending to adjust my tote strap. A warm, gentle gust billowed across the landscape, rustling the palm fronds, blanketing me from top to bottom as the midmorning sun bore down from above. In the distance, the Caribbean Sea lapped at the shore. Birds twittered noisily, shooting between trees. I caught their reflections, their choreographed dances, in the tinted glass. Just through the window—that *table*. I hadn't maintained a professional distance that night. I'd been lost in the moment. Drowning in Dean, in the way he did what he wanted to me, coaxed out such a ridiculous high...

Swallowing hard, I turned away. Going forward, I had to get better, find a way to create professional boundaries between us—yet still appear one hundred percent present.

Somehow.

Because Dean didn't want a faker. He'd made that clear with all the times he had told me to be myself, as best I could. To not put on an act. I wasn't on stage anymore.

But...

Ugh.

Let it go, Belle.

Because today was Sunday.

And Sundays were all for me.

Mercifully, my surroundings soothed me. While the snow and slush and ice and hail of Manhattan's winter made me introspective and distant, the chorus of Ixora Isle's nature had me unfurling like a flower in bloom. The breeze carried away my worries. The symphony of whispering leaves and skittering wildlife quieted my racing mind. And the sight of the sparkling blue waters ahead—well, it was good for the soul. By the time I navigated the jungle path between Dean's mansion and the waterline, pausing at the peak of the little hill that slanted down to the white sandy beach, my anxiety had dissipated.

For now.

And, for now, I'd take what I could get.

Barefoot and smiling, I sauntered down the slope, kicking the sand as I went, and stopped midway between the trail and sea to dump my stuff. Soaring green islands rose up across the water in the distance. Dean had told me we'd take day trips every so often, and I had a whole secret wish list scribbled in my diary with all the things I wanted to do. At no point would I thrust my personal agenda onto him—because Monday to Saturday, we did whatever Dean planned.

Still. As I surveyed the horizon, a hand hovering over my eyes to shield them from the glare, the possibilities really were endless.

Just as I bent over and dug into my tote, searching for the sunscreen to get the spot on the back of my neck that I always forgot about, a very distinct rustling sounded behind me. Shooting up, I whirled around to find Dean Donahue— because who *else* was on this island? *Honestly, Belle*— strolling toward me with a folded black chair under one arm, his laptop under the other. He sported an army-green panama hat on his head, beige board shorts, no shoes...

And a completely bare chest.

Corded muscle snaked up his arms. Defined pectorals. One, two, three, four—*six* clear-cut abdominal muscles and a deliciously sharp V-cut slicing down beneath his shorts.

Guh.

I swallowed hard, suddenly fidgeting with my bikini top straps as he strolled toward me. Unhurried. Confident. He moved effortlessly—like he owned the place.

And he did.

He owned me, too.

The thought had a flicker of arousal bolting through me, my heart beating just a touch harder.

"Hi," I managed, waving shyly when I realized I'd just been gawking at him—gawking like I'd never seen a hot, shirtless guy before. Which wasn't true. The Children of Hades were always in various states of undress at Elysium, men too. I'd seen the abs. I'd seen the rippling shoulders.

But no one made them look quite as mouthwatering as Dean.

As he carried on toward me, I couldn't help but think about what we'd been doing at this time yesterday. According to the house schedule, right now would be office work time for Dean—he had a thousand irons in a thousand fires, so I couldn't fathom how he had managed to swing a two-month vacation—and taskwork for me. Yesterday's task had been polishing all of Dean's dress shoes, naked, while he worked away at his desk. He had about a dozen for me to do, which I'd done sitting up on my legs, ankles crossed beneath me, chest out—just to give him something to look at.

Only he'd barely looked at me. Not while I polished, anyway. It was when I was finished that his dark stare found me. He'd then instructed me to take all the shoes back to the rack in his bedroom closet. One at a time. And I could only carry them in my mouth. No hands.

Thankfully, I hadn't used *actual* polish to clean the already fairly-clean shoes; just a cotton rag and my own elbow grease. So, one by one, I'd picked up each shoe, the scent of leather and sophistication fusing to the insides of my nostrils, and crawled from the second-floor office to Dean's bedroom. Straight to his closet, no snooping around. Still naked. Knees screaming from all that time on the tile. Twenty-four times I made the trek. Dean had sauntered after me for every single one of them, a few feet behind, occasionally ordering me to move faster, slower, to stop so he could slip a finger between my damp folds...

It was fun. For all my worrying and stressing, yesterday *had* been a lot of fun—and there had been exactly *zero* sex involved. After the morning session, we'd had lunch. Dean massaged my legs during pool time, admiring my faintly bruised knees, and then we'd played another game for our afternoon session.

While not as pleasurable as his first game on the jet, we'd both gotten something out of it.

With the coffee table moved aside, Dean had scattered ten foam balls around the sitting area on the first floor. Some on the plush throw rug, others on the tile. He would then time me for fifteen seconds, and I had to grab all the balls I could, hands clasped behind my back, and put them in a bowl on the couch. However many balls were left dictated the number of times he'd flog me.

The first time I'd missed six, and I think he went easy on me.

Four the following time.

We played for about a half hour, taking breaks here and there for Dean to check on my poor butt and thighs, neither of which was fully recovered from my punishment the day before. In fact, I had a feeling that was why he'd gone easy on me with the flogger, which stung a little but could have been much worse.

By the time we'd finished, Dean had a tent in his shorts. My hips, butt, and thighs burned pleasantly, and my slick inner thighs told us both just how much I'd enjoyed myself.

But neither of us had found relief in the traditional sense. For aftercare, Dean had massaged some cocoa butter into my skin—and that was that. I'd gone to bed horny and flustered but had resisted the urge to find my much-needed release.

House rules and all that. I couldn't imagine Dean would be all that thrilled with me sneaking into his bedroom at three in the morning, begging him to just let me come.

Or—actually—maybe...

No. I blinked quickly, chasing the thought away, as Dean set his folded chair in the sand beside my things.

"Is everything okay?" I asked. A small part of me worried that I'd made a mistake, that I'd missed the memo and today *wasn't* an off day for me like all the other Sundays. After all, we had only been here a day and a half. Maybe I was supposed to be up in his office, waiting for my daily task.

"Fine, fine," he said with one of those breezy, handsome smiles that had me weak in the knees. "I just don't have a lifeguard down here, and I don't like the idea of you swimming by yourself."

My arms fell to my sides, relief quashing the anxiety. "Oh."

Dean was worried about me. He'd come down to watch me swim, to play lifeguard while I explored paradise. Warmth fluttered in my chest, the same sensation that bloomed at the sound of his praise.

"I know it's your day off," he said, handing me his laptop briefly while he unfolded his chair. He then took the device back and set it in his seat—and I tried not to drool over his muscle, over the faint scent of a musky, masculine cologne. How the guy managed to work as hard as he did *and* stay in such stellar shape was beyond me. I knew he jogged in the mornings before breakfast—I'd caught him yesterday after I called the office to confirm I was still alive—and there were a bunch of free weights in a storage bin by the pool.

Maybe I'd get to watch him work out while I lounged.

What a way to kill an hour or two.

"Well, yes, it's my off day, but—"

"Just pretend I'm not here," Dean remarked, his tone casual, like he wasn't asking the impossible. "If I stayed up at the house, I'd just worry. I'll be catching up on some work—but if you're under for too long, I'm coming in."

"Noted." I grinned, fiddling with the hem of my bikini bottom. To his credit, he hadn't once ogled me like I'd done to him.

Not that I'd mind if he did.

I'd bought the bikini *for* him. He'd requested all my lingerie be either pink or white, so I had applied that directive to bikinis too.

"Well, go on then." He grabbed his laptop before settling into the chair, appraising me from behind the shade of his aviators. "Enjoy the water. Sometimes we get turtles in the shallows."

"Oh, cool!" My cheeks coloured at the pitch of my voice —and the fact that I'd had to stop myself from clapping with delight.

What?

Turtles *might* have been my favourite animal. Sue me.

So, I unpacked the rest of my things, spreading out my towel and plopping my tote in the middle to keep it from blowing away. Dean even shuffled over enough so that his chair leg caught a corner. I then tossed my sunglasses, pulled my brand-new mask and attached snorkel on, and brushed my sandy feet off before slipping them into my pink flippers.

Brimming with excitement, eager to explore the clear blue waters of the Caribbean Sea, I waddled down to the surf, my steps exaggerated courtesy of the feet fins. However, rather than charging straight in, I paused. The water surged up to my ankles, warm and inviting. Nibbling my lower lip, I glanced over my shoulder and found Dean watching me.

Or maybe not.

Who could tell with those sunglasses?

Still, the thought had that *feeling* bubbling up again.

Which triggered my anxiety—my absolute need for professional distance.

So, I looked to the island to distract me again. To the sunlight glinting off the water. To the waves breaking against the shore. To the distant cries of birds.

And, with a steadying breath, I waded in with that *feeling* still warming my chest, clinging to me, at the thought of Dean Donahue watching my back.

8

DEAN

Tuesday, February 12th

"*S*trip."

Out of the corner of my eye, I spied Belle drag the beach cover-up over her head, then toss the shapeless cottony fabric onto the poolside lounge chair, barefoot on the cement. She fluffed her hair, as she always did, and I shifted myself away so she wouldn't see the effect that her naked body *still* had on me, two weeks in.

Not that I shouldn't get hard at the sight of a stunning naked woman who bowed to my every command.

As her Dom, I just expected myself to have a little more control. Over my feelings. Over my body. Over everything.

Hands planted on my hips, I refocused on the pink inflatable ring at our feet. The pool floatie was one of many I'd stocked the house with in anticipation of Belle's arrival. Pool time was a scheduled part of our day, as I wanted her to relax between sessions, and she had proven preferential to the enormous flamingo floatie; it had the perfect seat for her to curl up with her e-reader beneath the sunshine, and she always looked especially cute when she straddled the flamingo's neck, her feet kicking ineffectually through the water.

Today's floatie of choice was more traditional, though imagine my surprise when I inflated it for the first time and discovered the damn thing looked like a fucking *donut*. While pink, it also had a chocolate glaze and sprinkles on top. Belle had thought it was adorable, completely missing my unimpressed look as she fawned over it. On the next grocery run, I had been sure to include a box of near-identical donuts—just to see her smile.

Naturally, the donuts were rewards. I loved spoiling people with food, but two months straight of sweets and treats wasn't good for either of us. Thus far, I'd kept our desserts healthy and only brought out the chocolate, the ice cream, the mini-cakes when Belle had earned a little something extra that day.

Which she did quite often. Belle was a fucking dream as a submissive—in all categories save one. While she listened well and did as instructed with only minimal, occasional hesitation, she still came whenever she damn well pleased.

It was driving me nuts.

And her poor bottom couldn't take another spanking, honestly. A quick glance showed she was still pink from yesterday's. I sighed, hoping today's afternoon play session might finally help us get some control over that.

Wanton little submissive, coming on a whim—on *her* whim.

My cock twitched at the thought.

"I think if I sink into it a little more," she said suddenly, contemplatively, pointing at the inflatable donut, "and put my hips up on this end, we should be good."

"I was thinking the same thing."

For two glorious weeks, I'd been able to live out some of my longest-standing sexual fantasies, the kind that I'd need months and months of trust-building with a submissive in the real world to accomplish. While Belle and I had been on speaking terms since last August, we'd only had limited experience in the kink game. Still, she performed beautifully—especially when she wasn't *trying* to perform. Even now, she stood beside me with her shoulders back, her stomach taut, but not overly posed as she had been when we first started. And she was sublime.

I hadn't blamed her for the initial posturing. Most of Belle's submissive experience came from her interactions with other escorts onstage at Elysium. She was accustomed to performing for a crowd, not for a single Dom. I'd let it slide the first week, thinking she might need the comfort of familiarity, but had called her out on it this week. She didn't need to arch her back, thrust out her tits, her ass, just to please me. I preferred her like this—au naturel, but still at attention.

"Well, let's see if we can figure it out, shall we?" I offered a hand to help her onto the ring; I'd always wanted to fuck someone on one of these things, and we'd spent last night's dinner going over the logistics. Belle settled in gracefully with my assistance, scooting her butt up onto one side of the ring, her back and shoulders sinking into the middle, her head resting against the other side. I stared down at her, sans sunglasses, and frowned. Clearing her throat, she reached up and gripped the pair of handles on either side, which I intended to tie her to once we had our positions figured out.

I didn't like the strain on her neck. She'd be in that position for as long as I could have her, and the thought of her pulling something made my chest tight. So, we reworked ourselves, shuffling her about, trying different versions of the same pose until we found one that she was more comfortable in. Her pretty little cunt sat just on the edge of the ring, her legs dangling over the side. I could work with that.

"Are you all right?" When she nodded enthusiastically, her cheeks flushed the same adorable pale pink they always were before a scene, I grabbed the silk ties and ordered her to grasp the handles. Once she closed a fist around each, I tied her in place, topping each wrist off with a decadent bow—which was, of course, all for my viewing pleasure. She was just so pretty in pink. Bows were an added bonus to such a perfect package.

"Ready?" I asked with a raised brow.

"Yes, sir."

"Good. Sit up. Lift yourself—good girl, just like that." I grabbed the ring and dragged it toward my prized infinity pool, the one with the six-million-dollar view, temperature-controlled to perfection. However, the stamped buttermilk-beige concrete surrounding it could hurt Belle's back, and I moved carefully, slowly, ensuring that risk was minimized. Once I had her at the edge of the pool, I lowered her in, grinning when she squealed softly at the *very* miniscule splash, then nudged the floatie toward the shallow end.

Stripping off my charcoal-grey tee, I tossed it onto the lounge chair next to Belle's cover-up. I really did love this part of the house. It overlooked the water on the east side of the island and came equipped with an outdoor pizza grill—still unused—and a half dozen cushy lounging chairs, though only two were out of storage for the time being.

Not only did peace find me, but I'd been looking forward to fucking Belle here in some capacity—on a chair, over a chair, in the pool—for two weeks now.

With a grin, a private one not for the eyes of my submissive, I dove headlong into the deep end, cock a veritable iron rod under my swim shorts. Gliding below the surface, I stroked through the slightly chilled water, using Belle's pink toenails for guidance. She let out another squeal when I burst forth, breaking the surface with a splash and shooting up right between her legs. I flopped onto the inflatable ring like a brute, drenching her, blanketing her, our noses only a few inches apart as she giggled, then pushed up to accept my quick kiss. Mollified, lips tingling, I eased away. In the shallows, I could stand, but I settled in the gap between her thighs, draped over the side of the floatie, and lazily kicked my feet to paddle us around the pool.

"How's this, Belle?"

"Good, sir," she insisted, pool water glittering in the sunshine, streaking across her skin away from her pebbled nipples.

"Anything uncomfortable?" A question different from *painful*. I knew she wasn't in pain, and I certainly didn't mind a little discomfort in my submissives. She shook her head.

"No, sir."

"Good."

I smoothed my hands up her thighs, relishing the way her skin prickled in response. Deciding to stick to the shallow end, I planted my feet, then lifted her legs over my shoulders; this was the easiest position to accomplish what I wanted. Belle lay there in the ring, tied down, splayed open, her folds wet—but not with pool water. I fought the urge to just dive in, bury myself in her perfect pussy. Instead, I circled her clit with my thumb, drawing slow, languid circles around the little bud. Her eyes drifted closed, but a sharp *tsk* had them shooting open again.

"Tell me about yourself, Belle."

Her confusion was lovely. Brow furrowed, forehead wrinkled, lips slightly downturned. She likely hadn't come out here expecting to talk—not about herself, anyway. I'd learned in these last two weeks that Belle certainly liked to talk, or, at the very least, be talked *to*. She responded eagerly to filth whispered in her ear, especially from behind.

But today I hoped that conversation would accomplish something—that it would distract her enough to hold off an orgasm, or at least force her to ask *permission* when one was on the horizon.

"About myself? What do you mean, sir?" She shifted about, but I kept at her clitoris, circling it, stroking the plump lips around it.

"Family, friends, childhood, favourite uni class," I rattled off, watching her closely. "I want to know more about you."

"Uhm." She pressed her lips together with a wince; I hated *uhm*. However, rather than chastising her this time— she seemed to have caught herself—I merely moved away from the little bundle at the crest of her thighs, massaging her outer lips, my forefinger and middle finger in a wide V.

"Go on, Belle."

"Well, I was a military brat," she said somewhat tentatively, her inner thighs twitching when I focused on a spot that always seemed to rile her up—the right pressure, the right consistency, the right tenure. Her pussy and I had become rather familiar these last two weeks.

"Really?"

"My dad was in the army." She swallowed hard. "He's retired now, but we moved a lot. Usually somewhere new every two or three years. Mom worked part-time on the base, if she could, at the shops and things. We were in Germany for two years while I was in high school—ninth and tenth grade. In Heidelberg. I loved it."

I'd gleaned she had something of an adventurous streak, piecing together the bits of her personality and history that she had been willing to share on our coffee dates. To account for that, I had several day trips planned this month; not only did I want our play sessions to stay fresh and exciting, but I wanted her to see the islands, too, as my treat.

So far, we'd gone out into deeper waters with a team from Saint Croix, wherein Belle had swum with dolphins, turtles, and tropical schools of fish. I'd hovered nearby, both enjoying her excitement *and* keeping an eye out for danger as the hired divers showed her around. Last Saturday, we had explored the caves along my island's cove, and yesterday we'd gone hiking in Saint John's national park, then shopping in Cruz Bay. She had walked away with the teeniest string bikini—I just knew I was going to rip it to pieces the first time she wore it.

Sure, I was using some of the time I'd bought for nonsexual purposes—but being a Dom wasn't strictly sexual. We maintained our dynamic, even off the island, and I honestly couldn't remember a time I'd been happier.

Which—was a bit depressing.

What the fuck had I been doing all my adult life that I couldn't have had *this* ages ago? Working? Being ordered around by my father? Reviving the catastrophes my brother had left in four of our major resorts?

I could have had this bliss. I could have had *her*.

I swallowed hard, tuning back in to Belle's reminiscing about Heidelberg with a soft smile. Well, I had her now. That was all that mattered.

"And do your parents know you escort?" I asked after a

moment of silence, one punctuated by two sharp breaths from Belle as I swept my thumb back and forth across her clit.

"Y-yes," she whispered, then cleared her throat, her hips bucking up to meet my hand. "I sat down with them after my i-interview with Candace, actually. We made a pros and cons list."

I chuckled. "How very logical of you."

"We—" She squeaked again when I slipped a finger into her wetness, in and out, then returned to her clit. "They're my emergency contacts on my f-file at Elysium, actually."

"And they don't oppose it?"

"Well..." Her cheeks flushed, and I snuck two fingers in this time, thrusting deep inside her heat as her eyes widened. Honestly, she was positively *dripping*. I could have used that—embarrassed her, lowered my voice as I whispered about how sordid and wrong it was to be so wet during a casual discussion of her family life. But Belle didn't get off on humiliation, nor did I, so I left it at that.

"Belle?"

"Dad doesn't exactly broadcast it," she said breathlessly. I milked a long, low moan out of her when I removed my fingers again, spreading her arousal across her folds. Her right arm jerked up, perhaps to brush the hair out of her face, but her cheeks darkened when she found herself stuck. "They tell people I bartend in the city, but they don't mind asking me about my work. Foot fetish stuff seems safer to them, after I explained it, than, you know, what most escorts are known for."

This. I nodded. "I imagine so, yes."

"I didn't tell them I'd been, uhm, cross-trained into other areas," she said, squealing when I pinched her thigh. *Uhm.* "Sorry, sir."

"And your friends?"

"My friends were actually really judgmental," Belle admitted with a frown. Her blue gaze swept across the house as she nibbled her lower lip briefly. "Like, *really* judgmental. I just don't tell them about it anymore. I mean, after we graduated, we all kind of drifted apart anyway. There are only a few I keep in touch with. Most of my friends now are in the same profession."

"It must be easier that way," I told her before I dipped down and engulfed her clit. She whimpered, her heels digging into my back, and I sucked hard in response. The pressure lifted seconds later, heels undug, but I could imagine her curling her toes instead, eyes clenched shut.

While it was disappointing to learn that Belle had experienced some personal tension, it didn't surprise me. Escorting wasn't exactly a profession the world smiled upon —even when the world hadn't a fucking clue what went on half the time. Not all escorts slept with their clients. Some were exclusively show pieces, like Belle used to be. Some professional Doms never took their clothes off, never touched a client's bits. Maybe I was too deep into it. I'd been a patron of Elysium for years, after all, visiting anytime I was in New York. Maybe I had just normalized it.

Still, the thought of Manhattanite fucks being rude to *my* Belle over what *she* chose to do with her life—a surge of protectiveness, possessiveness, flared deep within me, and I gripped her quivering thigh, hard, hoping to leave a mark as I swept my tongue the full length of her sex. Belle moaned, lifting her hips up to meet it.

I ought to pull back. From the sound of her breath, from the greediness of her hips—I had her in my thrall. This was the precipice, the tipping point, the exact moment she ought to realize she was close and *fight*. Fight the pleasure. Fight the fall. Prolong it. Heighten it. Leave it in my very capable hands to dole out as I saw fit.

Belle didn't get off on humiliation—but surrender. Surrender to my touch, to the pleasure of it, to the pain. If she stopped jumping the gun, she'd realized how much *better* she could feel.

I, in theory, should also back off. It was my responsibility as her Dom to guide her, teach her, instruct her with a firm hand if necessary.

But I so adored her little breathy moans, her squeals— the way she flailed helplessly in my grasp.

Unlike any submissive I'd had before, Belle made me weak.

And a Dom couldn't be weak.

I pulled back begrudgingly, easing up, moving away from the spots that drove her wild to ones that merely made her feel good. She sucked in a ragged breath, the tension in her body dissipating somewhat.

"How did you get into escorting?" I asked thickly, hoarsely, my voice like gravel—the Dom voice that always made her shudder.

"Penny!" she blurted, arching up and all but shouting the name when I flicked her clit. Her cheeks flushed bright crimson when I arched an eyebrow at her, and she settled back into the floatie with a whimper. "I... We, uhm—"

I smacked her thigh this time, forgoing the chastising pinch for something sharper. *Uhm*. There were so many other, *better* words to add a pause to one's speech.

"Sorry, sir," she whispered, her eyes closing tightly for a moment as my thumb found her clit again, circling it, sweeping over it. Before she could get another word out, I added two fingers to her heat, massaging her inside and out. "*Oh*."

"Belle."

"Penny got me into escorting," she whimpered. Her hips writhed against my hand, her nipples hardened to perfect stiff peaks. "We m-met at a human sexuality seminar at NYU. At first we were just seat buddies, but then around Christmas we s-started talking about what she did for a living. It intrigued me. Plus, I had student debt, and she told me, *ahh*, that I could make money just by letting people t-touch my feet."

She tried to retreat, to pull herself away from my grasp, but she wasn't going anywhere. I pressed down on her clit, working her inner walls harder.

Curiosity had forced me to ask the question. Belle was such a natural submissive, albeit an unrefined one. The stars had aligned for us; she'd been added to Elysium's submissive registry only two weeks before I started looking for a vacation companion. As soon as we had begun all this, I couldn't help but wonder why she hadn't gone straight into it. Perhaps she hadn't known—hadn't realized that she was made for this lifestyle.

What a terrible waste, her first three, four months at Elysium, pawning her pretty feet off in a dark room.

"And did you like it?" I murmured, reaching underwater with my free hand and clamping onto her big toe. "Strangers, fetishizing your feet?"

She giggled when I squeezed, the sound making the corners of my mouth curl up.

"I like escorting. I like making people feel good," she admitted, then moaned and arched her back up when I resumed working both clit and G-spot simultaneously. She'd started to quiver, a lovely pale flush spreading from her cheeks to her breasts. "Escorting has structure. It has rules. People think it's a-ambiguous, but to me, it's b-black and white."

I caught the hitch in her words, and a distressed look flashed across her face. Before I could ask, it was gone.

"Both you and the client are on the same page," Belle continued. "You both know what you're doing there. It isn't shades of g-grey. There is order, and we...oh, *god*."

A part of me wanted to press the issue. Something about the distinct lines between client and escort—something was bothering her. I hadn't noticed anything amiss these last two weeks, but that flicker of dismay had piqued my interest. I made a note to ask again, another time, not mid-scene.

"And do you like this?" I growled, pumping her harder. "Being my pretty little submissive?"

Our eyes met and her cunt tightened. Her lips parted. Her breath stuttered. She nodded and I nipped at her thigh.

"Use your words, Belle."

"*Yes*, sir," she choked, "I like being your pretty little sub."

My smile turned predatory—for I, the hunter, had truly cornered my prey. "Good girl."

This was her moment. This was her chance to learn, to improve, to take her pleasure into her own hands and—

"*Ah!*" She bucked up, her pussy rippling around my fingers, and her sharp cry startled a trio of yellow-breasted bananaquits from the nearby foliage. In that moment, I knew I'd lost her. Again. Without permission. *Again*.

I exhaled noisily—on purpose. "*Belle*."

"I'm sorry, sir," she whimpered, her thighs quivering atop my shoulders. "It came out of nowhere. I didn't mean to—"

"No excuses, Belle." I tried to keep the disappointment out of my voice—but not all that hard. She licked her lips, chest rising and falling unevenly.

"Yes, sir," she said miserably. Good. At least she knew she had made a mistake. Mind you, she sounded upset every time she came without permission—which had nearly been every time—but she was always drenched after her punishments. My eyes narrowed at her when she threw her head back, gaze to the sky, with a defeated huff. Maybe Belle was a secret brat. Maybe she *wanted* the punishments. I didn't mind doling them out, but hearing her *beg* me to let her come was part of the fantasy. I'd like to hear it, and not just in our final week.

Apparently, I needed to get more creative with her punishment this time. While she yelped and cried when I spanked her, tried to wriggle away with every strike, her skin heating and coloring like something from a divine tragedy, her body didn't lie—her cunt *couldn't* lie.

This next punishment needed to make her suffer, my miscreant submissive.

So, I dragged her and the floatie toward the stairs at the far end of the shallows, the water parting against my chest like waves crashing over the hull of a boat. Tonight, I'd have a good think on her punishment. She'd take it tomorrow, during my office time. No task for her. Just penance—a good one, too.

For now, however, I had a *very* pressing matter to see to. Leaving her floating there without a word, still tied, her legs splayed weakly over the curve of the ring, I climbed up the stairs and stalked over to the lounge chairs. From the breast pocket of my discarded tee, I grabbed a condom and tore open the foil. My cock sprang free, falling like a lead weight once I yanked my soaked trunks down, and I rolled the condom on with a barely contained groan.

Silently, I stalked back to the pool and stomped down the first few steps. Water splashed up, sprinkling the slowly spinning floatie. Belle watched me curiously, almost with concern, and she squealed when I grabbed the float and yanked it to me. I spun it around, resisting the urge to do it a few times, and then hoisted her hips higher onto the ring, arranging her in our initial position. She was forced to lift herself with her arms, a small challenge, to avoid catching her neck at an odd angle.

Stepping between her parted thighs, I raised her hips a touch more before sinking completely into her. Again, we became a symphony, my groan and her cry echoing across the pool area, the trees, maybe even down to the beach—if I fucked her hard enough.

And I had no intention of going easy on her. While her punishment might still be pending, she hadn't earned gentle, indulgent lovemaking, not with such a wanton disregard for our house rules. So, I was merciless. Brutal. Each thrust, each pounding of my hips, coaxed exquisite sounds from her lips, so much so that I went harder, the pink donut ring bouncing against my thighs, just to hear her cry.

Water sloshed around us, and as one of my hands kept a firm grip on her thigh, the other found its way to her nipples —none too gently, either. A tweak for each, followed by a rougher plucking. Belle let out a strangled sound, glaring up at me for the first time, her teeth gritted. Her legs kicked out when I did it again, and I smirked. *Bratty* submissive indeed. The display earned each plump breast a swat, followed by a flick for both nipples. Defeated, as if realizing there wasn't a damn thing she could do about it, Belle tipped her head back, her blush deepening. She huffed again. Her toes curled.

My smirk turned dark—and my hand drifted up to her throat.

She heaved a strangled breath as my grip around her neck tightened, her eyes wide—but not in panic. In delight, almost. *Fucking Christ, this woman...*

I squeezed harder, slamming into her, then, when her mouth fell open with a gasp, I slipped my fingers between her parted lips—used her mouth as my anchor, hoping she could still taste herself on my fingers.

She started to clench around me again, her limbs stiffening. While her lips closed around my hand, I had yet to feel a hint of teeth. *Good girl.* So ridiculously beautiful, flushed and moaning and shaking—but she didn't get to come again. It seemed even less likely that she'd remember to ask for permission with four fingers shoved in her mouth.

So, I had my way with her—selfishly. I sought my own pleasure, thrusting hard, over and over again, until I found release. It was the kind of orgasm you feel in your teeth, that leaves you seeing stars, and I barely managed to keep myself upright, not to plummet right on top of her. Knees weak. Pleasure thrumming through my veins. I could have ground against her, prolonged it, but that might have been the final push she needed to climax herself.

I retreated instead, pulling out of her with a hiss, then pushed the floatie away before plopping down unceremoniously on the top step. Off she went, still stuck in place, a writhing mess of a submissive, gasping for breath. Pussy glistening in the late-afternoon sun. Blonde waves and long legs hanging over either end of the ring. Ruined. Left in the throes of pleasure, unable to find her release.

What a pretty picture. Exhaling briskly, I sat back, propped up on my elbows. The concrete bit straight down to the bone, but I could barely feel it. I could barely feel anything. Teeth briefly gritted, I sat up out of the water to pull the condom off, knotted it, and tossed it back toward the chairs.

I swept a wet hand through my hair, skin prickling as I settled into the water a few steps down. As easy as it would have been to sit here and languish in my phenomenal climax, I had a submissive to punish.

And how—in what way would it finally *stick*—I had no fucking idea.

HOUSE RULE #16

Belle will call a time-out for any problems, concerns, or issues she is having with this arrangement. She will not keep her fears from Sir, otherwise Sir cannot make them better.

9

BELLE

*D*amn it.

I'd been trying so hard. For two weeks, I *really* had been trying.

Why couldn't I do this?

This one silly little thing—don't climax without permission. I knew the rule, yet I'd broken it every chance I got.

What was wrong with me?

I lay on the slowly rotating inner tube in silence, listening to the chatter of birds, to the distant crash of white-capped waves. A stunning shade of blue sky stared down at me, cloudless, the same as it had been yesterday, and the same as it would be tomorrow. At the sound of a splash, of Dean diving into the pool, I clenched my eyes tight, embarrassment rippling through me, taking the place of what would have been a pretty awesome second orgasm. I'd fought it this time, as Dean pounded away. I really had.

Not that it would have mattered.

I probably would have come eventually, no matter how hard I tried not to.

What was *wrong* with me?

When I felt wet fingers undoing the satin around my wrists, I opened my eyes again, only to find my vision blurred by unshed tears. *Don't cry. Don't cry. Don't cry.* As soon as Dean had one of my hands loose, I wiped it across my face, pretending to scratch an itch.

Two weeks I'd been his sub. Only once had I managed not to break the first house rule. *Once.* It was a wonder he hadn't sent me back yet, claiming he'd received a defective submissive.

With my other hand free, I sat up, my body stiff and sore from being *taken* on a pool ring. I'd been excited for the scene when we talked about it last night. I hadn't expected it to end in tears and soul-crushing guilt.

Seriously. What was wrong with me?

Dean held the tube still as I moved about. While we'd floated over to the edge of the gorgeous infinity pool, palms swaying in the distance, we were still in the shallow end. It had been one of Dean's precautions—to keep everything in the shallow end, just in case the tube flipped over, or something. He was big on safety precautions. For all the pain and pleasure he inflicted, safety always sat at the forefront of his mind.

Which I appreciated.

In fact, I appreciated a *lot* about Dean Donahue. In the last two weeks, he had cooked all my meals, even on Sundays. Somehow, he had procured a list of my favourites —a feat that shouldn't have surprised me, given the limitless resources at a billionaire's disposal—and prepared them all sublimely. Best of all, he seemed to *enjoy* cooking for me. Not only that, but he took me out on day trips, all of them exciting and fun in their own right. Cave exploration.

National park hikes. Bikini shopping and dinner in Cruz Bay.

While I didn't need to call him Sir off the island, we still functioned as Dominant and submissive, even around other people—and I liked it. I liked that he navigated the world always looking out for me. A hand on my lower back. Walking in front of me in new places. Triple-checking my diving equipment before the professionals took me under to swim with schools of tropical fish.

Some might have considered it overbearing, Dean's persona, but he never spoke for me. He never ordered my food when we were out. He never steamrolled my voice in front of other people. He did little things, like fixing my ponytail when it had fallen loose. Crouching down to tie my shoelaces when they came undone. Asking how I was feeling. If I was okay. If I was hungry. Did I need some water? *You need to reapply sunscreen—it's been two hours, Belle.*

With Dean I felt—treasured. Protected. Appreciated. Desired.

All he wanted in return was for me to follow the freakin' rules, and I couldn't even stick to rule number one.

Lips pressed together in a tight line, I managed to get onto my knees, my sex both pleasantly sore *and* swollen with need, aching, and then slip through the hole in the tube. Dean still steadied me, standing and holding both hand grips when my toes nudged the pool's tiled floor.

"I really am sorry," I said quietly as he steered us toward the deep end. I knew he was frustrated with me, and I wouldn't have blamed him for walking off, but Dean was a stickler for aftercare.

Just another little thing I appreciated about him.

"I know, Belle." Water sloshed up around the sides of his face when he released the ring and started treading in place.

I just hung there, floating, bobbing along, the chilled pool doing wonders for my slightly battered lower half.

"I just want you to know that I've really been trying," I told him, wishing I sounded stronger, hating the way my voice threatened to crack at any moment, "and I don't mean to break the rules, and I'm genuinely really sorry—"

Damn it. My vision blurred as tears swelled, and suddenly they were spilling down my cheeks before I could stop them. I blinked hard and sniffled, purposefully looking away from him—but not before I caught the shift in his expression from unreadable to something softer. Just like that. All it took was a few tears—tears I wished would just stay in their stupid ducts.

"Oh, *Belle.*" Dean paddled back to the floatie, his voice all warm and velvety. It was his coddling voice. I *loved* his coddling voice. He usually adopted it after a scene—or a punishment—and it had a way of making my insides turn to goo in two seconds flat.

Unfortunately, in that moment, I didn't *deserve* to be coddled. I'd screwed up, again, and I didn't deserve his velvet. Sniffling, I tried to turn the ring away so we weren't facing each other anymore, but he climbed onto it before I could kick fast enough, his added weight holding us in place.

"I'm sorry," I croaked, tears clinging to my lashes as I hesitantly met his sage-green stare. Inside, my stomach kept knotting itself, over and over again, to the point that it hurt. "I don't mean to cry."

"Don't apologize for your feelings," he murmured, tone straddling the line between commanding and comforting. "They're all valid."

Before I could get another pathetic apology out, he took my face in both his large hands. Softly. Gently. His thumbs swept across my cheeks, collecting the fallen tears, and then, much to my shock, he peppered my very red, slightly puffy cheek with a storm of quick, feverish kisses. I let out a little squeal-giggle, squirming to escape his grasp.

Ignoring the way my heart skipped a beat, something electric dancing beneath my skin.

It was only after he'd kissed every bit of my face not covered by his hands that he pulled back, smiling that handsome, panty-melting smile of his. I managed a weak one in return; I just didn't deserve his kindness, even if it *did* make me feel better.

"No, Dean, I'm sorry." I cleared my throat as his hands drifted from my face to the ring. He'd settled directly in front of me, and I could feel the gentle pulse of each kick below the surface. I shook my head, knowing what I had to say would spoil the illusion of us being here, but it had to be said. "You're paying me to be your sub, and I keep breaking the first house rule you made, and I'm sorry—"

"Belle." He caught my chin with one hand, his hold firmer this time. Forceful. Domineering. Lifting me to meet his gaze. "You're doing a wonderful job as my submissive."

"But I keep breaking the rules, and I don't mean to—"

His soft chuckle had my cheeks warming. "No submissive is perfect. No Dom is perfect either. We're human. We make mistakes—unintentional ones, most of the time. I'm not angry at you," Dean gripped me harder, forcing me to crouch over the ring so that our faces sat no more than a few inches apart, "and I don't want you to be angry with *yourself* either."

Relief coursed through me. Sweet, gentle, soft, warm *relief*, that kind that unknotted my stomach and sapped the tension from my limbs.

"I know you're doing your best," he continued, releasing

my chin. I stayed right there, hands resting on top of each other, hunched over the tube's side so I could be close to him—so I could keep feeling that unexpected yet overwhelming sense of relief I hadn't even realized I'd needed. Dean tucked my hair behind my ear, his eyes exploring my features slowly, like he had never seen them before—a strange thought, given we were both stark naked. When his thumb grazed my lower lip, I ducked my chin in, suddenly shy.

Another strange thought, given, well, *everything*.

"It's on me, as your Dom, to push you to do *better* than your best," he murmured. "It's my responsibility to guide you, to help you achieve something. We'll get there. I'm not an impatient man, Belle, nor would I ever be an impatient Dom."

I bit the insides of my cheeks when my lower lip trembled.

"I'm sorry," I whispered. His gaze hardened, and he lifted my face back up with a rigid finger under my chin.

"Stop saying that."

"Yes, sir."

There was a moment, as I forced myself to meet and hold his stare, when all this felt very *real*. Everything. Our situation. Our dynamic. Our—relationship. I didn't feel like I'd just been comforted by a client, but someone else. Someone closer. A friend? A *boy*friend? No. I swallowed hard. No, I couldn't think that. I couldn't...

As if possessing a mind of its own, my hand crept up and brushed his hair back, smoothed the sandy brown locks, made darker by the water. Dean held perfectly still, watching me, his gaze never once leaving mine.

It hit me then—the intimacy of it all. Here, on a private island. Two people alone. Naked. *Giving* each other a piece of their soul. My submission. His dominance. Freely given, willingly taken.

He might have been paying me at the end of all this, but what I did with Dean, what we did to each other—I would have done it for nothing.

So much for professional boundaries.

Sucking in a sharp breath, I retracted my hand when I realized it was still up there, fiddling with his hair like it was mine to fiddle with.

"I—" My lips pressed together before *uhm* could slip out. "I'm going to go freshen up, then grab a drink. Do you want something? I can make you a smoothie."

He was partial to peach—with a hint of vanilla and honey, a pinch of nutmeg and ginger. Dean might have cooked all my meals, but I knew my way around a blender. And by now, I knew what he liked. All too well, I knew.

"No, Belle, I'm fine," he said softly. Not in his Dom voice. Not in a voice I recognized at all; in fact, I could have sworn he was *frowning*. Ignoring the spike of panic, the sudden tightness in my chest, I forced a smile so bright that it hurt my cheeks.

"Okay!"

Then I was off like a shot, dropping through the middle of the donut floatie and scrambling underwater for the staircase. Amidst the quiet of the faintly salty water, surrounded by glittering white and grey tile, tears stung my eyes again.

And for the life of me, I just couldn't figure out *why*.

10

DEAN

Wednesday, February 13th

...and while I realize you are on vacation—your assistant has made that perfectly clear the fifteen times I've called this week —I really do think you should take a look at what is happening at the resort. I'm afraid Richard isn't exactly stepping into his old position as easily as everyone hoped, and I know you have a vested interest in the success...

*E*yes narrowed, jaw clenched, I deleted the email without reading the rest. I knew what it would say. I could have written *all* these emails from managers and GMs as soon as my father told me we were all about to play musical chairs with our roles in the Donahue empire. Word for word—I could have written everything. Just because Richard had tricked the enablers at his latest costly rehab center into giving him a clean bill of health didn't mean he'd *changed*.

My brother—the con artist, the manipulator, the sloth. The last time he had been *clean* was when he was twelve. It had all been downhill from there, and I still couldn't understand why my parents didn't see that. Adelaide understood my brother's habits just as well as I did, and she was only twenty, for fuck's sake.

Closing my eyes, I dragged in a deep, calming breath and relaxed into my high-backed leather office chair. When I refocused on the twin monitors in front of me atop my sleek black desk, the email was gone. I could forget, momentarily, that the resorts I'd lovingly cultivated for the last seven years were going to shit in a matter of weeks. I could block it out. Pretend it wasn't happening. Pretend that the general managers I'd left in command could handle my brother once they learned how best to *manage* him.

A woman. A limitless credit card. A bottle of scotch. A kilo of cocaine. A locked door.

Simple, really.

Once they realized the only way to limit the chaos was to give in to its worst vices, things would run smoothly. I had to let go, even if instinct told me to take charge. Call someone. Shout at someone. Reorder things. Confront my father. Step up from the lowly middle-child rung and usurp my brother.

My instinct had steered me well before.

But those fuckers had forced me—

Never mind. I was on vacation. I had Ixora and Belle and an ongoing list of fantasies to explore.

Let the rest of them put out their own damn fires for once.

Sitting forward, I scrolled through the rest of my very full inbox. My executive assistant Eliza would answer the bulk of these, but I still liked the option to read each and every email I received. While the Donahue global empire was expansive, I had my own empire to run outside of the real estate and resort business.

I'd invested heavily in start-ups over the last few years, ranging from tech to med, nearly all of which had provided substantial returns. I owned several luxury apartment buildings in London, Venice, and Hong Kong that all needed managing, along with about two dozen restaurants in Manhattan and Los Angeles. Unlike the rest of my immediate family, I wanted as diverse a portfolio as possible. Sure, real estate had given us Donahues a cushy security net through the years. It was almost a guarantee now; Donahue + real estate ventures = a new trust fund for the next two or three generations, at least.

But I wanted to spread out—and thank fuck I had. If I'd stuck to the party line, thrown my whole self into my father's ventures, I'd be shit out of luck by now.

And bored. Terribly, terribly bored.

Silent partner. In my *own* family's business. What the fuck do you even do as a silent partner when your name is on the bloody building? Sit back and wait for the check to arrive every month? Infuse the business with cash when needed? I wasn't a fucking bank. Even my investees looked to me for input, and I had my own personal teams—branding experts, graphic designers, patent lawyers—assisting along the way.

Still, I was just a man—a man with irons in nearly every fire. I prided myself on my ability to delegate accordingly. The restaurants ran themselves for the most part, but I still required weekly and monthly figures from management. My inbox was never empty. Everyone reported to me, albeit indirectly, through my CFO and his team. Even on vacation, I had allotted myself at least an hour of work time in my second-floor office each day.

Usually, in that time, Belle had taskwork to do. Something to keep her busy, but always within sight. Those outside the dynamic might find it demeaning, but submissives enjoyed keeping busy. They needed structure, purpose, and praise for a job well-done. Some subs preferred being babied, doted upon—littles, mostly—while many others felt a need to contribute to the household. A sense of purpose took them far, and nearly all looked to their Dom to dictate that.

It was a part of the relationship I had always relished. Pushing a submissive's boundaries. Helping them set and accomplish goals. Seeing the look on their faces, in their eyes, when they conquered a challenge. The success of a submissive reflected the skill of their Dominant. Given the nature of the relationship, outsiders thought us Doms bossy, demanding, the kings of micromanaging. Little did they realize that in the grand scheme of things, our submissives called the shots. They set the limits. They produced the goals that we in turn would help them reach.

So, yes—taskwork for Belle may have consisted of things others thought demeaning. Dusting my office with a feather duster, which she could only hold in her mouth. Naked, of course. Polishing my shoes. Reorganizing all my bookshelves into alphabetical order one day, then by colour the next. Tidying my desk.

Or, sometimes, just sitting patiently at my side—waiting for the next instruction.

She needed orders. I needed to give them. Otherwise, we were both restless. I saw it on her days off; usually around lunchtime on Sundays she came wandering back to me, looking for something to do. Her time after dinner was also her own, but generally she still sought me out, offering to play cards or stargaze or watch a movie together in the cinema room.

Today, however, taskwork was out the window. I'd spent

the night thinking about our interaction in the pool yesterday, from her failing once again to ask permission to orgasm right down to her tearful apologies in the aftermath. While it frustrated me that she still wasn't following such a crucial rule, I hated to see her cry. I *never* wanted to see her cry, honestly—unless the tears followed a spanking, or a vigorous round of fucking. Tears were the body's natural response to overstimulation, to emotional anarchy in the brain.

To realize she had been crying in frustration, anger, perhaps even fear that she wasn't pleasing a man paying her to submit—well, it had broken me a little. It made me feel like a failure, like I had let her down as her Dominant.

Then there had been that *moment*, after she'd settled. After I'd told her to stop apologizing. A flicker in time. Over so fast that it gave me whiplash. We had looked into each other's eyes—and I'd seen the woman inside. *Belle.* Not just Belle, my escort, my paid submissive.

It stirred something inside me, something deep, raw, primal even. I'd never felt more myself, more a true Dom, than when she toyed with my hair, when I gazed into her eyes and saw—her. Belle Bennet. Compassionate. Worldly. Intelligent. Beautiful. Warm.

The submissive I'd been searching, waiting, hoping for all these years.

And then it was over, just like that, with her scampering back to the house.

I'd been left there to float by myself, thinking, pondering the strange turn of events, the break in our illusion, the realization. Chance had brought us together. Maybe even fate—not that I believed in that sort of thing.

Yet she'd said it herself: Belle needed the structure of the escort-client relationship. It was simple. Straightforward.

Easy. I suspected she preferred to keep her heart safe, that the lack of real *feelings* had its appeal.

But I knew, right then and there, that this woman—my beautiful, intelligent, worldly, warm submissive—was where she was meant to be.

Here. With me.

Kneeling at my feet while I worshipped her submission.

Perhaps she had realized it, too.

Perhaps it scared her.

With that in mind, I let it go. I tucked the epiphanies away for another day. Belle needed order, first and foremost. She needed routine, defined expectations, a clear-cut role for us both to play. So, I would give it all to her because I *could*—until I could broach the subject without the risk of her running again.

I had spent the rest of the night crafting her punishment. No taskwork today. *Punishment.*

Obscured by the computer monitors that took up the bulk of my desk, Belle whimpered. Not for the first time this morning, either. We had been in the office for about a half hour, and her punishment would last until she had completed it.

Eight orgasms.

This morning's punishment was my equivalent of the old—you wanna smoke, kid? Well, smoke a whole *carton* of cigarettes!

If Belle wanted to climax, then she was *going* to climax.

But she was going to do it on my terms.

Eight climaxes, right here in my office. No rest between —eight distinct, separate orgasms. One right after the other. She couldn't do anything else today until she had seen the punishment through.

The *look* on her face when I first told her—it was like

she'd won the lottery. Although she had tried to fight it, to remain calm and docile, Belle couldn't stop that bright, infectious grin from spreading across her sweet mouth. I'd let her have it, that elated moment at the thought of all that pleasure.

She mustn't have realized how torturous it would be, three or four climaxes in, forcing herself to keep going, to thrust her sensitive little clit against the vibrator over and over again until she wanted to *scream*.

This was a punishment, after all.

I leaned around my second monitor. Behind it sat a neat, sparsely furnished office. I hadn't put as much time or care into its design as I had the rest of the house; this was supposed to be a *vacation* home. If the office was too comfortable, too welcoming, I might never leave it. Stunning floor-to-ceiling windows lined the wall behind me. Matching bookshelves sandwiched in the doorless entryway, the hall silent beyond. One of my landscapes— the Caribbean Sea mid-storm—hung on one wall, an enormous twelve-by-twelve-foot canvas. A two-seater white couch sat against the other.

And in the middle of it all, Belle.

It had taken us some time to get the pillow arrangement beneath her right. Even though this morning's session was all punishment, I didn't think it fair for her to have to kneel on the merciless tile for however long it took her to finish. So, we had collected all the cushy, plush pillows from the indoor seating areas and stacked them into a pyramid of sorts—at the peak, a rather large vibrator. Not the kind for internal use, of course, although some inexperienced asshole Dom might attempt to shove it in a hole at some point.

I'd been cursing myself since I dreamt up this

punishment for not furnishing the house with a Sybian. In its absence, we'd had to improvise. Belle sat straddling the pillows, the vibrator between her thighs. The device rumbled along at its lowest setting, batteries freshly charged. It could go for hours. Belle couldn't.

When she realized I was watching, her watery blues snapped up, begging, *pleading* me to relent. I said nothing, neither verbally nor with my expression. Flushed and quivering, she looked lovely this morning in her tightly cinched white corset. I'd laced it up myself, fastening it tighter than comfortable; this *was* a punishment.

The corset crushed her creamy breasts, forcing them up, the delicate skin trembling as she rocked back and forth across the vibrator. Her hands were out of the question; she knew how to pleasure herself. If she had full use of them, the punishment would be over too soon. So, they remained tied behind her back with pink satin, the usual bow.

I'd opted for the bit gag again, enjoying the way it cut across her mouth, her cheeks. Besides, she'd likely want something to sink her teeth into after, oh, orgasm number five? My ball gags weren't quite as pliant.

Blonde waves drawn up in a bouncy ponytail, she shuddered, rocking her hips, the corset demanding near-perfect posture. She hadn't started to dribble too much from her mouth yet, just a bit of saliva glistening on her chin, but that was coming. The slickness along her inner thighs turned my semi into a full erection. Last night, I had debated allowing her to wear panties. Although she wasn't permitted to wear them ordinarily, I worried the vibrator might prove too uncomfortable without a barrier, even if it *was* just a slip of fabric.

In the end, I'd decided against it. *This* was a far prettier picture.

Although I hadn't given any terms should she climb off, topple over, or in any way give herself some reprieve, the implication that she wouldn't be able to sit for a week was there. I'd alluded to it—in the dark look I gave her as I arranged her on top of the pillows, in the steely bite of my words when I told her she couldn't stop until she'd had her eight climaxes.

I couldn't see her while I clicked through my inbox. It was on *her* to take the punishment.

Trust—crucial in all things.

Needing a break from the ceaseless barrage of emails, I switched off both screens and stood. My shorts tented noticeably, and I made no effort to hide it as I strolled around the desk, hands in my pockets. Belle tracked each step, peering up at me with tear-filled eyes. To her credit, none had fallen yet, and she held my gaze as she ground her hips into the pillow beneath her, the vibrator muffled.

"So," I said, stopping directly in front of her, tent bulging in her face. "What sort of progress have we made?"

"'Ree," she mumbled back, the gag hindering her speech just beautifully. I smiled, my chest tightening, and then crouched down.

"Three?" My thumb grazed her lower lip, then stroked her cheek. "Look at you, Belle. Nearly halfway there."

She let out a strangled moan as I stood, then bowed her head without prompting when I reached for the gag's clasp. I undid it with one hand, then curled the saliva-soaked thing into my fist. Belle straightened when I unzipped my shorts, and her mouth opened, on cue, as soon as I dug my stiff cock out. Without a word, I thrust it between her parted lips, groaning as she took me in, my head falling back, my eyes drifting closed.

Her mouth was heaven.

Her pussy was paradise.

And Belle was my very own goddess—the kind I could keep on a leash.

She gagged only slightly, her technique much improved from the first time she'd dropped to her knees for me. While teaching her how to deep-throat hadn't been on my to-do list these two months, it had been something that happened naturally over the course of our sessions. I found myself murmuring little hints—stick your tongue out, breathe through it, hold it a moment longer, a gag reflex can be conditioned to settle. From the way she engulfed me now, the head of my cock briefly nudging the back of her throat, she had been paying attention.

Her nostrils flared slightly as she dragged in a deep breath, her gaze soaring to mine. That was one of the house rules: if my cock was in her mouth, she had to be looking at me. Watching me. Waiting for the next instruction. Beyond that, there was just something so fucking *stunning* about a submissive gazing up as she took me, almost down to the hilt, her pretty pink lips circled in a perfect O.

As I wrapped her ponytail around my free hand, a slight lift of my brow encouraging her to move, I noticed something amiss: the vibrator. I could hear it, suddenly. Frowning, I glanced down and found her hips off it completely. Belle sat up on her knees, still watching me, her head bobbing up and down my cock—as if that might distract me.

Bratty.

My Belle was bratty when she wanted to be. I believed that now, no longer sidetracked by her brilliant smile and demurely fluttering lashes, her proclivity for pink and lace.

Brat.

I forced her down my cock, waiting until she stopped

gagging, and then narrowed my eyes at her. "What do you think you're doing?"

There it was—the fluttering of those dark blonde lashes.

"Do you think that because you've got my cock in your mouth, the punishment stops?"

She shook her head ever so slightly, her arms erupting with little bumps. My cock pulsed, and I took a deep breath, forcing myself not to react.

Which was difficult as fuck, given how obviously her body responded to my Dom side, to the gravel in my voice, the flint in my stare.

"Put your hips back down," I ordered, slowly, precisely, each word enunciated. She tried to pull back, eyes shut, but I only gave her an inch, my fist around her hair, and waited as she sucked in a few deep breaths through her nose. When her eyes opened again, a tear slid from each down her cheek. I smirked. "Tears aren't going to help you. Put your hips back on the vibrator, Belle. This isn't a reprieve. Your punishment is still ongoing. *Down.*"

She sank with a huff, then squealed the moment she touched the vibrator again, her whole body spasming. Mercifully, I didn't feel a hint of teeth.

"Good girl." I pulled her back by her hair, removing my cock. "How are your arms? Are the restraints too tight? Anything numb?"

"My pinky is a little numb, sir, but everything else is okay."

I acquiesced with a small smile. "After your sixth orgasm, I'll remove the silk. You'll just need to tell me when it happens."

She pursed her lips sourly, then hastily relaxed her face, as if realizing she'd been sulking up at me. "Yes, sir."

"Good girl. Now—open."

I sank back into her with a sharp exhale. To make things a little easier, and to keep her on task, I bent my knees just enough so that her mouth and my cock were at the same height, so she wouldn't need to reach. For some time, I let her do what she did best—that swirling thing with her tongue, the extra suction around the tip, cheeks hollowed, her pace pleasantly torturous. I lost myself in her, in the build of my own pleasure, until I decided she'd had enough control over me for one day.

Submissives. No one realized just how terribly wrapped around their little fingers we Doms really were.

Grasping the base of her ponytail, I set the pace, the speed at which I fucked her mouth. Rocking against her, the room silent around us save for her gurgling, for the wet slurp of her mouth and the subdued hum of the vibrator, I chased the high.

Until she came.

With my cock buried between her lips.

Her high-pitched cry hummed up my shaft, and I nearly doubled over, my knees weak, as she shuddered and writhed at my feet. Her entire being tensed with pleasure, her blushes burning bright red across her sparsely freckled skin.

"Four," I croaked, my voice thick and threatening to quake. Belle looked up at me again with those watery eyes, breathing hard, trembling—and I was a goner. Two more gentle pumps and I broke, spilling myself into her, choking out some hoarse cry of my own. Pleasure rippled up from my core, instantly turning me lightheaded.

No. Just *light*. Like I could float away at any moment, courtesy of the goddess at my feet.

Her throat worked as she swallowed every last drop, and I cupped her chin when I pulled out—only then realizing I was squeezing the bit gag so hard in my other hand that it made indents on my skin. I switched my hold up, clutching it by the straps instead.

"Clean me, Belle," I murmured. This time, I let her off the pile of pillows, away from the vibrator, as she licked my cock from top to bottom. Head tipped to one side, I waited until *she* decided she was through—that I was clean enough. As she settled back down, shivering at the resumed contact with the vibrator, I let out a tight breath; if she had gone on much longer, I'd have been saddled with another damn erection that refused to quit.

I tucked myself away, then crouched in front of her, still a little spacey, and reattached her gag. Belle accepted it with a furrowed brow. While I had no qualms about untying her hands after her next two climaxes, the gag stayed.

"Four more to go," I said cheerily after I'd adjusted the gag's tightness. Her eyes widened slightly, and I booped her on the nose, just for good measure, before I stood. A drawn-out, strangled moan followed me back to my chair, and I settled into it without looking over the monitors. She was on her own again—at least for a little while. I could keep myself distracted all day with busywork; there was always something to do in my professional life.

But I'd set it aside—hell, *burn* it all—to watch her struggle through that eighth climax. I knew she could do it. Belle had the determination. And when she succeeded, I had a batch of chocolate-covered strawberries I'd been saving, just for her.

Turning both monitors back on, I found my inbox refreshed—and a new email waiting for me at the top of the list.

From my father.

Entitled *RE: Richard*.

My jaw clenched. Oh, *now* he wanted to discuss my brother? *Now* he wanted my opinion—the truth?

No. He had made his own damn bed—and he could fucking lie in it. My vacation hiatus extended to pretentious fathers, too. With a deep breath, I swallowed the rush of anger and deleted the email without opening it, ignoring the spike of guilt sharpening in my gut.

I then shut off the monitors again. Grabbed a book from the fiction bookcase. Settled on the loveseat. Cracked open the book. Pretended to read—but instead watched my little submissive take her punishment over the top of the page, her gaze fixed on the painting of the ocean's unrest across the room, my father's email already forgotten.

11

BELLE

Thursday, February 21ˢᵗ

"Would you like another glass of wine?"

"Half glass, sir," I said, trailing my finger over the rim of my wine glass. I'd never been much of a drinker, and neither was Dean, but he had made *the* most delicious white wine sangria to go with our homemade sushi tonight—I just couldn't resist. Each sip was like sunshine and daisies on my tongue, and I had already called dibs on all the fruit in the bottom of the pitcher. So far, I was buzzed but not drunk—just tipsy enough to stop thinking, which was a relief.

Three and a half weeks into the two months: I had hoped I'd have a handle on everything by now. The dynamic between us. The professional bubble I needed to cast around myself. Logically, I needed to hoard my Sundays like I would never have a day off again. Sure, I swam, hiked, read. I emailed my parents about my "vacation." I talked with Penny on the phone. I made smoothies. I stayed out of the way as the ladies from the cleaning service scrubbed our temporary home from top to bottom. But even on my off days, I always drifted back to Dean, to the comfort of his smile, the familiarity of his rigid routine. He had a gravitational pull that I couldn't ignore, one that made me feel safe, secure—one that terrified me.

It terrified me to think I couldn't get through the day without talking to him—that I *needed* the structure he provided, that I craved his praise. *Good girl.* Suddenly I imagined a day without hearing those two little words and it physically *hurt*. Even on breaks during the rest of the week, I wanted to be around him, doing something as simple as sitting together on two different lounge chairs by the pool, each of us reading something on our own. Him on his tablet, scouring the Financial Times and every other Times outlet available. Me, on my e-reader, racing through the love and lust of my new favourite fictional characters.

I just wanted to be with him.

And I had thought, by week three and a half, that I would be over him by now. That he wouldn't be so bright and shiny. That I would want my space. That I'd be sick of him—of the way he tsked at me when I made little mistakes during our sessions, the way he steered me around in public with a hand on my lower back, the way he chose my outfits for day trips.

But I wasn't over him.

I wasn't even annoyed by him—by the way he cleared his throat or cracked his knuckles or drummed his fingers on every freakin' surface in the house.

Roommates in the past had driven me bonkers. People who'd started off as friends had quickly become acquaintances at university, our forced proximity in one of Manhattan's shoebox apartments sullying the relationship beyond repair. Back then, I only ever saw them in the mornings and at night, classes occupying my days.

I saw Dean all the time. Unless he was jogging through the trails, or working in his super-secret, super off-limits third-floor lair—we were together. And I wasn't sick of him. Just the opposite, in fact.

And that scared me. A lot.

Still, I played my part. I tried to shove the fear out of my head, to instead think about how much fun I was having— that I would have been Dean's submissive for free if he'd asked me. Focusing on the present, getting lost in our sessions, our games, it all helped.

But the fear still flared. Whenever I let my guard down, it was there, whispering about professional boundaries, about how I was at risk for becoming one of those stupid escorts who fell for a client—a client who only saw them for their body and what he could do to it. A client who didn't love them back. A client who would leave them with nothing when the job was over—nothing but money.

Sometimes, I tried the aloof thing. It never lasted long. Not when he smiled at me, touched me, kissed my temple and told me I was his good girl. Then, I was jelly. Putty. Boneless and happy, pliant in his hands. Here, on the island, I wasn't a professional. I was a woman who gave up a modicum of power and control over my body, my mind, my heart because Dean made me feel safe. During our sessions, he made me feel *free*, like I could finally accept that I enjoyed being dominated and punished, that the illicit fantasies spun by tawdry romance novels weren't *bad*. Twisted. Sick. They were—fun. Exciting.

Somehow, I could almost admit to myself it wasn't just money that had steered me into a lucrative kink at Elysium. Dean had the ability to make me feel like my truest self, a self I hadn't even realized existed before the start of this month.

I had gone and made all this personal—I was weak.

I was on the path to becoming *that* escort, and I had no idea how to get back to the other path, the safer path, the path well-traveled.

Although she was my only source of real-world communication, I had stopped telling Penny any of my concerns. I could barely admit how much I liked—needed, craved, desired, *wanted*—Dean out loud; there was no way I could say it to Penny.

The *lecture* that woman would give—no way. Not doing it.

Even if it *would* have been nice to talk to someone about it.

Dean would be great to talk it through with if he wasn't the reason I was free-falling in the first place. The guy was wonderful at acknowledging and accepting whatever emotion struck me during our sessions. I always felt safe with him.

Still, no.

Dean was the last person I could talk to about the maelstrom brewing in my brain.

I flinched when his hand settled on the nape of my neck, and then smiled up at him as he refilled my glass. Only halfway this time, the fruit and ice cubes jostling around inside the pitcher. Dean topped off his glass too, still grasping the back of my neck—not threateningly. Possessively. Affectionately, his thumb brushing across my skin. When he left, I sagged a little, the warmth of his palm lingering as I grabbed my wine glass and took a little sip.

"Thank you, sir," I said when he sat back down at the head of the table—the same table he'd tied me to the first night, the table where we had nearly all our meals. He shot me an easy smile and winked.

"You're welcome, Belle." While he picked up his glass, he didn't drink it. Instead, he merely swirled the white, sharply citric liquid about inside, watching me. "I have lemon and raspberry sorbet for dessert."

A moan slipped free before I could stop it. "*Yum.*"

"Just for you."

"Not for you?" I shifted in my high-backed chair to face him when he shook his head.

"No, Belle. None for me." In an instant, the easy smile vanished—replaced by something darker. Something that shot straight through to my core. That skittered down my spine, frigid, yet pooled piping-hot between my thighs. It was incredible, the change between regular Dean and Dom-Dean. Incredibly *sexy*, that is. His features seemed to sharpen, darken, those sage-green eyes filled with wicked deeds, his smirking mouth speaking a thousand sinful things without uttering a word.

I adored Dom-Dean.

Too much.

That was my problem.

"You're my dessert tonight," he rumbled, settling back in his chair—slouching into it, lazily, like a man who knew he owned his domain and every living thing in it. I shivered, clutching my wine glass so tight that it easily could have shattered. With a quick flick of his gaze from me to the spot directly in front of him, Dean murmured, voice like silk, "Finish your wine—and then get on the table."

I downed the entire glass in two huge gulps. Then, gathering my billowy sundress in hand, I climbed up. He hadn't told me to strip, so I left the dress on—a dress sheer enough to see my nipples, the fabric white with pink hearts, strapless, nothing more than a simple bathing suit cover-up. I had a whole arsenal of them, all of which I'd purchased for this trip, figuring Dean would enjoy the fact that he could see my puckered nipples so easily through the material.

A theory quickly proven correct my first week here.

"Lay down on your back," he instructed softly, words so low that I had to strain, *really* concentrate, to hear, "so that I can see all of you. I'd like to watch you come."

My cheeks burned—still—as I exhaled sharply. His accent always sharpened when he was Dom-Dean. Lilting, simmering just below the surface. It drove me wild.

Facing him, I pulled my dress up to my hips, then leaned back, settling on the table. I peeked around my bent legs, and the sight of him watching me with such intensity, drumming his fingers slowly on his chair's armrest—it was enough to make me come right then and there.

Legs open, folded, tipped over on each side, I knew I was wet. I knew it before my finger first slipped between my folds. I could *feel* the heat, the need. Maybe he could too. The thought had me shivering again, my skin prickling, my stomach somersaulting.

Dean had never asked me to masturbate for him before. I knew it was on our approved list of activities, but I hadn't given much thought to actually *doing* it. At first, my movements were all for show. Spreading my lips. Circling my clitoris. I wanted him to enjoy the view.

However, as I lay there, open, touching myself for him, I thought back to the beginning of this month—when he'd told me, frankly, that I didn't need to perform for him. What I had learned acting on a stage for Elysium's patrons was all fine and good, but it didn't translate to a one-on-one session. So, I had dropped all that. Stopped sticking my butt out. Stopped worrying about how my breasts looked, if my stomach was sucked in, whether I was rocking a set of sultry bedroom eyes. As the days went on, as my time with Dean lengthened, intensified, I focused on being *present*.

So, that was what I did now. I stopped performing. I closed my eyes and took a deep breath, then slowly let it all out. After that, I touched myself for pleasure. I touched myself how I might in the privacy of my own bedroom. I pictured Dean—the look in his eye as he consumed me.

That was the best mental porn out there.

Slowly, my hips started to rock, to grind, to writhe against my hand. My movements became jerky, chasing the high, pursuing the flicker of bliss for something deeper. I found myself pinching my stiff nipples through my dress, imagining it was him—pinching harder to make it seem real. My back arched. My mouth dropped open. My brow furrowed. My body *tightened* so deliciously that I moaned, pleasure prickling through every limb. Pleasure that was so exquisite—but also not what I needed. Not what I wanted. Pleasure that burned like a hissing, spitting, crackling bonfire, when the pleasure I chased burned like the sun.

"Sir, c-can I—"

"*Yes*," he growled before I could even get the question out. Ever since I had been forced to endure *eight* climaxes in a row—a task that had taken me nearly an hour and a half to accomplish, my clit on fire and my energy spent—I remembered to ask. The lesson had stuck. I knew when to beg, when to speak up, so desperately familiar with my own climaxes now. I'd learned what I needed to. Dean had seen to that. No more coming without permission. These days, my Dom seemed all too happy to give it, so long as I asked first.

Yes. Dean's voice rattled around my head, that single word opening the floodgates. I pressed harder. Bucked my hips up, my fingers homing in on that one *perfect* spot until—

"Oh, *god*!" Until I peaked. Until I tumbled into the abyss, fireworks fizzing behind my eyelids as a glorious wave of pleasure washed over me. My fingers continued to work, operating with a mind of their own, prolonging the high for as long as I dared.

I squeaked when Dean's hands suddenly locked around my ankles. He yanked me down the table, straight to the edge. Heart pounding, I sat up on my elbows, only to fall back down when he buried his face between my thighs. The first sweep of his tongue across my swollen, slick folds had me crying out, hips arching up to meet him.

Arms wrapped around my thighs, he licked, licked, *licked* me through another flood of pleasure. My hand threaded into his hair, grasping and tugging. I was a woman possessed, and Dean's tongue called all the shots, right up until the last delicious moment.

When the world finally stopped exploding with colour, I sheepishly removed my hand from his hair, hoping I hadn't pulled too hard. My legs quivered, but I couldn't help smiling when Dean dragged his mouth the length of my inner left thigh, not stopping until he reached my knee—and pressed a firm kiss to it.

"Thank you, Belle. That was lovely."

"Thank *you*, sir," I managed, taking his hand when he offered it and sitting up. My grin, all post-orgasm loopy, had Dean smiling, shifting from that dark, sensual creature into something lighter, warmer.

The aftercare Dom. Still Dom-Dean, still sexy—just different.

"Sorbet?"

"Yes, please."

Seated at the edge of the table, I pushed my dress down as Dean stood and saw to my dessert. Out of the corner of my eye, I watched him putter around the kitchen, grabbing a bowl and a spoon, scooping a single helping of each flavor. When he returned, so had my composure, the feeling of being grounded again after that wonderful high. I accepted my bowl with a small smile, the ceramic cold to the touch. Then, much to my surprise, Dean wandered back to the kitchen to retrieve a huge ladle, which he stuck in the nearly empty pitcher of sangria.

"For all the fruit at the bottom," he insisted as he set it on the table beside me. His wine glass, still full, sat precariously close to the table's right corner, and I tried not to breathe him in *too* deeply when Dean stretched across me to grab it.

"I'm going to watch another Sherlock episode tonight," I said as he straightened, his musky cologne lingering between us. "You in?"

Since I spent most of my daytime breaks reading by the pool, I had opted to make full use of Dean's gorgeous home theater room in the evenings to catch up on all the shows I'd missed since starting at Elysium. I usually worked six nights a week at the kink club and caught up with sleep during the day. Between that, running errands and trying to maintain some semblance of a social life, there wasn't much time for TV-bingeing.

Enter Dean's huge library of movies and TV shows.

When he first showed me, I'd thought I'd died and gone to heaven. Not only did he have a wealth of stuff to watch, but plopping down in the cushy, enormous chairs felt like being cradled by a cloud. There had been plenty of nights where I'd completely passed out within minutes of curling up inside one of those bad boys, courtesy of a full day with Dean and the Caribbean sun.

If I woke up in my bed with zero idea of how I got there, I could safely assume Dean had carried me there after I conked out, whether he had been watching the show with me at the time from the comfort of his *own* cushy chair —or not.

Just one more of the many things that I liked about him —that I could fall asleep, full-on snoring, drooling sleep, and not have to worry about him hurting me. Misusing me.

As I spooned a bit of lemon sorbet into my mouth, I couldn't help but think how strange it was to trust someone so completely in such a short time.

When I nudged Dean's thigh with my toe, lifting an eyebrow to my question, he shook his head.

"Not tonight, Belle. You go—enjoy yourself."

He gave my chin a quick pinch before sauntering toward the stairs, wine in hand. Bowl sitting on my lap, my gaze trailed after him, through the glass railing, along the alabaster staircase. One flight, around the corner, second flight. Then he was gone.

And I didn't need to follow him to know what he was up to. Anytime Dean turned down an invitation to do something together during what was technically free time for me, it was because he planned to lock himself away on the third floor for the rest of the night.

I let out a huff. It wasn't that I *needed* to know what he did up there. Dean had a right to privacy, just as much as I did. But I still *wanted* to know. It was driving me nuts, honestly—even though it shouldn't. I ought to let it go. Dean had made it very clear that the third floor was off-limits. In fact, that was one of the house rules—no third floor.

But I just...

I just wanted to know—*him*. It wasn't about the mystery, the allure of the ambiguous third floor. Dean always emerged in a good mood. He went up there distracted, maybe even a little distant, then returned carefree and smiling. Something up there mattered to him. Something up there soothed him, relaxed him. It took his worries away, even if it was only for an hour.

A part of me wanted to be that for him. More than just the escort he'd pay to act out his fantasies. I wanted...

Frowning, I set my sorbet bowl aside, still seated on the table, and went for the pitcher of ice cubes and leftover sangria-soaked fruit. The giant ladle managed to snag a grape, a strawberry half, and a slice of kiwi. I shoved all three into my mouth—but didn't chew right away. Not when I heard the door to whatever the heck was up there closing. A curt, echoey *click* in Dean's enormous house. No lock. Never a lock. He kept it open, as far as I could tell.

Slowly, I smooshed the fruit around with my tongue, each flavor laced with enough absorbed sangria to make me pucker. Sensing that it was just me and ol' Holmes for the night, I gathered up my dessert and drifted to the home theater room, wet thighs brushing together. At the top of the stairs, I paused, bowl and jug precariously balanced in one arm, and used my dress to wipe each leg.

And as I carried on, I realized that while I might have wiped the evidence of Dean's dessert away—*he* still clung to me, his lips ghosting along my thigh with every step I took.

HOUSE RULE #17

The third floor is strictly off-limits. Punishment for breaking said rule *will* be more severe than any other offense. Belle should consider herself warned.

12

BELLE

Thursday, February 28th

"Now, remember, while I'm gone, no swimming out here."

I leaned back against the pier's wooden railing, grinning as Dean prepped his flashy little boat for the trip to Saint Thomas. A warm midday breeze toyed with my hair and dress, and I held a hand over my forehead, shielding my eyes despite wearing sunglasses. "I know, sir."

He marched about, throwing ropes onto the bobbing dock. "And I've left something already prepared for lunch in the fridge. You'll just need to put it all together when you're ready."

My lips pursed. Yup, I'd seen all the salad prep he had done when we normally would have been having fun in his office. However, Dean was headed out for some meeting in Saint Thomas, the details of which had all been vague— apparently, I wasn't need-to-know. And that was fine. But today was a Wednesday. I didn't want—or need—the day off, and a ridiculous part of me already missed him.

Which was, you know, *ridiculous*. He'd only be gone for two hours, three max. He had promised to call if things ran late, and I had free run of Ixora while he was gone. If I really wanted, I could *nap* for the full two hours and wake up to his return. But I'd been on edge all morning; who'd have thought I would come to crave the stringent routine Dean had in place six days a week?

I gathered the loose fabric of my sundress up in one hand, then picked up Dean's laptop carrier case with the other when he seemed to be going down for it.

"Sir, I know how to cook," I said as I handed it to him, the boat rising up and down between us. The wind made the sea choppy today, and while I didn't want to see him go, I was also pleased he hadn't asked me to come with him. I'd only *just* gotten my seasickness under control and could now officially sit in the damn thing without needing to take a handful of anti-nausea pills beforehand. Given we had done a few more day trips this past week, coming up on the end of our first month—movie night in the park in Saint Thomas, a luxury spa day in Saint Croix, kite surfing off Cruz Bay, and an ice cream date in Coral Harbor—I considered it a win.

"You, cook?" Dean's eyebrows shot up over his aviators. "That's debatable, Belle."

"Hey!" I swatted at him with a giggle, lightly smacking his butt when he leaned over to slip his bag in the pocket on the back of the driver's seat. He shot up and whirled around at the contact, and I hid my hand behind my back with an innocent smile.

"You know," Dean mused, "I'm only basing my opinion off the evidence at my disposal—"

"Well, if you would just let me cook one of these days—"

"We tried that, remember?" He leaned on the boat's

chrome handrail, taut muscle climbing up his arms, rippling shoulders hidden beneath the floral-print button-up tee. "Fajita night?"

"Okay, well, your burners run a lot hotter than the ones in my crappy studio," I argued, hands planted on my hips. "Fajita night doesn't count. That was a trial run."

"Fine." He beckoned me forward with a crooked finger, and I tiptoed along, both hands behind my back now, unable to stop grinning up at him. Dean smoothed a hand over my wild blonde mane, wrangling it back to earth as the wind continued to whip it into a frenzy. With a soft sigh, I leaned into his touch, into the way he cupped my face, thumb stroking my cheek as he said, "We'll do another Belle night—you'll cook everything. I'll be totally hands-off."

"Well..." I shrugged, fighting the urge to clutch his wrist, to turn and kiss his palm. "Maybe not *totally* hands-off."

His rich, full laughter had me blushing, and I stood up on my toes as he came down, presenting my cheek for what I thought would be a quick kiss. Instead, he lingered, his breath hot against my skin, his hand suddenly back in my hair, threading through it, fisting it just hard enough to tip my head back.

"We'll see," Dean murmured. He trailed his nose along my jaw, my neck, then up to my ear. "Be a good girl while I'm gone."

I swallowed hard. "Yes, sir."

He pressed one final kiss just below my ear, then straightened. "Shall I bring you something back?"

I bit my lower lip as I smiled, wide and adoring, the kind of smile that came naturally around Dean. "If you want to."

"Then I suppose we'll have to see." He shot me one last grin before casting off the final bit of rope anchoring him to the dock. As he went for the keys to get the engine going, I started forward, grabbing the metal railing of the large bowrider.

"Don't forget to call," I said, hating how worried I sounded as Dean crossed back toward me. "I mean, if you're going to be late. It's a bit windy, and I just..." I trailed off when he cupped my chin. "Don't forget to call."

"I won't, Belle. Even if I'm not running late, I'll call the house phone before I go."

We held one another's gaze for a beat longer than necessary, reflections caught in our sunglasses. Finally, begrudgingly, I took a step back and crossed my arms.

"Well, you don't want to be late."

"No," Dean said as he straightened. "I suppose not— although I can certainly think of a few acceptable reasons *why* I might be late."

He wanted to have me on the boat. It was in our dossier, one of the sessions we'd both signed off on. Arms bound with intricate knots behind my back, he wanted to set me on his lap and slowly have his way with me from here to Saint Croix. The thought made heat flare in my cheeks, in my core, between my thighs.

"Go on, sir."

"And when did my submissive get so bossy?"

"I think I've always been a little bossy," I said as I sauntered backward, going until I bumped into the wooden rail on the opposite side of the pier again. "Maybe you just haven't been paying attention."

He smirked. "Hardly."

Yeah, that sounded about right. Dean wasn't a man who missed much.

I drifted to the beach as he backed the boat out, but stayed put until he was past the shallows, puttering into the horizon. Before he went too far, Dean slowed and waved at me. I stood up on my toes and waved back, smiling. Then he was off, headed toward the towering isles of green in the distance.

With a heavy sigh, I wandered back toward the house, kicking through the mounds of near-white sand, stopping here and there on the trail to admire a flower or a flock of birds in the trees. The whole place felt bigger without Dean, more imposing—intimidating, even. Like the island knew I didn't belong, that I was just a visitor. Gathering my dress in one hand, I headed for the house at a good clip.

In the hour that followed, I did my best to keep busy. I tidied my bedroom. I put away all the dishes that had been left out to dry on the rack next to the sink. I ate the salad Dean had prepped. Made a smoothie—one for me, one waiting in the fridge for him. I read by the pool. I entertained the idea of a little skinny-dipping in his absence, but eventually decided against it. Somehow, it didn't feel right—doing the things alone we usually did together.

So, I retreated indoors, to the wonderfully cool interior, the tinted glass walls a surprisingly good buffer against the heat. While February had been incredibly comfortable, as we crept closer to March, so too did the daily temperatures rise. It was all still manageable; Dean had chosen the winter months for a reason. I couldn't imagine doing half of what we'd done outside in, say, July. Ugh.

As I headed for the stairs, I caught a glimpse of my reflection in the nearby wall. My cheeks looked fuller, my skin freckly—on its way to golden. I liked the look, although my wide-eyed innocent persona was harder to pull off when I wasn't porcelain white. Dean didn't seem to mind. He always prompted me to put on sunscreen, and then to reapply it, but we had wasted many a Sunday afternoon down at the beach, lying under the sun together, napping, reading, chatting.

E-reader in hand, I scaled the alabaster staircase up to the second floor, purposefully *not* looking over as I went. While I had no issues being on the upper level, I still didn't like looking over the glass railing. My stomach knotted at the thought, and I scuttled away, headed down the corridor to my bedroom.

After tossing my reader on the bed from the doorway, I drifted back toward the stairs, trying to decide how best to kill the rest of my Sir-less afternoon. Behind me stretched the long hallway that housed Dean's bedroom, his office, and a few other empty guest suites. And to my right, just as I neared the top of the main staircase—another set of steps that took you up to the third floor.

I paused.

I shouldn't have paused.

I should have just kept going—to grab my smoothie, then go to the cinema room, like I'd planned, to waste another hour before Dean came back.

But I did it. I paused. And suddenly I was climbing the steps nestled in a narrow, closed-off stairwell. Ten steps up to a dark landing, then another—I counted quickly, my heart beating just a little faster—eight steps up to that door, whose sturdy *click* echoed throughout the entire house whenever it closed.

Nibbling my lower lip, I lingered on the landing, peering through the darkness. Light outlined the door. Maybe it was a rooftop lounge? Maybe it was just somewhere private for him to go—somewhere to get away from *me*.

The thought made my stomach twist harder, and I pressed against it, pretending the ache came from those weird nuts Dean had added to my salad and not actual *feelings.* Hurt feelings—at the thought of him needing to escape me.

"Don't go up there, Belle," I whispered, my hand on the wall. "Just go back downstairs."

But downstairs didn't tell me anything new about Dean. It didn't help me get to know him better. I had examined this house from top to bottom over the last four weeks—but beyond that door was uncharted territory. It was a piece of Dean I might like, maybe even love.

Or it might be weird.

I swallowed hard. Given that Dean and I engaged in kink play on a regular basis, we'd had our fair share of weird. Nothing had scared me yet. Or, better yet, nothing had left a bad taste in my mouth. Every day, Dean Donahue did something, said something, that made me like him, want him, more than the day before. Even when he pulled out the really kinky stuff. Even when he tasked me with folding his clothes, naked, while wearing a sizeable butt plug. Dean and his desires didn't scare me. They thrilled me. They excited me. They had me wet and wanting before we'd even started.

So, what if something beyond that door really *was* weird?

What if it made things weird between us?

Maybe that's a good thing, my little voice of self-preservation hissed. *Maybe you need that push to build up your professional walls again. They're about a foot tall right now.*

Rule number one in the escorting handbook: don't fall for the client.

And I was dangerously close to breaking it.

Maybe if something up there freaked me out, I'd be able to get through the next month without damning myself, without risking my job and my heart.

Maybe whatever was up there would be the deciding factor. Maybe it would finally nudge me in one direction or the other.

Maybe—

Oh, hell, I was already walking up the stairs.

The handle gave way easily when I pulled down on it. No lock. Just as I'd thought. With a deep breath, I pushed the door open, standing two steps down from it. The wide-set panel swung away, illuminating the narrow corridor around me with sunlight. I squinted but stayed put.

If I climbed those final two steps, I'd be breaking Dean's trust. Even if he never found out, *I* would know. It made me queasy just to think it.

But, but—all my *reasons*.

Just a quick peek.

No snooping. Just—in and out, quick scan, then off to the cinema room to watch a show with my smoothie.

Heart pounding, I climbed the last two steps slowly, then poked my head into the room.

Only it wasn't just some old room. I gasped, not caring how dramatic it felt to literally *gasp*—because it was just that beautiful. A gorgeous sunlit gallery greeted me, the domed ceiling made entirely of paneled windows. My peek turned into a gander as I stepped inside, eyes wide as I took in the dozens upon dozens upon *dozens* of paintings. Stacked in rows, canvases of all different sizes, colors poking out from every direction.

The style—it was just like the painting in his office. I loved that painting of the ocean's unrest. Looking at it gave me strength whenever I was stuck doing a punishment during office time. It gave me focus.

It made me *feel*.

And that was because *he* had painted it. That painting

was a piece of him, and I'd been unwittingly drawn to it for weeks.

Twirling a long strand of blonde hair around my finger, I drifted in.

Paintings like these deserved *more* than a peek, that was all. They were stunning. Breathtaking, definitely, with vivid canvases of the natural world—flowers from his gardens outside, trees from the island's forest, the clear blue water and white-tipped cliffs down by the cove. And the *birds*: he had captured every single one I'd seen around Ixora since I arrived. Beautiful. Here and there, the occasional cityscape, with bleak, smoky fog or explosions of yellow, orange, and red light. Sunrises. Sunsets. A fuzzy white and grey sheepdog, eyes obscured. That one made me laugh.

I didn't know much about art, but I'd taken an intro to art history class at NYU to fill my humanities credit. The distinctive brushstrokes, all that color, the blurred lines between objects and their surroundings. Dean Donahue was a secret impressionist.

He was an artist—a brilliant one at that.

As I studied his work, carefully holding each canvas by the corner, greedily digging through the rows, this seemed right. It was what I had thought about Dean all along. He wasn't white and grey with accents of black like his jet. He might run an empire, be worth billions—but to me, he was his paintings.

What was that old Monet quote?

"I would like to paint the way a bird sings."

An apt description. A quote that put words, eloquently, to the strange, wobbly feeling in my chest that I felt while poring over his work.

In the center of the room, it appeared he had a new work

on the go. While the background needed colour, the rest of it was—

Me.

Dean was painting me.

He had the cluster of freckles on my right shoulder down. The figure in the painting had her back to her audience, though she peeked over her shoulder mischievously. A long blonde plait trailed down her back, tied off with a pink bow at the end. He had done a rough tracing in pencil first; her face—my face—still needed to be filled in.

Well. I'd been right about one thing: this room had certainly made my feelings for Dean clearer. As I stood there, tearing up like an idiot, a pleasant burn on my cheeks and a tightness in my chest, I decided that my feelings were almost *painfully* obvious now.

Which suddenly made this trip, our dynamic, so much harder. It complicated things. It—

"Belle."

My blood ran cold. I tensed, then slowly turned on the spot to find my furious Dom in the doorway. Sunglasses on top of his head, a thin box of pink macarons in hand, Dean stood there silent, rigid, his figure seeming to fill the entire doorway.

"What do you think you're doing?" he asked, his words dangerously quiet—precise.

As I stared back at him, lightheadedness struck. My knees threatened to give out. I couldn't think straight. My tongue felt too big for my dry, sandpapery mouth. I started to tremble.

And two seconds later, I made everything a thousand times worse when, in a mousey little voice, I squeaked, "Uhm..."

HOUSE RULE #2

Belle will use her safeword (apricots) if she is feeling unsafe, has encountered an undiscussed limit, or is too uncomfortable to continue—no exceptions.

13

BELLE

"*G*et downstairs."

Ohmygodohmygodohmygodohmygod.

Head down, I power-shuffled across the room. The heat of Dean's stare scalded, tracking me the entire way, and he stiffly turned to the side so I could squeeze by him through the doorway. My clammy hands tightened to fists as I hurried down the stairs, going from light to dark—to darker still when Dean slammed the studio door and thundered down after me. His figure loomed behind, a phantom in the shadows, and I practically ran the rest of the way down.

"Left," he ordered sharply. Okay, so not *downstairs*, downstairs. I turned, hesitating, unsure of where he wanted me, cowering out of the way when he stalked down the hall. "Your bedroom."

I nodded. There was no point in trying to say anything in my defence. I'd been caught snooping—I'd been caught breaking a house rule. One that threatened severe punishment if broken.

For the life of me, I couldn't imagine *why*. His work was

magnificent—but it was just that: *his* work. Not every artist wanted their soul plastered across a billboard in Times Square.

Lying was always an option. I could say I heard a noise—wanted to make sure everything was okay, that nothing was broken, that, I don't know, a bird hadn't crashed through the studio's glass ceiling.

But I'd damaged Dean's trust enough today. A lie would make everything worse. It'd taste sour and foul on my tongue—and I'd probably end up crying, anyway, inadvertently outing myself.

"*In.*"

I scampered through my open bedroom door, wondering if I was being given a time-out. Dean always seemed to enjoy administering punishments—and I, for the most part, liked enduring them. Today, however, as he slammed the box of macarons on the little dresser next to the door, he didn't look like he was enjoying himself. In fact, this could very well be the first time I had ever seen him truly *angry*, his features granite-hard and his eyes stormy. My lower lip quivered at the thought, but I steeled myself. I had done the crime. I deserved to do the time—whatever that might entail.

"Dean, I'm sorry. I just—"

"Strip," he snapped, then marched out of the bedroom. With trembling hands, I tugged my dress over my head, folding it a few times over before tossing it on the bed. Waiting for him to return—was agony. I thought I had experienced the pain of *waiting* during our sessions; anticipation could be just as delicious, just as glorious, as the act itself. This, however, was torture.

Five minutes stretched on like five years, but I just stood in the same spot he had last seen me in, fidgeting with my nails, my insides twisting. When he finally stalked back in, a brief shining moment of relief flickered through me—only to extinguish almost immediately. He hadn't returned empty-handed.

In one hand, a spreader bar, the cuffs at either end made of leather. In the other, a paddle. A large, hefty wooden paddle that I had never seen before. My heart leapt into my throat; why did he have *both*?

"Dean," I started, my breath hitching, "sir, I'm really sorry—"

"Lay back on the bed."

I hesitated, not liking the size, the weight, of that paddle. Our eyes met briefly, and his were all storm and steel and disappointment.

I hated the last one the most. So, with a deep breath, I climbed onto my squishy queen, then settled on my back, heart hammering. He said nothing as he attached the spreader bar's cuff to my right ankle, pulling it tighter— possibly tighter than he needed to. I winced, staring up at the ceiling, regretting how I had gone about discovering the third floor.

Because I didn't regret what I'd seen. In fact, learning about that side of Dean only made my feelings for him stronger.

But I had done it the wrong way.

He wrenched the left cuff tight too, and I flinched, suddenly finding my legs spread open—wider than I'd anticipated. It was hard to measure length just by looking at something, but *feeling* it, legs open, every part of me on display, was a different story entirely. The bar certainly felt bigger than it looked.

Dean stomped over to the bedroom window, then yanked back the curtain I always kept closed, all in a brooding silence. I sat up on my elbows, frowning when he lifted the window open and locked it in place.

"What are you—"

Before I could even get it out, he was back at the bed, yanking me down to the end by the spreader bar. He then scooped me up, an arm around my waist, and half walked, half carried me over to the window. I waddled along beside him, struggling to move with the bar in place, so focused on that that I couldn't prepare for what he did next.

For when he pushed me right up against the window ledge, facing the sea of blush-pink oleanders below. I looked up immediately, anxiety spiking. Beside me, Dean knelt down and fastened the spreader bar's cuffs to two clasps on the floor I'd never noticed before—probably because I avoided that window like the plague. Spaced roughly the width of the bar apart, two little metal hoops stuck out of the floor, no more than a finger's width around, attached to which were the clasps.

And attached to the clasps—me.

I couldn't move. Not even if I wanted to. I was stuck— right up against the window ledge.

"Dean—"

"You cannot fall." He stood and hooked an arm around my midsection, lifting me as far as the clasps would allow, pulling me to show that I wasn't going anywhere. "You will not fall. Do you understand?"

I hated his tone. It was crisper, sharper. This wasn't Dom-Dean. This definitely wasn't aftercare Dom-Dean. This was—*angry* Dom-Dean. I'd never met him before, and as he set me back down on the ground, none too gently, I wasn't sure I liked him very much.

"Do you understand, Belle?" There it was: a *hint* of Dom-

Dean. A whisper of the velvet I had come to expect, want, *need*.

"Yes, sir," I whispered, my hands death-gripping the window ledge as I continued to stare up, not out. I wasn't sure why it mattered if I knew I couldn't fall—

"Good. Now, bend over the ledge, out the window."

Oh. My heart dropped from my throat straight to the pit of my stomach in two seconds flat. He wanted me to—*lean* out a second-floor window? Naked?

Well, the naked part didn't bother me, but the, what, twenty-foot drop below—

"Belle."

My voice wobbled. "But, sir—"

"Do you know what rule you broke today?" His words had me shivering. That voice. Like steel. Like flint. Like a knife. I nodded miserably.

"Yes, sir."

"Good. Then do as you're told."

Teary-eyed, I looked through the opening before me. In the far distance, waves lapped at the beach. They whitecapped and crashed in the open sea. Closer to home, palms swayed in the breeze, bowing to the right, flourishing beneath an unrelenting Caribbean sun. The breeze kissed me, too. It brushed across my face, ruffled through my hair. But I didn't bow. I stayed upright, my lips trembling, staring off into the horizon. Hoping that would calm me. Hoping that would make this easier—if I just watched where the sea met the sky.

Dean pushed against my lower back. Not harshly. Not insistently. The weight of his hand had an oddly soothing effect, nothing more than a reminder that I had a job to do —both literally and figuratively.

Still, I couldn't believe that he was making me do this.

Heights were *not* my friend. They never had been. He knew that. He'd known that from our first day here.

So, he had either forgotten—or he remembered and didn't care.

In that moment, I wasn't sure which hurt more.

You hurt him first, whispered Logic and Reason, two nagging voices at the back of my mind who usually worked in tandem with Self-Preservation. All three had been sounding meaner lately, more critical of my choices, my feelings, but they were right. I had broken his trust first. I had broken the rules. Maybe I had even broken *us*.

With some difficulty, I pried my hands from the window ledge, then reached down and pressed them flat to the outside wall. My clammy skin skirted over stubbly concrete, and, slowly, with Dean's hand still resting on the small of my back, I bent over. The wind picked up as soon as I eased through the windowpane, tossing my hair about, throwing my balance for a loop. I panicked. I started as you do just before succumbing to sleep—when you feel like you're suddenly falling, falling, falling into the black and startle awake.

I pressed hard to the wall, bending at my waist. A pair of tears fell—straight down, *splat*, onto the cobblestone pathway through the garden. My stomach turned. So high. So precariously high.

You cannot fall.

You will not fall.

He might have been angry with me, but Dean hadn't forgotten safety. He hadn't forgotten to remind me that I was still safe with him.

But then his hand was gone, its heat lingering across my lower back. My skin prickled in his absence, and I squeaked when my sweaty palms lost their grip and I fell another inch or two down the wall, my breasts compressed against it suddenly. Tightening my core, I braced myself again and straightened, looking up—up and out, straight to the blue horizon.

My head threatened to spin, but each deep, purposeful breath quieted my panicked brain. Just don't look down. Don't look down. Don't look down. Don't—

I stilled when Dean placed the paddle against my butt. It spread the full length of me, encompassing both cheeks. The weight of it, the firmness, had my lips trembling again, my eyes tearing.

"Ten strokes," he said coolly from inside. "You will count them, Belle."

"Yes, sir," I replied, wishing my voice didn't shake, but knowing that was too much to ask for right now. He gave my backside a little pat with the paddle, and I found myself wondering if maybe, just maybe, he planned to go easy on me. Usually it was three sets of five, not two.

The smooth wood of the paddle vanished. I braced myself, staring across the horizon. Then I heard it, the faint *whoosh* of air, followed by...

Thump.

I screamed—more in surprise than anything. It was so different from the stick he had used the first day; the stick stung, same as his bare hand. They were both just a kiss of fire across my skin, one that quickly faded. The paddle *ached*, then burned. Quickly, at that, its reach widespread.

"O-one," I whimpered, my gaze swimming. The second hit was no less shocking, but I managed not to scream this time. Squeal. I had no qualms about squealing—and squeal I did. Over and over again, with each hit. Three. Four. The fourth squeal tapered off into a wail.

"Open your eyes, Belle."

I hadn't even realized I'd closed them. Dean slipped the flat face of the paddle between my forcibly parted thighs, rubbing me. Soft, lush seeds of pleasure unfurled through my core—only to vanish the moment I opened my eyes. Because there was the ground, all the way down there, and I couldn't keep still long enough to comfortably prop myself up. I tensed at the rush of air. I flailed with each hit.

Whoosh.

Thump.

"Five!" I shrieked, standing up on my toes, shifting my weight between my legs—trying to move out of reach, only to find myself stuck. One hand reached back to grab the window frame, but as I started to straighten up, there was Dean again on the small of my back.

"Halfway there, Belle." No velvet this time. All steel. I would have killed for velvet.

Hot, wet tears sliced down my cheeks, falling heavily to the cobblestone below. The remaining five hits came in rapid succession, all concentrated on the same burning, throbbing spot on my backside. By the tenth, I was still counting, but there was no telling if the words coming out were coherent. To me, it was mostly just squeals and screeches that bore a passing resemblance to the English language.

My entire lower half was on fire. Even if he hadn't paddled my thighs, everything hurt. *Everything.* My shoulders ached from the strain of holding myself up. My core felt like a spring that had been stretched too taut, seconds away from snapping. My thighs—my thighs wanted to close, but they couldn't.

Even the slightest attempt, the faintest movement, however, told me I was wet.

What the hell was wrong with me?

I dragged in a shaky, stuttering breath, nose blocked, tears streaming steadily now. A final watery look toward the garden below somehow didn't feel as bad as it had a few minutes ago. I could stare at the ground, at the tear splotches, and, for the first time in my life, not feel like I was going to fall—or die.

Dean's arms wove under mine, and slowly, carefully, he guided me through the window and stood me upright. My back ached. My backside burned. My thighs quivered. And I couldn't look at him. Shaky, suddenly lightheaded, I grabbed at Dean's shoulder before I collapsed, leaning my full weight on him as he reached down to undo one ankle strap. Once free, my leg sprang toward the other, the movement intensifying the burn, and I wavered, fisting the starchy fabric of Dean's floral button-down tee.

He moved tentatively, probably slower than he needed to, as he went for the other cuff. When the thick, oppressive bite of leather disappeared, I pushed off him, stumbling back into the wall next to the window. Dean didn't follow. He made no move to draw me to him, to cuddle me into his arms. Once he had unbound me, the spreader bar on the tiled floor between us, he just stood there.

Stiff. Looming. One hand in a fist.

I pressed both of mine flat to the wall. Thick, silent tears trekked down my cheeks, my mouth set in a trembling line. When I finally found the courage, I looked at him. At the hard lines of his face, the terse frown of his lips. His sage-green gaze lifted to mine, and I didn't see aftercare Dom-Dean. Not even a flicker. Just this unrecognizable, surly Dom whom I didn't like. I didn't want. And, you know what, I didn't *deserve*.

Not after *that*. Not after—I glowered at the paddle on my bed, at the way it sank into my thin comforter, rumpling it.

That thing had been the worst of my punishments. Worse than forced orgasms. Worse than bare-handed spanking. Worse than some stick Dean found in the woods.

And he couldn't find it in him to muster an *ounce* of the soft, warm, comforting persona he put on for aftercare? For something so important, not only to my physical health, but to my mental, emotional health too?

My tears fell harder, hurt turning my heart hard.

"Get out." As much as sudden movement pained me—I lashed out, shoving at his arm. "Get out."

The jolt seemed to startle him back to reality, startle him out of that awful *look*, the steely glint vanishing. He stumbled, catching his foot on the spreader bar, faltering. There he was—my Dom. My Dean. I saw him now, like a ray of sunlight *finally* forcing its way through the storm clouds.

But I didn't care.

"Get out! Get out. Get out. Get *out*!"

Sobbing, I shoved him again—and again, and again, and again. Right out my bedroom door. Dean made no move to stop me, to catch my hands, to pin my arms—nothing. He let me push him across the room; we both knew I couldn't have physically moved him unless he let me. He let me shove hard. He let me scream at him.

And finally, he let me slam the door in his face.

14

DEAN

*F*uck.

This wasn't how today was supposed to unfold.

I'd had it all sorted in my head—arranged.

First, I would have lunch with my father's crusty old business associates, the kind who flocked to the Virgin Islands every year around this time. As expected, they would float an invitation to the gala they held during the annual regatta in Saint Thomas, and I would hem and haw, but eventually accept. Father forced me to go every year.

"You have a house out there! It'll be *easy*."

Like spending an entire evening with the sharks of our world was *easy*—like it was no trouble at all. Usually, I was expected to network. I was expected to brag. I was expected to talk up the family and forge new connections—or reignite old ones—with anyone worthy of our time.

I had anticipated the invitation. I had gone every year. But professional responsibilities had always forced me back to Europe, or Britain, or New York—I never had the *time* to stay more than a night in "that little house" my father always referred to with a sniff.

Today's luncheon had been accepted out of respect. While I had no intention of answering any of my father's emails regarding my brother's poor performance—the shock of the century—I also had no plans to embarrass him in front of his old school chums, now the business elite across Europe and America.

The plan had been simple.

Show up. Smile. Chat—be talked *at*, more like. Boost my father's latest venture. Accept an invitation to the gala. Pick up something sweet for Belle. Go home. Cuddle my submissive into the evening.

I had an easy day in mind after the luncheon. Simple. Relaxing. Intimate. I'd feed her macarons and she would sit in my lap, purring like a kitten—because *that* was where I'd thought we were after a month together. Things had been going so well. It felt so natural. I had already ordered the—

And then I'd come home to find her in my studio.

To find her snooping, prying.

To find her breaking a rule I had thought was so simple to follow that I nearly hadn't included it in our list of twenty house rules at all. Just telling her the third floor was strictly off-limits should have been enough.

Lunch had wrapped early. I hadn't called because I'd wanted to surprise her—look, darling submissive of mine, I wasn't gone all that long!

Then I'd found an empty house. An empty pool. An empty beach. An empty bedroom, her hiking shoes in their usual spot in her closet. I'd panicked. My first instinct was that something had happened—and I'd fucking panicked.

Then I'd spotted light trickling down the staircase to the third floor, and just like that—panic off, rage on.

She had been so good at following the rules lately.

Yet today's rule-breaking felt personal, somehow. A breach of our very carefully cultivated trust.

And I'd—gone too hard on her. She didn't know the history of that room. She didn't know the years of bullshit weighing on me.

Numb, I slid down the length of her closed bedroom door. On the other side, she was sobbing.

I ran a hand through my hair.

You went too far.

I'd always sneered at Dominants who got into this so they could take their problems out on someone who got off on pain, on submission, on following orders. Yet, here I'd gone and done just that. I had let my own personal shit influence the way I disciplined my submissive. That paddle had been too heavy. I shouldn't have done ten counts—not consecutively, anyway.

But she—

It didn't matter what she'd done. Poking around my gallery wasn't an act of malice; Belle didn't have a malicious bone in her body. Yet I'd responded to her, disciplined her, like I was finally confronting the maliciousness of my past, like I could *feel* the flames of that fucking horrible night even though we were thousands of miles away from where it had all happened. Even though it was Belle, not Richard, who had discovered my canvas cache.

I had taken the anger from before and let it out today.

I'd fucked up.

She had been crying and apologizing, and I'd ignored her—because I could. Because she was my submissive and she had broken a rule, ergo, I could punish her however I saw fit.

Pathetic. Just like all the rest of them.

I closed my eyes, my heart aching. My head thumped back against her door, and I forced myself to listen to her —sobbing.

That paddle hadn't been intended for a *real* punishment, yet I had dug it out and used it. Abused it.

Hurt her.

My jaw clenched as I squeezed my eyes tighter, falling forward and burying my face in my hands. If anyone had shot all the trust we'd built straight to hell today, it was me.

The floor hooks had been installed about a month ago— a last-minute addition when I'd finally decided which room I would put Belle in. I had this fantasy that involved a very naked Belle, spread wide, and attached to those hooks while I fucked her over the window ledge. After we had arrived, however, I'd nixed that, not bothering to even broach it with her when I'd learned—

Oh my god.

Heights. When I'd learned that she had a fear of heights. I'd taken out everything in my itinerary that had to do with heights: parasailing in Saint John, a tour of the islands via a rickety little four-seater piloted by a friend of mine, hikes that took us too high in the national parks...

And then today—I'd gone and done it anyway. Fucked her, metaphorically, right over that window. It had slipped my mind, which, at the time, had been running on a single loop: *crime, punishment, crime, punishment.* Over and over again, demanding I *do* something, my actions compounded by a surge of long-festering emotional bullshit. I'd hardly been aware of it, the way history influenced me in the moment.

The way it tainted my ability to act as a level-headed Dom.

The way it fucked everything right up.

My insistence that she wouldn't fall had stemmed from the fact that no matter the situation, I felt it prudent to remind *any* submissive that she was safe with me. Given I'd decided to bend Belle over a window ledge two stories up, my one-track mind still demanded I show her that she wasn't about to plummet to her death, that I wouldn't let *real* harm befall her. Beyond that, I'd just been some charging bull, fueled by *feeling*, still scalded by the flames of that fucking night—and I had forgotten that my doting, beautiful, kind, warm submissive had an issue with heights.

Fuck. No wonder she was so emotional. No wonder she was so upset. When she'd kicked me out—I had never seen that look in her eyes before. Never heard that pitch when she screamed out her counts.

"Damn it, Donahue."

Not only had I forgotten a very real-world fear of hers, but I had invaded her personal space, thinking only of the fact that the hooks were there so the punishment ought to be there, not about the privacy of Belle's bedroom. My thought process at the time hadn't been complicated or sophisticated. I hadn't been thinking of every angle, every measure, like I normally did. I just—*did*.

She would ask to leave—why would she stay? It was in the contract: she could cut ties at any point, for any reason. I had insisted it be in there because I wanted her to feel safe.

Now she was going to leave—and she had every right to, every reason to turn tail and run. I had brought it on myself. I had ruined this. Right now.

With a deep breath, I pushed up to stand. Belle's decision to stay or go would be entirely up to her. In the meantime, I was still her Dominant—and she was in desperate need of aftercare. I needed to apologize. I needed to fix what I had very likely broken. And then she could go —today, if she wanted. I'd have it all arranged.

And I'd watch her go, let her walk out of my life, pretending that I wasn't falling for her. Pretending that I hadn't imagined a future for us, one beyond these two months. Pretending that I hadn't gone and bought her...

Never mind. None of that mattered now.

Belle mattered.

Stopping her tears mattered.

Apologizing mattered.

Aftercare mattered.

I moved through the house in a flurry. As I grabbed the cocoa butter I liked to rub on her flaming-pink skin after a spanking, I knew she could refuse to open the door. As I fished out some strawberry ice cream from the freezer, I knew she could ignore me. As I gathered the silky-soft blanket she liked to cuddle with in the TV room, collecting it from her chair, a chair that would smell like her long after she left, I knew that she could tell me to fuck off.

I wouldn't.

I was still her Dom. Her well-being was still my responsibility, and I would make sure, even if she fought me tooth and nail, that she didn't spiral. That she didn't blame herself. That she knew it was all my fault. That while she had broken a house rule, I and I alone had let us down today.

Arms overflowing with care items, I hurried back up to her bedroom, taking the stairs two at a time. By the time I returned, I was breathless, my heart pounding, my mouth dry. Inside, she continued to sob. The door didn't do much to muffle it. With a sigh, I shifted everything to one arm, then rapped my knuckles against the wood. The sobs quieted. No response. Swallowing thickly, I knocked again. "Belle?"

Nothing. It had gone silent inside—and I fucking hated the silence.

Pressing down on the handle, I popped the door open about two feet—and my heart broke at the sight inside. Belle, curled up in the middle of her bed. Trembling. Naked. Her backside raw, already showing the faintest hint of scattered bruises.

Donahue, you fucking bastard.

I inhaled deeply, forcing the anger out—anger directed at me, not her. Because even though it was focused squarely at me now, she would be sensitive to my tone, to the clipped way I spoke. So, I swallowed it, saving it for later, when I was truly alone. "Belle, can I come in?"

While she said nothing, her head bobbed up and down in a nod—a noticeable one at that. Suddenly, my heart felt a little less broken. Just like that. Nodding back at her, even though she couldn't see, I slipped inside and gently closed the door behind me. I set her aftercare things on the left corner of the bed, then made a beeline for the paddle I'd abandoned on the right. She shouldn't have to look at it. I snatched the damn thing up and slipped it under her bed, planning to put it away properly later. I then closed the window and drew the blinds, all in a flourish of quick, precise movements.

The white, double-layered curtain did a fair job of blocking out the sun. Shadow descended across the room, and a part of me thought I should just leave—that I should let Belle dictate how all this would go. She was, after all, a *professional* submissive, not my own personal one.

But before all this, I had very much hoped to change that in the future.

And I had no intention of letting that hope die because of today's fuckery.

So, I faced her, schooling my features, hiding my feelings as best I could, and found Belle watching me. Tears clung to her eyelashes, making them darker, clumping them together. Blotchy patches marred her freckled face. Redness tinted her swollen eyes.

"Oh, Belle..." I'd never wanted to cradle her to me more than in that moment. Instinct told me to scoop her up, to hold her tight, but propriety preached caution. Still, I climbed onto her bed, slowly, making no sudden movements, with the intention of wiping her thickly falling tears away. "I'm so sorry."

Before I could graze the backs of my knuckles across her cheek, she was up and moving—*toward* me, not away. Shocked, I stilled, kneeling there on the bed with my arms out to the sides—like I wouldn't touch her, hurt her, again— as Belle pushed up and pressed herself against me. Arms around my neck, face buried in my chest, the top of her head just under my chin, she clung to me—and sobbed.

Instinct kicked back in, and I let it. I gathered her shuddering body to me, lifting her so that her chin rested on my shoulder—so that she could *breathe* through all those tears. It was me who hid my face away, burying it in the crook of her neck, inhaling her scent, holding her tight. An arm around her waist. A hand cradling the back of her head. I held her, even though I hadn't meant to— and she held me back, her arms around my neck like a noose.

A welcome noose, one I never wanted to be free of.

We stayed like that for some time, surrounded by shadows, the outside world muffled. I stroked her hair as she cried, and in time, her delicate hand threaded through mine, twisting it as her sobs eased. I winced, but the physical pain was minimal—secondary to the emotional.

"I'm sorry, Belle," I whispered against her skin. She continued to shiver in my arms, her hand still fisted in my hair. "I'm so sorry."

I murmured it over and over again, my lips brushing her shoulder, her neck, the shell of her ear. I said it until she stopped crying entirely. Until her breath stopped stuttering. Until her lips stopped quivering.

Slowly, she unwound herself from me, and I held her arms as she settled onto the bed, a visceral response to pain flashing across her face the moment she sat back. Wincing, Belle settled onto her side instead, her head pillowed by both arms.

"Belle," I murmured, still kneeling before her, "I *am* so sorry for—that. That punishment was completely over the line."

"The house rules said it would be severe," she said, her voice catching. Looking away, she cleared her throat. "And I went up there and broke the rules, knowing what I was doing—"

"No." I cupped her chin, thumb stroking her soft, damp cheek. "No, that was uncalled for, and I'm sorry that I hurt you. There should be a punishment for breaking that particular rule, but not that." I started to retreat, to bring my hand back, but she grabbed it, clutching at my wrist. My chest tightened, and, with her unflinching gaze on me, I offered a quick apologetic smile. "I'm sorry I forgot about your issue with heights, too. It was careless of me, and I'm sorry—for being careless with you."

Never again.

A tear slid from the corner of her eye. The other pooled and crept down her nose. Sniffling, Belle released my wrist and brushed them away. She then sat up on her elbow, scanning the pile of supplies I'd brought up with me, and picked up the small, round container of cocoa butter. Ordinarily I would have had it in the fridge before a punishment; a spanked bottom so enjoyed the caress of something cool. Today, it had all happened so fast.

"Belle, would you like me to rub that in for you? I'll be very gentle."

She studied the container for a moment, then handed it to me with a nod. Slowly, she sat up on her knees, careful not to let her ass touch the backs of her calves, then went for the strawberry ice cream and spoon. I bit the insides of my cheeks to keep from smiling, the tightness in my chest, the *fear*, giving way to something softer, warmer, indulgent.

"Would you like to eat that while I tend to you?"

Another silent nod. I smiled gently this time when she peeked at me from beneath her lashes.

"Well, all right then. Come here."

We arranged ourselves at the head of the bed, reorganizing pillows to Belle's optimal comfort. I sat with my legs out, back to the padded headboard, and Belle draped herself over my lap, her slowly darkening ass resting on my thighs. A pillow propped up her legs, which crossed at the ankles, and she cuddled the silky-soft cinema room blanket under her front half. When I was sure that she was comfortable, that nothing was stretched or pulled in a way that would make her ache, I uncapped the little round container and dipped my fingers into the cocoa butter.

At the same time, Belle popped off the lid of the ice cream tub, then set it on the side table nearby. Ordinarily she would have a limit on the amount of sweets she could eat in a single sitting, but I had no intention of giving one —not today.

Well, maybe. That was an awful lot of ice cream, and my girl loved her sweets.

I started massaging where the skin was its pinkest—where it was its lightest. As I worked the cocoa butter in, I still wasn't sure if I would touch the darkest parts today. When I had unleashed hell on her poor bottom, I had aimed the paddle at the fleshiest bits, as one does to minimize damage. Much to my relief, my aim had been on point, although that didn't make me feel any better about the colour blooming across her skin.

If she decided to stay, I would insist we take the next four or five days off, just to give her time to recover. Or, at the very least, play gently in the meantime.

"I'm sorry for going up to the third floor," she said in a very small voice about five minutes after we'd started. In the preceding quiet, I had busied myself with working the butter into her skin, massaging away the soreness. Belle, meanwhile, had eaten about a quarter of the ice cream in the pint-sized tub.

I paused, my throat feeling tight and dry again, then settled my buttery hand across her thighs. "Thank you, Belle. I accept your apology."

Given the nature of our dynamic, apologies came in the form of serving one's punishment. When Belle had finished her punishment, she had truly apologized for whatever she had done to warrant it in the first place. Here, she didn't need to say it again—but the fact that she did had me at a loss for words.

"I broke your trust," she continued, scooping the baby-pink ice cream onto her spoon, staring down at it. "I'm sorry."

"I think we both did a bit of trust-breaking today," I muttered as I slipped my thumb between her upper thighs, more habit than anything. "I have a complex relationship with my art. It isn't an excuse—I shouldn't have done what I did. It's just..." I swallowed hard. It was just that I hadn't shared my art with anyone since that fucking horrendous day. And now my work had become the center of another potentially relationship-ruining moment. With a soft throat clear, I went back to massaging her, avoiding the spots that made her tense. "I shouldn't have reacted the way I did."

She said nothing as she ate another quarter of the container, and I had to bite my tongue to keep from telling her to slow down. Instead, I slipped out of my Dom persona, just for a moment, to bring a harsh glint of reality to the conversation.

"There is a clause in the contract," I started, hating myself for bringing it up, but knowing that I should—that I would hate myself more if I didn't. "You can leave for any reason. You'll receive payment for February and March all the same. I... I don't want you to stay somewhere you feel unsafe."

Belle faced forward, her spoon in her mouth. When I peered around, I found her gaze unfocused. The silence had my heart thundering, beating so hard it threatened to burst right out of my chest. Fire prickled beneath my skin, growing hotter the longer she said nothing, and I paused once more, drawing in a soft breath.

"Belle—do you want to leave? I can have the plane ready to go by this evening."

In a few measly hours, she could be gone from my life forever.

"No." She stuck her spoon in the slightly melted ice cream. It sloped to the side of the container. "I don't want to leave."

I finally exhaled that soft breath. *Thank god.*

Relieved, I went back to massaging her, touching her with the knowledge that she was still mine—for now. That I had a responsibility to do better, to *never* let what happened today happen again. I stilled, however, when she looked over her shoulder at me.

"I want to know you."

My eyebrows shot up. Know me? Belle knew me better than some of my closest friends at this point. She knew the *real* me. Not the mask I wore in the boardroom. Not the one I adopted for my father's associates. And not the one I begrudgingly carried for years, cleaning up my brother's messes as a legion of staff watched on.

"I want to know *Dean*," she continued, sounding surer of herself this time, "not just my Dominant. I...need to know *you*."

Why?

I bit my tongue again so I wouldn't blurt out the first thought that came to mind. Whatever she needed to feel secure with me, I would give it to her. After all, I had pried information out of her that one afternoon—lapping at her pussy as we bobbed along in the pool. I had a halfway decent picture of who Belle Bennet truly was; it seemed only fair to return the favor.

But then again, I *needed* to know. I was her Dominant. I ran the show. I was responsible for her—for her well-being, her safety. Her body *and* her mind.

Submissives look after their Doms, too, you pretentious prick.

I glared up at my forehead, all the while knowing the little nagging voice was right. In a true Dominant-submissive relationship, we were equally responsible for each other. Perhaps it was time to finally let her in.

"I can do that," I whispered when I realized she was still

staring back at me. My small smile had her cheeks pinking up, and she turned away, gone back to her ice cream.

"But I don't want to know today," Belle said after another spoonful, her voice thick, heavy. I resumed massaging her, working each side of her hips with both hands.

"All right." I bit back *sweetheart*, catching it just in the nick of time. Because she wasn't my sweetheart—not really, not yet.

Still, the title suited her. It suited us.

"What do you want today, then?" I asked instead. My hands drifted up to her lower back, avoiding the darkest bruises on her cheeks in favor of a back massage. When she kept quiet, spooning more ice cream in, my Dom side flickered back to life. "Belle, do you want to be left alone?"

She shook her head.

"Do you want me to stay with you?"

She nodded.

"Okay," I murmured, not bothering to hide my smile this time. The silence that followed lacked the anxiety of the last stretches, and I fell into an easy rhythm, working her back, her thighs, her poor bum with my hands. I eventually grazed the sharpest, brightest of the bruises, knowing the butter would do the skin some good, but only applied a very slight pressure. If Belle's whimpers suggested anything, it was that she wasn't ready to be touched there—which was fine by me.

What wasn't fine, however, was that she had nearly gone through three-quarters of that pint of strawberry ice cream in less than a half hour. Finally, even though I'd sworn I would indulge her as much as she wanted today, I took it away—and Belle let me. As much as she deserved to eat an entire pint, I worried she might get a stomachache. With some difficulty, I reached over and set the container on the night table, then popped the lid on, my hands soft and slick.

Sometime later, she asked, "Did you get those for me?"

Kneading the base of my palm up her back, I followed her line of sight—straight to the macarons.

"I did." My fingers splayed when they reached her neck, then fell back together to slowly slink bit by bit up the long, slender column. "They reminded me of you, all pink and sweet."

A luxury, macarons. A treat that required a skilled hand to craft. I hadn't really chosen them because I thought Belle was pink and sweet—more because she was my luxury, a submissive who required a skilled hand, one who made me a better Dom, today's behavior notwithstanding.

She stared across the room at the box, nibbling on her lower lip, and I felt my resolve weakening.

"Do you want them now?"

She nodded. Sighing, grinning, I carefully extracted myself and crawled across the bed, *just* able to reach the box on the dresser without climbing off. As I made my way back, I found Belle curled up on her side, hugging the blanket.

"I want you," she started, but then her voice caught, and there was this *pause* that had me stopping mid-crawl. Our eyes met, and once again I saw the depth in those blues— the stunning levels of intricacy, of intimacy, behind a single look.

Those blues took my damn breath away.

Belle blinked hurriedly, flushed, and sat up on her elbow. "To have a macaron, too. I want you to have one."

"All right." What I wouldn't give for just a flicker of what was going on inside her head. Instead, I undid the satin bow around the long, thin box and gently pushed it open. When offered, Belle took the first pink macaron in the row, carefully, handling the delicate meringue pastry like it might crumble.

A bit like how I'd expected to find Belle when I returned for aftercare. Broken. In pieces.

But—my girl was made of tougher stuff. She had surprised me. She had captivated me.

And, most of all, she had made *me* feel safe. Relieved. Needed.

She had made the choice to stay, despite everything, and as I plucked out my own soft pink macaron, I vowed that she wouldn't regret it.

I vowed that I would never be careless with her again.

"Cheers," I murmured, holding up my macaron. She nibbled her lower lip, perhaps weighing the shift in tone, then tapped her pastry to mine. I fought the urge to kiss her. "Here's to March."

Belle smiled shyly, but there was strength, too, in the way she held my stare and tapped our macarons once more. "To March."

MARCH

BELLE: PART 2

*"Thanks to Elysium, I was a child of Hades--and
Dean had dominion over me. From day one,
I had already belonged to him..."*

It's March on beautiful Ixora Isle. Flowers bloom just as
surely as matters of the heart, and Belle and Dean recover
from their breach of trust one step at a time.

In the coming days, the couple must face:

A dinner date that takes a turn for the dangerous.
An unwelcome family reunion.
A birthday surprise.
A black-tie affair.
A promise.
A death.
A gift.

HOUSE RULE #5

Communication is essential, both in and out of playtime.

1

BELLE

Monday, March 4ᵗʰ

People were going to call me crazy for staying.

After all, my client—not my boyfriend, not my husband—had bent me over a window ledge, ankles restrained, legs spread, and paddled me until I was a screeching, wailing mess. It was only now, four days later, that I could sit without wincing. Anyone else would have left. And had anyone else forced me to confront my fear of heights, albeit indirectly, I probably would have left too.

But it had been Dean—and for some reason, one I had yet to put my finger on, I couldn't walk away from Dean Donahue. When he had come to check on me that day, shortly after everything had happened, I hadn't wanted to shove him out and slam my bedroom door in his face again. I hadn't wanted him to leave me alone. I'd wanted to crawl into his lap so he could comfort me. Coddle me. I hadn't expected an apology—but the one he gave, over and over again, made the storm of emotion inside disappear. Instead, I found peace in his arms.

Which was insane.

I knew that.

Even after everything, I still trusted him.

Over dinner that night, we had discussed invoking my safeword. We talked about appropriate punishments, and the role both a Dominant and a submissive played in implementing them. While I wanted to curl into a ball and not leave my bedroom, Dean had me up and moving about —and talking. About safety. About trust. About personal limits and boundaries.

I'd gone to bed that night feeling safe—which was also insane. I knew that, too.

Over the last few days, we'd passed the time lazing around. In the pool. In the cinema room. In the kitchen, where Dean continued to ply me with all my favourites, like he was *still* apologizing.

And, honestly, *that* was why I stayed.

Because the man who'd paddled me wasn't the man I knew. He wasn't the Dom I knew.

I believed that wholeheartedly, despite the nagging voice at the back of my mind, always whispering as I tried to fall asleep. *He hurt you. He bruised you. He forgot your biggest fear and used it against you.*

All of that was true.

It was the way he responded afterward, however, that made me stay. Dean could have locked himself in his office. We could have gone days without speaking, the house tense, the island paradise devolving into a tropical nightmare. We could have then begrudgingly resumed Dean's rigid daily schedule—and I would have done it, because I was a professional, but I wouldn't have put so much of myself back into it. Not again. I would have been Belle, The Escort—period. No more wavering back and forth. No more straddling the line between professional and personal.

But Dean had talked. He had listened. He had comforted and soothed and apologized.

So, here I was again: a tightrope walker, trying to toe the line and remain professional, always a second away from careening down into Bellelandia, where I was just me—*me*, who wanted my Dom back, whether he paid me or not.

Even though I was ready to get back in the ring, Dean had insisted we take a full five days off after the incident so I could properly recover. I'd almost protested—I didn't *need* five days of recovery—but then I'd sat down and my butt had *screamed*, the bruises an ever-present reminder that I wouldn't have been able to play like we usually did. So, begrudgingly, I had accepted that the first week of March would be full of lazy days spent at the pool, on the beach, in the theater room, and on any padded surface we could find.

However, just because we weren't playing didn't mean the dynamic needed to stop entirely. I still called Dean sir— because he was *my* sir. And he cared about me, cared *for* me. He carried the guilt of that afternoon with him wherever we went, and I wanted to distract him. I'd gotten past it; I'd made it clear I never wanted to be paddled again, because it was *nothing* like the for-show paddlings Penny doled out at Elysium, but I wasn't afraid of future punishments.

I *liked* my punishments.

I wanted to get back to them.

I wanted to get back to *us*.

In an effort to distract him, after lunch today I'd grabbed Dean's hand, steering him away from the pool, and walked him up to the third floor. If anything was going to help us move on, it was confronting the room that had triggered the reaction. Standing at the top of the dark stairwell, I'd waited, holding Dean's hand, looking up at him—patiently, not expectantly, wide-eyed but supportive, strong, until he finally pushed down on the handle and threw the door open.

In an instant, we'd been bathed in sunlight—and there was no going back.

For the last hour, he had taken me through each of his paintings. Work he'd had shipped in from his house in London. The pieces he had finished since we'd arrived on Ixora Isle. Landscapes. Cityscapes. Some canvases taller than me, others the size of a postcard, haphazardly painted, like he'd been in a hurry, desperate to get his vision across. Rough outlines, completed masterpieces—and me. We ended the walkthrough on the still-unfinished portrait of me.

"I don't normally paint people," Dean admitted softly, that gorgeous sage-green gaze roving the canvas. My cheeks warmed when it slid to me. "But you have a face that demands to be painted, Belle." He tucked my hair behind my ear. "A body too."

My blush sharpened. "Thank you, sir."

"Actually," he said as he faced me, "it was your smile that made me want to paint you, but then I started and realized I wasn't talented enough to capture it."

"Don't be silly." Dean's work was breathtaking. What he could do with a brush—it was as masterful as what he could do with his tongue. I smiled at the thought, my heart skipping a beat when he cupped my face.

"There it is," he whispered, "that smile..."

Try as I might, I couldn't stop myself from leaning into the touch, into his palm's warmth. Something felt different between us since the incident. Not bad—just different. I might have been calling him sir, but he was less dominant than usual. Sure, he still cooked all our meals. He reminded me every two hours, on the dot, to redo my sunscreen. He had a timer going off twice a day so he could apply cocoa butter to my backside, to my thighs—a gesture that always evolved into a full-body massage that left me prickling with heat.

Beyond that, however, Dean seemed more—normal. He wasn't the CEO. He wasn't the restaurateur. He wasn't the man with eight billion to his name. And he wasn't completely my Dom. We talked more freely about everything. Laughed more openly during our movie nights.

Almost like—friends.

Which, again, was insane. I *knew* that.

But knowing hadn't stopped it from happening—and I certainly didn't want it to stop.

I wasn't sure what had changed, *who* had changed, but maybe it didn't matter.

Maybe, months from now, when I had some distance and time, I'd figure it all out.

Maybe I wouldn't want to.

Maybe it was time I stopped thinking, analyzing.

Because whatever had changed, whoever had changed, I liked it. Period.

My breath hitched when Dean stroked his thumb along my lower lip, his eyes stormy, but he made no move to close the gap between us. I didn't either. We stood like that, each of us too still, in front of his easel, his half-finished portrait of me and my pink bow, his hand cupping my face and his thumb ghosting over my mouth.

I fought the urge to catch it, to suck it in.

"Sir?"

"Yes, Belle?" he murmured, our voices barely rising above the distant hum of the air-conditioning. I tipped my head into his palm, smiling that smile he seemed to like so much.

"Will you paint me?"

Dean chuckled, the sound skittering across my body and pooling between my thighs. The storm had ebbed in his eyes, replaced with something warm and lush instead— something I found myself drawn toward as he said, "I *am* painting you."

"No..." I took his hand with both of mine, his five fingers somehow meshing seamlessly with my ten as I led him around the easel to the small desk behind. I'd missed it on my first visit to his sunlit gallery, so enraptured with his work that I hadn't had time to take in *everything*.

The desk had the same finish as the deep, rich tones of the dining table downstairs, though it was nearly impossible to appreciate it under all those tubes of paint. Cans of paint. Toolboxes—filled with airtight containers of paint. Every colour. Every shade. Unique blends and brand names. He kept his brushes there in metallic tins, their pristine bristles facing the cloudless blue sky above, the gallery's domed glass ceiling leaving nothing in shadow.

Freeing just one hand, I picked through the tubes I'd only glanced at when we first arrived, when Dean had finally welcomed me into his private world, then plucked the one I was looking for—the shade that had caught my eye. Coral Rosé—nontoxic body paint. He had a whole collection of colours. I held the tube up, label forward.

"I saw these earlier," I told him. Our hands remained loosely entwined, hanging between us. Dean let out another little chuckle, one of surprise this time, and took the tube in his free hand, turning it over to scan the back.

"I painted models for a friend's fashion show a few years back," he said with a wry grin. "Felix Renaldi. He did this ridiculously risqué spring line in Milan and he had me paint the cosmos on thighs and arms—"

"Oh, what, no model boob for you?" I dropped my chin demurely when his gaze snapped to mine, sharp—dominant. "Sir."

"No, Felix had *most* of the torso covered."

Felix Renaldi. My brow furrowed. "Why do I know that name? Renaldi?"

"Felix lives in New York most of the year," Dean told me as he set the coral rosé back on the desk. "He frequents Elysium—he was actually my sponsor when I first joined."

Elysium membership was by invite only, and established members risked losing their privileges if their sponsored choices acted inappropriately. We held open-house events once a month, but they were considered tame evenings in comparison to what usually went on.

"Felix and I have similar tastes," Dean mused, fiddling with the ends of my hair, his voice like velvet. "Though I'm afraid my tastes have gotten quite specific over the last few months..."

The prickle of heat simmering beneath my skin surged to a full-blown wildfire. How easy it would be—to get lost in that voice, in those eyes. Instead, I picked up the coral rosé again and held the tube out to him.

"Sir?"

"Yes, Belle?"

"Will you paint me?"

He said nothing, but his hand tightened around mine. Swallowing hard, I pressed the tube to his chest, waiting until his hand settled over it to retreat. I slipped away from him, taking a few steps back, then grasped the flowy fabric of my strapless yellow dress, the kind that stopped at my knees and cinched around my chest, and dragged it over my head. His gaze raked across my nakedness, stormy again.

"Paint me?" I asked softly.

The thought of sharing this with him made my chest tight. So far, Dean had told me all about his paintings. He had explained techniques, colour palettes, the differences between acrylics and oil paints. We had talked shop—but I needed to get inside, to know why he painted, why he hid it.

Why he'd freaked out and turned into a completely different person four days ago.

We'd talked a lot here, surrounded by pieces of his soul, but not about the things I *wanted* to talk about—things I wasn't sure I'd earned the right to ask about.

Maybe it would be easier for him if he just *showed* me this side of him.

I ran a hand through my hair, gathering it and letting it fall down my back.

"Sir," I said, my nipples puckering as he lifted that wild gaze to mine, "I want you to paint me."

Dean inhaled sharply, clutching the coral rosé in a tight fist. I bit the inside of my cheek, waiting, worrying that I had pushed for too much. It was one thing to *tell* me about his art, to go into detail about the technical side of things—it was another thing entirely to *show* me this part of himself. But I waited, ignoring the little voice at the back of my mind that told me to take it back, to pretend I hadn't asked—that I was just standing there, naked, for kicks.

Finally, an eternity later, his movements precise, measured, Dean set Coral Rosé on the desk, and anxiety prickled through me, until—

"All right."

My eyebrows lifted, along with my heart, my smile. "All right?"

"We'll need a few things first," he said, sounding more Dom-Dean than he had all day. "Run downstairs and fetch as many pillows as you need. I want you lying down. There are spare linens in the storage closet just off my bedroom—pick the ones that can do with a bit of paint on them."

I nodded, hopping to without being prompted. My backside gingerly protested the swift movements, the bouncing down tiled stairs, but I ignored that, too. Beaming, I went to the storage closet first, picking through the neatly folded sheets, all creased and smelling like lavender laundry detergent. Next, I grabbed every pillow off my bed, including the for-show ones that always ended up on the floor each night.

My heart thundered as I scaled the stairwell to the third floor, and I stopped in the doorway to catch my breath—to watch Dean as he picked through tubes of paint and tossed the chosen few into the middle of the room. To his credit, he didn't appear stiff or anxious about sharing this with me. Instead, he seemed—focused. Brow creased, mouth in a thin line. It'd be easy for someone to read the look as anxious, stiff, but I *knew* that look.

It was the same look he wore whenever he was working out the logistics of a scene—when he was trying to determine which knot was appropriate for my restraints.

It was the kind of look that made my heart oddly happy.

Swallowing thickly, I padded in, and, without a word, started arranging our workspace—maybe playspace—on the floor, directly beneath the crest of the domed glass ceiling.

"You'll be on your back," he remarked, striding over and dumping an armful of paint tubes beside me. "I want you to be comfortable, so use all the pillows you need."

His gaze flickered to my lower half briefly before he went back to the desk, picking through brushes now.

"Yes, sir," I murmured, unsure if he'd heard me. Then, clearing my throat, I asked a little louder if I should take the pillowcases off.

"We'll throw it all in the laundry," he said over his shoulder, distracted, seemingly weighing the pros and cons of two brushes—one thick, weighty, the other thin, perhaps for detail work. "Don't worry about anything. I'll do my best not to make a mess."

You always do. Nodding, I finished organizing the pillows, then settled atop the line. With a wince, I shifted them around, lifting my hips, legs, and shoulders as needed to make sure everything was supported. Head, shoulders, lower back, butt, knees. My faded bruises ached dully once I finally stopped moving; their bite had dissipated over time, but I still made sure to position the area so that I wouldn't be adding too much pressure to it.

Dean continued to rustle about behind me, stalking to and fro, adding brushes to the pile of paint. At one point he disappeared down the stairs, his footsteps like thunder, and I took a deep breath, staring at the gorgeous blue above. Not a cloud in sight. Another perfect Caribbean day.

He returned a few minutes later with two bowls of water and a paint-spattered palette—a *parallel* palette, he explained when he noticed me looking curiously, so that he could hold it in his free hand, the paints in the same light as his canvas. Me.

Gently, Dean cradled my chin. "I won't touch your face, but I'll go from your neck to the tops of your feet. Is that all right?"

Was that all right? *He* was the artist, not me. Dean could

do whatever he desired with that brush. So, I nodded, my smile seeming to soften his gaze. "Yes, sir."

He lingered there, his grip briefly tightening around my chin, before withdrawing and getting to work. Head lolled to the side, I watched him spurt paints onto his palette, but then thought better of it. The final outcome should be a surprise—although it *wasn't* exactly a surprise that the first four colours he added were various shades of pink.

Dean leaned across me, starting with the fingers of my right hand. I jumped, the first sweep cold—startling—and then giggled. "Oh, that's a bit cool."

Dean smiled as he worked, the same easy smile I had found myself missing these last few days.

"I'm afraid I can't heat my paints like I do with the oils."

"It's fine," I insisted, shifting about on top of the pillows, making myself comfortable beneath the swirl of his brush. "It was just a surprise."

He worked in silence after that, his hand flying, moving back and forth between the palette and my skin. Every so often, I heard the tinkle of the brush's metal against the side of the bowl, the *dab, dab, dab* of it in the water. I stared straight up, not wanting to ruin the surprise for myself. I closed my eyes when the sky felt too bright. I let him work.

Until I couldn't sit in the silence anymore. Until my curiosity finally got the better of me.

Dean had just crested my right shoulder, swirling the thinner of the two brushes he chose around the curve, when I said, "You told me you had a complicated relationship with your art."

He exhaled softly, his breath warming my skin. The paint chilled my entire right arm, leaving it cool and sticky. I didn't dare move a muscle, even though my elbow had started to itch and my fingers suddenly needed to crack every joint. Instead, I focused on the furrow of his brow, the downturn of his lips, waiting once more.

"My parents never approved of it," he admitted at long last. His eyes narrowed slightly, as if recalling the memories. "They didn't mind the *doodling* when I was young, but then I was gearing all my classes toward it, asking to be sent to visual arts boarding schools and the like. I wouldn't shut up about it—the Royal College of Art in London, Slade, Goldsmiths, Saint Martin's. America. Britain. I had citizenships for both, so my search was vast." He chuckled coolly, dabbing his brush on the palette before sweeping it up the column of my throat. "Suddenly it wasn't just doodles anymore—it was serious. I had a whole guest room transformed into a studio before either of them realized what was going on."

"Bold move." That had him smiling again, albeit briefly.

"My passion made me bold." Dean sighed. "I think, when they realized I wasn't going to grow out of it anytime soon, things changed. They stopped supporting my little hobby. My father sat me down one day, just as I was choosing my subjects for the final two years of secondary school, and stressed the importance of more grounded specialties, along with an insane number of extracurriculars. By the end of the conversation, he had me enrolled in business, political science, advanced French, and higher-level mathematics. The workload and all the clubs I was suddenly in left no room for painting or sketching."

"That sounds like my nightmare." Seriously. I hadn't been a top student by any means in either high school or university, but I was slightly above average and stuck mainly to the social sciences. Extracurriculars were out; I preferred to work part-time after school—to earn my own money.

Dean nodded at the nightmarish sentiment almost

obligingly, but his gaze seemed far away as he continued to work.

"I wanted to please him and my mum," he insisted, shrugging one shoulder. "I did well in all those subjects. High marks. Strong GPA. I was good at them. I could *do* them. I just never wanted to—I was happiest in the art room."

I nibbled my lower lip and looked skyward. My parents had always been so supportive of whatever I wanted to do— even when I showed up at their condo in Portland with the news that, hey, your baby girl wants to escort! They had been behind me one hundred percent my whole life, even when I made mistakes. In fact, they welcomed mistakes if it meant I learned a lesson. I couldn't imagine either of them quashing something I was as passionate about as Dean was with his art—but then again, my dad didn't run a multibillion-dollar empire.

"When I finished, I applied to university like they wanted," Dean told me. The shift in his tone caught my attention—the tightness of it, the curt way he spat a few of the words. "They were thrilled—academic scholarships to Stanford, Oxford, Cambridge, Yale, Harvard. And I just wanted to paint.

"I tried to combine the worlds. I... I even," he chuckled, "did a presentation for them with my proposal to open an art gallery in New York. Business and art. I thought it would make me happy. Mum thought it was cute. Dad told me to pick a school.

"I wanted to make them proud. They had such a rough go of it with my older brother. That had always been the way, and I never wanted to be a burden. I saw what they went through reining in Richard—I couldn't do that to them. So, I agreed to the path they chose: I did a joint degree program at Harvard for law and business. Walked out with a Juris Doctor and a Master's in Business Administration. Not a speck of the creative anywhere, unless you counted the odd graphic design course."

"That sucks, sir." It didn't suck that he was fortunate enough to have a world-class education in *two* different fields, both of which allotted him the opportunity to make some serious money. What sucked, in my opinion, was the fact that his family had stomped on his passions, his dreams, and forced him into something that he didn't want. Dean was a gifted artist, and while I knew nothing about professional artists, maybe he could have gone into graphic design, or book illustrations, or *something* that made him happy.

Something that he didn't feel the need to run away from for two months with an escort.

"Before I decided on Harvard, I toured the campuses I was most interested in with my mum and sister," he continued, softer now, distractedly, almost like he was telling the story to himself. "My father told my brother to clear out my studio. He figured I'd given up on art—and that it would be easier if someone else moved my work for me while I was gone."

Dean paused, leaning in with the smaller brush to do something that felt very intricate at the base of my throat. When he straightened, he set that one aside on the sheet and went back to broader strokes with the larger brush.

"My... My brother had a party on our property. Got drunk with a bunch of his friends while our father was at a conference. Trashed the house. Had a bonfire out back...and used my work for kindling."

"*What?*" I nearly bolted upright, and would have, my eyes wide, had it not been for Dean working on my chest.

Still, my heart thundered, waves of anger crashing through me. "He—he burned your work?"

"My parents insisted he just misunderstood what was expected of him," Dean muttered, each word laced with bitterness. "They blamed the alcohol, his friends... Never mind that he was probably drunk *and* high at the time. He was supposed to move it all into a storage unit at the back of the property. Richard had other ideas."

What an asshole. I bit the insides of my cheeks, my unpainted hand curling into a fist.

"Every last thing was gone. Sketchbooks. Oil paintings. Wood carvings. Canvas, paper—all of it. We came back from a midnight flight and walked into chaos. Mum lost it. I tried to corral all the drunk uni students away from my sister, who was only eight at the time. Then I saw the fire. I smelled..." He swallowed hard and shook his head. "Richard told me himself. Asked why the paints smelled so bad when they burned. When I walked in on you in my gallery, I had some absurd flashback, and all the emotions I didn't get to show that day... It's no excuse, but—"

"Dean, I'm so sorry." I touched his knee, seeking out his gaze, even if he refused to meet mine. "That's awful. What he did—that's...psychopathic."

I winced, knowing I probably shouldn't insult his brother—but there was that familiar smile again, like a ray of sunlight breaching the storm clouds.

"Ah, yes, well, that's my brother for you," he told me. Sitting cross-legged at my side, he lifted his knee, then leaned down to kiss my hand on top of it. When I returned that hand to the ground, resting it flat atop the sheet, the heat of his lips remained.

"Kind of makes me happy I'm an only child."

"Well, siblings aren't all bad," Dean remarked, smirking

a little. "My sister is lovely. Spoiled. A bit petulant sometimes. But we're worlds away from Richard. Always have been."

"Do they know you still paint?"

"No," he said without missing a beat. "If my doodling comes up in conversation nowadays, it's usually a joke. I've made a lot for myself in my career, so I suppose it's funny to my parents—the idea that I wanted to be an artist instead. I do most of my painting in private now. You're the first person to have seen any of my pieces in years, actually."

My eyes watered at the news, and I looked up, purposefully, blinking a few times to keep the tears at bay. The fact that he trusted me enough to show me this—it had me all warm and fuzzy inside. I mean, he could have told me to go screw myself. He could have called Candace when I broke the rules and rooted through his private, personal art collection. He could have sent me home. Dean didn't *need* to do what he had done today.

Despite what had happened, the paddling, the anger, I still felt safe with Dean. He had been making me feel safe for weeks now, which was so crucial in our relationship. Trust. Safety. Openness. The fact that I, in turn, had made him feel safe enough to share this side of himself with me...

Well, the idea had tears welling again, swarming my field of view.

"Thank you for showing me all this, sir," I murmured, twitching when his brush swirled around my left nipple. "And for telling me... I'm sure it isn't easy to talk about."

Another one-shouldered shrug as he switched to the smaller brush. "It's been years since the fire. I should be able to talk about it."

"Still—"

"Don't look so upset for me, Belle," Dean said, fixated on

his work. While he might have been smiling, his shoulders remained tense, lifted. "For all their nonsense, my family means well most of the time. I love them. I wouldn't work as hard as I do for them if I didn't, but..."

"What happened to you, no matter how many years ago, wasn't right. It wasn't fair. It was cruel, sir. You didn't deserve that. You didn't deserve to lose—" *Pieces of your soul?* I made a face; that was a bit dramatic, even if it was true. "You didn't deserve to lose all that hard work and dedication."

All because his brother had gotten drunk with his friends, at that. If I had a sibling, and he or she did that to me, destroyed something I had poured my heart and soul into, that I loved as much as Dean loved his work, my dad would ream them out from here to kingdom come. It wouldn't get swept under the rug. The guilty party would be punished—severely.

"Yes, well, it's done now. It happened. I'm afraid none of us can take it back."

I bit the insides of my cheeks again to let the conversation go—because it seemed like Dean wanted it to end. Lying as still as I could, I stared up, unfocused, ruminating on the injustices of his past. Sure, Dean had led a very privileged life, but that didn't take away from the fact that what they'd done to him, to his passion, was wrong. It wasn't okay. Not by a mile.

Not that my opinion mattered, either.

Dean worked in a heavy silence for some time after that, finishing my chest, my left arm. By then, I was dying to know what he was doing—how he'd decided to paint me, and if I didn't keep talking, I might sneak a peek.

"Sir?"

"Yes, Belle?"

The paintbrush whispered down my belly, over the new

little roll below my navel courtesy of all the delicious meals my Dom had prepared for me.

"Can I ask you another question?"

"Besides that one?" He glanced over his shoulder, grinning impishly when my eyes narrowed. "Of course, Belle. Go on."

"Why did you hire an escort for this trip?" I'd wondered it from the moment I met him—why a man like Dean needed to *hire* someone for company. Couples played Dominant and submissive in the real world, sometimes part-time, sometimes every second of every day. Dean required a somewhat intense partner, someone willing to play the part no matter the situation, and I personally had been enjoying myself—too much. Couldn't he find a willing partner elsewhere and save himself two hundred and fifty grand?

"I've actually never had much luck with submissives in my day-to-day life. I've had a few, but they never lasted long," he admitted after a moment's consideration. Cool, thick paint slicked up the V formation between my thighs, and I squirmed, biting back a giggle.

"Really?"

"Hmm. For the last, oh, six, seven years I worked all the time. It wouldn't be fair to expect the kind of submission that I need from someone when I couldn't be there properly —physically or emotionally." The larger brush swept across my skin, up and away from my sex, as if painting the area all one colour while he spoke. "I dated here and there, but only a few fit the disposition to be a submissive, and most of them found the dynamic a bit—degrading. Like I was trying to control them or micromanage their lives, like I wanted to dominate them for sexist reasons or what have you. It never really worked out."

The fact that someone unfamiliar with the lifestyle might consider it controlling didn't surprise me. After all, Dean was a fan of routine. He liked to schedule the entire day if he could, down to the very last detail, something he usually told me about over breakfast. Power, control, dominance, influence, possession—the whole combination was his kink, from the way he commanded me during playtime to the way he cooked my every meal.

To someone who didn't understand—it was a lot to take on. *Dean* in that state was a lot to take on.

I understood. Doms didn't boss their submissives around to control them; they did it because their submissive needed them to.

Because subs enjoyed routine and structure too. We gave up a piece of ourselves to our Dominant because we knew they wouldn't abuse it.

At least, that was my reason for doing it.

Dean made me feel safe in my submission.

The realization hit me hard, but I tried my damnedest not to let it show. I lay there, perfectly still, my mind wandering, drifting, roaming over the kind of relationship Dean needed—why he had turned to an escort instead.

Once again thinking that I would have done this for free.

I would have done it in my personal time—but only with him.

All the while knowing what a dangerous thought that could be.

A thought that could wreak destruction on my professional life, my personal life, my heart.

So, I blocked it all out and focused on the sweep of his brushstrokes, the even rhythm of his breathing, my eyes closing, until, eventually, unintentionally, I drifted off to sleep.

2

BELLE

"*B*elle—"

"I'm sorry!" I jolted, startling between dreaming and awake at the whisper of Dean's voice in my ear, only to have him hold me down by a lone finger on my shoulder. Still on the pile of pillows, I blinked quickly, fighting the hold of my midafternoon nap.

"Don't move," he murmured gently. "You're all painted up—though it's nearly dry."

"I didn't mean to fall asleep," I told him, an indirect apology. As I recalled, I'd nodded off just after he explained why he had hired an escort—and I had given no response to that. Ugh. "I'm sorry—"

"Don't apologize, Belle. There's nothing to apologize for."

I wanted to press a hand to my forehead. Sit up. Scratch at my head. However, my skin felt thick, blanketed in paint. Instinct told me to look down, to confirm the foreign substance coating my body, but I forced my gaze to stay on Dean's handsome face.

"How long was I out for?"

He removed his finger from my shoulder, the tip coated in shimmery purple. "About three hours."

"*Three* hours?"

No wonder I felt so stiff. Suddenly I needed to *move*. I wiggled my hips from side to side, my butt sore, even cushioned by the pillows, and then did the same with my neck.

"Let's get you up, shall we?"

"But I don't want to ruin your work," I protested as he slipped a hand under my shoulders, his palm's warmth settling between the blades. "Shouldn't I wait a bit?"

"No, you're fine, Belle. The paint dries quite quickly."

A part of me didn't believe him, like he was somehow devaluing his work—but that was ridiculous. Maybe I was still half asleep. Clearing my throat, I held out my arms, straight as boards, when Dean lifted me. His lips twitched, as if holding back a smile, and once he had me sitting relatively straight, he gripped the underside of my arm, then heaved me up the rest of the way with his other arm across my back.

The world spun as soon as I was back on my feet, and I immediately toppled into him. The fact that I refused to look down only made things worse.

"You're all right," Dean murmured, helping me clumsily shuffle off the pillows and onto the tile again. "Anything asleep?"

"My butt, a little," I told him as the pinpricks started to hum beneath my skin. "Otherwise I'm okay."

"Good."

"Can I see?" My eyes, wide and imploring, shot up to him, and he nodded with a soft sigh.

"Of course."

"The mirror in my bathroom is bigger, sir."

A little smile kicked up the edges of his mouth. "That it is."

We crossed the gallery together, Dean still steadying, his hands on my arm and lower back. His studio felt too bright, the sun beating down on it, and the narrow stairwell was too dark, my eyes struggling to adjust between them. Once we were back in the second-floor hallway, alertness crept over me, and I shed the remnants of my nap with a steadying breath and roll of my shoulders.

Dean had worked on me for almost four hours; I shot him a wary look as we crossed into my bedroom. He must have been exhausted.

But if he was, he showed no signs of it. In fact, he walked with a spring in his step, his head held high, his shoulders back, his grin lingering. It was nice to see him again —my Dom.

I closed my eyes when we neared my bathroom, relying on Dean to lead me the rest of the way. My feet shuffled across the cool tile, and the light faded behind my eyelids as I crossed between rooms. We stopped, my thighs bumping against the granite countertop. Dean left, his presence notable—and missed. The light switch clicked. Brightness. I waited. Waited until he was at my side, his hand on my back, his warmth, his presence, with me again.

"You asked me to paint you," he whispered, his breath tickling the shell of my ear, his voice coaxing goosebumps to skitter down my arms, even beneath the paint. "So, I did. I painted what I see when I look at you, Belle."

I licked my lips, swallowed heavily, and took a deep breath.

Then opened my eyes.

"*Oh.*"

His work was stunning.

I shouldn't have expected anything less. Eyes wide, I drank it all in, scanning myself in the mirror, wanting, *needing* every detail.

To be honest, I had expected a lot of pink. Pink, white, beige, gold—girly but decadent, innocence personified. Instead, Dean had painted me like a sunrise.

The edges of his work, along my arms, my hips, my legs, were a blend of purple, black, and blue, like the sky at dawn as the sun chased away the night. I stepped back as far as I could from the counter so I could see his work reflected in its entirety. The colour scheme integrated beautifully to soft oranges and yellows as it moved inward. Over my heart, my sex—pink and red. The rest of me was the cosmos. It was the rising sun, the dawn sky, the welcome light of morning. Dark, rich tones throughout.

"Wow." I was a masterpiece—my favourite of all his works. I didn't want to move, to bend. Looking down, I noticed small details that were lost in the overall canvas: twinkling, swirling stars—black amidst the darker colours, gold within the lighter.

Dean leaned against the counter, his arms crossed, his smile a little less easy now. "Do you like it?"

"I *love* it," I breathed, hurrying back to him, my hand falling to his chest as I stared at myself in the mirror. "Dean... It's stunning."

"You're stunning, Belle," he murmured. Gently, he placed my hand on the granite, fingers splayed, and stood beside me, a little behind me, and brushed my loose blonde waves over my shoulders. "I just worked with what I was given."

I almost told him he was being modest, but I faltered, instead, at the caress of one lone finger down my spine. In the mirror, I watched him watching me, his sandy brown lashes, lush and thick, flickering as his gaze swept along my body. My nipples pebbled tighter as his finger ghosted across my bare skin, suddenly so sensitive, every nerve heightened, with the other half of me covered in his artistic genius.

My heart skipped a beat when Dean caught me, sage-green snapping to my dark blues in the mirror. Holding my stare, he moved in closer, electricity dancing under my skin when our bodies touched—when he wrapped my hair around his fist and gently tugged. My lips parted, my breath hitched. I tipped my head back as he nuzzled my cheek, his soft exhale warming my skin.

I turned my head toward him, as far as I could, as far as his fist would allow. Heat pooled in my core, flashing when Dean trailed a long, torturous open-mouthed kiss along my jaw—until it finally found my lips. Moaning, I stood up on my toes to meet him, to kiss him like I'd wanted to all day. He dipped down, claiming me, tongue thrusting between my lips, flicking at mine, before retreating—encouraging me to chase.

The heat in my core surged outward, the first tingles of arousal prickling between my thighs as I reached up and trailed my painted fingers along his jaw. Dean nipped at my lower lip, hard, and I squealed, the tingles exploding to white-hot jolts lapping at my sex.

I needed more.

More of him.

More of his skin against mine.

More of us.

More.

My hand dropped from his stubble to his shorts, fingers plucking open the button with surprising ease. With the movement, the bend, Dean's work cracked, the paint splitting over my knuckles. As I wrenched open his shorts, I tried—maybe not as valiantly as I could have—not to catch his artwork on the belt loops of his cherry-red Bermudas, on the zipper stretched taut over his shaft.

Exhaling sharply, Dean dragged his lips along my jaw, the scrape of teeth making me shiver, and then stopped at my ear.

"Belle…"

In the mirror, I watched him close his eyes, leaning into me with an almost pained expression. I stilled, fingertips nudged beneath the tight, smooth waistband of his briefs. Did he want to stop? Hopefully not for my sake—because I didn't need him to do that.

The incident—it had happened. We'd talked about it. He'd given me nearly four days of aftercare. It was done.

"Please, sir," I whispered, my words a soft whine that had his cock swelling *more*. Swallowing hard, I took the risk, my heart racing, and bumped my nose against Dean's, coaxing him to look up. Before he could tell me to stop, I kissed him—and held nothing back. My desire spiked as his lips parted, as he leaned into it, as he let me say everything I desperately needed to say without uttering a single word.

I tasted it—his surrender. To the moment. To me. To us.

My Dom's surrender wasn't gentle. It wasn't a soft acquiescence, a gentle agreement to go with the tide. It was rough and harsh, a surging tidal wave, a relentless summer storm. Dean kissed me like he wanted to hurt me, his fist jerking at my hair—and I loved it. Every merciless second of it. The way he angled his body toward me, his need digging into my hip. The way he steered me, guided me—conquered me. I melted against him, dissolving into a weak-kneed puddle of a submissive, a whimpering, moaning creature in his arms.

One hand in my hair, Dean closed the other around my throat, towering over me, forcing a slight bend in my knees. I pulled away, still close enough that I could feel the heat of our mouths, of their proximity. Close enough that a strand of saliva stretched from his lip to mine. I fluttered my lashes, gazing up at him, and sucked in a strangled breath—just for him, just so I could see the storm rage in his sage-greens.

His mouth crashed back to mine, his growl humming between us. My neck craned beneath him. My hipbones protested, unimpressed with being shoved up against the granite. I ignored them both. Instead, I focused on my hand —slipping under his briefs and finding him at full mast. He groaned when I grasped him, when I slid my hand from head to base and back again, stroking him.

If I hadn't been so forcefully held in place, I would have dropped to my knees and begged him to let me take him in my mouth. I wanted to thank him. I wanted to worship him, to show him how grateful I was that he had painted me as he saw me. Not the girl next door. Not the wide-eyed innocence schtick I'd been slapped with at Elysium. He saw something more. Dean painted *me*. He painted depth and passion. I needed to thank him, to let him know how much that meant to me—and I wanted to do it on my knees. But Dean held firm, kissing me, consuming me.

Until one hand dropped. It skimmed down my back, over the swell of my ass. It skirted the still-healing bruises, though a brief sharpness flickered when he grazed one in passing. I shifted my legs open when that hand slipped between them, my skin prickling when he cupped me. Dean groaned, pinching my swollen clit between two fingers, my desire smeared across his palm.

"*Fuck*, Belle," he growled into my mouth, his hand constricting around my neck when he broke away. His gaze slid across my face, from my watery eyes to my fully parted lips—the head of his cock slick when I swept a thumb over it. His jaw muscles flickered for a moment, lips in a thin line, fingers pulsing over my clit, watching me as my body twitched in place. Suddenly, his grip around my throat loosened, and I gasped down a breath as he slipped two fingers into my sex with ease. He groaned, sinking all the way in. I widened my stance further, dropping lower, as pleasure bloomed across my body.

"You're so wet," he murmured, voice low, gravelly. His thumb slid up my neck, cresting my chin and plucking at my lower lip. "You're so wet for me."

"Yes, sir," I said—sighed, more like. Sighed *dreamily*. "Only for you."

"*Belle.*" Nipping at my earlobe, Dean snatched my hand out of his briefs and pressed up firmly behind me. I braced myself on the mirror with a whimper, torn between my need for him and the sudden protests of my bruises. Need won out, my legs drifting further apart as I leaned over the counter, my cheeks flushed as I watched him shove his shorts and briefs down muscular thighs, his cock nudging against my ass insistently when he straightened. Our eyes met in the mirror, and my fingers curled against the glass when he wet himself between my folds, sliding back and forth, his dark, lusty stare holding mine, before thrusting deep inside me.

Pleasure surged, intermingling with pain—the pain of the intrusion, of his hips pressed to my bruises. My head hung heavy between my arms, and I swallowed hard, clenching around him.

"Belle?" Dean smoothed one hand up my back as the other gathered my hair away from my face. I bent lower, my painted breasts skimming the counter, and arched my back.

The shift relieved the pressure, and we both moaned as Dean sank in just a little deeper, peppering my shoulders, the nape of my neck, with languid kisses.

"Sir—" I yelped when he retreated, then *pounded* back into me with enough force to make my teeth chatter. My bruises ached, but some of the sharpness had ebbed. Slowly, I lifted my head, searching him out in the mirror. One hand on my shoulder, the other on my hip—never mind the artwork—Dean raised an eyebrow.

"Belle—"

"I'm all right," I insisted. Because I was. My healing bruises were still sore, but I could manage. More than manage. I clenched around him, a flurry of little pleasurable tingles rippling through my core, and noted how his jaw muscles wavered in response. With a nod, I pushed back against him, pain somehow sharpening the pleasure. "I can take it, sir."

"Tell me your safeword."

"Apricots." I squeaked when he thrust again, harsh as ever, but kept my head up, holding his gaze in the mirror, determined not to flinch. Dean studied me for a moment, then wrapped my hair around his fist.

"Say it again." Another teeth-chattering pump of his hips. I winced when mine slammed into the counter, focusing instead on the blaze licking its way from my nipples to my clit.

"Apricots." My voice didn't falter; I swore I saw a flicker of *pride* in his eyes. Dean bucked his hips against me, over and over again, yanking my hair back as he abandoned the single, poignant thrusts for something more consistent—but no less rough.

"Use it," he growled, the bathroom filled with the sounds of slapping flesh, with my little squeaks and whimpers. I tried to shake my head, the movement restricted by his fist.

"I don't want to." I exhaled sharply as his pace quickened, every glorious muscle in his reflection taut as he pounded into me. "I don't *n-need* to... Oh, *god*, sir—"

Dean snapped an arm around my waist and buried his face against my neck. He pulled me back somewhat to spare my hips, all the while murmuring *my Belle* softly against my skin. With my head wrenched back, caught in his grasp, all I could do was stand there and take it. Take him spearing me again and again, harder than ever before. Take his teeth on my throat, his hand around my hair. Take Dean, my glorious Dom, using me for all I was worth—

I cried out, the last thought pushing me toward the edge. Heat soared through my body, paint chipped and cracked and smeared.

"Sir, can I—can I *please* come?" I whimpered.

"*Christ*, Belle," Dean hissed, dragging his mouth up my neck, his pace relentless. "You fucking better."

With one hand still propped up on the mirror, prints smeared everywhere, I reached back with the other and clutched at his form-fitting tee—navy blue patterned with little pineapples. It had made me laugh earlier this morning. Now, I fisted my hand in the material, not caring when the seams stretched in protest. Not caring that I'd twisted it, maybe even ripped it as Dean forced me closer to the abyss. One last brutal thrust sent me plunging into darkness, my eyes snapping shut as I came, fireworks spiraling behind the lids.

In the abyss, there was no pain—only pleasure. Waves upon waves of *pleasure* lapping across me, through me, pooling in my core and surging all over again when Dean refused to let up. The physicality of it overwhelmed me—the force of my climax, Dean's cock filling me, his breath on my neck, his fist around my hair, his dominance all had me squealing out my thanks.

"*Thankyouthankyouthankyousir*—oh *god*, thank you!"

"My Belle," he murmured in response, holding me tighter, taking me harder, until finally he stilled, his body tense, groaning as his shaft pulsed inside me.

And while I might have been delirious, trapped in a post-orgasm haze, maybe even subspace, I could have sworn I heard him hiss: *mine.*

Just the idea had me shuddering.

My head popped back up as soon as he released my hair, and I drooped forward, both hands on the mirror again, my arms trembling. Still buried inside me, Dean stroked my hair, smoothing it down my back. Something felt different this time around. The sex, the way we held each other—the way he gently kissed and nibbled my shoulder, resting on me just as much as I relied on his arm around my waist to keep me up.

We hadn't planned this. Nowhere in either of our dossiers would you find *quick, rough screwing over the bathroom sink, Belle covered in paint*. It had just happened. Naturally. Organically. Dean telling me, commanding me, to climax had made this one the best yet. I could still feel it; from my lightheaded giddiness to my tingling toes, it clung on fiercely, refusing to let up. Each slight movement we made had heat crackling inside me, and if exhaustion hadn't struck like a freight train, I could have stayed like that forever.

Or, until he was ready to go again.

This—*scene*—it did feel different. Better.

Right.

As if this was what we would do without a detailed outline at the back of our minds.

I gulped at the thought. Farewell forever, professional distance.

When Dean stirred behind me, straightening, I turned over my shoulder to smile at him, fingers grazing his stubble. He grinned back, softly, sleepily, like we had just woken up from the best nap ever, and before I could stop myself, I caught his lips in a gentle kiss. Neither of our eyes fluttered completely closed, preferring instead to watch each other as our mouths met for just a beat too long.

Somehow, that extra beat didn't scare me like it would have a few days ago.

And that should have *terrified* me.

I parted my lips instead at his prompting, sighing when his tongue grazed mine before retreating.

"Thank you, sir," I whispered, our foreheads resting together. Dean's arm had moved from my waist, stretching across my chest, between my breasts, so he could hold my shoulder. Safe, secure, I no longer propped myself up on the mirror, relying on him instead.

"For what, Belle?" He grinned. "For letting you come?"

My cheeks darkened, and I wasn't sure who initiated the next kiss—him or me.

"Well, yes, that," I mumbled against his lips, easing away just enough so I could get the rest of the words out—so I didn't get lost in him. "But, thank you for *seeing* me."

Dean set his forehead against mine, brow furrowing— likely at the wobble in my voice. I swallowed down the emotion and stole another quick peck instead, knowing I didn't need to say more than that. He caught my chin just as I nipped at his lower lip and held me there.

"I see you, Belle."

My heart beat just a touch faster. "I see you too, sir."

Because if I had to paint him, I knew two things for certain. One: I would do a terrible job, because art wasn't exactly my forte. And two: I would paint the colours of his soul, the colours that I saw shimmering beyond the surface. Not all the white of his house, the grey of his jet, the accents of black and gold. Honestly, I would have used most of the same colours he used on me, oddly enough, excluding the pink.

Well, maybe just a dab of pink. Right over his heart. For me.

For the way he saw me.

"Shall we get you cleaned up?"

I pressed my lips together. I didn't want to move—to break apart and shatter the moment. It was slipping away from me faster than I would have liked.

But I let it go, because we couldn't spend all day here, like this.

Right?

So, I nodded. My heart still beat faster when he kissed my cheek, but there was a sudden emptiness, loneliness, when he eased out of me and stepped away. In his absence, I studied his creation in the mirror, burning the stunning details into my brain. Behind me, Dean saw to the rainfall shower, the sudden burst of water pummeling the tile floor, steaming the glass walls.

I only turned away from the mirror, from his smeared and cracked masterpiece, when he called my name. Arms wrapped around myself, I padded across the spacious ensuite bathroom, each step heavy as physical, emotional exhaustion weighed me down.

But some of it lifted when I settled into his arms. With my back to his chest, Dean held me, and I reclined against his shoulder as the shower rinsed the first coat of paint from my skin. Purple, blue, green, black, red, orange, yellow—pink. They all swirled around the drain, around our feet.

I leaned into Dean as he pressed his lips to my temple, water rushing down my body, and closed my eyes.

Exhausted but satisfied.

Sore—but safe.

HOUSE RULE #11

Belle will be a good girl, or expect punishment for bratty
behaviour.

3

BELLE

Friday, March 8th

Sometimes I forgot how boring taskwork could be
—especially when Dean wasn't watching.

Actually, *most* of the morning taskwork he assigned was
boring, but I still enjoyed it for several reasons.

One: there was a sense of pride in accomplishing a task
set out by my Dom.

Two: I liked proving to myself that whatever Dean asked
of me, I could do, because I was growing into a good
submissive.

And three: the look in Dean's eyes as he watched me
work—it made my heart race and my panties damp.
Metaphorically. Because I usually did taskwork naked.

Today, however, I wasn't naked—and Dean wasn't
watching me. Not that I could see him, but Dean had the
type of gaze, the type of *focus*, that I could feel. It made the
hairs on the back of my neck stand up, made me work
harder. I hadn't felt it once today, and I wanted to stomp
my foot and pout, honestly. Like a child. Like a bratty,

pouty, petulant *child* who wasn't getting the attention she craved.

At some point I'd wondered if that was part of the game, but then I would hear him sigh at his desk, the huff followed by heavy keystrokes or a rapidly tapping pen.

I had been at this for a half hour. Laced into a frilly pink corset, white stockings up to my mid-thighs, connected to a baby-pink garter that belted around my cinched waist. Dean had called me a treat when I arrived in the office. He had even fastened the corset a *hint* tighter to make me squirm.

Then he had put me in the corner, slightly bent at the waist, back arched so my bare butt was on full display, hands behind my back—not tied, mind you—and balanced a quarter on my nose.

"Do *not* drop the quarter," he'd whispered gruffly in my ear.

"Yes, sir," I'd murmured back, instantly aroused, instantly excited for this new task.

That had been ages ago. Since then, he hadn't checked on me. His bare feet had stridden confidently across the tile, straight to his desk. I'd heard the plop of his body into that high-backed leather chair, the soft whirr of the desktop. Then—nothing. No, *how are you doing, Belle?* No, *did you drop the coin yet, Belle?* No, *is my submissive being a good girl?* Not even an *are you wet yet, Belle?*

Dean *always* chatted with me during taskwork. Sure, he had actual work to do on the computer as well, but I never felt like I'd been forgotten.

And after reconnecting in my bathroom, covered in paint, and resuming our previous dynamic with gusto—I didn't want to be forgotten.

It turned me into a brat.

And I *wasn't* a brat. I was a good girl.

Across the room, Dean sighed again, and I slowly shifted my weight between each leg. The movement alleviated some of the stiffness, but I'd also hoped maybe he would notice—maybe my bare ass would ensnare him.

Nothing. I pursed my lips, going cross-eyed for a moment to look down at the shiny silver quarter balancing on my nose. There hadn't been a single close call so far; I could probably stand there for the next hour and not drop it.

But that would mean another hour of being forgotten, maybe even ignored.

Beyond that, *something* had been bothering Dean this week. Now that we had moved on from the incident, I'd hoped we could fully resume our relationship, and for the most part, we had. Dean was present during playtime. He was my Dom, the same Dom who cooked all my meals and reminded me to reapply sunscreen, but in our free time, something was distracting him. He was on his laptop more often, checking emails more frequently. I had seen him send calls to voicemail, his eyes stormy—and not the fun kind of stormy I enjoyed. The bitter, sharp storm of anger, frustration.

While he had invited me into his world, shown me a glimpse of himself no one was fortunate enough to see anymore, I still wasn't sure if I had the right to ask him what was wrong. Anything happening in an email was real-world business—and I, Belle Bennet, his escort, was for fantasy. Could I cross that line so soon after the incident?

Dean tried to hide his moods. If he caught me watching him mid-storm, up went a somewhat forced smile, followed by a game or a treat from the kitchen—a distraction, as if whatever was bothering him didn't exist.

I didn't mind being his distraction for now, but I hated

seeing him so upset, so visibly bothered by whatever was in those emails. It hurt me. His distress hurt my heart.

So, if I couldn't outright ask—then I would distract. Two could play at this game, sir.

Still balancing that damn quarter on my nose, my face shoved in the corner of the office, I fought back a smile as an idea sparked to mind. It'd be fun. Probably a bit painful. Hopefully he would see the cheek behind it—and not take it too seriously.

So, I dropped the quarter.

On purpose.

The coin clattered and spun on the tile for a moment, round and round, until it flopped flat on its side. Behind me, Dean's forceful assault on his keyboard stopped. Silence. With a deep breath, I peeked over my shoulder and found him leaning around his dual monitor setup, frowning. My adrenaline spiked.

"Belle." He nodded down at the quarter. "Pick that up."

Taking my time, I doubled over, bending at the waist to show off—everything. Once I had the quarter, I straightened just as slowly and faced him with what I hoped was a seductive little smirk. Whether it was or it wasn't, Dean's face gave nothing away.

"Now, put that back," his eyes narrowed somewhat, "and get in the corner."

I bit my lip for a moment, knowing my smile read more naughty than seductive, and held up the quarter. "Heads I do it. Tails I don't."

Dean rolled his chair to the side of his desk. "*What* did you just say?"

You heard me, sir. I didn't dare say *those* words, of course —I wasn't that brave. Instead, I balanced the coin on my finger, then flicked it up with my thumb. It shot higher than

I intended courtesy of my nerves, but I still managed to catch it and slam it down on the top of my other hand.

Heads.

"Oh, sorry, sir..." I pursed my lips at him and shrugged. "Tails."

My Dom stood—slowly, just as I'd done when I bent over, only he did it to terrorize, not arouse. Little did he know, the movement provoked both in me: fear and desire. He looked so powerful behind that desk, looming over it, fingertips *just* pressed to the surface.

"If you don't get back in that corner," Dean growled, pointing at me, "*your* tail is going to be in serious trouble."

I shivered. Maybe this wasn't such a good idea. If Dean had been in a bad mood already, maybe misbehaving *wasn't* the way to distract him.

But, heck, I was committed. No going back now.

"Belle." His voice cracked across the room, sharp as a whip and twice as deadly. "Get. In. That. Corner. *Now*."

I cocked my head to the side, holding up the quarter again. "But I flipped for it—"

"There is no *bargaining* in taskwork!"

Heat flashed in my belly as he stormed around the desk, and I scampered off with a giggle, racing for the door as fast as my stockinged feet could carry me. I skipped at first, not taking it seriously as I headed down the bright, airy corridor, past my room, toward the outdoor lounge overlooking the pool. From there, a spiral staircase would take me downstairs—one I'd never dared use before, but that also hadn't seemed so terrifying since the day I'd hung out the window.

Only I didn't make it that far.

Dean's footsteps thundered after me, bare feet pounding the tile now, and when I glanced over my shoulder, flicking my curls as I did, I found him charging me like a snorting bull. I yelped and *ran* this time, fear slicing through the heat pooling in my core. Seconds later, his arm snapped around my waist like some steel vaudeville hook. I lurched forward, going nowhere, trapped, my rigid corset keeping me from folding over, and then squealed when he hoisted me up and carried me into his bedroom.

A bedroom that wasn't much different from mine. The colour scheme matched the rest of the house. A king-sized bed instead of a queen. Two dressers instead of one, a writing desk under a window that overlooked jungle, not a garden tailored to his submissive. A closet full of clothes and shoes, not intricate lingerie and flimsy swimsuit cover-ups.

Dean tossed me on the bed, and I bounced off my hands and knees, rolling onto my back, suddenly plagued with a horribly-timed case of the giggles. With both hands clapped over my mouth, I tried to smother the sound—to hide the smile, especially when Dean looked like he did.

So serious.

So...

So Dom-Dean.

So *punishment* Dom-Dean.

Jaw clenched. Mouth set in a thin line. Brow slightly furrowed and gaze hard. Why did that look make me wet? It shouldn't. It should make me anxious. It should send me squirming to the other side of the bed, full of apologies and tears.

Instead—I giggled.

Dean climbed onto the bed, straddling me, blanketing me with his hard body as he snatched my wrists and yanked them away from my face, then slammed his lips to mine. His kiss stoked the wildfire scorching inside me, the kind of kiss that both stole my breath away and breathed *life* back into me. Firm, rough, ravishing, yet torturously brief—over too soon. I whimpered, pushing up onto my elbows to trail after him.

He said nothing as he climbed off and rolled me over, pinning me roughly to the bed.

"Sir—" I yelped when he spanked me, hard, one smack for each cheek. He *had* promised my tail would be in serious trouble, and as he clambered back on top, straddling my lower back, I realized that I probably should have taken that threat more seriously. I squirmed, hopelessly trapped beneath him, his thighs clenched firmly on either side. My corset's tightness paired with his weight had me gasping for air, and Dean lifted himself up to alleviate some of the pressure. Hands fisted in the duvet, I sucked in a full breath, the frilly pink corset, deceptively innocent, refusing to let my ribcage expand as much as I needed it to. Dean sat up further, allowing me more give, before hellfire rained down on my poor bare ass.

The blows were relentless, one right after the other, over and over again without rest as I squirmed and squealed beneath him. My skin was on fire some ten seconds in, and Dean hadn't even told me to count—he was spanking too fast, too hard, for me to keep track.

This—may have been an incredibly stupid idea.

My legs folded, though I knew it was pointless to try and shield myself. He soon had them flat on the bed again, one hand capturing both ankles as the other continued its unholy assault. Tears blurred my vision, falling thickly when I blinked, and I fisted the bedcover harder, wailing.

"I'm sorry! I'm sorry! Sir—I didn't mean to—*ahhouch!*"

Dean gave me nothing but his firm palm, landing each smack so that it *hurt*. My apologies morphed into high-pitched squeals and incoherent cries, the punishment dragging on for an eternity.

He ended it with a sharp full-handed slap to each cheek, and by then I was just tears and strangled breaths, sobbing into his bed. Rather than climb off me right away, Dean waited, sitting up completely so that his weight was gone, but his thighs remained clamped around my hips. I whimpered when he smoothed the backs of his knuckles over my traumatized skin, and batted watery lashes when he blew on each cheek, at a distance, the air cool and very much welcome.

Soon, my pulse stopped thundering between my ears. My mind cleared. My ass burned, but it was nothing compared to the sharp, throbbing ache of the paddle. I could handle a spanking. Dean had never given me one this intense before, but as I propped myself up on my elbows, I decided I could take it—that this was survivable.

That even after it, I still wanted him. That if he palmed me, he would find me wet.

As he climbed off and kneeled beside me, I ignored the cruel little voice at the back of my mind asking what on earth was *wrong* with me. I focused on the thought of Dean taking me, brutally, *right* this second, pounding me into the mattress while I sobbed and thanked him for letting me come—twice, probably. The heat surged again, and after he gently rolled me onto my back, my hands went straight for his shorts, for the bulge that had been pressed into my lower back.

"*Belle.*" Dean caught me just as I popped open the button, and, with an exasperated sigh, swiftly trapped my wrists to either side of my head. "What has gotten into you today? You aren't usually a bad girl."

While there was a hard edge to his voice, it wasn't as

steely as I deserved. My mouth fell open—but I had nothing to say. I *wasn't* normally a bad girl. I liked being a good girl for him. I lived for his praise during playtime. Amidst all that wildfire and heat, an ice-cold kernel of guilt made itself at home. I swallowed hard, unable to meet his eye.

"I…"

"Tell me," he demanded. "Right now."

His tone brokered no room for argument, and I couldn't have mustered one if I tried. I couldn't have *lied* if I tried. There was no fight left in me—because I wasn't bad.

"You…" My lower lip quivered, but I took a deep breath and made myself meet his eyes. I might have been naughty, but I could still be brave and own up to this crazy scheme. "You seemed like you were in a bad mood again."

The words flew out of me, soft and quick, and when Dean said nothing, I wondered if he'd even heard them. Then, frowning, he released my wrists and planted his hands on the bed, still caging me in on either side of my head.

"*What?*"

"You've just seemed a bit upset this week, and I could hear you getting, uhm—" I clenched my eyes shut before he tapped my nose. Stupid *uhm*. I'd almost stopped saying it lately. With a sigh, I peered up at him, at his handsome face, the tension easing out of it as I spoke. "I could hear you getting upset again. You—you tap your pen, and you type really hard. Sometimes you jiggle your leg. We were having a really nice morning before you got on your computer, and I just thought I would…"

"And you just thought you would, what, distract me?" Dean's eyes narrowed slightly, but the beginnings of a smile had started to creep across his lips. He grabbed my chin when I tried to look away. "Belle, were you being a bad girl, on purpose, for my benefit?"

I nodded. Dean exhaled sharply, the last of his serious, stern Dom expression disappearing with it.

"Oh, Belle." His voice like honey, Dean kissed my cheek. "That's very sweet of you."

As he settled down beside me on his back, I realized my hands were still up by my head, where he'd pinned them. Blushing, I threaded them together on my stomach, then brought my knees up to relieve the pressure on my lower back—and to lift my poor behind off the duvet. The whole area burned, but it was easy to ignore when my Dom suddenly offered an apology. To me. For *his* behavior.

"I'm sorry I've been so distracted," Dean told me, his hands mirroring mine atop his chest. "If I've been short with you, please know it's not because of something you've done. I try not to let it affect us, but—"

"You don't." I rolled onto my side to face him, pillowing my head on my arm. "Really. You've never been short with me, either. I just notice it sometimes, when you think I'm not looking."

I wished we were having this conversation in the pool. My ass seriously needed an ice pack—stat. Even though it was getting harder to ignore, I did, because this conversation mattered more than my discomfort.

"You don't have to tell me anything," I insisted, finding the courage to offer a willing ear by focusing on his handsome face, his tentative smile, on the way my heart fluttered at the sight of both, "but you can, if you want to—if you *need* to talk to somebody, I mean. I can listen. I'm a good listener."

"I know you are, Belle." Dean stretched toward me, and I leaned forward so he could kiss my forehead, both of us grinning like idiots when we pulled away. My stomach looped when he set his hand on top of mine, thumb stroking me. "Thank you."

I nodded, not trusting myself to say something cool and collected in return—expecting, instead, something babbly and embarrassing. We stayed like that for a long moment, studying one another, the hum of the air conditioner filling the room, until Dean sat up and checked on his handiwork.

"Go on, fetch the cocoa butter," he said with a sigh. "You're all red and pretty down there."

"Yes, sir." Grinning, I scooted down the bed and scampered off, feeling as light and airy as the sun-soaked corridor outside his bedroom, sunshine streaking in through the four skylights along the way. Light and airy and *helpful*, I skipped along, like my plan had worked—like I had finally found a way to make my Dom feel good, to make him smile like he did when he lost himself in his art.

You let him spank you, the mean-girl voice at the back of my head muttered, *calm down. No Nobel Prizes for escorts, remember?*

And, just like that, all the light and airiness—gone.

Damn it. Swallowing thickly, I carried on toward the stairs, off to get the cocoa butter from the fridge, with just a little less pep in my step.

4

DEAN

Sunday, March 10th

"*D*ean!"

Belle's panic cut through the house, through my heart, like a knife. I shot up, pulse racing, and threw myself around my desk, stubbing my pinky toe on the corner.

"*Fucking* hell shitpissfuckballs *ow*," I hissed, hopping a few times, then power-limping out of the office. She called my name again, her voice high-pitched and strained, and I picked up the pace. It was Sunday—she should have been lounging by the pool. Last I recalled, she *had* been lounging by the pool, wearing that ridiculous little string bikini that I'd bought her last month.

"I don't want tan lines," she'd said innocently, sauntering by the kitchen on her way out, towel thrown over her shoulder. I'd gawked like a caveman, like an ape, dropping the breakfast pan I'd been washing, sudsy water splashing everywhere. Honestly, I ought to be used to her naked figure by now; she pranced around the house half naked most of the time anyway, but god *damn* she just looked so *good* wearing next to nothing.

I'd wanted to throw her onto the dining table, pin her down, and rip those strings to nothing.

Then, of course, have my way with her. Thoroughly. Harshly. Things were nearly back to normal between us, which meant I could fuck her how we both wanted again. Now, if only I could say the same for my professional endeavors.

Unfortunately—or, perhaps, for the bikini's sake, fortunately—work had called me away for most of the morning. Not only was I managing my own investments, luxury properties, restaurants, and the legion of staffers who reported directly to me, but I had conceded a few days ago and was currently neck-deep in Richard's fuck-ups. Just a few spreadsheets, a few forms, a few expense reports. I had told my father I would help a *little*. Nothing crazy. Only on Sundays, so I wasn't taking time away from Belle. I had never been very good at saying no to either of my parents, and my father was fucking relentless when it came to getting what he wanted. I'd finally broken down and agreed to do a *bit* of damage control.

What he had sent me—it was at least a month's worth of work.

I still wasn't sure if I would do it all, but this morning I had sat myself down and waded in. After all, I cared very deeply about the people my brother's laziness affected. Not just my father, but the general managers of the resorts, the staff working under them—Richard held their livelihoods in his addict hands, and from what I'd seen, he either hadn't realized what an enormous responsibility that was, or he just didn't care.

Knowing my brother, I erred toward the latter.

But now something had happened to Belle, and I would never forgive myself if it had happened because I was once again bowing to my father's wishes and fixing my older brother's mistakes.

Never. I'd never forgive them, either.

As I raced down the stairs, my pinky toe screaming, I half expected to see Belle leaning heavily on the kitchen counter, covered in blood. Somehow. Shark attack in the pool—that was what her tone had suggested as she wailed for me.

Instead, I found her standing there, her eyes wide and panicked, her hands cupped—with a little bullfinch inside.

My gut response was to ask her why the *fuck* there was a bird *inside* my house, some five feet from my pristine kitchen —but her eyes brimmed with tears and her lower lip started to quiver as soon as I stepped off the last stair, so I opted for a softer approach instead.

"Belle," I said gently, holding up a hand as one does to settle a startled filly, "what's happened?"

"She was flying funny around the pool and then she hit the window and fell down and she got back up but then she wasn't walking right and then she just stopped and I don't think she's breathing and we have to do something for her!"

"Oh, Belle," I murmured. Normally the bullfinches stuck to their flock. Given the amount of glass encasing the first floor, this wasn't the first bird to have flown into it by accident, but this little one was likely the first Belle had seen who hadn't survived the collision. I moved closer, grasping a frantic Belle by the back of her neck. Yeah—the bird was definitely dead. But my submissive was looking at me with those big blue eyes, like I would just know how to make things right. With a sigh, I offered her what I hoped was a reassuring smile. "All right, take a breath, Belle. Give me a second..."

I jogged into the kitchen and dug out a dish towel from one of the drawers next to the sink, then hurried back and held it out.

"Put her in here."

Belle stroked the tiny brown bird's wings, the feathers streaked with a faint red, then did as she was told. I made sure to cradle the bird just as she had, only wrapped in a towel this time.

"Now, go wash your hands."

"But—"

I mustered a stern expression. "Right now, Belle."

With a huff, she darted around me into the kitchen and went for the lavender dish soap. Honestly—picking up a bird with her bare hands. What was she—no. I knew what she'd been thinking. She had watched a helpless bullfinch hurt herself smacking into a window, and Belle's instinct had been to help.

"Now, run upstairs and fetch one of the shoeboxes from my closet," I told her, pleased to find her less frantic now. "We'll give her something safe to sit in, and...then we'll see."

Belle was off like a shot, zooming up the stairs, taking them two at a time before disappearing around the corner. In her absence, I examined the bullfinch—a Lesser Antilles bullfinch, if I remembered my avian taxonomy correctly. She was small, her feathers a blend of brown, orange, and red to help her hide in the fruit trees. Upon closer inspection, I found her beak cracked. If it hadn't happened when she hit the window, then she might not have been eating.

And she certainly wasn't breathing anymore.

"Tough day, old girl," I whispered, stroking her velvety

feathers with the towel. "We've got you now. You're safe here."

I looked up sharply at the sound of Belle racing down the stairs—carelessly, almost. Frowning, I bit back the urge to tell her to slow down.

"Is she breathing?" she asked, one of my coral Prada boxes in hand, the logo emblazoned across the lid in gold. "She hit the window so hard. Is she okay?"

"I don't know, sweetheart, but I don't think so."

Heat flashed across my cheeks—*sweetheart*. It had just slipped out, natural as anything. I pressed my lips together as Belle breezed by, taking the shoebox to the dining table, seeming not to have noticed.

Every time I had said her name in the last few weeks, I'd really wanted to say *sweetheart*. She called me sir. Belle *was* my sweetheart—my inquisitive, kind, beautiful submissive who deserved such a sweet pet name. It suited her.

I'd been cautious, however, remembering that day in the pool when she'd expressed how much she liked the clear-cut division between escort and client. I hadn't wanted to cross that line with her, put her in an uncomfortable situation, especially after the paddling incident. I had been so cautious. So vigilant.

And now—it had just happened.

I'd called her sweetheart, and our world hadn't fallen apart.

Fuck it. I was going to do it again. Because, honestly, some of our lines had already blurred, and neither of us had done a damn thing about it.

And Belle was my sweetheart. *Mine*. Using her pet name, staking my claim, took us one step closer to me giving her—

It.

Her gift.

The gift hiding under my bed, still wrapped in the box. The gift that could make or break us. The gift that was entirely inappropriate for a client to give his escort—the gift that I'd bought two weeks in when I just *knew* Belle was meant to be mine.

I had every intention of giving it to her before the month was through, when she was ready. If she was ready, and *if* she accepted it—well, we'd cross that bridge when we came to it. I didn't want to get my hopes up. Not yet.

For now, we'd start with the name. Sweetheart. *My* sweetheart.

Once she had the shoebox lid off, I set the dish towel inside, gently lowering the bullfinch in, careful not to jostle her. Belle hovered beside me, twisting her hands as she peered anxiously at her rescue.

"She's not breathing."

"No, sweetheart, I don't think she is."

As right as it felt to call her what I wanted, my heart ached when Belle burst into tears, her hands over her mouth, her shoulders shuddering. I wrapped an arm around them, pulling her close, and kissed her forehead.

"I know it's just a b-bird, but she hit the window so hard, then got up and walked around a bit before she fell over again," Belle said breathlessly from behind her hands, wet streaks cutting down her cheeks, "and I just thought...I just thought maybe..."

I knew exactly what she'd thought—that maybe she could do something to save her.

"I know." I pulled her closer and she nestled under my chin, gripping the front of my T-shirt with both hands. As she continued to cry, I held her tight, not wanting to ever let go—not wanting anything else in the world to make her cry like this. If I could, I'd shield her from everything. I couldn't, of course, but I would damn well try. My eyes closed briefly. Belle in my arms felt right. If I was being honest with myself, it had felt right from the first day we met, surrounded by lawyers, her delicate hand sliding into mine, those royal blues shyly gazing up at me as she smiled.

That had been it. I'd been done for—hook, line, sinker.

And I'd been falling for her just a little bit harder, day by day, since then.

Fuck *me*. Belle sobbing in my arms about a bird, feeling so deeply for an otherwise insignificant little creature, coming to me for comfort, for guidance, for support...

No denying it anymore—I loved her.

"Why don't we bury her somewhere on the eastern trail?" I said, finding my words at last. They might have been thick with feeling, my throat tight, but I got them out. I remembered who I was to her. I was her Dom—and a Dom took charge in a situation like this.

Slowly, blinking those watery lashes, Belle looked up at me, her cheeks pink, and I smiled.

"The finches make their nests along that trail. We'll put her out there—so she can watch the sunrise with them."

Belle considered it for a moment, nibbling on her lower lip, and then nodded. "Okay."

"Okay."

I held back a chuckle when she wiped her tears away on my shirt—as if doing so without even realizing that she'd done it. Begrudgingly, I let her go, then went for the shoebox lid; the dish towel was organic cotton—it could be buried too.

"Wait." Belle held her hand out over the box, and when I stopped, she tucked the corners of the beige towel in too. "Maybe we could give her a nicer coffin?"

"Is Prada not to her taste?"

She looked up at me sharply, the edges of her mouth twitching. "No, it's just not very unique."

"Right." I set the lid down on the table again, nodding. "And she was a very unique little bullfinch. Shall I go get my paints?"

I'd been joking—but then Belle sank into the dining chair in front of the box, that hint of a smile gone, and muttered, "Yes, please."

Well then. I guess we were painting a bird coffin today.

Before I left, I planted another kiss on the top of Belle's head, pulling her hair behind her shoulders and needlessly wiping her cheeks dry one last time. She leaned into my touch, but her focus was on the bird. So, without a word, I darted upstairs, ignoring the call of my office completely. Fuck work. Belle needed me—and together we were going to make the best damn bird coffin the world had ever seen.

Or, at the very least, make one that looked less like a shoebox from the back of my closet.

When I returned a few minutes later, arms full of paint and brushes, Belle had wrapped the bullfinch and removed her from the shoebox. The little bundle sat in the middle of the table, out of the way, and I made a note to have this afternoon's cleaning crew do two rounds of detail work on the first floor.

Together, we decided to paint the shoebox to look like the bullfinch, which meant the basecoat was a blend of tawny and russet. Belle worked on that while I chose the detail colouring—mahogany, sienna, ash grey, bronze, sandstone, and marigold. At first Belle insisted I do all the shading, but with some pointers, she managed just fine on her own as well.

"I know I'm being silly," she said about an hour later,

sweeping marigold across the lid. "I know it's just a bird, and I'm being—"

"It's not silly," I told her without looking up, dabbing at the shoebox's corner to smooth an edge. "You're not silly, Belle."

She could be giddy and excited over little things like turtles or Swiss chocolates, but I had never considered her silly. Beyond that, silly suggested frivolity, and to me, Belle's feelings had never been and never would be frivolous.

As I worked, I felt her studying me briefly before going back to the lid—and that was that. We finished up the bullfinch's coffin in a timely hour and a half. After, we left it to dry, and Belle changed into a black romper I'd never seen before. Fare thee well, string bikini. Until we meet again...

While I'd tried to swing lunch as we waited for the paint to set, Belle hadn't been interested. In the end, however, I managed to persuade her to nibble on some chopped carrots and cucumber, and by the time she finished, we could touch the shoebox without smudging our efforts. Belle set the bullfinch inside, reverently lowered the lid into place, and carried it out while I grabbed a metal shovel from the storage shed.

She lagged a few paces behind me as we walked the trails, saying nothing until I asked if she liked the spot I chose at the foot of a leafy tamarind tree. Standing beside me, she gave the tree and its whispery, bright green leaves a once-over, and then nodded.

"Yes, this is good."

I dug a small grave, about four feet deep, careful not to tear any of the larger roots I met along the way. When I was finished, Belle handed me the shoebox and I gently placed it at the bottom. Together, we filled the hole, the dark earth painting our arms and knees. Sweat dribbled down my back, and I wiped at my forehead, smearing dirt there, too.

She disappeared for a few minutes after, leaving me without a word, and I stood, waiting, hoping she hadn't gone back to the house without telling me, worrying about her disappearing into the forest alone. However, when she picked her way out of the foliage with an indigo hibiscus bloom in hand, my mild annoyance faded away.

"You were a very beautiful bullfinch," Belle said as she arranged the flower on top of the dirt mound.

"Yes." I watched, unable to hold back a smile this time, as she stood and wiped her hands on her romper. "She was."

And yes—she is. Beautiful. Inside and out.

Belle looked up at me, then giggled, standing up on her toes to brush the dirt off my forehead. With a grin, I bowed down to let her.

We stood before the grave another minute, silent, the shovel resting on my shoulder, before slowly meandering along the trails, back toward the house, hand in hand.

Just me and my sweetheart.

5

DEAN

Tuesday, March 12th

The bar buzzed with patrons when Belle and I strolled in, and I led her through to the only booth left in the far corner, our hands clasped, positively giddy. Because it was all going according to plan. Fantasies in public settings were hit-and-miss, as there were, unfortunately, so many variables I *couldn't* control. But tonight had been perfect. Belle's skintight little outfit. Her glossy blonde waves. Her smile. Dinner—our conversations. Sunset on the beach with the submissive of my dreams. And now a packed bar with a booth just waiting for us to christen.

The stars had truly aligned for my sweetheart's night of forced public orgasms.

It was one of my list-approved fantasies: taking Belle somewhere off Ixora and making her climax surrounded by strangers. She'd be all dolled up, looking scrumptious. Men wouldn't be able to resist ogling her no matter what we did. Dinner. Dancing. Drinks. We'd retreat to some shadowy corner of a bar where I'd whisper filth in her ear as my fingers worked her under the table. She'd fight to keep a straight face, to appear composed and proper, like we were any regular couple on a date night, and then I'd drag her into a *screaming* climax, one she'd have to keep quiet.

Just thinking about it—I had been flying at half-mast all day.

Belle must have noticed, because she had been brushing up against me since breakfast. Bending over in her near-sheer cover up, luscious figure on display. Talking back to me, all the while wearing the cheekiest of grins—just *begging* for me to take her over my knee. I hadn't. I intended to pay her back by making her climax as many times as I could tonight.

Because this evening's outing was technically our playtime, we had yet another lazy day around the house. Belle's taskwork had been to sit at my feet while I worked through the mind-numbing bullshit my father had sent me. Whenever I'd started to huff, not even realizing I was doing it, she would put her head on my lap as if to comfort me. Quiet me. Settle me.

It had been lovely.

But then the rest of the day she'd been a total teasing brat, and I couldn't wait to put her through the ropes.

We'd had dinner at a cozy little seaside restaurant on Saint Thomas, both of us eating light. From there, we strolled along the beach at sunset, Belle in her short, pink, form-fitting dress—an outfit that clung to her gorgeous figure like it had been painted on. I especially enjoyed the back cutout, which let me rest my hand directly against her skin as we walked off dinner.

Oh, and I also thoroughly relished the fact that she'd worn the perfume I'd bought her before my vacation had started. Dabbed delicately on her wrists, her throat, it had greeted me as we left the house this evening, and she had giggled when I grabbed her and buried my face in her neck. That perfume—yet another subtle reminder that she was mine.

We'd gone from beach to bar when the sun finally dipped below the horizon. The location I chose was small, intimate. Made entirely of reclaimed wood from the island, its shacklike appearance belied the fantastic drinks and appetizers inside. Located within walking distance of a few of the island's hotel chains, Sunset Beach Bar, as per usual, had bustled with tourists when we'd arrived. Crescent booths lined the back wall overlooking the bar. Beyond that, the place was totally open, lacking a fourth wall. Instead, we were greeted with views of the patio, the beach, the water. Twinkling strands of soft yellow lights illuminated the outdoor seating. It was just what I had imagined, just what I had fantasized about for ages...

Now, if only Belle would stop people-watching and actually *focus* on the fact that my hand was on her thigh.

Was she tipsy? I eyed our empty glasses, wondering if I shouldn't have asked the waitress for a refill already. This would be Belle's fourth drink tonight—perhaps the alcohol was making her distracted. She had just been so *cute* squealing over the little umbrellas when we'd first arrived that I couldn't help myself.

Not great Dom behavior, but occasionally I was allowed to be indulgent.

I shuffled closer, then squeezed her leg. "*Belle.*"

"Hmm?" She startled out of wherever her head had been, blinking a few times before shooting me a shy smile. "Oh, sorry, sir."

Her thighs parted, hitching her dress up to reveal more

delectable skin ripe for caressing. Her eyes, however, shot back to the bar, focused intently on something else. I watched her for a moment, then resisted the urge to huff like a child. *This* wasn't part of the fantasy. I was supposed to have her in my thrall, whimpering and shuddering as my fingers tormented her under the table.

"What's wrong?" I murmured, nipping at her neck instead. She giggled when my teeth grazed her skin, then sat up a little straighter, cheeks stained pink, as the waitress stopped by with our drink refills: scotch for me, fruity blue cocktail with little floral umbrella for Belle. We both smiled distractedly while the waitress added a stack of napkins to the table as well before flitting back to the bar. Belle's gaze followed her as she pulled her drink closer and wrapped her lips around the straw.

"Belle. Tell me." My hand left her inner thigh for the tumbler of scotch instead. I kept my tone firm, but conversational. "Do you not want to do the—"

"Oh, no!" She sat up sharply, straw bobbing in her drink. Her blush sharpened, the colour more noticeable beneath the dim mood lighting, and she shifted on the wooden bench to face me. "I mean, *yes*, I want to." Clearing her throat, she lowered her voice and snuggled closer as I looped her hair around my finger. "I *really* do."

My cock stirred at her eagerness, and I leaned forward to kiss her forehead, then trailed my lips to her temple, to her ear, where I licked the shell and whispered, "Good girl."

She shivered, her lower lip caught between her teeth as my hand smoothed back over her thigh.

"It's just," she said tentatively, peering up at me through her lashes, all kittenish and adorable. I paused and lifted an eyebrow, adopting that stern Dom expression that always had her melting into a puddle of gooey, pliant submissive.

This time, however, she merely nodded toward the bar, neither gooey nor pliant. "There's this woman sitting over there—the redhead in the teal dress? She was here when we sat down, and then those guys just showed up, and I've been watching them feed her shots for the last fifteen minutes."

We'd been in our secluded corner booth for about a half hour, enjoying our drinks, the ambiance. I hadn't wanted to start the scene the second we sat down, not when anticipation could be so utterly delicious. I'd wanted to make a night of it, drag it out, have her squirm and wonder, make her *wait* for me.

But apparently my doting submissive had found something to distract herself with instead.

"She just looks really uncomfortable now," Belle continued, playing with her drink's umbrella, snapping it open and closed. "And they keep touching her."

I exhaled softly, then retracted my arm from its comfy place across the back of the booth. Ordinarily, I wouldn't give two fucks about what strangers were doing to each other at a bar. However, Belle seemed genuinely concerned —and what concerned her concerned me.

Leaning forward, I scanned the very full bar, which ran nearly the length of the building and had three bartenders managing the somewhat-organized chaos. I spotted the woman in question last, even though she was right under my nose at the corner some ten feet away from us. Just as Belle had said: red hair, teal wrap dress, yellow flip-flops— one had fallen off at some point and was sitting under her barstool. She couldn't have been much older than Belle, and two men sandwiched her in place, one seated on the stool around the corner, the other standing beside her.

Men. I hesitated to call them men, not when they barely looked old enough to legally order drinks here. My frown hardened when the larger of the two plaid-shirt-wearing preps ordered another round of shots, which the bartender promptly delivered. The woman's arm shook as she brought the glass of clear liquid to her lips—well, she missed on the first attempt, catching her chin instead. Still, she downed it in a single gulp, coughing as her companions cheered her on. One had his hand on her knee. The other's was on the small of her back, then up to her shoulders when she swayed slightly.

"She looks..." Belle trailed off when the woman teetered off her stool. We both watched her zigzag past our booth, one yellow flip-flop forgotten under her barstool, before disappearing through the doorway to the bathrooms.

I glared at the trio of bartenders. They really shouldn't be serving her anymore.

But then again, those fucks shouldn't be ordering anything for her either.

Belle set her clutch on the table. "I'm going to go check on her."

She was halfway out of the booth when she paused, lower lip caught between her teeth again, and then settled back in beside me.

"I mean... *Can* I go check on her, sir?"

Warmth washed over me, my chest tight. Just as I'd felt the day that poor bird hit the window—love. It filled me up from the inside, choked me, smothered me, blinded me, threatening to spill out between us. I wanted to kiss her. I wanted to drag her out of the booth, throw her over my shoulder, and whisk her out of here. Off to some dark corner, far from prying eyes, prying ears, where I could make her scream.

Where I could show her exactly what she, Belle Bennet, did to me.

And what I wanted to do to her, long after our two months expired.

"Of course, sweetheart, that's fine." I tucked her hair behind her ear with a soft smile. When was the last time a woman had made me all warm and fuzzy? Never. Doms didn't *get* warm and fuzzy—right?

Maybe we did. Maybe we did when we'd finally found the right submissive. "Go make sure she's all right. I'll be here when you come back."

Belle planted a firm peck on my cheek, her smile dazzling, her cheeks flushed, before scooting around the table and hurrying off to the bathroom. I leaned forward, watching her go, and then sat back with a sigh. Did she know the effect she had on me? She had to—I wasn't exactly being very subtle with my affection.

Did it frighten her?

Did it make her want to run—to draw the line in the sand between client and escort?

It hadn't happened yet, but we still had three weeks left on Ixora. The hammer could fall at any time.

Clearing my throat, I downed half my tumbler of scotch in a single gulp. The liquid scalded the whole way down, scorching my core—making my case of the warm and fuzzies worse. In Belle's absence, I stole another glance at the bar boys. Tall, lanky—plaid shirts and board shorts on each of them. If I had to guess, I'd put them at twenty or *just* twenty-one. College students getting an early jump on spring break. While some schools were out now, over the next few weeks they would swarm the islands like locusts, adding to the bedlam that the annual regatta brought to Saint Thomas. I intended to avoid all that, if possible.

The pair stood jostling each other, laughing, smiling. The blond—already with a bald patch at the back of his

head, the poor fuck—even picked up the abandoned yellow
flip-flop. They had a good chuckle over that, too, and my jaw
clenched when Blondie tossed it back under the seat. His
brunet friend—freckly, wearing a seashell necklace and
socks with his sandals—nudged it under as far as it would
go, pushing the shoe up against the bar.

Which would likely force a severely inebriated woman
onto her hands and knees to retrieve it.

Immature little pricks.

I batted around the idea of going down to fetch it myself,
maybe bringing it to the bathroom so the poor woman
wouldn't have to stumble around half barefoot. However, by
the time I'd picked up Belle's pink clutch, a perfect match
for the neon of her dress, my submissive had reappeared at
our booth, her expression tight.

"Is everything all right?" I set her clutch down, making
room for her on the bench, but she made no move to climb
back in next to me.

"They keep buying her drinks and asking her to come
back to their villa," she said stiffly, arms crossed as she
briefly glared at the pair over her shoulder. When she faced
me again, her features had shifted to something softer,
pleading—that of a submissive indirectly asking my
permission for something. "She's crying in the bathroom,
and she's really drunk."

Damn it. I'd so looked forward to making Belle squirm
and come and squirm and come—from now until closing
time, if I so chose it. Instead, we were going to have to deal
with this. Because it was technically the right thing to do—
and because Belle wanted to. Because she wanted my
permission to.

And here I was, a warm and fuzzy Dom, finding it
harder and harder to say no to her outside of our scenes.

"All right." I passed over her clutch, and she held it to her chest, waiting. "Let's take her home, then."

"I think she's here for work," she told me. From her tone, I couldn't tell if she was addressing me, Dean Donahue, or *me*, her Sir. Truth be told, I didn't mind either way, not when she looked at me like that—like her partner in crime, the one to stand beside her through what was bound to be a messy endeavor.

"Likely staying at one of the hotels then," I managed as I slipped out of the booth, then smoothed a hand down my button-up black tee as Belle nodded.

"She said something like that, but I couldn't really understand which hotel she was saying." Her features shifted again to something apologetic. "She's...really drunk."

Fucking perfect. I grinned wryly. "We'll figure it out. Go fetch her."

"Are you sure, sir?" She stopped two steps away from the booth, hesitating. "I'm sorry we're not doing—"

"It's fine, Belle. Really." And I meant it. Sort of. "We can always try again after."

She flitted back to the bathroom door, hurrying along on the tips of her toes at a half run, her white flats a little worse for the wear after all this island living. Once she disappeared, I grabbed my scotch and downed the rest, exhaling a mouthful of fire afterward. It really was a drink that deserved to be nursed, but apparently I no longer had that luxury.

And that was fine, now that I thought about it. As long as I was with Belle, I didn't care what we did—even if it meant accompanying some belligerent tourist back to her hotel.

I could always make my submissive squirm and come and blush somewhere public after today. We had time.

Not as much time as I would have liked, however.

I slipped a hundred-dollar bill under my empty tumbler, then pocketed both my wallet and the tiny blue floral umbrella from Belle's drink—which I intended to stick behind her ear sometime, maybe when she was expecting a flower, just to make her laugh.

Belle emerged a few minutes later, one arm around the redhead's slim waist, clutch tucked under the other. The pair at the bar noticed them immediately, a homing beacon activated the second they stepped out of the bathrooms.

"Oh, hey, who's your friend?" Blond Prick pounced first, seeming not to notice me as I fell in behind the girls, ready to take the redhead off Belle's hands.

"I'm taking Juliet home," Belle said stiffly, headed straight for the barstool with the shoe. When she left Juliet to her own devices, I moved in, balancing the teetering woman with a hand on her back. Mascara streaked down her freckled cheeks, her eyes red and unfocused. She tipped back toward me, and I hastily grabbed her elbow, too, getting her upright again just as her lower lip started to quiver.

"Aw, come on—it's so early." Ah, and here was Brunet Prick, right on schedule. They circled like vultures, closing in on both Belle and Juliet's personal space, totally unaware that I even existed.

"She's too drunk," Belle said before bending down to grab Juliet's flip-flop. Two sets of eyes settled on her heart-shaped rear, and anger darted through me. I'd wanted her to be the center of attention, but in a completely different circumstance—preferably with my hand between her thighs, milking her third or fourth climax as people started to glance toward us, wondering what all her poorly muffled squealing was about. This—two brats perving on her while she helped a lady in drunk distress—had me fuming. My hand curled to a fist, jaw clenched.

Still, I wasn't about to make a scene. Fist unfurled. Jaw unclenched. Belle had a great ass. Let them look. I was the one who got to have all the fun with it.

She straightened and returned to Juliet, dropping the flip-flop at her feet. We both helped the woman into it, me with a hand between her shoulders and Belle with an arm around her waist. Honestly, when you couldn't push a sandal strap between your toes, you were too drunk.

"She's *fine*," Blond Prick argued as we dove headlong into the crowd separating us from the exit. I kept Belle and Juliet in front of me as best I could in the sea of people, following within an arm's distance, and the pair of plaid-wearing prats trailed after us, trying to scoot around me on either side. I squared my shoulders and stuck out my elbows a little, barring them.

"Why don't we get a table outside?" Brunet Prick offered, stomping along in his horrific socks and sandals combo, his breath rank with cheap vodka. "We could even go down to the beach."

I rolled my eyes. Because putting this intoxicated woman near a body of water seemed like a *genius* idea. Honestly, if Belle hadn't stepped in, Juliet's safety could have been compromised.

"No, gentlemen," I said finally, looking between them as they hovered in my peripherals, "I don't think so."

Both frowned, as if just realizing that I was a part of this.

"Look, man, we're just trying to have a good time."

Ahh, there was the shift in tone. Blond Prick had gone from some pathetic faux-seductive rasp to an *I'll put your head through a wall if you so much as look at me* growl. How macho. How terrifying.

As we picked our way through the crowd, Brunet Prick finally managed to skirt around me, his lanky frame darting by a trio of women suddenly barring my path before I could stop him. It put him one step closer to Belle. Scowling, I kept my eyes on him, unable to make out what he was crooning as we muddled through the densest part of the bar, Blond Prick still suggesting we detour to the beach behind me.

A few moments later we were out the front door. The din of countless conversations ceased, silenced as soon as the door swung closed. Our feet crunched across a sandy, gravel-ridden parking lot, and the night's cool breeze ruffled my hair, soothing my rising temper. Behind us, smokers huddled just off to the side of the main entrance, chatting quietly amongst themselves. To my right, a vacant road sporadically lit by lampposts, the concrete bathed in a soft yellow light. To my left, dark outlines of palm fronds danced against a starry night sky. Beyond that, the sea.

And in front by a good five or so feet—some twat who had placed himself between me and Belle. If only he realized what a stupid fucking move he'd made. My pace quickened.

"Do you guys want to get food? We know a great place," Brunet Prick offered, power-walking suddenly as if to outrun me—as if to keep up with Belle's brisk stride.

For fuck's sake.

"Or we could do room service," Blond Prick added, practically nipping at my heels. He wiggled his eyebrows suggestively when I looked back at him, incredulous. "We can swing this if you can."

My glare hardened. Right. Time to verbally eviscerate this bar gnat—

"Hey!"

Belle's startled cry had my heart leaping into my throat —and the sight of Brunet Prick's hand wrapped around her forearm had me seeing red. Blood-boiling, heart-thumping, caveman-brain, possessive-Dom *red*. Two long strides later I'd reached them, and I slammed a hand down on the little shit's shoulder and wrenched him away from Belle.

"Fuck off, bro," he snapped as he staggered back, unsteady on his feet—drunk, probably, but not quite as drunk as the woman he'd been feeding shots. Worried he'd trip over his own fucking feet and crack his head on the gravel, I kept a hand there to steady him, a verbal lashing on the tip of my tongue—

And then he took a swing at me.

This lanky, sock-and-sandals, seashell-necklace-wearing *boy* took a swing at me.

His fist, not even properly formed to protect his thumb, flailed wide, missing my nose by about three inches, but the look in his eye told me he'd try again.

So I decked him. Square in the face.

Pain radiated through my hand as soon as my fist met his jaw, and I reared back with a hiss as Brunet Prick went down.

"Holy shit—Travis!" Blond Prick rushed to his friend's side, and I stepped out of the way, teeth gritted, shaking out the dull ache that had engulfed my hand. My first thought was Belle—and I found her watching me, eyes wide, brows up, lips slightly parted. There was no telling whether she was impressed or terrified, but I wanted neither. It was stupid, punching some drunk kid because he got handsy with my—

My what?

My escort?

No. My girl. My sweetheart. My Belle.

I'd never been in a bar fight before, nor had I wanted to, but I would have taken on assholes twice my size for her without flinching.

Behind us, a few of the smokers cheered, but I ignored them, face hot, adrenaline pounding, as two of the bar's security team stalked toward us. Hands raised, I stepped away from the scene.

"We were just leaving."

"He grabbed me," Belle insisted, her voice about two octaves higher than usual as she pointed a shaky finger down at Slowly-Regaining-Consciousness Brunet Prick. "*And* he swung first!"

"That's enough, Belle." I hadn't meant to sound like I was chastising her, but my fight-or-flight response was still kicked into overdrive and it made my words sharper. A flicker of warmth returned at the thought of her defending me, but it wasn't necessary. Not wanting this to drag on longer than it already had, I fished a business card out of my wallet and offered it to the nearest bouncer. "If you have any questions—"

He waved me off as his partner played the *how many fingers* game with this Travis character.

"Not necessary, Mr. Donahue."

My business card lingered between us, but rather than question the first stroke of good luck in the last hour, I slipped it back into my wallet and gave the man a curt nod. When I faced the girls again, ready to get the hell out of here, Juliet doubled over and puked on her feet.

Fucking. Perfect.

Belle darted out of the splash zone, face crinkled with disgust. I ran my hand through my hair, then flexed it at my side.

"Well, let's get her cleaned up, I suppose—"

"Is your hand okay?" Belle asked, hushed, fretting over me like she had the bullfinch as I approached. "Dean—"

"I'm fine," I told her, shifting upwind and trying not to gag when the vomit smell hit me. "Really. It's nothing."

"Are you sure? Maybe you should have it looked at."

"It's *fine*, Belle." I closed my eyes and took a breath. *Stop sounding so aggressive, you fucking knob.* When I opened them, I found a frowning Belle gathering Juliet's stick-straight red hair away from her mouth. She glanced at me shyly when my fingers brushed against hers. "I'm sorry. I don't mean to be short. I'm fine. My hand hurts a little, but at least I know how to form a fist. If he'd hit me, he might have broken his thumb."

"Water," Juliet wailed as she flicked vomit off her feet. "Need *water*."

I exhaled crisply, and Belle shot me another apologetic look.

This night had started out *so* perfectly.

"I will be back in two minutes—with water and paper towels and hand sanitizer," I said, slowly, tautly, swallowing my frustration, because it wasn't meant for Belle. I wasn't upset at *her*. She was the one who had rescued Juliet from two assholes, one of whom was rolling about on the ground, howling about how I'd shattered his nose. Idiot. I hadn't hit anywhere near his nose.

How had we gotten here?

All I'd wanted was make Belle come, repeatedly, in public.

And now we were cleaning up a drunk mess, the scent of vomit stuck up my nose, while some college kid screamed about suing me for all I was worth.

Scowling, I made a beeline for the bar and hoped— *please*—that they had hand sanitizer.

Not exactly my best night out ever. However, as I glanced back and spotted Belle comforting a sobbing Juliet, her expression earnest and gentle, as though administering her own form of aftercare, I decided that it certainly wasn't my worst, either.

6

BELLE

*D*ean hadn't said a word to me since we left Saint Thomas.

I stood waiting for him, my feet in the sand, clutch in one hand and shoes in the other. Silently, Dean navigated his bowrider, casting lines and tying the boat to the gently bobbing wooden pier—doing all the things with all the ropes, things that I had seen him do a dozen times before, but couldn't tell you what he was doing, or what he still needed to do.

If I hadn't learned any of it by now, a month and a half into our trip, I wasn't about to learn at one in the morning after the strangest night so far. My cheeks burned at the memory, and I stole a quick look at Dean's hardened expression in the faint light of the dashboard. Was he angry with me? I couldn't tell. The silence didn't bode well, and I hadn't wanted to push him after—well, everything.

He'd had such a nice night planned for us. Sure, it had featured a little embarrassing kink for me in particular, but I had been excited about it all day, just as he had. And then I'd gone and ruined it by sticking up for Juliet, and things just went downhill from there. First those two drunk idiots at the bar, following us, harassing us, grabbing my arm— taking a swing at Dean. He had never struck me as the violent type, but he'd stepped up to defend me without hesitation. Dean had knocked the guy out cold. My knight in shining armor.

The moment had been swiftly ruined by Juliet throwing up every last ounce of vodka churning in her stomach. That guy—Travis—promptly started screeching about suing Dean, pressing assault charges, and we had been stuck at the bar for about an hour while they sorted it out with the local police. Witnesses stepped forward, thankfully, to confirm my story, but by then Juliet, a personal assistant from Minnesota, had become an absolute drunken disaster. She'd kept trying to curl up on the ground to sleep, but then, as I attempted to sit her back up, she would vomit again, then cry about needing sleep.

Getting her back to her hotel had been a nightmare. Not only had she lost her room key and phone, but she couldn't remember where she was staying. Dean and I had hopped in a cab and taken her around to six resorts before we found the right one. By then, mercifully, the staff on duty offered to take over from there, calling her boss as Juliet wailed about getting fired.

Dean had given her his business card, with a scribbled note to call him in the morning. She'd be too drunk to remember, but he'd also offered to speak to her boss and let him know that her situation tonight hadn't been her fault.

We cleaned up in the hotel lobby bathrooms, took the same cab back to the docks, then climbed into Dean's boat and headed for Ixora. At no point had he suggested we return to the bar to resume our night. Midnight had come and gone, and from the look on his face, I'd assumed he just wanted to go to bed.

I couldn't help but feel like tonight's chaos had been all my fault. I could have just alerted bar security that Juliet was being hassled and fed shots by two creepy guys, but I had wanted to handle it personally. I felt it was my duty as a fellow woman who was *also* frequently bothered at bars—one of the reasons I never went out anymore—to see her home safely. But that had dragged Dean in, and then it had just been one mess after another.

As he turned off the last lights on the boat and hopped over the edge onto the dock, I wavered between apologizing profusely and letting it rest until tomorrow morning. Maybe we both just needed to get some sleep and forget tonight had ever happened. But this was the first of his fantasies that we hadn't accomplished together, and guilt twisted my stomach to knots. Guilt over failing as his paid escort—*and* as his submissive.

More so the latter. The way his eyes had glittered mischievously as he'd talked about tonight at breakfast, I really *had* wanted to play. I'd wanted to please him. Heck, I'd been walking around the house all day in a constant state of arousal just *thinking* about what the night had in store.

Reality had been nothing more than a freezing-cold shower—for both of us, probably.

I blinked quickly, adjusting to the darkness, the beach illuminated only by moonlight. Stars glittered overhead too, thousands of them, beautiful and dotted across a pitch-black sky. Dean's dark outline stalked down the dock, his footfalls heavy, each one timed to my pounding pulse. The island filled the silence still hanging between us. Wind rustled through the palm fronds. Waves crashed against the shore, against the cliff faces just beyond the pier. The bird population had gone quiet, their songs saved for sunrise.

As he closed the distance between us, moving from wood to sand, the hard lines of his face became clearer. The cheekbones, the strong jawline. Dark eyes, unreadable. Not wanting to press my luck, I just turned and worked my way across the beach, headed toward the trail that would lead us back to the house. My heart yearned to speak—to say something, anything. To apologize. But his face—it was almost like he didn't want the apology. I held my clutch to my chest, white ballet flats hanging off two fingers at my side, worried.

Scared, honestly, that I had messed this all up.

That we were about to have a repeat of the gallery incident, and this time it *would* be all my fault.

The hairs on the back of my neck stood at the sound of him closing in, heavy, firm footfalls thumping behind me.

No. I won't let this turn into that. I would use my voice this time. I would fight to be heard so we wouldn't fall apart. I'd wanted to do a good thing tonight, but I had done so at the cost of Dean's fantasy—at the cost of our time together. It was, after all, limited. Eighteen days left.

My heart sank at the thought.

So, I stopped. I faced him, lifting my chin, determined— only to inhale sharply at the look in his eye. Moonlight glinted off the sage, his gaze made dark and dangerous, otherworldly, flecked with stars. I started off so strong, holding my ground, shoulders back, but with every long stride he took, I found myself shrinking—shrinking down before my Dom.

When he stopped in front of me, I expected words, no matter how curt and crisp. Velvet or steel, I could take them both. Instead, Dean grabbed the neckline of my skintight dress, its fabric stretchy, yielding, and yanked me to him. I stumbled, feet catching in the sand, and pitched forward into his body, solid as a marble statue, my own personal Greek god. God of lust. God of the underworld. Thanks to Elysium, I was a child of Hades—and Dean had dominion over me.

From day one, I had already belonged to him.

Our lips met harshly. My shoes plopped into the sand, forgotten, as he dragged me into a kiss that set my body on fire. Toes curled in the sand, I pushed up, guilt forgotten, and surrendered—at first. I plunged into the savagery of his kiss, the bite, the passion, the possession. Dean kissed me like he wanted to claim me, mark me, consume me, our mouths parted, souls exposed. I let him—until I fought him.

I had no idea why I did it. Never had the idea to push back crossed my mind before, because I was a good girl who did as she was told. Yet I shoved him, both hands to his chest, momentarily throwing him off. I backed away, gasping, but he caught me before I made it more than a few steps, yanking me to him again with a growl. His mouth crashed to mine, merciless, and I bit back. His lips, his tongue—nothing was safe.

We were a hurricane, stumbling along the beach, bathed in moonlight. Louder than our surroundings, stronger, too, Dean and I were an unstoppable force—fighting one another. I fought for my freedom, tugging at his shirt, his collar. He fought to keep me, an arm snapped around my waist, fingers tangled in my hair. Heat pooled in my core, striking out each time his teeth caught my lower lip—when he grabbed my ass and *squeezed*, reminding me that he could.

Reminding me that I was his.

With a moan, I struggled harder, grabbing the front of

his button-up tee and pulling. Much to my horror, I ripped clear through the first two buttons. Dean's grip loosened around my waist, and I fled, staggering back, panting, eyes wide at the carnage I'd left behind.

Not only had I ripped the buttons clean off, but I had torn the fabric, too, right above the third button.

Ohmygodohmygodohmygod.

Slowly, Dean looked down at the wreckage, both of us gasping for breath. I hugged my clutch to me, terrified and more aroused than I'd ever been before. Without my panties, each gust of wind, each island breeze, whispered across my slick sex. My bodycon dress had crawled up my thighs, barely covering me. I was about to tug it down, my cheeks as pink as the fabric, when Dean looked back up— and smiled.

My sex pulsed for that smile, for the danger clinging to it, for the way it said, *You've done it now.*

"Oh, kitten..." Dean closed the gap between us in two torturous strides, then yanked the clutch out of my hands and tossed it somewhere up the beach. "Wherever did you get those claws?"

"Sir—" I gasped when he yanked at my dress's neckline again, this time wrenching it down my body, tucking it under my bare breasts. With the built-in support, I hadn't needed a bra; something about going without my bra *and* my panties had made me feel so damn sexy earlier tonight. Now, as my nipples puckered, I felt exposed. Helpless. Cornered—by a predator whom I *wanted* to stalk me, hunt me, catch me.

Devour me.

Trembling, I lowered my arms to my sides and lifted my gaze to his. He held it for a moment, that smile haunting and beautiful as ever, before he pinched my nipple and *twisted*.

"Ow!" I slapped his hand away, eyes watering. His smile sharpened—and his hand went for my throat this time. Faster than I had anticipated, faster than I could respond to, Dean clamped down around my neck, then hauled me up to meet his mouth. Just like that, we were a hurricane again, two forces of nature colliding. Only one of us could come out on top.

As he slipped his tongue between my parted lips, I went back to his shirt, ripping it the rest of the way down. Three more buttons peppered the beach. His hand tightened around my throat, and when I dared open my eyes, I found Dean watching me, brooding, glowering. A challenging flick of my brow had him marching me across the sand, its texture shifting from feathery-soft to unyielding wet grit as we crossed into the surf.

The sea surged, reaching, reaching, reaching—crashing over our feet, my ankles. A shiver raced down my spine, my hands smoothing up Dean's chest. My *nails* raking up his chest. I stopped right at his nipples, ignoring the pressure on my windpipe, the ferocity bearing down on my lips, and wondered if I *dared*—

Before I could decide, Dean somehow knocked my feet right out from under me. I toppled over with a squeal, plummeting in a controlled fall as Dean guided me down— quickly, like he wasn't actually holding me, his arm around my waist, his other hand on my throat. I let out another undignified, high-pitched squeak when my back touched the wet sand, the crashing surf hurtling toward me.

But Dean had me up and flipped over by the time the water reached me, surging across my wrists, my knees, my ankles. Huffing, I tried to wriggle away, crawl to freedom, only to be dragged back and thrown over Dean's knee. He knelt in the surf, pinning my draped body in place, positioning me where he wanted—like I weighed nothing at all. Like I really *was* his kitten, small and malleable in his strong hands.

I steadied myself on the sand, hands sinking deeper by the second, and then attempted to straighten up. Dean's arm across my back was like lead, forcing me to stay just so— dangling over his knee, face only a few inches from the sand, and my butt in the air. The surf surged, crashing back into us, and I lifted my chin to avoid the spray. Then, unwilling to accept my lot, I yanked at his torn shirt as his fingers ghosted up my thighs, and pounded my feet against the sand.

Dean responded by pinning them down with his other knee.

He chuckled at my strangled moan of protest, then roughly tugged my dress up, exposing the rest of me to the moon, the stars—to his hungry stare. I yelped when his teeth raked across my skin, over the curve of my backside, clamping down on one globe as I squirmed uselessly in place. Another dark chuckle, the sound licking its way straight to my sex, his fingers trailing up my thighs, between them. I made no effort to open for him, but he found my slick folds anyway, sliding across them, flicking at my clit. Over my shoulder, I watched him, still smiling like the cat who'd caught the canary, and, as he met and held my gaze, Dean thrust two fingers into me.

"Ah!" I tightened around the sizeable intrusion, but he met little resistance, my arousal drawing him in, beckoning those fingers home. Dean hissed softly, stroking my inner walls, caressing that little spot that made me twitch and whimper. My fingers curled into the sand, my hips rocking of their own accord, greedy and wanton.

Wait. We had been fighting—and this felt like surrender.

I tried to swat him away, but I couldn't reach his arm, nor did my ineffectual smacks at his side, his back, have any effect. Dean retaliated, nipping at my ass again, hard enough to make me squeal and thrash about. His firm, sensual caress inside shifted to something harder, his fingers pumping in and out as I struggled, as I moaned in frustration. The surf continued to crash into us, salt water sloshing up to my chin, my lips. Fire crackled and spit in my depths, its heat coaxing me to clench, to grip Dean's fingers with every harsh thrust.

As if he wasn't busy enough, the fingers of the arm locked over me started to play with my right nipple. Rogue agents, inching closer while I was distracted, they plucked and pinched, refusing to budge even when I grabbed him by the wrist and *pulled*.

"No," I half cried, half moaned, my traitorous thighs falling open slightly when his pace increased, each pump shuddering through my body. Dean's smile turned mocking.

"*Yes*, kitten."

My head fell with a moan, and I was forced to watch him cup me, knead me, as his two fingers drove me closer and closer to an earth-shattering, heart-stopping—

He withdrew just before I could ask him for permission to come. I sagged over his knee, gasping, shaking, like a spring pulled too tight, ready to snap. Just as before, Dean effortlessly moved me, arranged me, lifting me off his knee and setting me on all fours as the surf retreated. For a moment, I stayed where he put me, hands and knees and toes dipping into the sand. Dress hiked up, yanked down, hair a mess from both the wind and my Dom.

The sound of his belt buckle opening snapped me out of it. With a slight shake of my head, I started to crawl away, parallel to the water, until two firm hands clamped around my hips and dragged me back with the rush of the next tidal surge. As soon as he released me, I was off again, crawling faster, splashing water as I went.

This time, when he caught me, it was with his belt looped around my waist. It cinched tight, forcing the breath out of me at first. Over my shoulder, I caught Dean's smile—hungry now, positively ravenous—as he notched the leather on the third hole, then used the tail end to smack me. First the side of my thigh, then my ass, harder. I flinched, yelped, but when I tried to crawl away this time, I got nowhere. He just needed to grip the belt wound snugly around my waist with one hand and I was *stuck*. Bound. Trapped. Captured.

Collared and *loving it*.

Head down, I hid in my hair, not wanting him to see just how much fun I was having—wanting to maintain the charade, the façade, that had us both ensnared. Me dripping down my thighs, Dean hard as he ground against my ass.

I sucked in a soft breath at the sound of his zipper, at the brush of clothing as he pushed his shorts and briefs down his thighs. That breath shot out of me, sharply, when he slapped my inner thighs, one and then the other. I knew what he wanted—he wanted them opened wider. He was going to take me like this, belted, captured, on the beach after midnight with no one but the moon to hear me scream.

Heat pulsed through me at the thought. I bit my lip. *Please don't let him know how badly I want him to do that.*

Determined to stick to my character, I didn't move. I stayed perfectly still, the water rushing up to me—until he smacked again, one cheek and then the other, harder, sharper, the sting intermingling with the need between my thighs. I gritted my teeth, wondering just how far both of us were willing to take this. Dean could go harder. *Much* harder. So, I yielded, adding a slight arch in my back, parting my thighs *just* a little. Unsatisfied, Dean pushed my right one open another few inches, then filled me with a single, brutal thrust.

My cry echoed across the water. Eyes wide, mouth hanging open, I fisted my hands in the sand, the sea surging. My inner walls clung to him, like I had been designed to fit him, to cater to his cock. Faintly, over the crash of the waves, I heard Dean's short, brisk breaths as he stilled, perhaps giving me the courtesy of time to adjust to him. I whimpered, dropping onto my elbows as the water rushed away.

He started to move with the surf's next surge. Gripping the belt with one hand, Dean rocked his hips, even the slightest movement forcing lightning bolts of pleasure through me. As sea water charged the shore, I propped myself up on my hands again, begrudgingly, lifting my chin at the crash. A shiver skittered down my back when he slowly, achingly, eased out of me, only to pound back in a breath later. I cried out, jolting forward as far as the belt would allow, breasts bouncing.

After a brief reprieve, he did it again. And again. And again. Each time, the lapse between shortened, until finally he found his rhythm—the one that would send me careening over the edge in about a minute if I wasn't careful. I moaned with each harsh thrust, wishing the belt had been around my neck instead, but still delighting in it, this little addition to our routine. Over my shoulder, I found him grasping it with one hand, the other hanging at his side. I'd expected to meet his dark stare, his teasing smile. Instead,

Dean had his head thrown back, lips parted, eyes closed as he lost himself in me.

Maybe he hadn't been angry about tonight after all.

I yelped when the next crash of surf hit, splashing up my arms, spattering my pebbled nipples. My sir took me brutally, his hips relentless, his cock pumping deep inside me, grazing all the places that made me squeal. I stomped the tops of my feet on the sand, whining, as heat licked its way across my sex, my core—so wonderfully close to the kind of orgasm that would have me seeing more than just stars. Suddenly, all ability to think straight vanished. I was lost in a sea of promise so exquisite that I would let myself drown again and again. I closed my eyes tight, head dropping forward with a sob, my sex rippling around him. Almost—there. Almost—

"Don't you fucking *dare* come without asking," Dean snarled. My eyes shot open when he spanked me, each pitiless smack of his palm inciting a new kind of blaze across my skin. Vainly, I tried to wriggle out of reach, only to earn another two spanks on each side. The belt tightened around my waist when Dean gripped it with both hands, his pace quickening, the slap of flesh to flesh drowning out the crashing waves.

"*Please*, sir," I whimpered. "Please, can I come?"

I couldn't hold out. So—close. So—right *there*.

"No."

I collapsed onto one elbow, bobbing along with his relentless rhythm, and peered up at him. No? Had he just said *no*?

His smile was back. That dark, mocking sort of smile that made me want to cry in despair and scream with need. Dean cocked his head to the side, issuing an unspoken challenge.

"Please?" I whispered. His smile sharpened.

"No, sweetheart, you can't."

I folded down with a sob. "*Please*—"

"What is it about no," another two smacks, "that you don't understand?"

"Sir, I c-can't—"

"You can." He dragged me back up by my hair, not letting go until I braced myself on my hands again. The surf surged. I cried. Dean hammered into me.

He had never told me no before. He had never denied me. I—I didn't know what to do.

Not come. That was what I was supposed to do.

Or come and be punished for it. No. I couldn't do that again. I couldn't. I'd die.

But this was *torture*. All that heat, the crackling fire lapping at my insides, every part of me on edge.

"*Sir*," I wailed, stomping my feet again—like a brat throwing a tantrum. Dean chuckled, dragging one finger up my back before threading his hand in my hair.

"All right, Belle." He gave a little tug, forcing my head back. "If you can last *one* more minute, you can come as much as you want without punishment."

"O-one minute?" I gasped. Sixty whole seconds? That was an eternity!

"*That* is my only offer."

I whimpered and nodded as best I could, then tried to distract myself with the stars. Only, as soon as that minute started, Dean pounded harder.

"*Sir!*" My betrayed cry ricocheted off every piece of the island, accompanied by the faint echoes of his laughter. This wasn't *fair*! I stopped feeling the water, the wind. I couldn't see the stars anymore. I was adrift—adrift in the River Sir, where all good submissives go to surrender.

There was just me and him, *us*, alone in the black. Through the haze, through the fire scorching my insides, I counted. Forty seconds to go. Twenty. Ten. Five. Three. Two. *One*.

"Good girl," Dean murmured, slowing at last, the hand in my hair moving straight to my clit. "Come for me, sweetheart. I want to hear you scream."

I twitched and moaned as he played with me, but it wasn't until both his hands found their way back to the belt, his hips slamming into mine, that I finally imploded. I gave him my screams, some incoherent blend of his name, his title, and *oh god* leaving my mouth as I plummeted into bliss.

"*Good*." Two more smacks, my pleasure-addled body a rag doll at his disposal. "My, don't you look pretty, coming so sweetly all over my cock—under the moonlight. Don't you think that's poetic, kitten?"

"Y-yes," I sobbed, hiding in my hair again.

"Yes, *what*?"

Dean gathered my blonde waves and yanked them back, driving an arc into my neck as tears rolled down my cheeks.

"*YesIthinkitspoetic.*"

"What was that?" He jerked my hair. "Sir can't hear you when you don't enunciate."

"*Yes*," I cried, my body sated yet *starving*, desperate for him to grant me my freedom—to let me go, to stop pounding into me, but also to let me come again a dozen times over. "Yes, I-I think it's poetic."

"I wish you could see how perfect your cunt looks with my cock fucking it."

"Y-yes, sir."

"Maybe next time I'll put you in front of a mirror—and you can watch." His voice hitched, his pace stuttering. "Would you like that, sweetheart?"

"Yes, sir, please, please, *please* I want to watch you take me—"

"Say it right, Belle," Dean growled. His cock pulsed inside me, and as he slammed in one last time, stilling, I gave him what he wanted—what *we* wanted.

"*Please*, sir, I want to watch you *fuck* me—"

"*Fuck!*"

A second burst of pleasure drowned me just as Dean's first consumed him. We collapsed into the surf, me on my elbows, his hands planted on either side of my head, blanketing me without smothering me. Suddenly, I couldn't breathe. The belt—too tight. I heaved in a ragged gasp, but before I could reach back, Dean was up and removing it. He tossed the strip of fine Italian-crafted leather aside, then heaved me up, supporting me with a hand across my chest, open-mouth kissing my neck.

"Such a good girl," he whispered, panting, both of us fighting to catch our breath. I clutched at his wrist, his elbow, and leaned into him—light as air. If he let me go, I'd float away.

"Thank you, sir," I murmured back, turning just enough to kiss his cheek.

"A very good girl, sweetheart."

I closed my eyes, smiling.

"*My* very good girl."

I nodded, fearless in his arms. "Yes, sir."

Slowly, we untangled ourselves. Once free, I pulled my too-tight dress over my head and threw it back up the beach, then sucked in a lungful of salty sea air. Beside me, Dean kicked off his shorts and briefs, but left his torn shirt, the fabric billowing in the breeze.

Then, just as I was about to suggest a quick dip in the water, he scooped me up and threw me over his shoulder—

like I really *was* his kitten—and carried me back to the house without a word.

———

Barefoot and spent, I padded downstairs at 5:30 that morning in search of a bottle of water. For the first time since I'd arrived, I hadn't crawled naked out of my bed—but Dean's. Chilled by the blast of the AC, I had slipped into his ripped button-up tee, the one he had so casually tossed aside before hauling me into the shower. It smelled like the beach, like a heady combo of Dean's sweat and his musky cologne, a blend that drove me wild.

And I liked that it was torn. He hadn't tossed it in the garbage, just on the floor. Maybe he wouldn't throw it away.

I wrapped the shirt around me as I stepped off the last step of the first alabaster staircase, rounding the landing and carrying on down to the second. Just beyond the lounge area, one of the glass doors was only partially closed. Grinning, I tiptoed across the tile and finished the job. No wonder the air-conditioning was going crazy this morning.

As I clicked the lock into place, then scanned the first floor for any wayward geckos or iguanas, I couldn't help but flush at the memory of when I had last passed through that door. Only four hours ago, Dean had carried me inside, over his shoulder, naked—full caveman mode engaged. We'd gone straight up to the glorious shower in his master bath, but for the first little while, there hadn't exactly been much freshening up going on.

More like ravenous lovemaking against the tiled wall. On the little bench seat. Bent over, bracing myself on the glass as he—

I shivered, my smile hurting my cheeks as I double-checked all the corners. Not an iguana in sight. Geckos, the rascally little things, would be harder to track down in such an enormous house. A silent house this morning, save for the air-conditioning—and the hum of the fridge, which settled as I made my way around the walnut dining table.

I ought to hurt more than I did. Dean and I had played a lot in just a few short hours—a *lot*. In the shower. Over the chaise chair next to his balcony. On the floor—apparently I was a sucker for getting onto my hands and knees for him— in bed, over the bed, tied up to the bedpost. I should have been sore and exhausted. Instead, I was still floating along, content.

Pleasantly full, if you could even feel like that after a sex marathon. Full and complete and whole. And happy. Blissfully, stupidly, *happy*.

Fridge door propped open, I pushed through the containers of leftovers and snagged one of the cold glass bottled waters at the back. Rather than guzzle it down right there, I closed the fridge and all but skipped over to the stairs, eager to get back to bed. Dean's bed. Not my own— maybe for the rest of the month. I just couldn't imagine crawling back under the thin duvet in the guest room while Dean slept just a few doors down.

I wouldn't push it, of course. Our individual bedrooms were the one bit of privacy we both had from each other, but if he invited me in again, I wouldn't say no.

"Belle?"

I flinched, stumbling onto the bottom step and clutching the bottle to me, so not in the mood to clean up scattered shards before 6 AM. Peering up, heart hammering, I spied Dean leaning over the glass wall that lined the two staircases. Hair tousled, bleary-eyed, he looked like he had rolled out of bed the second he woke up.

"Are you all right?" he rumbled. I bit my lower lip, grinning; his voice had a croaky purr first thing, one that made me shiver—made me wet.

"I'm great." I lifted the bottle as evidence. "Just thirsty."

We set off in unison, me climbing up, him sauntering down, and met on the landing in the middle. As soon as I rounded the corner, I inhaled sharply: Dean was buck naked, sporting a sun-kissed glow all over, and I couldn't help but wonder if he had been tanning in the nude without me. Six-pack on display. The sharp, defined V-cut of his hips. Thick cock hanging between his thighs, not exactly standing at attention, but not entirely disengaged either. Beneath his ripped shirt, my nipples pebbled. This man. My very own bronzed Adonis, strolling down the stairs with the grace and ease of a king—the lord of all he surveyed, myself included.

We gravitated toward each other without a word, like two halves finding their way back to the whole. Dean backed me up against the shiny alabaster landing wall. Roughly a foot thick, it came up to my mid-back and had a rounded edge rather than a sharp corner like the stairs.

Our hips met first, mine arching out to greet his, molding to him as his shaft became more alert.

"May I?" he murmured, holding out his hand as I pressed back against the wall. Without hesitation, I gave him the bottle, watching as he cracked it open, then brought it to my lips. His eyes were warm first thing in the morning. Not full of schedules and dark deeds, the thousand other tasks a man like Dean Donahue had on his plate—just warm. Comforting. Commanding, even so. Perhaps that was just his natural state.

My lips parted, and he fed me a quick sip, then another, the frigid liquid sliding down my throat, washing over my insides. It did nothing to quell the embers flickering back to life within me, the remnants of this morning's *many* encounters sparking.

When I pulled back and licked my lips, he capped the bottle and set it on the ground, safely out of reach. The implication excited me, and my breath hitched as he caressed my cheek, then wove his hand into my loose blonde waves.

"Did you miss me?" I whispered, tipping my head into his hand, lifting a teasing brow. My smile faltered when he didn't return it. Dean studied me silently for a moment, not an ounce of tease in him, before tightening his hand in my hair.

"Yes," he murmured, then pulled me into an all-consuming kiss. Open-mouthed and deep. A kiss to claim, to consume, to brand—to mark me for his own. Possessive and hungry, a kiss I felt in my marrow. The kind that had me up on my toes, that made my heart skip a beat.

The kind that turned the embers back to flames, pleasurable heat soaring through me.

We had come together so many times already. I had *come* so many times already.

But I wanted him again.

Dean made me insatiable. And if the way he kissed me said anything—he was starving.

He kissed me like that for some time, slowly, deeply, tasting me like I was the only fine dining he would ever need. At one point, his hand slipped between my thighs, languidly massaging my sex as he swallowed every sound I made. Every moan. Every shudder. Every sigh. He made me feel like a rare delicacy—the sort no one would ever sample again, if he had his way.

I wanted that, just as badly as I wanted him.

And the realization didn't send me running. It had my hands in his hair, my mouth open to him, my thighs open for him. After a rather intense month and a half, Dean knew my body. He knew where to go hard and soft in equal measures, where to linger if he wanted to make me whimper. I was his canvas, his fingers the brush, and he crafted a masterpiece right there on the landing. By the time his hand smoothed over my hips, beneath the shirt and up to my breasts, I was a panting, trembling mess.

My eyes fluttered open when he pressed his forehead to mine. I was still met with warmth, but need, too. Darkness. A hint of danger and promise.

"Dean..." We had forgone his Dom title—just for this morning. I'd cried his name when he forced orgasm after orgasm out of me, and it only spurred him on. He hadn't corrected me. Not once. Maybe he liked the way it sounded. I certainly liked the way it tasted.

Even if I wasn't calling him sir, I'd asked to come. Every time. Even if he was dragging the climax from my body, I still begged. In fact, that was the only bit of our dynamic that remained. What we had done this morning—none of it was planned. None of it was discussed, assessed, analyzed for safety. We were just two people who did what they wanted to each other—and it felt different. Right. Normal.

Not that the sex was standard, by any means.

Apparently, when given the chance to improvise, Dean and I erred toward the dark side. Rough and hard. Pain and pleasure. We slipped into our usual roles naturally, but without all the formalities. I submitted, but I also fought. I inflicted pain, too, and was thoroughly chastised.

I loved it. I *loved* our sex.

And maybe—maybe I loved...

"Belle."

He had grown hard against me, his cock resting against my belly. The muscles along his jaw flicked when I stroked the silky head, smearing the drop of precum just as languidly as he had with me.

Stealing one more kiss, the kind that made my toes curl, Dean hoisted me up, large hands grasping my thighs. I reached between us and steered him into me, breath catching as he thrust up. *Oh.* My lashes fluttered closed. My head tipped back—and I didn't give a damn that he had me pinned to the landing wall, that if I looked over my shoulder, I'd see straight down to the first floor.

In Dean's arms, I wasn't scared anymore—of anything.

He mouthed hot kisses along my throat, and I locked my ankles, resting them on the small of his back. One hand continued to grip my thigh, but the other ghosted around my back, trapping me against him.

I felt full again. Physically, this time. Full and stretched —but still whole.

"*Dean,*" I whimpered, arms curling around his neck, our foreheads finding one another. He finally rocked against me, moving at my unspoken command.

No. A plea.

I couldn't command him, not when he owned me, mind, body, and soul.

The first rule of escorting—I'd broken it.

And I didn't care anymore.

Wrapped snugly in each other's arms, we made slow but intense love on that landing, breath mingling, mouths never more than a few inches apart. We rarely kissed during our scenes, but here, it was like neither of us could get enough. His kiss was a drug, and I was already addicted. Whenever he so much as brushed my lips, I was open and pliant beneath him. I was a willing captive in his grasp—and I needed so much *more*.

My climax snuck up on me. Like a great whitecap breaking against the shore, it crashed over me so suddenly, so swiftly, that I cried out. Clinging to Dean, I rode the wave, hips grinding against him as he smothered my noises with another desperate kiss that had me seeing stars.

His kiss turned sharper, harsher when he came shortly after, pounding through the final few thrusts, our symphony of sounds reaching a crescendo, filling the house.

Panting, gasping, holding one another, we settled together, Dean pressing slow, seductive kisses to my neck.

"Sorry I didn't ask for permission," I whispered, adoring his little chuckle. Dean nibbled at my earlobe, then planted a firm kiss beneath it.

"I'll let it slide this time."

We grinned at one another, and I brushed my fingers through the caramel-blond locks that had fallen over his forehead.

"Thank you, sir."

Dean watched my lips as I spoke, his gaze warm again, his smile soft. "You're welcome, sweetheart."

Sweetheart. The first time he'd called me that, I had been bawling over a dead bird. Anyone else would have made me feel like an idiot, because, after I'd distanced myself from it, I could acknowledge *maybe* I'd had a bit of an overreaction. But Dean had been so accommodating, so gentle that day. I'd thought the pet name might stem from that persona— that of the soft, caring Dom who hated to see his sub cry. Two weeks later, it had stuck.

And I really, really, *really* liked when he called me sweetheart.

With my legs still wrapped around Dean, my hips had

finally started to ache. I cupped his face, that gorgeous strong jaw, and kissed him—a hard, firm peck, our mouths closed—and then slid my eyes pointedly up the stairs behind him. Dean's eyebrows lifted.

"Are you telling me what to do, kitten?"

Oh, I liked that one too. *Kitten.* It made me feel bold and mischievous.

"Wouldn't dream of it, sir."

"No, I thought not." Grinning, he ducked down for me to grab the smooth, narrow neck of the glass water bottle, then hoisted me up a little higher, cock still buried where it belonged, and carried me upstairs to his shower, then back to his bed—where *I* belonged.

7

DEAN

Friday, March 15th

I hated waking to an empty bed now.

Especially an empty, Belle-less bed. Ever since she had spent that first night, she just hadn't left—and I hadn't wanted her to. Waking up to that sleepy smile, her royal blues warm and inviting, her supple, naked figure just *begging* me to do horribly wonderful things to it...

Well, it certainly made getting up harder. In fact, I hadn't climbed out of bed at my usual 6:45 start since she'd moved in. No 7 AM workouts. No breakfast prep. As soon as I was up, in more ways than one, I had Belle in my arms, happily smothered by her wild blonde mane, and we usually ended up dozing another hour away together. Sometimes fucking. Sometimes just spooning, sleepy conversations murmured, punctuated by her giggles—giggles that made my heart so fucking happy. It had been bliss, honestly. As I crawled in beside her each night, I couldn't imagine waking up without her.

I couldn't imagine a *future* without her anymore.

But here I was—without her. At just after six, a gentle dawn light spilled into the room, my near-sheer white curtains doing little to dampen it. Brow furrowed, I sat up, naked beneath the covers, and scanned the room for Belle. Not in the chair by the balcony. Not *on* the balcony—though that would have been a shocker, given, well, heights. I even checked the bathroom, but that was dark and quiet too.

Where on earth—

Something clattered downstairs.

Ah. Had she snuck out—to make me breakfast in bed? No. As much as she complained about not being allowed to cook, the little minx would be lost if I ever handed over the spatula. She was hopeless in the kitchen, and while bumbling amateur cooks usually made me want to rip my hair out, Belle triggered my inner Dom like none other. Her struggles encouraged the protective, assertive, supportive, patient side of me to the surface. I liked to encourage her when she tried, but in the end, nine times out of ten, I always salvaged her attempts into something edible.

So, she wasn't a cook, and I didn't mind, but I couldn't see another reason as to why she'd be downstairs. And that crash—it had sounded like one of my metal mixing bowls.

Something was afoot. The bedroom smelled like vanilla.

After relieving myself in the bathroom and washing my face, I headed down the hall, padding along on the balls of my feet, looking absolutely fucking ridiculous—a six-foot-two ass-naked man tiptoeing—so she wouldn't hear me coming. Something else clattered, the vanilla scent growing stronger, the commotion followed by Belle's very innocent little *oh, darn it*; I grinned. Hearing an expletive tumble from her usually demure mouth that night on the beach—*fuck* had it ever pushed me into oblivion.

I stopped at the top of the staircase, peeking over to the

first floor. Sunrise painted it in warm hues, and the light over the stove illuminated the open kitchen area. Just as I'd suspected, there she was, doing *something* at the long stretch of countertop closest to the stairs. My eyes narrowed.

Was that a...cake?

And my paintbrushes?

Wearing one of my shirts again, buttoned up this time, Belle looked positively scrumptious, her hair tossed back in a messy bun, a bit of blue colouring smeared on her cheeks —and now, when she wiped at it, her forehead.

The movement of wiping at her forehead, however, had made her look up, and the moment she saw me, she jumped.

"Oh—no!" She lurched over the cake, arms around it, hiding it as best she could. "Don't look! It isn't ready yet!"

"Belle, what on *earth* are you doing?" I sidled down the stairs, arms crossed, fighting an enormous smile as she continued to shield her work from my prying eyes. "It isn't even seven in the morning yet..."

"I've been up since three," she admitted weakly as I stepped off the last stair. "Stop—right there. Don't... You're going to ruin your surprise."

"I think that ship has sailed, sweetheart."

"Oh..." Her disappointment made my chest tight. "Right."

"What are you doing?" Strolling into the kitchen area, I finally noticed the stack of baking bowls in the sink. The dishwasher hummed, its heat warming my legs in passing.

"It's..." Belle set the paintbrush down, six bowls filled with different shades of blue and grey scattered around her. She'd used nearly all my lemon and vanilla extracts; the bottles sat empty next to the full sink. She scratched at her messy bun, then hastily pulled her hand away, fingers stained blue. "It's for your birthday."

I blinked back at her, shocked.

"I wanted to surprise you," she added, shyly almost, picking at her blue-stained nails. She then turned toward me, cocking her hip against the counter. "Happy birthday?"

I hadn't told her it was my birthday. I rarely ever told anyone. Clearing my throat, I leaned in and stole a quick, firm kiss, then looked at her cake. She had somehow managed to find the glass turntable at the back of a cupboard.

"How...did you know it's my birthday?"

"The dossier," she told me with a shrug. Right. Of course. We each had a copy containing all pertinent information about one another.

"Ah. Yes, well—"

"I can't believe you weren't going to say anything." Belle nudged my arm, grinning, her shyness forgotten. "I *love* birthdays!"

Her smile managed to lift my spirits. "Of course you do, sweetheart."

I, on the other hand, hadn't properly celebrated a birthday in *years*. Frankly, they had lost their sparkle. For the most part, I worked straight through them, and then, around midnight, my staff would creep into my office with some delicacy from the kitchen, a sparkler stuck in the top, and they'd all sing happy birthday while I counted down the seconds until I could get back to whatever task they had interrupted. The whole affair only lasted about five minutes, if I was lucky, and then the dessert—tart, cake slice, macaron, once a whole croquembouche—sat in my office's mini-fridge until I forgot about it and eventually gave it to my assistant.

But the look on Belle's face, the enthusiasm with which she professed her love for birthdays—maybe I didn't mind them so much today.

Hers was in July.

I already had gift ideas in mind.

Only a handful involved bondage.

Shaking my head, I leaned down, slowly rotating the turntable to give her work a closer inspection. "Belle...did you *bake* me a layered cake? And is that—fondant?"

It looked just shy of three tiers high, and I knew in an instant that the exterior wasn't buttercream. The fondant rippled and split, only smooth in a few patches—clearly handled by someone who had never touched an ounce of fondant in their life. But it was obvious that she had tried. Very hard. And—oh, it made my eyes sting with *feeling*.

Fucking hell, Belle was turning me soft.

"I've been researching it for two weeks," she admitted, her enthusiasm and smile infectious. Her eyes practically shimmered. "I snuck my list of ingredients to Jackson when he dropped off the groceries, and then last Sunday he brought me everything I'd need. We hid it all in the pantry."

I smoothed her flyaways down, impressed with her ingenuity. "I wondered why you were so keen to unload the bags."

And she had suggested ideas for a lot of our meals this past week, most of which could be made from whatever we had in the fridge. At the time, I'd just been pleased with her enthusiasm for meal-prep when she usually showed none. Clearly it had all been a ploy...

Minx.

"One of the layers didn't rise as much as the others for some reason," she continued, brow puckering slightly, "but I just put it in the middle. I'm sure it's fine." Belle slowly spun the turntable back around to what I assumed was supposed to be the front of the cake. "It's a vanilla lemon layer cake." She hesitated, her little frown deepening. "I wanted to be more adventurous, do something with bourbon, but I didn't know... I don't really bake, so..."

For someone who didn't bake, she'd had the foresight to use the ring molds, which were also in the sink, and the house smelled spectacular. So what if one layer hadn't risen as much as the others? Just looking at her, I was so fucking proud—I wanted to take that cake, as is, and show it off to anyone who would put up with me.

"Lemon and vanilla sounds delicious," I told her, drawing her to me with an arm around her shoulders. I kissed her temple, breathing in her natural scent, now paired with her efforts in the kitchen. Exquisite. "Thank you, Belle. I can't wait to try it."

Really. My sister Adelaide had labeled me a food snob years ago, and the title had stuck, but I intended to eat every crumb of that lemon and vanilla cake. Lick my plate clean, too, even if something was off with the recipe.

Still, one thing didn't quite add up.

"And," I grabbed my paintbrush, holding it up in front of us, "this?"

"Oh, I hope you don't mind. I cleaned them all before I used them, and I'll put them back when I'm done. I forgot to add a brush to my list."

There were four brushes of varying sizes in one of the cupboards, specifically tailored for the culinary arts rather than the *actual* arts. I bit my tongue. It didn't matter.

"I wanted to paint it like the painting in your office," she admitted. "You know—the ocean?"

Initially I had thought she'd just bought blue fondant, or maybe used blue dye, but now I noticed the brushstrokes;

she had struggled her way through the fondant setting process, and *then* decided to paint it. Ambitious, my girl. To her credit, she had chosen the colours well, and she appeared to have just started layering them. I wanted to tell her, however, with the scheme she had chosen, that she ran the risk of it looking muddied if she did too much.

But no. I wasn't here to critique; this was Belle's project, and she was doing a spectacular job. She would feel much more accomplished if she did it all by herself.

"It's lovely," I said with another kiss to her temple. She stood up on her toes to plant one on my lips, then nudged me away.

"So, go back to bed," my submissive ordered, the bossy little thing. "I don't want you to see it until it's finished."

I didn't want to go. I wanted to pull up a chair and just watch her work. Belle had a beautiful tousled, slightly rumpled look to her that I could stare at for hours—then ruin as I fucked her over the counter.

"But I'm awake now."

"Well, go away," her cheeks pinked when I arched an eyebrow, "*sir*. You can see it when it's finished."

Belle then plucked the paintbrush from my hand, dipped it in her ceramic bowl of cobalt-blue paint—edible paint, *please* be from the edible collection under my studio desk—and went back to work. I folded my arms, watching her for a moment with the most absurd, lovesick grin on my face. Ever the professional, my Belle. She looked right at home with a brush in her hand, even if she was globbing the colour a bit.

Resist the urge to fix it for her.

Slowly, my gaze wandered from her messy hair to her paint-smeared cheek, then on down to where my shirt cut off at the middle of her thigh. No pants. My cock twitched appreciatively, swelling to life at all the filthy things I could do to her in that outfit.

Down, boy. The idea I landed on didn't involve the appendage, as much as it adored Belle.

"Well," I said innocently, "I'll need to do *something* to keep me busy, I suppose."

She hummed in agreement. "It's nice outside. Maybe go for a run."

"No, I think..." Smirking, I stepped around behind her, then sat on the floor and scooted back. Belle squeal-giggled when I forced her legs apart, lifting her by the hips so I could sidle right into place. My back nudged against the cupboard—and my nose nudged at her pussy.

"*Dean!*" Toes barely touching the tile, Belle swatted at me, wriggling about as she balanced somewhat precariously on my shoulders. "What are you *doing*?"

As loath as I was to admit it, I liked when she called me by my name. In fact, I didn't even mind that she was breaking a house rule. *Sir* had a time and place. Hearing her giggle my name—it made our relationship more intimate, *real*.

"Just go back to painting," I insisted, tipping her body back so I could see over her mound. She peered down at me, smiling incredulously, and the pink in her cheeks darkened when I wiggled my eyebrows. "Pretend I'm not even here."

Belle squealed when I moved her back into place and smothered her cunt with my hungry mouth, dragging my tongue between her folds. I loved her noises. Every single one of them. I loved her taste. I loved the way she felt.

I just loved—*her*.

By now, I had a whole routine in place when it came to pleasuring my submissive orally. If I spent too much time on her clit right away, she'd come in about two minutes, and I much preferred to drag it out for as long as I could. I worked her slowly to start, arms wrapped around her thighs. A little lick here. A little lick there. A nibble. A flick. A dip inside her. I found my rhythm in slow, lazy teasing.

I had no clue if Belle was getting any painting done up there, but she certainly was making an awful lot of noise. Another long, languid sweep of my tongue, followed by a hard suck of her clit. Her body shuddered, and slowly, the longer I worked her, the more she leaned her weight on me for support. The more her thighs quivered. The higher-pitched her noises became. When she tangled her hand in my hair and rocked her hips against my mouth, I knew I had her. My motions quickened, and two sharp smacks to her pert little ass had her moaning, long and low, the title she was supposed to call me.

Good girl, Belle.

When I had her like this, all I wanted was to slip a thumb up her ass—just to test the waters. Anal hadn't been strictly forbidden, but Belle had classified it as a soft limit. Given I had become quite the connoisseur of her cunt, I didn't mind. Still, I had a feeling she would enjoy the fullness of both holes put to use. I spread her cheeks as her hips trembled, her juices sweet on my tongue, and then smacked her again. Another time. We could broach the subject slowly, gently. When and if she was ready.

As her gasps grew sharper, shorter, I wrapped my arms back around her legs and crushed her cunt against my mouth. While my jaw had started to ache, I put it to good use, tormenting her thoroughly, until I finally had her squealing exactly what I wanted to hear.

"Oh, *god*, sir, can I please, please, please, *please* come?"

I pulled back just enough to drag in a lungful of air and growl, "*Yes*, Belle."

Nuzzling her clit with my nose, I made sure to lick, lick, *lick* her through her climax. My cock lay rigid against my abdomen—pouting, likely, as I so enjoyed the feel of her rippling around it whenever she came.

No matter. I'd make her come again today. After all, it *was* my birthday, and somebody professed to *love* birthdays. My entire schedule had just shot right out the window, a fresh batch of wicked games dancing across my mind. Games of pain and pleasure. Games that would make her sob and mewl and *beg* me to come, and I'd deny her again and again until I was sure she was hanging onto her sanity by the skin of her teeth.

Then I'd bury my cock deep inside of her—and she would come around it as many times as I told her.

Because today was my birthday.

And I was finally going to savor every sweet second of it.

When Belle's white-knuckle grip on my hair loosened, I scooted out from under her, ass numb from sitting on the tile, and caught my breath. I was seeing stars, but probably because all the blood had gone from my head to my dick.

"Oh my god," Belle moaned, hunched over the counter.

I stood with a smirk. From what I could tell, she hadn't accomplished much on the cake since I'd started, save a few sweeps of the cobalt across the top. Face thoroughly flushed, her hair sat skewed atop her head—like she had been pulling at it, perhaps just as hard as she had been yanking mine. Her climax coated her thighs, and I wanted to lick her clean.

"*Thank* you," she said as she pushed herself up, still bracing on the counter, her toes curled. Our smiles mirrored one another, and I swooped in, pressing a quick peck to her cheek.

"You're very welcome, sweetheart." I gave her butt two

little pats. "All right. Off for a run. Can't wait to see the cake when it's done."

Belle slumped over the counter with another moan, paintbrush seemingly forgotten, and I sauntered off with my head held high, still painfully erect but grinning like an idiot.

Because I was the birthday boy—and my day was just getting started.

8

DEAN

Sunday, March 17th

*A*s soon as I spied that mega-yacht on the horizon, I knew today was fucked.

At first, I'd told myself not to jump to conclusions. While the silhouette was familiar, it could have been *anyone's* mega-yacht. The Virgin Islands, both American and British, were full of the uber-rich this time of year. With the regatta taking place in Saint Thomas, plus all the American colleges giving the offspring of the pampered elite a week off, the islands were positively teeming with those who could afford such a luxury.

Hell, if I had more of an ego, Belle and I would have island-hopped on something similar. As it were, I much preferred my trusty little bowrider.

Perhaps mega-yachts had left a bad taste in my mouth, because the one person who I *knew* owned one had made my life a living hell for the last—oh, decade or two.

As I closed my laptop and sat up straighter on my lounge chair, squinting under the midmorning sun, there were a few blissful moments when I could pretend that yacht belonged to someone else.

Until it was within range for me to see the title painted across the side.

Big Dickie.

Because *Enormous Cock* was too obvious.

My jaw clenched as I set my things aside on Belle's towel. The water was calm today, but that monstrosity was too large to dock at the pier. I let out a long angsty sigh and stood at the sight of a familiar figure strolling out from the second covered deck.

Hands in my shorts pockets, shirtless, I scanned the shallows for Belle. Her head resurfaced a few moments later as she popped up briefly to wash out her goggles before diving back down, still unaware of the shitstorm headed our way.

It had been such a wonderful Sunday, too. We'd fucked first thing, with me slipping into her from behind after ages of sleepy, cozy foreplay, and then again in the shower. For the first time since she had arrived, Belle had consented to breakfast on the second-floor terrace. I'd been sure to position our chairs far from the railing, but it seemed her fear of heights had diminished a fraction, because she had been her usual carefree, gorgeous self, smiling and laughing and feeding me cantaloupe squares like this had been our life for years.

Unfortunately, Sundays also meant work—work that ol' Big Dickie over there ought to be doing himself, but instead he was here, flaunting his mega-yacht and hopping onto a little speedboat to come rain on my parade. While Belle did her thing, chasing after turtles and exploring the calm waters along Ixora's shoreline, I had plowed through emails, spreadsheets, and contracts for the last two hours. Give it another ten minutes and I'd have been ready to join her in the water, my own pair of fins and goggles waiting patiently beside my chair.

Well. So much for that.

I tracked Richard's speedboat as it peeled away from the yacht, darting back and forth, making waves unnecessarily —an echo of my brother's very existence. As per usual, he rode the thing too hard too quick; the engine would be shot before the end of this season, and it looked brand-new.

Belle's head breached the surface a little farther out than before, and my heart leapt into my throat—my brother was headed straight for her. Anxiety churned in my gut, and I hastily waved him to the left, stalking across the shoreline, beckoning him to follow. He did, eventually, after Belle zipped to the right, cutting through the water, waves sloshing in her face. The fear turned back to the usual angry knot, woven through years of frustration, that refused to leave me when it came to Richard. It was a miracle that it hadn't manifested into something physical; Richard could give anyone an ulcer—anyone who saw through his bullshit, that is.

The maroon and gold speedboat pushed right up onto the shore—and would require one of us to push it out when he was ready to leave.

Me, likely, while Richard sat in the driver's seat and barked orders.

A fair picture of our adult relationship.

"Hello, Deanie," my brother called when he cut the engine. After popping his black sunglasses atop his head of tousled brunet curls, he hopped out of the front seat, barefoot, and strode across the sand toward me. Arms crossed, I stayed right where I was.

"Richard." The surf surged after my brother, washing

away his footprints. Good. Richard had never set foot on Ixora before—I'd prefer to keep it that way.

While I was tall, Richard had always been taller. Leaner, his frame wiry but firm. My hair erred toward our mother's dark blonde, while Richard was a near replica of our father in his mid-thirties. He wore a white Lacoste tank and board shorts that matched his sleek maroon speedboat. The watch, which had belonged to our grandfather, was worth more than a house in suburbia and shouldn't be within a mile of the fucking water.

"You don't look happy to see me," Richard mused, drawling in our father's posh accent—like they'd just gotten off the phone. He then dragged me into a bone-crushing hug, my arms still folded across my chest.

"Should I be?"

Richard laughed, the sound deep and full like always, like he hadn't a care in the whole world, the sound accompanied by the faint aroma of beer.

"I'm surprised to see you functional," I remarked when he finally let go after holding me about fifteen seconds longer than necessary. It was a tactic; he did the same thing with handshakes. I took a few steps back up the beach, needing the distance, the slight elevation. "Isn't today your holy day?"

St. Patrick's Day. Not only were the islands crawling with regatta-goers and spring-breakers, but everyone would be out to celebrate the holiday—*especially* on the weekend. The carnage left on the streets tomorrow morning, empty plastic cups and crushed beer cans and discarded shamrock-shaped accessories, was reason enough for Belle and me to stay far, far away. Meanwhile, it genuinely shocked me that Richard wasn't buried in booze, coke, and a woman's cleavage by now.

In fact, he almost looked—functional. Not sober, not if his breath had anything to say about it, but he could fool the unobservant. He had been doing it his whole life.

"None of the good events start until two," my brother mused, sliding his hands into his pockets and rocking back and forth on his heels. "Figured I'd get business out of the way before pleasure."

I snorted, unable to help myself. *Business*? Like Richard had ever cared about our family's business. Sure, he enjoyed the privilege, the power, the prestige it offered, but when it came down to the nuts and bolts of the *business* itself? Ha.

The fact that I had been managing a large portion of his business this whole month spoke volumes to that.

"Ahh, and who is *this* gorgeous creature?" Richard turned on the spot, staring down Belle as she strolled out of the water, goggles on her head and flippers in hand. Glistening with seawater, she tossed both in the general direction of our belongings, the goggles managing to land on the towel. She looked positively adorable in her baby-pink bikini, which, mercifully, provided far more coverage than most in her closet. I didn't need Richard ogling her like a starved man eyeing his first meal in weeks.

In fact, when I cast him a sidelong glance, that was *exactly* the expression I expected to find. Instead, I found something else—something sharper, more *aware* than usual.

When he grinned at me, eyebrows lifting, the knot in my gut tightened. His smile straddled the line between smug and dangerous. I had the sudden urge to order Belle back to the house, up to her bedroom and out of sight.

She would do it if I told her to—but for some reason I couldn't.

Maybe I just wanted her by my side while I told Richard to get the fuck off my island.

What? One could dream.

"Belle," I said tightly, offering my hand as she padded across the surf, water rushing over her feet, "this is my brother Richard."

I went to her so that she wouldn't have to stand on the toasty dry sand. Our fingers threaded together, and I resisted the urge to dip her into a kiss that would make it obvious for anyone in a ten-mile radius that Belle was *mine*.

Richard's gaze crept across her figure, obvious as sin. To her credit, she didn't shy away. In fact, Belle stood next to me with her head held high, even under my brother's pervy perusing, her shoulders back.

"Oh, hi. Nice to meet you." She didn't offer him her hand, but she did flash a brilliant smile—one I realized in a heartbeat was fake. When we first started all this, I had tried to discern between the phony and the genuine expressions. Escorts needed to act their way through most client interactions, and I so enjoyed Belle because she didn't. As much as I had tried to memorize her reactions, all the varieties of smiles she had in her arsenal, I hadn't been as sure as I would have liked to be when all this started. By now, I just assumed they were all real for me.

Rightly so.

Because this smile, this phony, forced, too-wide smile that didn't reach her eyes—it was an obvious fake. To me, at least. Richard, accustomed to women fawning over him, seemed to lap it right up.

"Belle—a pleasure." He swooped in to kiss her cheek, which Belle offered, but she didn't move forward to meet him. Not so much as a step.

My hand tightened around hers. She squeezed back.

Richard, meanwhile, had pulled his sunglasses off his head and was currently running a hand through his chocolate-brown curls—a move that highlighted a toned bicep. Belle's lips twitched, her smile stretching wider.

"And we worried that Deanie came out here all by himself for two months," he said, chuckling, "like some hermit, or a disgraced celebrity the tabloids froth after."

"Well, you would know the tabloids, Dick."

My brother smirked. "Haven't seen any strange boats around, have you?"

"Just yours," I replied tersely.

"Oh!" Belle shifted so that she stood partially in front of me, our clasped hands resting on the small of her back. She wrung out her braid's tail with the other hand, water dribbling on my brother's toes. "Are you visiting for Dean's birthday?"

For the first time since he'd stepped onto my beach, Richard faltered. His slightly pursed, I'm-a-model-in-my-spare-time look fell, replaced with a blank, clueless expression that had me rolling my eyes.

He'd forgotten.

He'd fucking *forgotten* that I'd turned thirty-one just two days ago. Even our father had managed to send an email from his office account—Adelaide had done a video message with Mum and the cats.

True to form, Richard recovered from his brief fumble like it never happened. That sharp grin returned as he stared down his nose at Belle, one hand fisted around his sunglasses.

"Well, not exactly, but we spoke on the day, of course."

"Of course," she said curtly.

Belle's smile turned pinched, as if biting the insides of her cheeks, and I held in a chuckle. My birthday had been a nonstop sex romp. After she had finished the cake, which had been a touch heavy-handed with the lemon but still perfectly edible, I'd insisted she nap for a few hours. She'd need her strength for the day ahead, and by god I'd milked every last ounce of it from her. While I had only climaxed a handful of times, Belle had struggled to walk by nightfall, her legs jelly and her ass cherry red—beautiful. Just stunning, from head to toe. We'd eaten her cake under the stars, nestled together on a huge beach blanket, pillows piled high, surrounded by empty champagne bottles. It had been my best birthday *ever*.

And if Richard had actually called me, I imagined that wouldn't have been the case.

Not that he would have done it, mind you. I couldn't remember the last time we'd even spoken on the phone.

"I'd hoped we could have a chat, Deanie," my brother said, smoothly transitioning from the mildly irked playboy —perhaps at the discovery that he couldn't charm Belle as easily as the rest—to the haughty martyr in the blink of an eye. "I've been *drowning* in work lately, as I'm sure you're well aware, and I thought that maybe we could figure something out, something a little more permanent, while I'm here."

I ground my teeth together, releasing Belle's hand lest I crush it. *He* had been *drowning* in work? I was the one who had been doing his damn work, taking *hours* out of my Sundays just to get through it so hotel GMs would stop sending me panicked emails, so my father would stop demanding I cut my vacation short and come back to fix the fallout of the stupidest decision he had ever made.

"Actually," I said, forcing myself to release the anger with a sharp exhale, "Belle and I have a lunch we need to get ready for in Saint Croix. It starts in an hour, so—"

"That little dinghy can get to *Saint Croix* from here?" Richard nodded toward my bowrider, smirking. "I can always give you a lift, if you need it, Deanie. Seas are looking choppy today."

"They were pretty calm before you—" Belle caught herself, donning that beautiful fake smile again. "—before your yacht arrived. Smooth as far as the eye could see. Looks pretty nice now, too."

My brother hummed as he offered her the same look he might give a waitress who'd just told him his card had been declined—because it was maxed out. Again.

"Well, if you'll excuse me," I muttered, stalking off, unable to stomach him a second longer. Honestly, the fucking *nerve*—showing up here and expecting me to, what, offer to take *more* work off his hands? What the fuck did he even do with his day?

I needn't ever ask; I knew the answer. I'd known the answer to that question since we were teenagers.

"We'll talk more at the gala then, eh?" Richard's voice cut across the soothing rustle of palm fronds. I stilled, then faced him with a scowl. The gala loomed in the very near future, a yearly event I was always forced to attend to shill our father's next big idea, to network with the upper echelon of the business elite, to be photographed with all the *it* women in the society pages, and to put a cool, composed face to the Donahue brand name. Given I'd been running the bulk of our hotel empire in the Mediterranean these last seven years, my appearance had been mandatory.

That was Richard's arena now.

Yet somehow, I was still expected to go.

Belle slowly picked her way along the beach after me, arms crossed, frowning. Behind her, Richard wore a look I knew well—a look the said he recognized he'd just fucked up my day and got some sick thrill out of it. He shrugged, half turned back toward his speedboat.

"I assume you're going," he remarked. "Dad will be disappointed if you don't at least show your face."

I stuffed my hands into my pockets to keep them from balling into fists. "We'll see. Belle and I have other commitments that night."

My eyes narrowed as Richard laughed, slowly backing into the surf.

"Put in the *bare* minimum, Deanie. I know you're on holiday, but the empire stops for no one."

Oh, I could just hit him.

Outrage flashed through me like a dozen lightning bolts cracking all at once across a tempestuous sky. Me, do the *bare* minimum? I swallowed my rage, forcing my expression to remain neutral as Richard waved us both off and started to push the speedboat out. Belle stood between us, her arms still crossed, and watched him go. Meanwhile, a high-pitched whine had started between my ears, and my jaw ached from gritting it so hard.

I hadn't wanted Belle to see this side of me—the horrible, petty, childish side of me that reared its ugly head whenever my older brother made an appearance in my life. At family functions, I could avoid him, sometimes using our sister as a buffer. Given I'd been the one managing most of the empire he'd mentioned, we seldom ran in the same social circles, either. Generally, I could forget Richard even existed.

Until he thrust himself into my orbit again, reminding me why I avoided him in the first place.

Scowling, I marched up the beach, not breaking stride when Belle called for me, and headed for the trail back to the house.

"Dean!" She chased after me, my name echoing through the trees, and while I slowed, I didn't stop. I needed to move. I needed to expend this pulsing, racing *energy* pounding through my veins, threatening to slam one of my fists into a palm trunk.

Her soft footfalls squished along the path, but before I could tell her to give me space, to just go back to the beach —or inside, or wherever she wanted to go, because technically I couldn't order her around on Sundays—Belle caught me. Her delicate hand snagged my elbow, the slight pressure behind it making me stop. I huffed, glowering down the trail, palms and shrubbery blocking the house. This needed to be tended to; I hadn't had the landscapers out since we'd arrived. It was getting overrun.

"Hey," she murmured. When I didn't yield, didn't turn around as she tugged on my arm, Belle darted in front of me, threw herself around my neck, and hugged tight.

Not a word uttered, she just held me, her whole body blanketing mine. She squeezed—and suddenly the need to *move*, to run, melted away. My heart still hammered in its cage, but I could breathe freely again, the ringing between my ears gone. Burying my face in the nape of her neck, her skin sticky with sea salt and sweat, I wrapped around her and hugged back.

She stroked the back of my head. Her fingers whispered down my neck. At no point did she try to pull away, even though I knew I was holding her too tight, embracing her like I thought she'd die if I didn't. Only when my pulse evened out did I ease away, my hands still resting on her hips, my jaw aching.

A very real, very breathtaking smile crossed her lips, and she cupped my face with both hands. "Hi."

I kissed each palm. "Hi."

"You can talk to me—if you want," Belle said, eyebrows flickering up, the wind playing with her flyaways. "Remember? I can listen."

"I *want* to tell you—"

"So, tell me." She moved in closer, our hips finding each other. Her hands smoothed down my throat, my chest, then knotted together over my heart. "What's been going on this month? You're working so much more than you did before, and I know it's stressing you out."

"Work doesn't stress me out," I muttered, casting a dark look toward the water. "*Richard* stresses me out. My father stresses me out."

"Talk to me."

And as those royal blues bored into mine—I did. I told her everything. How I had been forced to step in seven years ago, after Richard had almost run four of our most prominent hotels into the ground. Mismanagement of funds. Allowing his enormous circle of leeches to stay for free, to drink resorts dry. Bad publicity everywhere; the Donahue name had taken a serious beating over Richard's very public shenanigans with women, with alcohol. Our father had spent a fortune paying off the man my brother beat to a bloody pulp in a blackout rage. While he'd never killed anyone, his DUI count was in the double digits across numerous countries; all of those had to be bought out, too.

I had only been twenty-three, barely out of university, barely a man, when my father shuffled the familial responsibilities around like I had thirty years of experience behind me. Suddenly I was responsible for *lives*. I was responsible for over five hundred staff members across four hotels, and I was desperate to shoulder the burden of Richard's failures, desperate to fix what my brother had broken for the sake of my mum's heartache and my father's headache.

Desperate to prove that I wasn't just the boy who had spent much of his childhood doodling—that I had more worth than that.

I learned on my feet. I hired smart. I implemented new procedures, effectively erasing the useless ones enacted under Richard's regime. Meanwhile, my father told everyone Richard had to step back for his health. He shipped him off to rehab clinics around the world, the best and most costly. I understood addiction was an illness, a disease, but my brother could stop. He could go cold turkey whenever it suited him, whenever he needed to sell the lie to someone—a doctor, a therapist, our parents—that he was well again and could be responsible for his own affairs, for his trust fund. When he was in the clear, out came the alcohol, the drugs, the women, the posse of yes-men who lived for my brother's every word.

Had I not done what I did, had my father and I not put our heads together and *worked* seven years ago, our hotels could have gone under. Instead, we thrived.

Then, eight months ago, my father had called me into his office and told me Richard was ready to step into his old job.

"He's really grown and matured," he had insisted when I started to protest. "He's ready."

Richard wasn't *ready*—my brother's finances had just needed padding, and my salary would add all the cushion necessary to ramp up his lifestyle. I had fought against it. If he really *had* grown, matured, seen the light, *whatever*, then I would have welcomed Richard into the business. I had enough going on in my professional life that I could step back and still have a very full plate.

But I knew then that he was going to fuck it all up. Undo years of blood, sweat, and tears that I had poured into our empire.

I'd refused. I wouldn't sign a damn thing. I threatened to tell our investors, our board of directors, anyone who would listen, the truth about Richard. I'd start a fucking petition if I had to if it meant keeping jobs safe and our hotel reputation untarnished.

And then my father told me that he knew.

He knew that I was a client at Elysium, despite the NDAs all members signed. He knew enough about my preferences for it to disgust him—just enough that when he threatened to out me, to cause a scandal, I had no other choice. Our investors wouldn't trust some pervert handling their money. Richard might have still been a party boy, but he kept the worst of his vices out of the press. Most accepted his extracurriculars.

Father wanted me to step back. Become a silent partner in the family business. Let Richard take the reins again—let Richard lead.

And if I didn't, he'd tell the world I liked to spend my spare time at a seedy fetish club in Manhattan, that I was some abusive asshole who hated women, who whipped them, choked them, to get off.

The truth wouldn't matter.

Deep down, he must have known Richard wasn't ready; why else would he threaten me? He used the business savvy he was known for, showed me why he was a shark. I'd been fucking blackmailed out of a job that I loved by my own father—just so his firstborn could have the spotlight again.

I'd eventually stepped down without a fuss, told people I wanted to focus on personal projects. I became the silent partner, literally, having barely spoken to either Richard or our father in months. When it was all over, I had Belle. The day we left New York marked the end of my brother's first month in my old position—and already they had all been clamoring for me back.

My father held out the longest.

Now that I had folded, because, despite everything, I still cared for him, for the Donahue name, he was demanding I clean up Richard's mess again. He hadn't apologized either, and like a schmuck, I'd been correcting my brother's mistakes for the last few Sundays.

Because I was weak. My family had always made me weak.

The only person I wanted to be weak for was Belle.

When I finally finished the entire story, start to end, I was lightheaded, my mouth dry, my throat tight. Belle hadn't interrupted once, though her incredulousness, her disgust, had played openly across her features. A part of me was ashamed to admit that I had bowed to my father's wishes again after everything, but I couldn't keep it from her anymore. She had wanted me to talk, so I did.

Maybe I had just talked myself right out of her life.

The whine returned between my ears as I waited. My hands had slipped back into my pockets at some point, allowing her the space to retreat if she so desired.

Much to my surprise, Belle pressed closer, her arms around my neck again.

"I don't like him very much," she said. I let out a breathy chuckle.

"Which him?"

She wrinkled her nose. "Both."

"Yes, well, I don't like them much either these days." Yet here I was, doing exactly what they wanted. Pathetic. Where the fuck was my spine? I looked away, unable to meet her gaze—until she stood up on her toes so that we were nearly at eye level.

"Dean, you are a fixer," she told me firmly, weaving her fingers into my hair. "You're a caregiver and a problem-solver. You're happy making other people happy. I've known that from our, like, fourth coffee date."

I forced a weak smile; I really didn't deserve her trying to rationalize my lack of a backbone. "Belle—"

"And your dad and your brother are taking advantage of that. They're taking advantage of *you*," she continued, speaking over me, her gaze strong—unflinching. "I don't want you to be upset with yourself because—because *they* are playing on these qualities that make you such a good, warm, kind, wonderful man. Okay?"

My eyebrows shot up. Was my submissive really giving me a speech about being too hard on myself? My lips twitched, yearning to stretch into a patronizing smile, but I put a stop to that and swallowed the laugh bubbling up my throat too.

As much as I wanted to dismiss the notion, to call it absurd, to insist I was being *just* hard enough on myself, I didn't. Belle wouldn't have said what she had if she hadn't meant it. During our scenes, she said what she needed to, what I told her to—only this wasn't a scene. She was still my submissive, but I wasn't holding *all* the reins. She was free to speak her mind, and she always did. Belle had a knack for making her opinion known without hammering me over the head with it.

And above all, I respected Belle's opinion. I respected *her*.

So, maybe, just maybe, there was some truth to all this. Maybe I hadn't *just* been putting in the hours required of me. Maybe I hadn't worked myself to the bone all these years because I loved my family—but because they had found a way to manipulate me.

"What they did to you is awful," she continued, wearing the same expression she had when she'd told me that Richard burning my paintings had been psychotic. My submissive wore her passion, her shock, out in the open when we were alone.

"Yes, well..." I was a grown man. A big boy. In theory, I could have put an end to it. But then again, if we were looking at this retrospectively—a man with a joint business-law degree from Harvard should have seen what was going on all these years. I should have seen what my father was doing to me, my brother, but my love for them and my desire to make them proud, to be the uncomplicated son, had blinded me.

My shoulders slumped. Did that make me a good man—or a feeble one?

"I'm so sorry that they put you through that." She wobbled a little, still up on her tiptoes. In an instant, all my thoughts of weakness vanished, and it was just Belle and me again, alone on this island. I snaked an arm around her waist, taking the weight off her poor toes.

"It's all right. I found my balm in you." My gaze swept across her face—across those sumptuous pink lips, the freckly constellations on her cheeks, the depths of her royal blues. "You have made all this much more tolerable."

Her cheeks coloured, and she pulled me into a kiss. Before I could deepen it, slip my tongue between those heavenly lips, she broke away, her eyes sad. "I don't want you to have to tolerate it."

I opened and closed my mouth a few times, a handful of snarky comments at the ready. Instead, I set her down with a smile, hands drifting to her hips again, and shook my head. "Neither do I."

Honesty. I hadn't been so open in years. Not even to my mum, who had always said I worked too hard, or to my baby sister, who complained that I was never around, that I was always busy, always stressed.

Frowning, I pressed a quick kiss to Belle's forehead, then pulled her in for another hug. As she gripped me back, arms wrapped around my torso, head nestled under my chin, I couldn't help but feel as though a weight had been lifted off my shoulders. When I opened my eyes again, the world seemed a whole lot brighter—and a whole lot simpler.

I didn't exist on this planet to work. I didn't deserve to die at my desk one day, the whole empire on my back.

I existed for this—for the little moments, for the love of a good woman.

For family too, but not a family who shoved me down and swanned across my broken body.

"And this gala?" she asked when she pulled away. We stood facing one another still, but our hands had twined together, hanging between us. Rolling my eyes, I gave her a very basic rundown of my responsibilities at the yearly event, emphasizing that now it was technically Richard's job, but I couldn't imagine him doing it. My brother could be a great face for the company, handsome and strong, the kind of man women swooned over and men aspired to be—until he opened his mouth.

"Well, why don't we just go and have a good time?"

This time, I let my incredulous laugh loose. "What?"

"Yeah," Belle said, shrugging, her cheeks still stained pink. "We'll get dressed up, eat some good food, dance—make a date night out of it."

A date night? We'd had playdates so far, many of them,

but a *date* night—somehow that seemed more intimate, even without the bondage.

"That way, your dad can't say jack about not showing your face," Belle continued, sounding giddier by the moment. "You can shake some hands, crack some jokes— but Richard will be the one to schmooze and sell and network and whatever. We can just have fun. Let him know that he didn't faze you today, that you aren't doing his job anymore."

Logic told me to agree. Self-preservation insisted I stand up for myself.

But my heart—it wasn't quite so eager to jump on board. Leaving Richard to his own devices could spell doom for my family's hotel empire. I wasn't sure if I could fully let go of that—if I could step back and watch my brother tank everything that I had worked so hard to rebuild.

Belle squeezed my hand, gently, curiously, and tilted her head to the side as she said, "Come on... It'll be fun."

I squeezed back. The night *would* be much more pleasant if I endured it with Belle. She had a knack for lifting my spirits, making me smile—grounding me.

"So, what you're saying," I started, eyes narrowing, "is that you are *willingly* throwing yourself to the trust-fund wolves?"

"This trust-fund wolf isn't so bad," she whispered as she leaned in, her grin turning impish—then innocent when I fixed her with my best stern Dom look. "Yes, of course I'll go with you. I didn't exactly pack for some upscale gala, but I'm sure I can swing something from my wardrobe."

I snorted. As much as *I* enjoyed all of Belle's lingerie and sheer dresses, she hadn't a thing to wear to something of this caliber. Still, I was certain Felix had a formalwear line this year—one phone call and I could easily fill a whole guest room with gowns.

"We'll figure something out," I told her, mind racing —*fixing*, solving the problem on the spot. She was so right: I always had been a fixer, tackling unforeseen issues before anyone else even realized they existed. And I *was* my happiest here, taking care of Belle, making her feel good, safe, adored—making her smile.

In that moment, as she peered up at me, positively glowing, I wanted to say it.

I love you.

I loved her for all that she did for me, to me, with me. I loved her for all that she was and all that she would be. I loved her so desperately that it ached, that it burned deep within, consuming me from the inside out.

Belle was the woman, the submissive, the partner I had never realized I needed.

All this, dancing on the tip of my tongue, and the best I could muster was a kiss. Soft and sweet, I pressed my mouth to hers, then murmured my thanks against it. Her eyes wide and bright, Belle peered deep into mine. Did she see it—the love? Did she spy it simmering just below the surface, how much I adored every single fucking facet of her?

She sighed dreamily when I cupped her face, my large hands caging her, my kiss engulfing her when our mouths opened. The heat spread, a wildfire raging between us, connecting us, forging us together in all this. Our kiss intensified, no longer soft and sweet. Harsh. Biting. All-consuming. My submissive whimpered, her body crashing to mine—a perfect fit.

Her delighted little squeal when I hoisted her up, wrapping her legs around me, only had my cock hardening faster. Hands cupping her ass, I swallowed every sound she made on the march back to the house. Her giggles. Her gasps. Her squeaks. Her moans.

While I hadn't been able to tell her just how deeply I loved her, I could damn well show her.

And I did—with a hand around her throat, tangled in her hair, between her thighs, I showed Belle Bennet exactly how I much I loved her, worshipped her. Over the dining table. On the stairs. In my bed.

Our bed.

I showed her over and over again, until neither of us could *move*, much less speak—until all my concerns about Richard, about our family's empire, at long last disappeared.

HOUSE RULE #3

Belle will be herself—or as much herself as she is comfortable being.

9

BELLE & DEAN

Monday, March 18th: BELLE

"You know, sir, it's kind of hard to focus on *anything* when you're doing—that."

Dean hummed in agreement, his voice low and velvety in my ear. "Ah, sweetheart, that's the *point*."

He circled my clit, then swept across it for emphasis, and my body jerked, twitched, *danced* on his lap, heat spiking in my core. Unfortunately, for every pleasurable wiggle I made, there was pain, too, my bare breasts bouncing—the nipple clamps doing their dark work.

"Anything else on this page?" he murmured, dragging his nose from my ear down the column of my throat. My skin prickled, responding to the featherlight touch eagerly as Dean's hand continued its languid assault between my thighs.

Right. The page. Frowning, I refocused on the computer monitor, fifty dresses to skim through. Felix Renaldi, Dean's fashion designer pal and fellow Dom, had several collections of gowns that I had been ordered to peruse in preparation for the gala next week. Rather than assigning me a task and then doing work of his own at his office computer, Dean had forgone his work entirely in favor of this: he'd pulled me onto his lap, naked, and told me to add whatever dresses I liked to the cart. Then, he would send the list off to his assistant so she could pull samples from Felix's showroom in Manhattan and fly them down here for me to try on—all in the span of about two days.

Initially I'd thought it was a bit much. After all, there were plenty of local designers on the nearby islands I could pick through if I *really* needed a dress this fancy.

But then I discovered Felix's gowns—and I was a goner.

Together, Dean and I narrowed down the search preferences. Formalwear. Couture. Floor-length. Pink, white, gold. For the last half hour, I had been going through all the options that left me drooling. Felix's designs were exquisite. He didn't shy away from lace, tulle, cashmere, silk, brocade. There was something for every woman, despite the outrageous price tags, and it was obvious that he knew how to flatter the female form.

I could have lost myself in his website, spent hours magnifying details, admiring the tailoring—if Dean hadn't added the nipple clamps, then slipped his hand between my thighs. At first, I hadn't been able to see anything beyond the pain. My nipples weren't overly sensitive, but the clamps induced a sharp ache that I felt with every breath. It wasn't until Dean started to stroke me, his fingers familiar with every inch of my body, that I was able to push past the pain.

But then the pleasure had started to mount, paired with the bite of the clamps...

How the heck was I supposed to focus on *dresses*, no matter how beautiful?

"I-I like this one," I said, swallowing hard when he

smeared my arousal over my folds. A gentle tap at my inner thigh had me parting them more, and Dean trailed my slickness down there too.

"Yes, you would look beautiful in that. Put it in the cart."

With a trembling hand, I tapped the touchscreen monitor, adding the peach-coloured gown with its lace-up corset and mermaid-cut skirt and ample front slit to the eighteen other dresses we had already agreed on.

"Good girl," Dean crooned in my ear, and my eyes fluttered closed, my hands death-gripping his sleek black desk. Even fully clothed, the heat of his body burned me, and I felt so little on his lap, so small and pretty. Like a little doll for him to fuss over.

Let's be honest: I'd been wet from the moment I perched on his knee. Wetter still when he yanked me back against him. His cock had grown harder and harder against my backside, and when all this was through, I so hoped he would bend me over the desk and do something about it.

The thought had me moaning, and I fell back, his chin tucked over my shoulder, totally splayed open as my sir stroked me, massaged me, tormented me so perfectly. When he found that *one* spot, just to the right of my clit, that always sent me spiraling, I clamped down on my lip and whimpered. The heat soared within me, between us. My breath quickened, and I reached behind, the leather of his high-backed chair groaning under my fingertips.

"Oh, *sir*—"

So much hazy, wonderful pleasure—and then *blinding pain* when he flicked one of my nipples. I jolted up with a long, low whine, one that arced into a squeal when he slipped two fingers into me.

"Not until you've looked at *all* the dresses, Belle," he

chastised. Tears in my eyes, I turned back to him, about to argue, about to beg him to stop pumping his fingers over my G-spot, but then thought better of it. I did *not* want another nipple flick.

But there were fifteen pages of dresses to get through, and I was so, so, so, *so* close.

Not that that mattered. Dean expected restraint.

And I was his good girl—most of the time.

So, with a groan, I returned my attention to the monitor, to the dozens more dresses on this page alone that I could choose from.

Only to squeal-cry again when, paired with the thrust of his fingers, Dean swept his thumb rapidly across my clit and raked his teeth up my neck...

Tuesday, March 19th: DEAN

Thwack.

Belle stood up on her toes with a high-pitched cry, most of it muffled by the neon-pink ball gag between her lips. I kept myself at a distance, admiring the lovely flush blooming along the side of her breast—no nipple clamps today, and fuck, did those gorgeous peaks ever stand at attention. Moaning, she dropped her head forward, chest heaving with each ragged breath.

Slowly, each step precise so that she could hear the *click* of my oxfords on the tile, I circled her, loosely grasping the riding crop at my side. We had only been at this for twenty minutes, but already my darling little submissive was painted up with marks. Her ass. Her thighs. Her breasts. Her hips. The bottoms of her feet, which, given the spreader bar, had been difficult to manage, but we'd figured it out. Belle had simply needed to grasp the rope binding her hands high above her head, lift herself up for just a moment, and then *thwack*—right on the soles.

So far, her breasts and inner thighs had coaxed the best sounds out of her. I paused directly behind her, then gently tapped the crop's leather tip against her right ass cheek. Her head shot up, her body tensed. I circled the area with whispery caresses, then dipped between her cheeks. She arched for me, the minx, offering her perky ass as a sacrifice, but I went for her inner thighs again with two sharp, exacting hits. Belle squealed, standing up on her toes once more.

"Down," I barked. And down she went. Smirking, I stroked my erection through my slacks. Physical release wasn't the goal today. This afternoon's session was just a bit of fun with the riding crop—although there was always room for a spur-of-the-moment burst of creativity that would somehow involve Belle's lips around my cock.

I'd gone shirtless so that when we were through I could cradle her naked figure directly to my skin. She could feel my heartbeat, slow and reassuring, and calm down in the safety of my arms.

For now, however, I enjoyed the way her greedy eyes raked across my figure—a figure I worked on for at least an hour a day, just to keep it toned for her. Belle enjoyed my definition; her fingers explored the dips and curves of my body in bed, sometimes before we drifted off to sleep, sometimes first thing in the morning, sleepy but insistent.

I'd tied her to a hook I'd had installed in my office. She hadn't noticed it until now, and I hadn't made use of it yet, but today: ropes around her wrists, stretched up to the ceiling, and then the spreader bar between her feet, nothing but naked Belle in between.

She was to *die* for. I'd gotten hard just tying her in place.

And she'd been wet by the third *thwack* of the riding crop, her cunt glistening for me in the late-afternoon light streaming in from the windows.

The spreader bar had been a late addition, but I had wanted to remove its stain by introducing it to her again— properly. Set out in front of her on a towel were all the vibrators we had in the house. I'd told her that if she was a very good girl and took all her strikes, then I'd let her choose the vibrator she wanted to come all over. The lovely creature was partial to the magic wand, and if she made it through the next fifteen minutes, I'd plug it in and massage the vibrating head against her clit until she shattered.

Still strung up, of course. Still bound in place, legs spread wide for me.

I struck the backs of her knees twice in rapid succession before strolling around in front. Tears streaked down her flushed cheeks, her eyes red. Holding her stare, I smoothed the tip of the riding crop along her belly, then slowly rubbed it against the crest of her pussy. She let out a stuttering breath, nostrils flaring, and then screamed—*fuck* what a gorgeous, muffled scream—when I smacked the crop against her wet lips. Not too sharply, not too harshly, but her cunt was probably so primed for any sensation now that even the slightest touch would be torture.

And I gave her the slightest smack six times in as many seconds before retreating. Each damp *thwack* of the crop elicited another scream. When it was over, her head fell back, her body sagging.

"Belle?" I had told her to pull her blonde waves into a ponytail today. Not only did I enjoy having something to wrench her head back with, but I wanted to see her face—to drink in her pleasure, her pain, but to also gauge when she was pushing herself too far. We had tested her verbal and nonverbal safewords already, but she had been open to *more* lately. Sharper hits. Larger plugs. Breath play.

I had to make sure she wasn't going too hard too fast— either to please me, or to prove to herself that she could.

Tucking the riding crop under my arm, I strolled over and lifted her head up. Her eyes were closed, her expression slack, but she seemed to come back to me when I undid her gag's clasp. I held the wet gag in one hand, Belle's saliva-coated chin with the other.

"Are you all right?" I made sure to stay in my Dom space, my tone neither warm nor friendly—but my intention genuine. She licked the dribble off her lips, breath stuttering again as she nodded.

And then *smiled*. Wide and beautiful and yielding, that smile reached her eyes—made them shimmer, even as tears rolled down her cheeks.

"I'm fine, sir," she whispered.

"Your hands?"

"Only a little numb."

"Can you make it the next fifteen minutes?" I checked on their colour—all looked well. "Or shall I bind them behind your back instead?"

"I can make it, sir," she told me softly, sweetly. I made a note to check on her again in five minutes, just in case, then brushed my thumb across her chin—not to wipe the drool away, but to smear it around more. Belle nibbled her lower lip for a moment, and then murmured something so quiet I missed it.

"What was that?"

"You can go harder, sir," she repeated, raising her hoarse

voice above a whisper. Her eyes glittered, but, for the first time, I noticed they glittered with darkness, with sin, with a depravity to match my own. Smirking, I reattached her gag, then took a step back and stroked the underside of each of her breasts with the crop.

"Are you ready, sweetheart?" I asked, tapping one breast, then the other, back and forth. She mumbled something, something that vaguely sounded like *yes, sir,* from behind the gag. I grinned, enjoying the way her skin rose with gooseflesh, her nipples tight little pearls.

"That's my girl..."

Thwack.

Wednesday, March 20*th*: BELLE

"I feel like a cupcake."

"Well, you look like a princess." Dean's executive assistant Eliza, who was sporting an asymmetrical bob and a stunning Chanel pantsuit, studied me for a long moment, her hands on her hips, lips pursed, and then nodded. "I mean, it *is* a bit poofy—"

I pushed down on the four-foot-wide skirt, a skirt that had fairy lights and a battery pack hidden amongst all the tulle. The fabric yielded, then sprang back up, propped in place by the mesh wiring underneath. We both stared at my reflection in the floor-length mirror, Eliza's expression suggesting this was a possibility—and mine screaming no way in hell.

Just as he had planned, two days after Dean and I picked through the hundreds of gowns on Felix Renaldi's website, the chosen forty had made their way to Ixora Isle courtesy of Dean's assistant. Poor Eliza was twig-thin and *maybe* pushing five foot two, but she had wrangled the entire collection down here from Manhattan. Flying in Dean's private jet and having four assistants of her own probably made the process easier, but it still seemed like a huge ordeal for nothing.

After all, I still believed I could have just gone to one of the boutiques on Saint Thomas and found a dress for this snooty gala there—but Dean wouldn't have it. So, here we were, in one of the unused guest bedrooms, which had been transformed into a Renaldi formalwear showroom. Four racks of gowns awaited me, some of which I didn't even remember choosing—like this one.

But then again, I hadn't exactly been coherent for a lot of the selection process. Nipple clamps and denied orgasms had a way of distracting a girl.

"Do you still want to show Mr. Donahue?" Eliza asked, head cocked as she stood behind me, fluffing out the enormous skirt. It wasn't a terrible dress: the bodice cinched around my waist and gave me great cleavage. Dusky rose *was* a great colour for my complexion. But that skirt. I wasn't even sure how to walk in it—Eliza had helped me climb in, then laced up the back while I'd stood there, horrified.

Thankfully, Dean had waived the *no panties* house rule today. I couldn't imagine the look on Eliza's face if she had to help her boss's half-naked sex friend in and out of dresses all day.

"I'll show him," I said after a moment's consideration. I'd show him, but only for a laugh. If he liked this—we might have problems. After all, his opinion really mattered to me. Next week, we were stepping into *his* world, and I wanted to look appropriate. The social elite would already be making snap judgements about me on Dean's arm; no point in adding fuel to that fire by looking woefully out of place courtesy of my fashion choices, too.

"Can you walk?"

The mesh boning under the thousand layers of tulle actually helped my mobility, keeping the bulk of the enormous skirt out of the way. I still had to kick at it with each step, but I managed, waddling out of the guest room and into the hall. This was dress eight of forty, and we had been at it nearly an hour already. Dean and I had agreed that I still hadn't found The One yet, but I dreaded the thought of spending the next four to five hours working my way through the rest of the gowns. Eliza had already peeled off the tailored jacket of her pantsuit, a thin sheen of sweat broken out across her face.

Who knew trying on clothes could be so exhausting?

Maybe we could take a pool break before lunch. Dean had acknowledged that this would be an all-day affair at breakfast, and back then I'd just laughed. All day to try on dresses? Was he crazy?

Nope. Just realistic, as always, when it came to time management.

I'd felt bad at first that he was sacrificing a day of our usual fun for me to try on gowns, but the look in his eye when I'd walked into his office wearing the first form-fitting dress, complete with a plunging neckline *and* back—well, that dark hunger had suggested he really didn't mind me playing dress-up.

The hunger had dissipated over the last hour, the novelty wearing off, but he still offered a thoughtful critique of each dress, stopping whatever he was doing to give me his full attention.

This dress wouldn't need much of his time.

The dress announced my arrival, swishing along with

each step, and Dean glanced up the second I squeezed through his office doorway. I stopped in the middle of the room, under the hook he'd hung me from yesterday, and blew the bits of hair that had escaped my bun out of my face.

"So..."

His lips twitched, as if fighting back a laugh. "Wow."

"Yeah." I pushed down the material again, watching it bounce up as Dean stood from behind his dual monitors. "I don't remember adding this to the cart."

"I thought it was a bit questionable at the time, but I let it slide."

"*Sir*. In what *universe* would I wear this—"

"You look a bit like a cupcake," he said thoughtfully, tipping his head side to side as he appraised me. My cheeks warmed: apparently we were riding the same brainwave.

I loved that—being so in tune with him. We'd had plenty of those moments lately, and while they were most powerful during our play sessions, my stomach erupted with little butterflies whenever it happened in our free time.

Gathering the giant skirt in both hands, I sidled up to his desk, grinning, and leaned over to kiss him. Just a quick peck—he had wanted to keep us *very* vanilla with all these assistants in the house; Eliza's four lackeys had even set up a makeshift command center for their usual responsibilities at the dining table downstairs. When I pulled away, Dean's brows shot up, his smile curious.

"*I* thought I looked like a cupcake too," I murmured with a giggle. "I'm going to say this one's a no."

Dean gave me a very serious, very studious nod. "Agreed."

Still blushing up a storm, I practically floated back to the door. At some point, what had started as a job had turned into paradise, into a dream I never wanted to wake up from.

Even the mean voices at the back of my mind had finally shut up.

"The next one will be better," I insisted, waddling around the corner, then leaned back to shoot him a smile. "Promise."

"I can't wait, sweetheart..."

Thursday, March 21st: BELLE

I couldn't see.

Even without the blindfold, the world was a blur around me. My gaze darted about, frantic, teary, unfocused. The sun —too bright. All the white furniture blended together. My chest heaved. Gasping. I couldn't breathe. I couldn't get enough *air*.

"Belle?" Like velvet, like honey. Like rich, smooth chocolate. Like the glow of a new day, just as the sun crested the horizon. "Sweetheart?"

And in the chaos, there was him. Dean. My Dominant. *Sir*. I sought him out—that voice, that comfort. Naked and shaking, my hands groped into the bright void, desperate for him.

Sage green. I found him. Those eyes. I saw them first, clearly, in brilliant focus. Flecks of gold in the afternoon sunshine. A hint of grey—lingering darkness from our scene.

No more frantic searching.

Just him.

I stared into those eyes, my breath coming easier now, in deeper gasps, filling my lungs, then leaving in long and slow exhales. He was doing it too—breathing with me. Was I mirroring him, or the other way around?

We fell into a rhythm, a familiar song, staring into one another, inhaling one another. My hands found his bare chest, the dip of his pectorals, my marble Adonis.

I blinked. The room came back into focus. We had played in the first-floor lounge today. The blindfold sat on the glass coffee table. Beside it, the leather switch, the vibrator, the gag, the plug, the clamps. Thick, squishy carpet cushioned my legs, my butt. Silence all around us, save for the drumbeat of my heart.

Slowly, Dean eased me onto his lap. I went willingly, happily, his pliant little submissive. As my cheek pressed to his skin, I closed my eyes, forcing the tears out again. They fell, brushing across my skin and his. Still shaking. Still —breathing.

Subspace. He had called this subspace.

It was terrifying and beautiful. I craved it. I feared it. I plunged into it with my eyes open.

He stroked my hair, murmuring soft comforts against my shoulder, my neck, my cheek.

"Tell me where you're at," he said—a gentle inquiry, a delicate command. My lids lifted, but heavily this time. Hands limp in my lap, I took in our surroundings. The white couch. The glass walls. The palms outside. When I came back to Dean, I nuzzled under his chin, finally able to move —but only just so.

Tell him where I was at?

I was naked and bruised.

But *euphoric*.

Tell him where I was at—I was in love with him. Didn't he know? I tipped my head back, staring into the sage. Couldn't he see?

An exhausted sort of cackle-snort slipped out of me, and I closed my eyes when he pressed his lips to my temple.

It was insane.

Loving a man who reduced me to this—this weeping, aching mess of a woman.

A woman who truly felt *free* for the first time in her life. Free in his arms. Free at the end of his lash. Free because he gave me permission to soar.

I loved him, even when he made me sob. In pain. In earth-shattering pleasure. God help me, I *loved* Dean Donahue.

So, no, I suppose it wasn't insane. It wasn't insane to love the man who had ripped the lock off my cage—a cage I had never noticed in all my life—then wrenched open the door and told me to fly. Who set me free. Free to live how I wanted, needed. Free to make my choice, to choose him, this, *us*. Free to feel like this—both broken and whole.

No judgements. No fear. Just acceptance and passion. *Love*. It filled the room, the house, the island. It filled my world until it threatened to burst, and even then I wanted more.

"Belle?" He breathed my name into my hair, which he had removed from its pink satin bow at some point. It splayed across my back. His fingers smoothed through it, undoing my braid.

Tell me where you're at.

"F-four," I stammered.

"Only a four?" Dean held me closer, tighter, the constriction so damn *good*, even after he'd bound me. "All this—for a four?"

Zero to ten, our new post-play rating scale.

Zero: I felt nothing.

Ten: I felt *everything*.

One to nine: I felt alive.

I nodded, mouth stretching into a shaky smile to match his as he smoothed my tears away.

"All right," Dean whispered, gathering me up again, tucking me under his chin. "All right, sweetheart. I'm here. You did so good today. I'm very proud of you."

"Thank you, sir." My heart smiled. I closed my eyes and breathed him in, listening, *feeling*, the steady thrum of his heart.

Free as a bird—in my Dom's arms.

Friday, March 22nd: BELLE

My heart pitched straight down into my stomach.

"Nope—nope. I can't. I officially *can't*."

Abandoning my half-eaten bowl of popcorn, I scrambled from my huge, cushy chair and into Dean's next to me. As I hastily curled up in his lap, my sheath dress hiked around my thighs, my face hidden in his neck, the heroine screamed.

"I can't do it!"

Dean let out a few uneasy chuckles, pulling me closer. "Well, I told you we didn't need to watch a horror movie—"

"Why would she go down to the basement?" Something groaned—something creepy and definitely dead. Goosebumps rippled across my arms, and we both jumped at a noisy onscreen crash.

"Because she's an idiot. There's a perfectly good pantry she could have locked herself in—"

"Ghosts can go through closed doors!"

"Oh, it's not a ghost. It's...some other...horrible...thing."

I snorted, risking a peek through my fingers—just when

the *thing*'s shadowy reflection caught in the dusty mirror the heroine strolled by, her trembling hand clutching the flashlight. Nope. Nope. A horror movie projected on the enormous wall in the cinema room—it had been a poor choice across the board. Dean's earlier vote had been for some ridiculously dry political thriller, so I'd gone in the complete opposite direction with what I *thought* might be some B-rated slasher flick that would make us laugh. Mistake. *Mistake*.

"Ugh, no, I can't either."

"*No*," I protested, tugging at Dean's wrist when he covered his eyes. "You have to tell me what's happening while *I* don't watch."

Something crashed again and I squealed, burying my face against him.

"Well, why do *I* have to watch it?" he grumbled, wrapping an arm around me, his entire body tense. Despite my racing heart and clammy palms, I grinned.

"Because you're the *sir*."

He sighed dramatically, and when I resurfaced again, he appeared to be watching through his fingers.

"Can we at least turn the light on?"

I shook my head. Dean's home movie theater was *amazing*, the seats comfy and the projected image filling an entire wall, but you had to watch everything in the dark. "If the light's on, then we can't really see the screen."

"You're not even watching it!"

"But you're watching it for me," I insisted as I snaked my arms around his neck, staring up at the stream of light emanating from the mounted projector overhead. Suddenly, it was too quiet. My pulse quickened. "What's happening?"

"*Belle*."

More onscreen silence. I waited, biting my lower lip, in

full brat mode and loving it. Neither of us said anything for a long moment, even after something creaked in the movie, the heroine gasping.

Dean huffed, his hand sliding down to cup my butt. "She's... She's opened some box, and now she's looking at a necklace. We're zoomed in on the necklace. It's this gaudy ruby thing. And now we're panning up to— Oh, fuck *me*. What the hell is *that*?!"

The heroine screamed.

The *thing* screamed.

I squealed, shoving my face into his shoulder—and Dean hid behind my hair.

Sunday, March 24*th*: DEAN

In the very faint light streaming in from the balcony windows, my submissive was looking at me like I was crazy.

"You've never been *flogged*."

"Of course I have." I tugged the duvet cover up, then threaded my hands together on my stomach. Belle, meanwhile, settled in, an arm crooked under her pillow, my eyes long since adjusted to the darkness of my—our— bedroom. We had said good night to one another almost an hour ago, but then she had asked something, and I'd answered. Another round of murmured good nights and sweet dreams and languid kisses, then something had occurred to me that I just had to share, and Belle concurred. On and on the cycle went, several times over. Good night. Kiss me. Oh, wait, what do you think about—?

And now here we were, chatting in bed, long after midnight.

"I don't believe that," she said with a giggle. I shot her a look, one she may or may not actually have been able to see, brows lifted.

"And why not?"

"Because... Because Doms don't get flogged."

"I'll have you know that I've been caned, flogged, whipped—the works," I told her. Years ago, sure, but that didn't change the fact that it had all happened. She was quiet for a moment, perhaps mulling over this startling new information, and then shifted onto her back.

"Why?"

"Because I wanted to know what it feels like." All the Doms I knew had done the same at some point. Perhaps not all within one week as I had, shortly after I'd been approved for membership at Elysium. Aged twenty-six, exhausted from work, and interested in taking my lifestyle up a notch, I'd planned to introduce more toys into my sessions. Toys that could seriously hurt a submissive if handled incorrectly.

"Why?"

I grinned. "Because I thought—if I'm going to do it to someone else, even if they ask me to, I ought to know how it feels. All of it."

"Nipple clamps too?"

"Nipple clamps too." Not that my nipples were anywhere near as sensitive as Belle's, but it hadn't exactly been a fun experience for me either.

"Butt plug?" She sounded like she was smiling.

"No." I chuckled. "I suppose I haven't tried *everything*. I've been bound, strung up, spanked."

"Huh." Belle sat up, the duvet falling away, her nipples pebbled—prominent, even in the darkness. "By who?"

"One of the Doms at Elysium."

"Which one?"

"He doesn't work on location anymore, I'm afraid."

"You were caned and flogged and spanked by a *man*?"

"Samuel," I said lightly, a faint admonishment. "I wanted to know how hard a man could go—so I wouldn't do it unless given the green light by my submissive. Samuel was very helpful. He knew it was just a learning exercise."

She crawled across the bed, the linens swishing beneath her, and I blinked rapidly when the bedside table lamp flickered on. "*Belle*—"

"How did it feel for you?" she asked, no longer incredulous—but dripping with curiosity. "To feel all the things you do to someone else."

I sat up with a sigh, arranging the pillows behind me to soften the bite of the headboard, and then beckoned Belle to me with a nod. She did as she was told, crawling into my arms and snuggling up to my chest. "I wasn't sexually aroused by it, but it helped me understand the feeling of, well, surrender, helplessness, to be completely at someone else's mercy. It allowed me to better understand my submissives and what they need from me."

And how hard to hit. That was key. Even though I had gone overboard with the paddle that fucking horrible day, I hadn't left any lasting physical damage on Belle's precious behind. I still knew where the wood needed to land. I knew how to bruise and not maim.

"Did you have a lot of submissives before me?" she asked, trailing her finger across my skin, some of her bright, exuberant curiosity dulled suddenly. I kissed the top of her head, my throat tight.

"Only a few—and none like this. None like you."

Her finger ceased its travels briefly, then started up again, her nail twirling across my chest instead, over my pecs, around my nipples. "And did it hurt?"

"What? The flogging? The caning?"

"Yeah."

I exhaled a laugh, drawing her closer. "Of course it did, and I'm afraid I don't enjoy experiencing pain—only inflicting it."

She hummed, then sat up, her hand on my chest, her hair a frizzy mess after our shower this evening.

"Do you think I could try it?"

"Try what—flogging me?" I arched my eyebrow when she nodded. "Why?"

"To see what it feels like...to be you."

Smirking, I smoothed her hair down, then cupped her chin. "And what if you like it more than submitting? What if *you* want to be the Dom?"

Her eyes widened, and she hastily shook her head, utterly adorable in her refusal. "I don't think that's possible. Not with you, sir."

"But you want to try it anyway, just to see what it feels like?"

"Consider it a learning exercise." Her royal blues gleamed as she smiled, sliding from my sweet little submissive to something—brattier. I hesitated. It was almost two in the morning, but she looked so fucking *interested*, so wide-awake.

"Get the riding crop from the closet," I said with a sigh, then held up a finger when she giggled and clapped her hands together. "*Only* around my shoulders and chest."

"Nipples?"

"No." I gave her a warning look before she hopped off the bed, even though I trusted her to respect my limits. "And my safeword is apricots, too."

"Oh, sir," she said, laughing as she skipped off to the closet. "You don't need a safeword with me..."

Only when it came to my heart.

She found her weapon a little too quickly for my liking, and as she smacked it against her palm, looking like a kid in a candy store, I couldn't help but wonder if I was about to seriously regret this...

Thwack.

10

BELLE

Thursday, March 28ᵗʰ

The last time I had actually styled my hair was the day we left New York.

Thinking back to the Belle of then, the one who had stood in front of her bathroom mirror, straightener in hand —so anxious, so afraid of failure—I wished I could have told her that it wouldn't be so bad.

I wished I could have told her that the next two months would be the best months of her life.

And that she would break the first rule of escorting. Crush it. Eviscerate it.

That she would become the stupid girl who fell for her client—and that at some point, she wouldn't care anymore.

That she was about to fall in love.

The Belle of then felt like a completely different woman than the one staring back at me in the mirror now. I liked this Belle better. Living in her skin, knowing what I knew, feeling how I felt—it was a whole lot easier, somehow.

After turning off and unplugging the styling wand, I set

it on its little stand to cool down. For tonight's gala, I had opted for a sleek shine, conditioning the heck out of my sun-kissed hair, my wild salt-and-sea-ravaged mane. Waves framed my face. The ends curled under. I'd managed to achieve a blowout look without spending a dime. Sure, it had taken a full three hours to get here. Barricaded in my old guest room, I had done my makeup and hair alone, wanting to surprise Dean with the final look when it was all one pretty package.

As per both of our preferences, I hadn't gone crazy with the makeup by any means. My face had a healthy glow to it, and I'd opted for neutral shades across my eyes—soft browns and golds to highlight my blues, but nothing dark enough to clash with my dress.

Stripping out of my bathrobe, I stuffed myself into the strapless bra that had fit like a glove two months ago, now a little tight, and removed the breathtaking Renaldi couture from its hanger on the back of the door. No panties, just in case Dean and I opted for a more exciting way to pass the time tonight.

Of the forty dresses I'd tried on, Dean and I had eventually narrowed it down to our three favourites. Then we'd taken a staff vote with the assistants. In the end, Dean had to break the tie—and he'd chosen well. Not only was the watermelon-pink gown so comfortable it felt like I was wearing nothing at all, it gave me the confidence to approach tonight's event like I belonged there. Like I fit in.

It made me feel like a queen, honestly. Not a princess. Not a fluffy, soft, sweet creature—but a queen.

Beyond that, I could get the gown on by myself *and* go to the bathroom without struggling through eight hundred yards of fabric. After zipping up the side, I gave my outfit a quick once-over in the mirror. Sleeveless with thin straps. A

V-neckline that made my hint of cleavage look spectacular. Fitted bodice, but not *so* fitted that I couldn't breathe. Layers of tulle made up the skirt, fluttering down to the ground like flower petals, the different hues of pink giving it depth and texture without the weight of a much heavier fabric.

Felix Renaldi was a fashion god. Dean had promised to introduce us back in New York so I could personally thank him for my day of dancing around in couture.

I swallowed hard at the thought, my easy smile falling away.

Back in New York—when all this was over.

My lower lip wobbled.

I didn't *want* this to be over. Three days from now, Dean's private jet would whisk us home. I'd return to Elysium over two hundred grand richer, my financial situation secure. He —would probably go on to fight some more with his family, hopefully stick up for himself.

And that would be it.

Tears welled, my face scrunching as I fought to keep them at bay.

I didn't want that—the *end*, the one all escorts faced. No fairy tales. Just money.

Even if I loved him.

Even if it seemed like he...

"Oh, heck." I grabbed some toilet paper and dabbed around my eyes. While I hadn't applied much makeup, the mascara would run and ruin everything if I cried—and we were only a half hour out from climbing into Dean's boat.

He had promised to take it slow so the wind wouldn't wreak havoc on my hair.

God, I loved him so much.

Sniffling, I tidied up my face and hoped the redness in my eyes would disappear. Tonight was supposed to be fun—

a date night. Drinks. Expensive appetizers. A little dancing, a little showing up Richard. Dean had been anxious about it all day, so much so that he'd cancelled our playtime in favor of lounging around the pool. Not that I minded—but he probably would have been more relaxed if he'd been able to, I don't know, bend me over the dining table and brutally have his way with me.

Just saying—an orgasm or five could do wonders for your nerves.

After a few more deep breaths in the mirror, I gave myself a thumbs up, determined not to let my feelings over all this ending sully what was bound to be an awesome night, then opened the bathroom door and—

"Oh, hey." And found Dean sitting on my bed. He quickly stood and faced me, looking positively scrumptious, the epitome of dapper, in an all-black suit tailored to perfection, his sandy blond waves tousled—a siren call to my fingers.

Him in black, statuesque and powerful. Me in pink, like I'd just tumbled out of the fairy court.

Hades and Persephone—ready for a night on the town.

My stomach looped.

"Belle..." Dean swallowed hard, perusing my figure slowly—taking his time, admiring every detail. His stare was possessive, greedy. Lord of the Underworld—and the way his wandering gaze blazed a path across my body, I was his queen. There was no doubt about it anymore.

I smiled shyly, tucking my hair behind my ear. "Well, don't you look handsome."

"You—are the most beautiful thing I've ever seen," Dean murmured, sounding both Dean and Dom, his voice making my knees weak. "Come here... Let me see you properly."

That *growl*. A shiver raced down my spine, goosebumps prickling as the chill turned molten in my core, between my thighs.

My shy smile turned coy, and I crossed the distance between us, slipping my hand into his when he offered it. Dean raised it above my head, eyeing me hungrily as I spun in place. Slowly, I performed for him, the heat intensifying, unfurling across my belly, licking its way down.

"Fucking magnificent," he murmured, each word like velvet steel. That was my Dean. The best of hard and soft, cruel and merciful. On my final turn, I noticed something seemingly innocent on the bed—a dark blue box. I paused, my hand falling from his, and brushed my fingertips across it. Given it was similar in size to the box he had first shown me on the plane, the one with that fun bullet vibrator, I couldn't help but wonder if he had something sinful in mind for the gala—something he had been keeping all to himself.

However, before I could ask, Dean sat at the end of the bed and set the box on his lap. Swallowing hard, I followed, perched beside him. My heart thundered at his expression —no longer hungry. Something else. Something shadowy and unreadable. I fiddled with the dress's top layer of tulle, rubbing the paper-thin material between two fingers.

"Sir, is everything okay?" If this was just another vibrator, another kinky toy, he'd be smiling. Mischievous. Eager. Dark, even, with that dangerous sort of glint in his eye—the one that made me wet every time. I didn't recognize the darkness here.

"Belle," he started, his words weighted, like he chose each one with the same intense care with which he always handled me. "I feel like I've been drowning. Always drowning, always fighting so fucking hard to get my head above water—and failing. I... It's like I've been dying a slow, painful death, one that's gone on for years with no end in sight, no sweet release." The bulge in his throat bobbed as he finally lifted his gaze to mine, the darkness vanquished. Bright, glistening sage greeted me. "And you—Belle, you were like the first *good* breath after finally breaching the surface. With you, I'm no longer drowning."

My gut told me to take his hand, to thread my fingers through his as we always did. But I stayed still, silent, hands fisted in my dress—my mind empty.

Until it wasn't.

Until I knew—

"I didn't realize I was drowning," I whispered, my eyes swimming, flooding, "until I met you. It's like I didn't know what *air* was, like I've never truly *breathed*, until you."

The seriousness, the stillness, hanging between us splintered as soon as his lips spread into an enormous smile. Warm and comforting. Dean beamed down at me, and I couldn't help but smile back, even if my stomach was in knots. A laugh slipped out, airy and carefree, and I gently wiped at the twin tears spilling down my cheeks, mindful of my makeup.

"I have something for you," he told me, shuffling closer and then lifting the navy-blue lid from the box. I leaned forward, gasping.

Inside sat two necklaces. One made of pearls and rose gold, a large circular gold pendant in the middle. The other looked more like a choker, crafted of rich-smelling pink leather, thin, with a similar loop of gold hanging off the middle.

"They're collars, Belle."

I blinked, heat rippling through me as I traced a finger across the pearls. Collars? Not necklaces, then. I looked to the leather, to the little hoop in the middle—like a dog collar, where you might attach a leash. My cheeks burned.

They were so beautiful—and they made me feel...

Conflicted. I pulled my hand back with a frown, twisting the tulle again.

"I don't understand, sir."

"Well," he shifted to face me properly, "a collar is a gift a Dominant presents to his submissive. It's a symbol of their bond, a symbol to others that you belong to your Dom." Clearing his throat, Dean set the box between us, handling it reverently, as though not wanting to jostle the pearls. "A collar... In certain circumstances, to certain couples, a collar can be equated to an engagement ring."

My tears fell freely now, probably dragging clumps of mascara with them, marking my freckled cheeks with dark brown. I wiped at them distractedly, my hands trembling, the knots in my stomach lacing tighter and tighter. "I still don't understand. You... You..."

"I want you. I want *us*. After this—I don't want it, us, to end when we step off the plane in New York." Dean dragged in a shallow breath, his cheeks flushed. Behind him, through the window whose curtains I no longer feared opening, the sun drifted toward the horizon, painting us a backdrop of burnt umber, burgundy, and apricot. It should have soothed me, seeing the shades of his soul stretched across the clear sky.

The knots twisted so hard they *hurt*.

I couldn't breathe.

"Is this—a joke?" I asked, choking on the words. Did he really mean—? Dean wouldn't joke about this. He wouldn't be that cruel. But *this* was the fairy tale escorts never got. This was the moment Hollywood dazzled audiences with, while the rest of us knew the harsh truth.

Dean's smile faltered. His brow puckered. The flush in his cheeks deepened.

"What? No. *No*." Exhaling sharply, he carefully shifted the box behind us, out of the way, and moved in so that our thighs touched. In that moment, the knots loosened—only a fraction, but his touch brought instant relief. I dragged in a deep breath, forcing myself to look at him, to meet his eye, to read between the lines. He smoothed a hand down my leg, a whisper of a caress, and grasped my knee. The knots gave a little more. "Belle, this isn't a joke to me. I'm being very serious. If you don't want that—I just thought, after everything we—"

"So, you're saying...you want this to be our real life?" I couldn't help it: I interrupted. I spoke over him. I finally found my voice, raising it to drown him out. "You want *this* to be our everyday...thing?"

His thumb stroked my leg as he smiled gently. "Well, we can define how intense we want our everyday life to be, but essentially... Yes. I don't want to lose you. And I know it's a cliché—a client offering to whisk his escort away from sex work. I'm not here to rescue you, Belle, and I don't mean to be a cliché. Not with you."

With great difficulty, I finally tore my gaze away from him, pinning it to a spot on the wall across from us instead. Ignoring the voice in my head, the one screaming *Yes!* over and over again, emphatically, I forced myself to *think*, to consider what it would mean to bring dominance and submission into my daily life. To bring Dean into my daily life.

It should scare me more.

That thought—it was my freakin' theme song for this trip. Dean ought to scare me more. My feelings ought to scare me more. All of it—should scare me more.

"Is this something you might—might want?" Dean murmured. His thumb had stilled, and I swallowed thickly as I looked back to him, unsure of how long I had been stuck in my own thoughts. For the first time since all this had begun, he sounded unsure.

And that uncertainty—it *killed* me. So, I nodded, desperate to bring his suffering to an end.

"Yes, but," I licked my lips, then shook my head, a dubious bark of laughter flying out of my mouth, "I don't understand why. I don't know why it makes me feel so good to do what we do. My childhood was fine—normal. I'm just a normal person—"

"Sweetheart..." Dean tucked my hair behind my ear, then trailed his finger along my jaw. "You don't need to be damaged to want this life. You just need to be yourself."

He was right; the patrons at Elysium were all normal. Sure, most of them had sizeable bank accounts, but outside of that, they were just regular people—who lived a secret life of kink.

"Belle, why did you get into BDSM at Elysium? Why become a paid submissive?"

"The money," I said, listing the automatic response I gave whenever someone outside of our world asked, skeptically, why on earth I would choose to be a fetish escort. Instead of offering me the knowing nod, the *ah yes, of course, the money* expression I knew so well, Dean merely arched an eyebrow, waiting. Waiting for the truth, for the real answer I'd never admitted out loud.

I could lie.

I closed my eyes and took a deep breath.

No. I couldn't lie. Not to him.

"And...to explore my sexuality safely," I muttered, picking at my nails, palms clammy. "Dominant sex and kidnapped heroines and spanking—I read about all of it in my romance novels when I was a teenager. The pain, the punishment, the desperate surrender to another person turned me on. It excited me. The darker the better. And I thought something was wrong with me, that I had some mental issues—that I wanted to be abused.

"Then at Elysium, the professional subs were doing what I fantasized about every night with their clients, and no one judged them. No one called them sick. I told Penny I'd always wanted to...to...*try*, and she was excited for me. Mostly, I think, because she knew I'd earn more, but I was excited talking about it again. I...I liked it. I don't know why—"

"You've just told me why, sweetheart." Dean's hand closed over both of mine, stilling my fidgeting. The weight of it, his firm grasp, had me sucking in a deep breath, and when I exhaled, the *release* had my eyes tearing again. Dean brushed one away when it fell. "And now? How do you feel now, Belle?"

"Now..." I clutched at his hand with both of mine. "Now, it feels like I'm free."

Dean's eyes seemed to twinkle as he smiled. "Not abused? Not sick?"

I shook my head, the last of my stomach knots releasing. "Never."

"I need you to know..." Dean untangled his hand from mine, then scratched at the back of his neck. "I wouldn't offer you a collar lightly. This isn't something I want you to wear for a month after we get back, and then it's done. It's... Well, it's more permanent than that, and it's completely your decision, Belle. But if you accept, it means you're mine."

Another shiver shot through me, shattering the nerves, the anxiety—the disbelief that this moment was even happening, that I was dreaming. *You're mine.* I was suddenly desperate to hear him say it again, and again—preferably while he was *making* me his, fist in my hair, pounding me into this bed. I swallowed hard, weaving my trembling fingers together, trying to quiet my hammering heart.

"If I'm yours," I said softly, carefully, needing him to say it, "are you mine?"

Dean blinked, as if fighting back tears of his own, and he grinned. "Yes, Belle. I would be yours, if you want me to continue being your Dom."

Lower lip caught between my teeth, I looked at the box, at the gorgeous pair of collars inside, then back to him, then down to the collars. The first rule of escorting—never fall in love with the client—whispered at the back of my mind, growing smaller, quieter, with each passing moment. Accepting his offer opened us both up to the potential for heartache and misery. For pain and suffering, the kind you never recover from.

But that was my head talking. Logic. Reason. Self-preservation.

In that moment, my heart was fearless.

I reached for the string of pearls and rose gold; it seemed like the more formal collar, something I could wear in public without anyone questioning it.

But Dean and I would know.

In our hearts, we would know what the pearls symbolized, what they meant to us.

"Can you...?" I swept my hair over my shoulder, handing Dean his gift, then turned my back to him. A beat passed in silence. Even my racing heart had quieted. Just before I could glance over my shoulder, I felt him—the heat of his body as he moved in close, reaching around me. The collar was cool to the touch, each pearl kissing my throat as he fastened it in place. My breath hitched, and I trailed my finger across the entire strand, stopping to circle the O-pendant in the center.

Wearing it—my first collar...

I felt like I could conquer the world.

Which was ridiculous, but screw it—that was how it made me feel. Powerful. I faced Dean again and found him smiling softly, his gaze warm.

Loved. Treasured.

Claimed.

"Now, Belle, I—"

I threw myself at him before he could get another word out, arms around his neck, clinging to him. To the safety he offered. To the confidence he incited. My lips brushed along his neck as he enveloped me in his arms, crushing me to the solid frame of his body. Drowning my senses in my sir, my Dom, in *Dean*. His musky cologne, distinctly masculine and powerful—a scent memory that would remind me of this exact moment for years to come. His breath across my shoulder, his lips, his tongue, his teeth as he showered me in hot, open-mouthed kisses. My name, whispered, murmured, growled, the velvet giving way to flint, to possession. *Belle. My Belle.*

Did this—the collar, his offer, the way Dean held me so fiercely, as if I might just disappear—mean that he...?

Yes, Belle. I would be yours, if you want me to continue being your Dom.

Of course I wanted that, but I wanted so much more than that, too.

I worked my way down to his chest and *pushed*, forcefully separating us, my heart drumming like thunder between my ears. This dress had made me feel like a queen.

The collar—like I could conquer the world. It was time to put that bravery into practice.

My lips parted, but no words came out. We just stared at one another, until my gaze dropped to Dean's mouth.

Say it, Belle. Say it, or regret it for the rest of your life.

"Dean," I started, terrified, exhilarated, clutching at his black silk lapels, "are you in love with me?"

Not *do you love me*. Precise language—it mattered. He was always so clear with me.

He stared down at me, mouth opening and closing, an echo of me ten seconds earlier. I tugged at his lapels, eyes prickling with fresh tears, lips stretched into what was probably a manic smile.

"Because I'm in love with you," I said, the words flying out of my mouth—maybe too fast, too jumbled, for him to understand. But then his cheeks flushed again, and I knew that he'd heard me. He'd understood. "And if these collars only symbolize our connection as Dominant and submissive, if they don't allow for—for *more*, then maybe I don't want—"

Dean smothered the rest of my frantic rambling with a kiss, his hands threading through my hair. Ruining it. Ruining the blowout effect. Ruining *me*—and I welcomed every precious second of it. We came together like we had on the beach weeks ago, two titans of nature colliding. He kissed me deeply, fiercely, marking me for his own.

Something he'd never need to do again.

Because I intended to walk the rest of my life, my hand in his—collared.

I was his.

He was mine.

And we belonged to each other, from this moment until the last.

"Of course I'm in love with you," Dean rasped before dragging his mouth along my jaw, over my ear, down my throat—searing the declaration into my skin. Permanent. A branding invisible to all but us. He cradled the back of my head in one hand, the other cupping my cheek none too gently. "I fell in love with you the first time I saw you in Candace's directory, that fucking *smile*, and I've been falling more and more in love with you every day."

He clutched my face in both hands, tilting it up, our eyes locked. All my knots, my butterflies, had burst into fireworks, explosions that threatened to lift me up and carry me into the night. Dean's words almost seemed to pain him, his gaze stormy.

Maybe he *was* a sucker for pain after all, just like me—but only when inflicted by the right hand.

"To me, the collar means love, sweetheart."

We clung to one another, Dean's expression mirroring the way I felt inside—like this wasn't happening, like it couldn't be real. In two seconds, we would both wake up in his bed, and all this honesty would have just been some wonderful dream. Back to reality. Back to real life, where there were no fairy-tale endings for escorts, and Dean would get sucked into working himself to the bone for people who didn't appreciate him.

I blinked—and he was still there. We were still Hades and Persephone, dapper and elegant, only with a touch of mascara smeared across Persephone's cheeks. Grinning, I tugged at his lapels, needing his fierce kiss again to ground me, to keep me from floating away. For I had become this buoyant, weightless creature, fueled by love, and if it weren't for Dean's biting kiss, for the way he pinned me to the bed, I might drift off and never come back to earth.

Only we did come back—later. With my dress's straps

yanked down my arms, my right breast out, nipple puckered and damp from Dean's mouth. My hair askew, dress hitched up, Dean's hardness settled between my thighs. We eventually remembered where we were, what time it was, panting, hearts racing, eyes bright.

"We could always stay here," he rumbled, dragging his teeth from the hollow of my throat up to my lips. I twirled a lock of his sandy blond hair around my finger, considering it.

"I want everyone to see my gift," I whispered back, guiding his hand to my neck, to the pearls.

It took us a little while longer to get off the bed—about the time it took me to come, Dean's hand between my thighs and his mouth on my throat, my breast. By then, my makeup needed to be completely redone, as did my hair. While Dean looked disheveled, he righted himself within a minute, the tent in his trousers slowly deflating. We'd both agreed we could have done something about *that*, but one thing would have inevitably led to another and we never would have left the island, not until sunrise tomorrow.

I, meanwhile, needed a solid twenty in front of the bathroom mirror again. My hair went into a ponytail, if only to show off the pearls, the rose-gold chain at the back. Because my cheeks seemed to have a permanent flush to them now, makeup was back to basics. No contouring. No layers of foundation or blush. A bit of colour on my eyes, my lashes, my lips. Dean stood in the doorway, watching, his mouth lifted in a sinful smirk, his gaze dark and suggestive.

Every so often, I caught those storm clouds in the mirror, and desire flashed through me. Temptation. Another realm Dean lorded over.

Darkness. Pleasure. Temptation.

Love.

"Sweetheart, you know that accepting my gift means you can't escort anymore."

I stilled, lipstick halfway across my lower lip, and then resumed applying the desert rose tint. When the colour was even, I capped the tube and set it back in my makeup bag, frowning.

In the heat of the moment, I hadn't even considered what would happen to my job if I belonged to Dean.

"I won't share you," he insisted, voice rough and thick as he strolled into the bathroom. He pressed up behind me, hands smoothing around my waist, mouth descending on my bare shoulder. "Not even with the clients who love you for your feet. You're mine."

I didn't want to share him, either. As my gaze drifted across the mirror, from my pearl collar to Dean's lips, I wondered if we ought to have a chat about *his* work life as well.

Not tonight. While his situation was problematic for me on a personal level, because I couldn't *stand* what his dad and brother had done to him, it wasn't the same. At all. So, with a gulp, I nodded, a sliver of anxiety cutting through my happy glow.

"I haven't really put much thought into what I want to do after escorting," I admitted. Ever since I'd started at Elysium, I had been living for the now, moving from one day to the next with no real plan, no real goals beyond paying off my debt, padding my bank account for a rainy day, and buying Real Adult furniture.

"We'll talk about it," he murmured, kissing up my neck. "Maybe find you a good career counselor."

My eyebrows lifted. He wanted to help me plan my life *outside* of our relationship? "Really?"

"Sweetheart, you're twenty-three." Dean nipped at my

ear, his bite sharp, startling, and then chuckled when I swatted at him. "I think most people your age have no idea what they want to do with their life."

"So, what?" I turned in his arms, smoothing my hands over his broad chest. "You don't want to keep me chained up in your penthouse, to be thoroughly used for your pleasure?"

"Only if you ask me to," Dean growled, tipping my chin up, craning my neck back as far as it would go while still holding my eye. He then flashed a dangerous smile. "And *please*, like a chained-up kitten would be for *my* pleasure alone..."

I squeal-giggled when he hoisted me onto the counter, pushed between my thighs, and claimed me again—his hands brutish, his mouth savage...

And I wouldn't have it any other way.

HOUSE RULE #19

The nature of Belle and Sir's relationship is private, not for public consumption.

11

BELLE

We arrived well after the gala had started—later than fashionably late.

And we were all smiles.

After needing to completely redo my hair and makeup three times, I'd opted to keep things about as natural as possible. The dress spoke for itself, anyway, not even the slightest bit rumpled from Dean's enthusiasm.

Sometime after eleven, Dean and I strolled into Saint Thomas's Sapphire Plaza Resort, my heels clacking across the grand entrance foyer. We were directed to an enormous ballroom facing the bay, a space which was usually reserved for gorgeous beachfront weddings, but tonight hosted the Annual Great Bay Gathering for the ultra-elite.

Stunning arched windows overlooked a well-maintained terrace outside. Gold, silver, and red pervaded every element of the décor: the curtains, the tablecloths, the cutlery, the plates, right down to the toothpicks offered by the roaming waitstaff. Soft yellow light from the chandeliers overhead blanketed the room, tempered it, made the sea of influential faces somehow seem more approachable.

Once we grabbed a flute of sparkling champagne each—champagne that cost more per bottle than my rent in New York—Dean pointed out the local wildlife, just as he had our first day on Ixora. Oil tycoons. Tech gods. Fashion mavens dripping in diamonds. Socialites and their inner circles. Weapons manufacturers, hotel moguls, restaurateurs who owned more Michelin-starred establishments than there were people in this room.

With my arm looped around Dean's, I took everything in without a word—but I was still all smiles as I nursed my champagne. As far as I was concerned, I had the best dress —Renaldi couture, don't you know—and the best Dom accessory. As I stood by Dean's side, the light, airy bubbliness from earlier still clinging to me, I almost *dared* someone to sneer. With my pearl collar hugging me, cradling me, empowering me, I felt like I could take on literally anyone in this room—Richard included, wherever he was.

When we finally wandered into the fold, however, I was shocked to learn I wouldn't *have* to hold my own. Dean dazzled everyone we met, and while most of the men deferred to him, their wives and partners chatted amicably with me. We complimented each other's outfits, gossiped about the circulating hors d'oeuvres, and chatted about our time spent on the islands. Most hungrily gobbled up my *very* sanitized stories about the last two months on Dean's private island, wearing their jealousy for all to see.

But beyond that, the people here were—well, *nice*. To be fair, I didn't have to swim with the sharks. Nobody wanted my business, my money, my expertise. Dean was left to field most of the tough inquiries, and to his credit, he handled it all beautifully. He kept the conversations light, seeming only to skim the surface of what could be very complex shoptalk.

In fact, he even boosted his brother, insisting that the business elite, all clad in perfectly tailored tuxedos, their polished shoes catching the light, direct their more complex questions to Richard.

I was so proud of him.

He was Dom-Dean here—cool, confident, self-possessed, and strong. He wilted before no one. He remained unbowed against a barrage of inquiries about the changes inside the Donahue empire. His expression gave nothing away. His cheeks dimpled when he smiled, but his gaze remained steadfast and unreadable. Dean played his secrets close to his chest for a full hour, brilliantly enduring all the barbed questions, the doublespeak from men who gambled millions like it was nothing, the probing from steely-eyed tycoons eager to find a chink in the Donahue armor.

Here I was, making pleasant, albeit vapid, small talk with wives and girlfriends and mistresses, thinking that I couldn't have loved Dean more. And then this new side of him surfaced, this business-savvy, utterly in-control man of the real world. The carefree, warm, velvet-tongued Dean who gave me tours of the islands, who went hiking in national parks, who waited patiently while I tried on bikinis —he was nowhere to be found tonight. Dean moved like a god, like the Dom I loved, surrounded by all these extraordinary people.

I was a smitten kitten, so enamored with the man by my side that my cheeks physically *ached* from smiling. And not some forced smile, not the kind I used to wear for clients. Sure, both hurt my cheeks, but I welcomed the pain here. I welcomed the burn, the quivering muscles. It was the pain of a woman in love, and whenever I caught Dean studying me, he wore a silly little smile himself—like we were the only two people in the room, like the rest of these circling vultures didn't faze him one bit.

I had a feeling that by the end of the night, I'd love him even more.

And more again tomorrow.

And the next day.

Love wasn't finite. Being with Dean had taught me that it was complex and limitless.

In a year's time, maybe five, ten, fifty—I couldn't wait to see how the love multiplied, to see how full my heart would be then, when now it was so close to bursting.

By the time Dean led me away to the dance floor, I was ready for a repeat of this evening's performance. Me, perched on some counter, legs wrapped around him as Dean pounded me through two climaxes, his hand in my hair, his mouth *everywhere*.

For now, one hand settled on my hip, the other supported my hand as he steered us into a slow, easy waltz. Surrounded by other couples, I let him take the lead, guiding me through the unfamiliar steps until we found our usual rhythm. Dominance. Submission. Surrender—to the music, to each other, to the dance itself. My smile had softened, and I couldn't tear myself away from those eyes, from his hooded stare that pierced right through me.

That reminded me, even here, encircled by all these elegant people, that I belonged to him.

I moved in closer, brushing up against him, feet moving without a thought. Dean ought to remember that even here, he belonged to me, too. My lip caught between my teeth, my hips found him, my breasts pressed to the hard planes of his chest. How we managed to move, to float across the dance floor so desperately close: it came down to his guidance, his ability to persevere even as my hand wandered down his shoulder, ghosting across his lapels, tracking the buttons of his freshly pressed shirt, until it reached leather—

"Kitten," Dean whispered thickly, his grip tightening, "behave."

Desire fluttered through me as I peered up at the flint, the steel, the granite of my Dom's stare—and smiled. His expression hardened, and I stood up on my toes, lifting my mouth so that it brushed his ear as I uttered two damning words.

"Make me."

A spasm skittered along his jaw, and I eased back with an innocent grin—all the while knowing he saw it, the mischief simmering just below the surface. We had put in our required time. We had chatted up the crowds. We had laughed at jokes that weren't funny. We had posed for pictures with people who *smelled* of money. Midnight had come and gone; it was a new day—and I wanted my Dom all to myself.

Selfish. Greedy. *Needy*.

I could be all those things, especially when I felt, *very* clearly, what that attitude did to him.

"Wait for me on the terrace," he murmured, his tone gravelly, rich—delicious. My sex clenched. My stomach flip-flopped, heat surging, stinging my cheeks.

"Yes, sir."

Ever the gentleman, Dean escorted me off the dance floor, then kissed my cheek before disappearing into the crowd. I couldn't imagine what he needed to fetch for a little moonlit-terrace canoodling, but the possibilities had me wet before I reached the glass door at the far side of the ballroom.

Much to my surprise, and relief, I found myself alone outside. The day's heat had dissipated, leaving the air cool and dry. Goosebumps rippled across my arms as I strolled to the far end of the terrace, headed straight for the cast-stone balustrade made of the same material as Dean's staircase. Visions of him taking me on those stairs danced across my mind as I leaned onto the smooth, flat railing. The bay was beautiful at night, the water peaceful, the twinkling lights of yachts and hotel verandas soothing my pounding heart, my racing thoughts.

Thoughts of my sir, what he could *possibly* be getting to make our night a little more interesting. Dean, pinning me to the stone railing, forcing me to count the lights across the bay—*making* me come, even as I protested, scandalized, while twenty feet away, behind a thin glass pane, the upper class nibbled on canapés and drank their weight in champagne.

I closed my eyes at the sound of the door clicking shut, at the even footfalls crossing the cement terrace. My breath hitched when I felt him, his hand smoothing down my back —hurriedly, like he couldn't wait, *squeezing* my backside like he'd been dying to pinch it all night.

Squeezing—not like he usually did. My eyes snapped open, and with the next gentle gust, the kind to rustle the shrubbery below the terrace, to make the torches along the shore flicker angrily—I smelled it. Bourbon. Bourbon and cigarette smoke, and cologne that was faintly sweet, whereas Dean's was always musky and full.

Heart leaping into my throat, I whirled around and clutched at my pearls—literally—when I found Richard Donahue gazing down at me, thin lips parted, eyes dark and hooded.

His hands on my waist.

"Oh. Hi," I managed, shoulders tensed as I squirmed as far back as the railing would allow. Given that my first encounter with Richard had been a disaster, his reputation from all of Dean's stories well-deserved in my mind, I had no doubt this second one would go just as poorly.

That day on the beach, I'd thought Richard and Dean resembled one another. Yet here, looming over me, staring down like he wanted to eat me, Richard couldn't have looked more different. Taller, leaner. Fouler. Sure, he was classically handsome. Women everywhere probably tripped over their own feet just for a flicker of his attention.

But he was rotten—right down to the core.

You could purge that rot. Fix it. Heal it. From what Dean had told me, it didn't seem like Richard cared to.

Dean's soul was jewel toned. Venetian rose. Azalea. Indigo. Ocean blue. Jasper red. I'd known that from the beginning. Richard radiated—nothing. His white linen suit, the shirt open two buttons too many, seemed an apt reflection of the nothing that was inside. Not purity or goodness, that white. It was just empty. Blank. Cold.

"Belle." He tipped his head to the side, and my mouth set in a thin line. He hadn't earned the right to say my name like that—to purr it, whisper it, like we were about to tumble into bed. Richard brought one hand to rest on the railing, leaving the other in his pocket, providing me an escape route. When I went for it, he blocked me with his body, chuckling, his smile not reaching his eyes. "Relax. I just wanted to formally introduce myself."

"We've met already," I said with a sniff. *Or are you too drunk to remember?* I clamped down on the insides of my cheeks as his smile sharpened. Oh, he remembered. He just wanted the chance to be gross about it.

"Yes, we've met, but not formally. Not," he pushed up against me, his enormous figure stiff as steel, "*properly.*"

"Ugh, get *off* me." I shoved at him—to no avail. He barely

moved an inch, but when Richard shoved back, I bent over the railing. Pain radiated up my spine, the alabaster digging into me; he swooped in, *Richard* digging into me.

"No." He caught my wrist when I tried again, trapping me there, his cock hard against my stomach. "I know who you are—*what* you are. I know what my brother likes. How would you like to earn a little more before you go back to that sex dungeon you work at? I can assure you that my bank account, among other things, is far larger than my brother's—"

I stomped on his foot, jabbing my heel into the white hemp, and this time when I shoved, he moved. Not much, but enough for me to get off the railing, to remove my spine from its unnatural bend.

"Just fucking listen to me—"

"Let *go*!" I shouted. I'd never had a client get handsy with me before, nor had an Elysium patron forced themselves on me. The helplessness, the powerlessness—it wasn't the kind that I got off on. Not by a long shot. Fear churned my gut, as nauseating as his breath, but I refused to shut down, clamp up. Just because he was stronger, bigger, just because he was one of the trust-fund wolves Dean had warned me about didn't mean he could just—

Just because I was technically still an escort, a sex worker, a paid submissive, didn't mean he could do whatever the hell he wanted with me.

Fuck this guy.

So, I fought like the kitten I was—nails out, teeth bared, feet stomping, arms flailing. Richard caught me by the elbow, wrenching it up; I went with the momentum, heart thundering between my ears, and lashed out.

"*Fuck*—"

Richard released me when I managed to clock him

square in the nose, a lucky swing and nothing more. Seizing my chance, I scrambled away along the railing, panting, my ponytail a little loose—my entire body numb, cold, buzzing the same way your foot does when you sit cross-legged for too long. My dress had survived intact. Trembling, I looked down at it, checked the thin shoulder straps, swept my hands across the tulle flower petals below.

Somehow, the dress's integrity seemed to matter.

Never mind that my wrists, my back, ached. My ankles wobbled in my heels, my feet clammy.

"Belle?"

With an unopened champagne bottle in hand, Dean stood halfway between the glass door and his brother, brow furrowed. In that moment, I wanted nothing more than to run into his arms—but I couldn't move. I couldn't speak. Humiliation spread like wildfire, engulfing me from top to bottom, choking me.

"Your whore almost broke my nose," Richard growled, leaning against the railing, splayed there like we had just gone ten rounds in the ring, like he had fended off an opponent twice his size.

Whore. I knew people thought it. Friends who disapproved of my decision to go into escorting, the people they told when they gossiped about this girl they'd met in university, the one who'd become a prostitute. It had never bothered me before. Let them think whatever they wanted. I knew what I did at Elysium. I *liked* what I did at Elysium—the people I worked with, the close-knit bond that had formed between us. Penny. Sex work had never shamed me before, but hearing Richard say it out loud, sneer it... Standing there, I suddenly felt very small—insignificant.

My embarrassment spiked, cheeks burning. Apparently I had been a sheltered whore, because no one had ever called me that before. Not in that tone. And if they had, maybe I wouldn't have cared, but this was Dean's brother. This—was the brother of the man I loved. Somehow it hurt so much more.

"Did she now?" Dean moved the champagne bottle from his right to his left hand. "Well, maybe I should finish the job."

Gingerly, I touched my pearls, finally finding the courage to look at him. Dean shook his head, scowling, my dark god in all black—my protector.

"Really, could you be more of a fucking stereotype of yourself, Richard?"

I hooked my finger onto the small ring in the middle of my collar, meeting Dean's gaze when it darted to me. If I could have curled up on the spot and cried, I would have.

"Belle, come here."

Dean held out the arm clutching the bottle, offering a safe port in the storm. I swallowed hard, sliding my fingers across my pearls again—and moved. One foot in front of the other, my body found its momentum, and I crossed straight to him. I hated to cower, to hide, but I just...

He felt so good. So solid. Dean enveloped me, his arm around my shoulders, and tipped my head up with a finger under my chin.

"Is that how it works?" Richard snorted. "You've trained her well. Got yourself a whore *and* a dog, eh?"

"Look at me," Dean murmured to me, and my eyes snapped back to him—I hadn't even realized they'd gone to Richard, to that smarmy face, to the creep in white linen. Dean did a quick sweep of my body, my face, my hair. "Did he hurt you?"

"No." I didn't have to think about it. Richard had startled me. Embarrassed me. But he hadn't hurt me—not like he wanted to, I assumed, the way he kept throwing *whore* around. I was shaken, not broken. I rolled my shoulders back and took a deep breath. "I'm okay."

Dean nodded, his mouth in a thin line—his eyes a raging storm. Like the painting in his office, fury seeped out of every pore, every detail: in his hand's slight tremor, in his powerful body's tension.

"Richard," he started, still looking at me—his voice whip-sharp and dripping with venom, "there are plenty of people inside waiting to speak with you, wanting answers. Some of Father's investors, his partners, his friends. They're all looking for you."

His brother chuckled dryly, then straightened and brushed a hand down his suit. "I'm afraid I don't have a head for numbers like you, Deanie. It's actually what I've been trying to talk to you about, now that you aren't knee-deep in pussy."

My blush sharpened, its intensity painful. Dean merely rolled his eyes and finally turned his full attention onto Richard.

"Let me guess," he mused, mirroring his brother's nonchalance, yet every word fell heavy between them. "You want the title and the perks that come with running things. You want the luxury of our Mediterranean properties, the staff at your beck and call—while I do all the work."

Richard clapped his hands together, so patronizing that it made my teeth hurt, I was biting down so hard. "You've got it. Even Dad thinks it's a good idea. I make a better face for the company—"

"No, Richard, that isn't happening. You want the salary, the benefits, the reputation—you have to actually *do* the job."

I pursed my lips. It was all pretty sound logic to me, but

Richard stared at Dean like he had insulted his mother. Their mother.

"Need I remind you what we have on you?" he hissed as he took a few steps toward us. "Do you want this, *her*, your little *perversions* to go public?"

In an instant, my humiliation vanished. Poof—into thin air.

Because *no one* threatened my sir.

Especially not some deadbeat jerk who couldn't keep his hands to himself. My eyes narrowed, and I stopped hugging Dean, stopped clinging to him like he was my life preserver in this mess. Arms crossed, I stood beside him instead and stared Richard down with my best impression of Dean's stern-eyed Dom look, the one that always made me just a *little* nervous.

"You know I was right to tell him," Richard carried on, oblivious to me staring daggers. "When my PI informed me what you do to these *women*, these poor, helpless, probably horribly *abused* women... Well, the whole arrangement is just twisted, Dean."

What a sanctimonious piece of—

I took a deep breath. This wasn't my fight. It might have started out that way, but this was Dean's brother, the man who had tormented him his whole life. Dean had earned the right to annihilate him, not me, even if he expressed his "concern" for my wellbeing like a patronizing ass, all the while lazily perusing my body like he had earned that privilege.

This guy made my stomach turn.

"Fuck you, Richard." To his credit, Dean seemed to have swallowed his rage. He even let out a little chuckle as his arm slipped from around my shoulders to my waist, the champagne bottle held in front of me like a shield, its golden tip shimmering in the moonlight. "Fuck you for *everything*. Do it. Tell them. Get on stage and make an announcement right now. Tell your skeevy tabloid friends— I don't care anymore."

"*What*? Dean, this is your life—"

"No, it isn't." He pulled me closer, wearing that soft, warm smile, the one that made my heart flutter. "My life is right here."

Unable to resist, I stole a quick kiss as Richard sputtered at us, cupping Dean's recently shaven cheeks. They were sharp. Not smooth, not when I brushed against the grain.

How would they feel between my thighs? I nibbled my lower lip, cheeks burning again for all the right reasons.

"*Please* tell me you didn't—? You don't fall in love with whores, Dean. You use them until they're all dried up, and then there's a newer, younger model waiting to take her place."

"I'm done, Richard," Dean said firmly, dripping with the calm, cool confidence I had seen inside earlier. He held my gaze a moment longer, then grinned at his brother. Ahh, the mocking smile. A secret personal favourite of mine. "I'm done with you, with our father—I'm done."

"Don't be so melodramatic, not for some—"

"Belle?" Dean pressed a hand to his chest, his expression wounded. "Am I being *melodramatic*?"

His inflection threatened to make me giggle, and I fought a smile as I shook my head gravely. "No, Dean, I think you're being *perfectly* civil. Reasonable. Sane, even."

"Hmm, yes." He nodded, his eyebrows furrowing deeper. "Yes, that's what I thought." When he faced his brother again, the farce dropped, replaced by something colder. "You've got a crowd waiting in there to pick your brain about the future of our family's legacy. They all heard I stepped down. A shift in the internal structure could spell a decline in an empire—or a surge. It's up to you now. Sink or swim, *Dickie*."

Dean flashed a quick, heartless smile as his brother gawked, then steered me back to the terrace door, a *hint* of swagger in each step. I added a bit of sway to my hips too, just to be a united front.

Once we were inside, bombarded with air conditioning and the drone of countless conversations, the string quartet near the dance floor playing something gentle and slow, Dean's weight fell on me. Not completely, but I suddenly needed to wrap an arm around his waist just to keep him from folding over.

"Are you sure you're all right?" he asked somewhat breathlessly. We cut through the crowd, ignoring anyone who called his name, and headed straight for the huge entryway with golden ivy crawling up its sides. I opened and closed my mouth a few times, lost for words, and nodded.

"I... Fine, I'm fine." The look on his face was so sincere that it *hurt*. "Bit shaken up, but it'll pass."

"Did he hurt you, sweetheart?"

"*No.*" I stopped us just beyond the arched doorway, shaking my head when one of the resort staff in a crisp red jacket strolled toward us, perhaps thinking we needed assistance. The guy did a one-eighty back to the noise of the gala without a word. Out here, everything seemed much starker, the corridor empty and bright in comparison to the ballroom. Each step echoed, and I pulled Dean off to the side, just behind some enormous Etruscan-inspired vase— Dean had been a little dorky about its history when we'd arrived.

He seemed to have no problem with me manhandling

him, and when I had him up against the wall, he sucked in a sharp breath, blinking rapidly, dazed.

"Sir?" I gently pried the champagne bottle from his hand. Had he intended for us to drink it on the terrace—or maybe put it to other uses? Clearing my throat, flushed, I clutched it to my chest with one hand and squeezed his arm with the other. "Are *you* okay? That—was really intense." I pressed my lips together briefly, hesitating, and then just decided, screw it: he wasn't my client anymore. "I'm really proud of you for, you know, everything you said back there. Really proud."

He swept a hand through his hair, his chest rising and falling slower now. "Thank you, sweetheart. I appreciate that."

"Of course." It was a big step: confronting the brother who, for all intents and purposes, had been emotionally abusing him since they were kids. When Dean had told me the airplane story, about how his fear of flying stemmed from Richard torturing him—well, I *should* have broken the jerk's nose.

Dean's gaze dropped to the champagne bottle. "Wish I'd opened that already."

"I could try—"

"Let's save it," he murmured, catching my hand when it went for the gold foil. "We'll celebrate back home. Because that—what I said—it was…"

I grinned, eyebrows twitching up. "Intense?"

"Liberating." Dean pushed off the wall and drew me to him. While I didn't need to support him anymore as we slowly meandered down the empty hallway—I could have. Arm curled around my waist, Dean let out a laugh, the abrupt sound bouncing off the walls, and shook his head.

"Everything I said back there—it's what I've wanted to say to him for years."

"Well, he deserved it."

Dean stopped suddenly, then swooped down and dipped me into a sharp kiss that had me moaning. Aching. Panting. Gripping his lapels, I chased after him when he pulled away, desperate for more—for his mouth on mine, his tongue thrust between parted lips, the threat of teeth ever-present.

"Let's get out of here," he whispered thickly. Heat flashed in my belly, gathering between my thighs, and I nodded.

"Yes, *sir*."

HOUSE RULE #8

Belle will not hesitate. She will trust that Sir acts with her best interests in mind.

12

BELLE & DEAN

Sunday, March 31st

The sea was calm today.

After a whirlwind two months for Dean and me, the sparkling blue lapped at the shore gently, easily. Not a great day for surfers, sure, but my goodness, was it ever beautiful. I couldn't take my eyes off it—at least, when they were open, anyway. When they weren't squeezed shut, the exquisite combination of pain and pleasure wreaking havoc across my body. Darkness and the sea. Both tranquil. Both a welcome sight.

If Dean hadn't offered me my collars, my mood today would have been vastly different. As the pink leather dug into my throat, I couldn't help but imagine how I would have looked at the sea today instead—if I hadn't been wearing my collar. My branding. My security blanket. My queen-maker. My tell to the world that I belonged to the man brandishing the flogger.

I would have been miserable. I would have looked at the sea, at the gently rippling blue, at the glitter of sunlight, and hated it. Hated that it was so calm, when inside me there would have been chaos. A swirling maelstrom of misery. I'd glare at it, all the while wishing time could slow, just for a day or two. Wishing one second was one minute—that one day was one year.

Wishing that I wouldn't have to leave him.

But he had said something. He had made a move. He had taken a chance, a risk—played Russian roulette with his heart. Dean had made me his, and so, today, I could look at the water and smile.

Well, smile as best I could—gagged.

Tomorrow we'd be boarding Dean's private jet once more. Two new people would climb those steps and buckle themselves in. Two individuals who had changed, in my opinion, for the better.

But we would still play our games.

Dean had two new ones to pass the time between Saint Thomas and New York. He'd been rather tight-lipped about it—and I couldn't wait.

Unfortunately, that hadn't been the only thing he had been tight-lipped about. After his run-in with Richard at the gala, after what he'd said, Dean had spent yesterday afternoon on a video call with his dad. Although he had left the office smiling when all was said and done, I still didn't know exactly what they had talked about. Dean had explained that he wouldn't be working with his family anymore, but the details beyond that were a mystery.

As far as I was concerned, they could stay a mystery until he was ready to talk. All that mattered to me was that he was okay.

And from the way he'd ridden me into the night, using my hair like reins, full of mocking smiles and denied orgasms—Dean had seemed okay.

Time would tell. He had seemed okay when we returned from the gala, shared the bottle of champagne between us, then made love on the beach until sunrise. But then he had gone quiet until his video conference. Even now, a day later, I still braced for the fallout. This was his family. This was his life. This wasn't fantasy anymore.

Well—*this* was fantasy.

The flogger cracked across my ass, mercilessly, and I yelped, squirming in place.

This, the trip's crowning glory, our grand finale, was pure, unadulterated, filthy fantasy—for both of us.

As pain bloomed, the blow warming my skin, I looked back to the sea again. So calm and peaceful—it belied the journey ahead. Sure, we were in love. While Candace would still get her cut of this arrangement, Elysium was out of the picture, and then what? Dean and I had talked about the fact that we were in a bubble here, that *this* paradise wasn't real life. As soon as we stepped onto the tarmac in New York, we were going to have to figure it out: our relationship, our dynamic, our professional futures. Nerves plagued me. Excitement burned me.

But fear...

Wearing my collar, there was no fear.

It might be a bumpy road, but I couldn't wait for the ride. I wasn't scared of it anymore—the unknown future.

Forget the first rule of escorting.

No. *Fuck* the first rule of escorting. I had fallen in love with my client. No more limbo. Now—now my life could take off like it was always supposed to.

Another ruthless crack of the flogger, the pain sharpening, the heat intensifying, blazing across my ass, my thighs. I wriggled in place, forearms tense, knees aching, and tried to move forward—but I was stuck. Dean had seen to that when he attached a leash to my pink leather collar and wrapped it around a tree trunk. I had expected that. He had walked me around on my hands and knees like a dog, naked, leash and collar and everything. I just hadn't expected the *second* leash.

It also attached to my collar—and tied around a palm on the other side of the trail. The towering twins that marked the end of the path from Dean's house down to the beach—he had tied me between them, the leather leashes taut, no give. I couldn't crawl away even if I wanted to.

I didn't want to, of course. But that flogger—I yelped, the sound muffled by my pink bit gag, when the tassels smacked across both cheeks, merciless and cruel. My sex clenched, an intense fire crackling in my core, radiating across every inch of me. I burned with pain, yet I dripped with pleasure, my pussy swollen and slick, need coating my forcefully parted thighs. Each gentle gust of wind was pure *torture*, but no more torturous than the squish of Dean's footsteps across the sand. *Squish. Squish. Squish.* I didn't dare look over my shoulder, because I wasn't sure I could take his mocking smile, his sinful gaze, his body taut and glistening, even here, beneath the canopy's flickering shade.

I wasn't sure I could look at him and not come.

The sea was better. Safer. It—

"*Ahhh...*" My hands dug deeper into the sand, toes doing the same, when he slipped two fingers into me—slowly, as if testing me. My cheeks stung painfully when he tsked, the admonishment paired with a dark chuckle.

"Oh, kitten, you're so wet." Dean pumped once, twice, my sex clinging to him as if to trap him, *make* him give me what I so desperately needed. I could practically feel his gaze drifting lazily across his handiwork—my red skin, my engorged lips. I could taste his smirk in every word he spoke. "Your cunt is positively *dripping*. Tell me, kitten, is it the flogger that's getting you off? Or is it this, how you're bound up tight, on your hands and knees—like a pretty present? Hmm?"

I bit down hard on the gag, drool dribbling over my lower lip and down my chin. Dean's fingers milked a strangled moan out of me in response; he already knew the answer. I was wet for him, for what he was doing to me, for the way he tied me in place. For the pain. For what I *knew* would be earth-shattering pleasure.

And for the journey between the two.

Birds twittered somewhere far away. Another sweeping gust of wind barreled along the path, rustling the trees, the shrubs. Not only did the breeze torment my exposed sex, kiss my flogged flesh—but, occasionally, it rustled the delicate gold chain dangling between my clamped nipples. I closed my eyes, tensing, as the wind did Dean's sordid work for him. While thin and delicate enough to snap with one pull, the chain tugged ever so gently at the clamps. Flickers of sharp, intense pain bolted through my breasts, not as powerful as my first encounter with the clamps—I had gotten used to it, to that very specific, awful, delicious sort of discomfort.

The bratty side of me wanted to reach up and remove them—or, at the very least, open them, just for a brief reprieve—but I couldn't.

While the leashes held me in place, clipped to my collar, the spreader bar between my ankles made it impossible to escape. And the cuffs around my wrists, attached by thin silver chains to that spreader bar, limited my mobility even *more*. Stuck on all fours. Spread open. Trapped, right here, right where my Dom wanted me.

His fingers slipped out of me quickly, as though his

clinical investigation of my wetness was complete. My body sagged slightly, the pleasure of him stroking my inner walls dissipating. Yet my clit pulsed, desperate for attention.

Had we done something like this the first week, my arms would have trembled, my shoulders ached from the exertion of holding this pose. I'd grown stronger—in more ways than one. I could take it. I could take *him*.

Hopefully. We hadn't discussed this scene in detail. It was supposed to be the *walk Belle like a dog and take her from behind* fantasy, but it had evolved into something so much more. Something wicked and wonderful, something so wrong that it was *beyond* right—

Crack. Crack. I straightened with a cry, eyes shooting open, breasts bouncing, clamps *clamping*, pain blooming once more, the embers stoked. Tears gathered. Now my thighs quivered, the sole focus of the flogger's wrath this time, and I whimpered as I tried to close them. Tried and failed—all for show, my squirmy, whiny escape attempts. Each failure made my heart race—made me wetter, hopefully made Dean harder.

I tensed, waiting for the next strike, only to hear—a hum. Over the crash of the waves, I heard it again: the buzz of the vibrator. A quick glance over my shoulder confirmed that Dean had switched tools, and I faced forward with a desperate, heady moan. At this point, I almost preferred the flogger.

I take it back. I take it back—my clit doesn't *need any attention*—

"Ahh!" I jumped as soon as the bulbous vibrating head of the wand pressed up to my swollen little bud. Squirming, wriggling, I did my best, but somehow Dean managed to keep up with the inch or two I danced out of reach. He pressed harder, massaging me in slow, steady circles. My head yearned to drop, to bury itself in the sand, but the leashes kept me upright. Pleasure surged, pounding through my system, picking up where Dean's fingers had left off. He had been edging me for what felt like *hours*. Dragging me to excruciating highs, only to stop with a chuckle, spank me, and bring the flogger back into play.

It was *torture*, but I wasn't allowed to come anyway. Not at all. Not until he gave me permission. If I asked before that, Dean had promised he'd deny me. No matter how hard I cried, begged, pleaded with the gag in my mouth, tears streaming—he would tell me no.

My hips jerked, even as I fought the spasms, even as I tried to arch away from the vibration. Heat pulsed through every limb, coming and going in waves. Sweat dripped down my face, gathered in the dip of my lower back. Couldn't he see how good I was being? How much I was fighting it? Didn't I deserve a little reward?

I exhaled shakily through my nostrils when Dean removed the wand from my clit—only to press it to the flat metal base of the stainless-steel plug currently occupying my ass. It was the smallest of the trio Dean had on hand, but my *god* did I ever feel stuffed.

"*No!*" My protest turned high-pitched fast, dragged out and strangled as the vibrations hummed through the plug, tickling something inside that shot electric jolts of pleasure straight to my clit. I lurched forward, the sensation too much, too overwhelming. The jarring movement jostled my clamped nipples, pain intermingling with the fog of pleasure, and my collar tightened, a stark reminder that I wasn't going anywhere.

"Ah, ah, ah," Dean chided, the hum stopping as tears rolled down my cheeks. He then patted my pussy, hand cupped, each light smack sounding wet as I tried to arch out of reach. The final tap was the hardest. "You'll take what I give you, naughty kitten."

Groaning, I added a slight bend to my arms, then shuddered when he stroked my folds, smearing my wetness down to my still-stinging inner thighs.

We had been at this forever with no end in sight. When Dean had first showed me the box of toys he'd brought on our little walk, I'd been excited. After all, we had played this game before, but with the riding crop. Smack, smack, smack, then, between my thighs, the vibrator, which I'd eagerly ridden, my arms strung up above my head. Only then, he had let me come whenever I wanted, so long as I asked first. That game had gone on forever, too, but at least I'd been allowed to climax.

Now, thinking back to the treasure trove of Dean's toys and restraints sitting somewhere behind me, I was starting to have regrets about agreeing so keenly when I didn't know what my Dom had in mind. This could, quite literally, go on for hours. Maybe he would take me for another walk, stretch my limbs, but then he could easily tie me back up between the two trees to start all over again. Pain. Pleasure. A climax denied. Pain. Pleasure. Repeat.

Oh, who was I kidding?

I loved it.

Hated the teasing, the denial, but loved the pain, the pleasure, the way Dean spoke to me. The two warring emotions were equal in every way, and then there was me, trapped in the middle, torn—desperate for it to finally end, yet thrilled at the thought that it could last all day.

Squish, squish, squish—his feet across the sand. Out of the corner of my eye, I watched him step over the leash. Then, slowly, walking like a god among men, he strolled around and squatted in front of me. When we had first come out here, Dean had worn a pair of black swim trunks. Now—nothing, his cock an iron shaft, sticking straight up from between his muscular thighs. His excitement glinted off the thick head; I swallowed hard, imagining my tongue sweeping across it, tasting his faintly salty essence.

His sage-green gaze drifted over my face, his head tipped to the side, then down to my breasts. I knew better than to bow my back, to try to tuck them out of sight. If he planned to tug on the golden chain, then there was nothing I could do to stop him.

Dean smiled, a hint of the mocking sort, a hint of the dangerous sort.

"Look at you..." He brushed his thumb across my lower lip, my chin, smearing my saliva down my neck. "You're a mess, kitten."

I blinked my watery eyes up at him, silently agreeing—silently thanking him for the state I was in, the state he put me in.

"I have another gift for you when we get back to New York." Dean grasped my cheeks, squishing them together, forcing them up against the pink silicon gag between my lips. "It's similar to this collar. Pink. Leather. Pretty, just like my Belle. But the ring in the center is much larger—and it'll keep that little mouth of yours open while I fuck it." My eyes widened slightly as he leaned in and nipped at the tip of my nose, *just* missing, teeth snapping together. "Would you like that, sweetheart? Something to keep your mouth open wide, so I can use it as long as I want?"

The thought made my stomach somersault pleasurably. I moaned and nodded as best I could, my gaze imploring. Dean held me a moment longer, stroking himself with his free hand, and then gave my cheek two gentle pats.

"Good girl. So *good* for your sir."

His growl had me aching—and I hated to see him go. *Squish, squish, squish*—his feet across the sand. Dean stepped over the leash, trailing a finger along my body as he went, until there was nothing.

Nothing—for so long that my heart hurt, that I was tempted to turn back and look for him, but frightened he'd be gone. My heart thundered. My teeth sank into the gag. My toes curled. I waited.

Then, just as I was about to stomp my feet and emit a *very* bratty squeal, the whispery tail of the flogger caressed me. It drifted up the cleft of my thighs, then up, up, between my pleasantly warm, pleasantly sore cheeks. Its touch was gentle, reverent—like the sea. Soothing. I looked to the great wide blue again, to the glittering sunlight and crashing whitecaps. The combination stilled me, centered me, gave me focus. I could do this. I could fight the desire to *shatter* into a thousand pieces every time he touched me. I could conquer the burn.

The flogger's tassels blanketed my shoulders, then trickled down my back, eliciting a storm of goosebumps despite the heat. As soon as they crested the curve of my backside, I closed my eyes and dragged in a deep breath before the inevitable—*crack*.

My right cheek.

Crack.

My left.

Crack-crack.

Both.

I screamed, clenching around the steel plug in my ass, little waves of pleasure rippling through me amidst all that fire. My collar, the leashes attached to it, held firm when I faltered, and I lifted my chin, eyes to the sea.

Bound on all fours, forcefully spread open, gagged, clamped, plugged—I still stood tall.

My Belle looked so beautiful right now.

A magnificent vision. Utterly divine.

And after all that had happened in the last forty-eight hours, I *needed* her beauty, her strength, her endurance. I needed her for support, for balance. After all, my life was changing—from here on out, nothing would ever be the same.

I wasn't sure where my bravery had come from at the gala. Perhaps it was seeing my brother put his fucking hands on the woman I loved—*that* was the straw that broke the camel's back, even if that time should have come long ago. Our relationship should have disintegrated the night I returned home and found Richard burning my paintings with his friends—that should have been it. Instead, I went on for years, biting my tongue for the sake of peace in the family, for the sake of our mum, our sister, who both loved us unconditionally.

But no more. Seeing Belle so distraught, her words bouncing around my skull...

That's psychopathic.

Your dad and your brother are taking advantage of that. They're taking advantage of you.

Dean, you are a fixer. You're a caregiver and a problem-solver. You're happy making other people happy.

I'd had enough. I'd finally said what needed to be said, and while it had knocked the wind right out of me, I had no regrets. No more would I work myself to the bone, sit at that desk and *bleed* for our empire, when neither Richard nor our father appreciated the fact that I had been killing myself. Nor would I do all the work while my brother swanned about at parties, taking all the credit. I needed more self-respect, and the gorgeous creature bound at my feet had reminded me of that.

So, I had scheduled a video conference call with my father's assistant yesterday afternoon. Naturally, I received an earful. It didn't surprise me that Richard had toddled off to daddy, whingeing about what a horrible little brother I'd been, that I wasn't willing to be his indentured servant anymore. My father had tried to talk me into it. When that hadn't worked, he had brought up the information he had on me—information that Richard had acquired, apparently, a year ago, through some PI in New York, back when he'd decided he was done with rehab and wanted to return to the job he had left in tatters seven years ago.

I hadn't yielded.

I remained unbowed. I'd smiled, calling my father's bluff. Tell the investors. Tell our staff. Tell the world. Those who had worked for me all these years knew what sort of person I was—I knew that now. I also had no qualms in finding a reputable entertainment rag to sit down with for an interview, alongside Belle if she so chose, to dispel any of the nastier rumors that were bound to arise.

My father, as I'd started to suspect, hadn't wanted to deal with the fallout.

In the end, I'd agreed to sell him my shares in the Donahue empire. The paperwork was already underway, and my legal team, my accounts manager, *my* CFO would handle the details. By the time I returned to New York, it would be done. All I'd have to do was sign on the dotted line.

My time working with family had come and gone, and I

had no interest in going back. Initially I'd planned to sell to investors, infuse the business with some new blood, but my father wanted to be the majority shareholder over Richard —we three had been equals before, but not where it counted. I had no idea what he planned to do with that majority, nor did I care.

At the end of the call, my father had seemed to understand, albeit begrudgingly, my list of grievances. He'd still offered some snide little comment about how I'd put my own happiness over the empire's well-being, but I'd let it go. I had no interest in fighting with him anymore. I would be civil at family gatherings, for the sake of Mum and Adelaide, but as far as I was concerned, I had nothing left to say to either my father or my brother.

Maybe in time, years down the line. Maybe when I had my first child, my father's first grandchild, we would find a way to mend what had been slowly destroyed over the years.

It wasn't ideal, wasn't a happy solution, but for now, I could make do. I could spend the final day of this vacation with Belle, outside of my own head, family tensions forgotten—and really just enjoy myself.

Flogger in hand, I stood admiring the scarlet flush across her ass and thighs, her cunt dripping. She was utter perfection like this. Even if I removed the leashes, she wouldn't get very far with her wrists chained to the spreader bar, though I would certainly love to watch her try. With a determined furrow in her brow, she'd scoot down to the beach to avoid the flogger's lash, a few inches at a time, while I meandered along after her. Escape was futile—just the way I liked it.

Smirking, I rained down another five-count of lashes, alternating between her thighs, her ass, and her feet. My restrained submissive squealed, pounding the tops of her feet in protest, the movement wiggling her ass, crowned with a gleaming steel butt plug, and jiggling her breasts, her nipples pinched between relentless clamps, connected with gold. I loved it, every torturous second—almost as much as I loved her.

Tossing the flogger back into the small metallic box of toys, I grabbed the vibrator again and clicked the button on the bottom. The wand whirred to life, and Belle's cunt tightened as I approached, her hips bucking forward to avoid me. Crouching behind her, I gave her ass two reprimanding slaps, one for each side, and then stroked the humming head between her folds. Belle jerked in place, whining, toes digging into the sand, then *squealing* so shrill, so loud, that she frightened a pair of birds from a nearby palm. I grinned, feeling particularly ruthless on our last day, and rotated the butt plug in slow, lazy circles by its base as I worked her clit with the wand.

Her entire body trembled, almost violently now, as she fought her climax. I had told her when this all began some forty minutes ago that I wouldn't let her come, no matter how sweetly she begged. If she *did* climax, and there was no way she could hide it from me anymore, I'd told her I'd fuck that pretty ass of hers with the handle of the flogger.

I wouldn't, of course. The lubricated steel plug was enough in that hole for today; but my threat seemed to have worked. She had held off for so long, her body coated in the evidence of her restraint.

Meanwhile, there was so much blood in my cock that it was a miracle I could see straight, never mind torment my submissive so beautifully. This was our most intense play session so far—but by no means would it be our last. I could have dragged it on for the next hour, pummeling her with the flogger, torturing her with the vibrator, until she was nothing but a dribbling, weeping wreck.

But I was mindful of the heat, of the strain on her body —of the fact that if I didn't fuck her soon, I might explode.

The day was young. Our flight wasn't until tomorrow morning. I could have her as many times as I wanted in the next ten hours, and I planned to make good use of the time.

"What do you think, Belle?" I asked, easing up on the vibrator so she could focus on my voice. "Shall I fuck you now? Do you think you've earned it?" I paused, grinning at the way she moaned over her shoulder at me, cheeks tearstained and lovely. I pursed my lips, nodding as though I spoke the language of sub-moans fluently. "Is that so? Are you sure? Does my pretty little submissive *deserve* my cock?"

Her eyes widened as her head bobbed up and down. Well, rather sure of herself, wasn't she? I pressed the vibrator to the flat base of the plug, enjoying the way her entire body tightened.

"Yes, I agree," I mused, my tone casual, distracted—like I wasn't dying to fuck her ten ways from Sunday. "I suppose you've done rather well, earned a bit of cock in your cunt. I think you've even earned the right to come."

But she could only climax if I was balls deep inside of her. I removed the vibrator, and with it the temptation to break the second she had permission. Belle sagged, her body begging to go limp, but the leashes attached to her collar forced her to stay upright. As I tossed the wand back into my box, I entertained the idea of tasting her, of licking her through orgasm after orgasm, *then* fucking her to my heart's content.

But I couldn't wait. I craved her tight pussy, needed to feel it ripple, *dance* along my shaft as she came.

The sand parted beneath me as I settled on my knees,

one hand on her hip, the other pumping two fingers in and out of her slick channel, rubbing against the teardrop-shaped plug in her ass. She bucked, half fighting, half grinding down for more, and I looped my arm around her waist and dragged her back into me. The leashes protested, their leather wincing taut as they held her in place. Her collar would dig in, merciless, constricting her windpipe. What I would have given to be able to see her face—her wide, watery eyes, her lips plumped up around the gag.

Our playroom back home was going to need mirrors—a lot of mirrors.

When she keened, a telltale sign that she was so *fucking* close, I withdrew my fingers, quickly replacing them with my cock.

"F*uuuuck.*" I hissed, long and low, as I sank into her, right down to the hilt. I hadn't taken her with her asshole plugged before, and it made her sinfully tight. Shooting stars ripped across the insides of my eyelids as my head fell back, eyes shut, mouth open. Her cunt convulsed around me, welcoming me home. For a few moments, a high-pitched whine singing between my ears drowned out the rest of the world. The crashing waves. Belle's moans. A creature of lust, I basked in the grasp of her wet heat, perfectly still—until she started rocking back against me.

My eyes opened. I smirked, watching for a few moments as her red ass ground back, trying to find her own pleasure. Bratty little thing. I smacked her twice, just for the fun of it. Leaned down and flicked each nipple, too, just to hear her scream—just to remind her who was in charge.

Then, grasping her firmly with both hands, fingers digging into her hips, I fucked her properly. Slamming into her, hard and fast, wishing I had tied a belt around her waist this time as well; I had so enjoyed having something proper to hold onto that night on the beach.

I pounded her through her first climax some fifteen seconds later, relishing every detail of her writhing figure. The way she shook, trembled, flailed. The way she fought her restraints, squealing and screaming and babbling incoherently against her gag. She was a woman possessed.

And I took that as a compliment.

I fucked her into another orgasm shortly after, my teeth gritted, my hips relentless as I leaned to the side to watch her clamped tits bounce. The pain would sharpen the pleasure, make it headier, make it burn so much brighter. I dug in, shortening my strokes, ramping up the intensity. Our symphony drowned out Ixora—the waves, the birds, the palm fronds, all silenced by Belle's cries, my grunts, and our bodies pounding together.

My climax took me by surprise. It had been building for some time, but the explosion happened so suddenly, so viscerally, that I choked and doubled over. Hips shuddering. Skin prickling. Jaw clenched as I spilled into her. My toes, my fingers—I couldn't feel any of them. I was just this limp, useless being at the end of an insatiable cock, and the temptation to collapse on top of her until I caught my breath was overwhelming.

Maybe next time—when I had her this tied up, this restricted, somewhere with air-conditioning and a dozen mirrors so I could take her in as I came down from the high.

Now, however, I forced myself to move. While I blanketed her, I did my best to keep my weight off her. The nipple clamps went first. They needed to be carefully removed, not the kind you could just rip off without doing serious damage.

I had the other kind too, mind you, and I intended to use

them very soon. Yanking them off *killed*, but then the pleasant afterburn of blood rushing back into place— speaking from personal experience, it was rather exhilarating.

Belle uttered a strangled cry as I removed each of the clamps, the second one sharper, shriller, than the first. Grinning, I tossed the golden clamps and chain aside, then undid her gag. It plopped unceremoniously into the sand, falling heavy, wet, slacked in drool. Kissing Belle's shoulders, her neck, her braid flush against her back, I listened to her suck in a few deep gasps.

"Are you all right, Belle?"

She hummed pleasantly, wearing a sleepy, adorable little smile when she glanced back. "Better than, sir."

"Good girl," I rumbled, then kissed her shoulder as I slowly started to regain feeling across the rest of my body. "I love you."

"I love you too, sir." She reached for me, and we pressed our foreheads together for a moment, catching our breath. When I retreated, straightening up on my knees, cock still buried inside her delicious cunt, she nibbled her lower lip for a moment, then giggled. "That was really fun."

My grin went nuclear, stretching into a lovestruck smile that hurt my cheeks. "Yes, it was, wasn't it?"

Just beyond, the midday sun twinkled across the water. I lifted my gaze with a heavy sigh, in need of a shower and a nap.

The sea was calm today.

"You know," I mused, leaning forward again and slowly, subtly, wrapping her braid around my fist, "we still have tonight." I unhooked her leashes, tossing them into the sand as she shivered. "*Hours* of it. How ever will we kill the time?"

Sure, this was our last hurrah, but I intended to make

slow, passionate love to her, without all the extras, at least once before we left Ixora. She would weep with pleasure again before the day was through.

"Tell me," I rasped. She stared down at the sand, her breath slowing, her expression peaceful.

"Tell you what, sir?"

"Tonight, after we've packed our bags, eaten our last supper..." I yanked her head up by her braid, savoring the way panic skittered across her features—panic giving way to desire. It glittered darkly in her royal blues, and suddenly my cock was ready for another round. I dropped down further, brushing my lips against her ear, and my smile turned wicked. "Tell me, after all that... How would you like me to fuck you, sweetheart?"

HOUSE RULE #21: ADDENDUM

Belle and Sir will show how much they love each other—
every day, no exceptions.

EPILOGUE: BELLE

Friday, August 15ᵗʰ

"*B*oth of my girls look so pretty in their collars."

I hoisted up Lily, our six-month-old ragdoll kitten, as Dean strolled toward us. Dapper as ever in a crisp all-black suit, including the bowtie I'd knotted earlier, he was sex on a stick—but I wouldn't be able to have my way with him, or vice versa, until the night was over. Torture.

"We're matching," I said, grinning as I lifted my chin to show off that Lily and I were sporting near-identical collars—only Lily's was faux crystal, virtually indestructible, and mine was Cartier.

"Magnificent. Both of you." Dean's hand fell to my lower back when he leaned in for a kiss, opting for my cheek instead of my lips to spare my efforts. As prone as he was to utterly *ruining* my hair and makeup on our nights out, which usually put us about a half hour behind schedule because we just couldn't help ourselves, it was in poor taste to show up late to your own gallery opening—especially one that was just a short elevator ride away at the base of our new home.

A whole lifetime had passed in the four and a half months since our sensual stint on Ixora Isle. Not only had I stopped working at Elysium permanently, but Dean had sold his shares in the Donahue empire to his father, relocated to New York, and bought us a building. Well, not *us*, per se. Sure, we had the penthouse all to ourselves, but he was in the process of converting the nine floors below into luxury apartments to be sold or rented out sometime in the next two years. While no one wanted to live on a construction site, the lift took us right to our front door, as it would with all the apartments courtesy of the resident's key card, and the walls were *just* soundproofed enough that we barely heard the clamor of drills and hammers, of men shouting back and forth over the din.

Soundproofed enough that none of them could hear me scream.

Dean had fortified our playroom anyway, a special space that came with a locked door and endless toys—endless things for him to bend me over, tie me to, and string me up from. Unlike the red and black private rooms at Elysium, our playroom was pink and gold, with plenty of mirrors, and included a fully stocked mini-fridge for immediate aftercare spoiling. It was my favourite room in the house.

Off-limits, initially, to Lily. We'd only had her a month, but anytime one of us forgot to close the door, there she was, crawling over sex furniture or batting at dangling flogger tassels.

"Are you sure she's going to be okay tonight?" I asked as Dean tickled our kitten's chin. Sporting the classic ragdoll patterns across her silky soft fur, Lily lifted her face obligingly, the end of her tail flicking, then slowly closed her enormous blue eyes. We had spent the whole week getting her accustomed to her little pink leash, which was currently looped twice around my wrist.

"She was fine at the housewarming party." Dean checked her collar—then mine, tightening mine another notch, just enough that I could feel the bite of each diamond. "She loved meeting all the people."

"We didn't have photographers then."

"Well, we'll keep an eye on her," he insisted, stroking a thumb up her tiny kitten nose, massaging between her eyes as Lily purred in my arms, limp and happy, fully living up to her breed's easygoing demeanor. "If she seems distressed, you can bring her upstairs or put her in my office." Sage green darted up to catch and hold my gaze. "All right, sweetheart?"

I smiled, head cocked. "Yes, sir."

Since leaving Ixora, Dean and I had needed to take some time amidst all the big changes in our lives to figure out the kinkier side of our relationship. Did we want to be Dom and sub twenty-four seven? Only in the playroom? When did the house rules apply? How intense did we want to take things?

I now had eight collars in my collection, and I never went anywhere without wearing one. We had eventually agreed to keep the wilder side of our romance in the playroom, though a very light, fluffy, fun Dominant-submissive dynamic filtered into our everyday lives, too. I was only required to call Dean *sir* when we were intimate, but I liked peppering it into regular conversation, just to see the shift in his demeanor.

While I trusted Dean to keep me safe, to act with my best interests in mind, we'd had squabbles like any other couple. Quitting my job, moving in with Dean, meeting his family, him meeting *my* family, trying to decide what the heck I wanted to do professionally as a Real Adult—as much as I loved my new life, it had also been stressful. Luckily for me, being bound spread-eagle, whipped, tormented with a vibrator, and then pounded into oblivion with Dean's hand around my throat was a *great* stress reliever.

What had helped the most for us during the last few months was that, because of our preferred kink, Dean and I knew how to communicate with each other. To be in a successful Dom-sub relationship, you needed to talk about everything, share your limits, your fears, and much of that translated into the rest of our lives, too.

And thank goodness, because if we hadn't been able to talk to each other, if we couldn't sense when the other was upset, stressed, or frustrated, this probably would have fallen apart months ago. I loved him, and Dean loved me, but relationships took *more* than that to succeed. With all that we had done in just four and a half months, all the change, all the professional and personal upheaval, we could have imploded. Any couple could have imploded.

But here we were. Dressed to impress, Dean in all black, me in fitted Renaldi couture, we had survived—and I was one hundred percent confident that we were going to keep surviving, thriving, for years to come. Decades. Just me and my sir.

And Lily, of course—who had fallen asleep, her head slowly dipping down until it face-planted on my palm. I pressed my lips together, smothering a giggle, and Dean appeared to be doing the same. When our eyes met, I cuddled Lily to my chest, and the kitten gave a little mew in protest. Dean, meanwhile, moved in to fix my hair, smoothing it down, adding more of a curl to the waves tumbling down my back. He had offered to bring in a professional for tonight, but I had no qualms in doing my own hair and makeup. All that practice at Elysium meant I could tackle the whole lot in an hour flat when I needed to.

Still, I appreciated him doing last-minute touch-ups, his sage gaze flitting across my appearance—not coldly, but astutely, carefully, his eye for detail surfacing. Naturally, I always preferred his slow, lazy perusal of my figure, where he inspected every inch of me at his leisure, reminding me with something as simple as a *look* that I belonged to him.

And he belonged to me.

When he finished with my hair, his hand smoothed down my back, over the fitted constraints of tonight's dress, and then stopped at my backside. Smirking, he gave it two affectionate taps, then a sharp squeeze, one that made me jump and giggle. My body clenched instinctively around the small butt plug I'd inserted at Dean's request before I got dressed. No panties, of course; we had kept a number of the more fun house rules from Ixora.

"If you're a very good girl tonight," he murmured, tucking my hair over my shoulder reverently, as though not to muss it. His lips brushed against the shell of my ear, his minty-fresh breath making me shiver. "I'll leave this in while I fuck you."

He squeezed my ass again, though I knew that he would have preferred to slide his fingers between my cheeks, maybe even press against the silicon plug's flat base. We both enjoyed the steel plugs for playtime, but this texture allowed the plug to contour to my body. Even though the dress I had chosen for tonight was restrictive, feeling much like a corset that constricted *everything*, the plug's base would remain hidden for the duration of the gallery opening. A little secret, just for Dean and me.

"Can we christen the office?" I murmured, quirking a

suggestive eyebrow as I covered Lily's ears. She reared back out from under my palm, then nibbled on the side of my hand. Dean chided her for me, and I readjusted my hold. The kitten was so good-natured that I could carry her around on my arm like one of those little yappy lapdogs. She enjoyed lounging like a sphinx, surveying her territory, before eventually falling asleep.

Dean scooped up my free hand once our little one had settled, then kissed the top of it. "Of course we can christen the office, sweetheart. Tonight seems rather appropriate..."

"Yay!" I nibbled my lower lip; he certainly *sounded* sweet, but his tone, his eyes, the way he smirked was downright filthy. I had no idea what he had in mind for our first time in his new base of operations at the back of the gallery—but I couldn't *wait*.

My giddy little giggle had Dean's smile sharpening, and, ever the shark, he dragged an open-mouthed kiss up my throat, the hint of teeth making me squirm, then nipped at my earlobe. Heat burned deep within me, and while I'd hoped he might do more, we really didn't have the time. Instead, Dean quickly arranged my hair once more to his liking, then shot me a wink before pushing the gold button next to the chrome elevator doors.

As the lift whirred up to meet us, the nerves that had been on the fringe all day exploded, making my stomach somersault—and not in the fun way. More in the *oh god please let tonight go well* kind of way. Still, amidst all the anxious churning, my excitement managed to poke through, too. I was nervous for Dean, for all the hard work he had put into this place over the last several months, but I was also beyond excited. Dean's New York gallery, the one he had tried to pitch to his parents before they shipped him off to Harvard, had had its soft opening last night for friends and family—and it had gone spectacularly.

Not only were my parents present, along with a bevy of Dean's Manhattanite friends, but his sister and her influential social circle had flown over from Oxford to round out the numbers. Thankfully, I had already met Adelaide the weekend before, so I knew what to expect of the youngest Donahue; we'd had a shopping day on Fifth Avenue, although I had tactfully avoided Candace's boutique, below which sat my former place of employment.

We had spent the day together while Dean worked overtime on getting the gallery ready. Adelaide was somewhat of a spoiled princess, but she was sweet, too, just like her older brother—and nothing like her eldest brother. She'd told me all about her plans to join an interior design firm when she finished with college back in England, and then dropped five grand on clothes in a single shop like it was nothing. Dean's little sis was the exuberant, bubbly, outlandish one of the family, and since I'd had a bit of experience with her, I had been able to warn Mom and Dad about her in advance.

She and her friends had been decently behaved last night, which had been a subdued affair with great appetizers and lots of laughter. Only one reporter had been invited, while the rest would be in attendance for the official opening tonight. My parents would have loved to see the place all dolled up for photos, but Dad had had a veterans' brunch thing back in Portland this morning that he couldn't miss.

Before he'd left, however, he had given Dean the stamp of approval—something he'd said only to me, of course. "Gotta keep the guy on his toes," he whispered conspiratorially, winking as our new building's doorman loaded his luggage into the car Dean had ordered to take him and my mom to the airport.

As we stepped into the elevator, Lily already asleep again in my arms, I knew tonight would be nothing like last night. This wasn't a subdued affair—this was a party. Adelaide and her girlfriends had been pregaming at a rooftop bar just up the street for hours already, and I had a feeling they were going to be the apple of every tabloid reporter's eye. Art critics, movers and shakers in the city's art community, local politicians, and Manhattan's social elite would be making the rounds tonight, made happy by the open bar, the trendy DJ, and the insanely pricey gift bags Dean's assistant had been preparing for months.

"Are you ready for this?" he murmured when the lift came to a gentle stop at the ground floor. I glanced at him, smirking.

"Are *you*?" This was Dean's baby, and I couldn't have been happier for him that it was finally happening. However, from the pinched look on Eliza's face as the elevator doors peeled open, I suspected there still might be a hiccup or two to work through before kickoff time.

"Just a few notes," his assistant said tightly as Dean stepped out. Her asymmetric bob looked especially severe tonight, her hair glossy and her shoes painfully high. She wore navy from head to toe, just like the waitstaff, and when our eyes met, she shot me a frazzled smile before hurling a thousand questions, comments, and concerns at Dean.

As expected, Dean fielded each one deftly. From soothing the DJ's ego to sending one of the lower-level assistants out to stock up on more champagne after a delivery guy had dropped a whole skid full of bottles five minutes ago, my Dom was in his element. Managing a crisis.

Handling the chaos. He thrived here—and I so loved to see him thrive.

While Eliza kept him on his toes for the ten minutes leading up to the doors opening, I had nothing to do but wander around and try not to ogle the guests waiting outside. Servers circulated the line with appetizers, while a pair waited on either side of the gallery doors with glasses of sparkling champagne—what little hadn't been destroyed by the delivery guy, anyway. The makeshift bar just off to the side of the elevators was fully stocked. The press wall would make a great backdrop for guests. The art was up. The DJ had started spinning quietly, getting his groove right before the crowd arrived. The air was electric—I could just feel it crackle and spark as I strolled about, taking it all in.

The space was gorgeous. It doubled as an exclusive entryway for the future residents of Dean's luxury apartments upstairs *and* a stunning gallery worthy to hold his artwork. Naturally, most of the work tonight belonged to local artists, but my favourite wall held three of Dean's impressionist pieces, all reflections of Ixora Isle, all painted after we returned to New York.

It was strange, and wonderful, and uplifting—all his newer work just seemed *brighter*, happier.

While the colour scheme didn't exactly speak to me, the gallery had a neutral enough palate to let the art shine. Pristine white tile as far as the eye could see met off-white walls. The marble accent pieces were flecked with gold and grey, and all the doors—elevator, office, and entry—were a stunning obsidian. Chic. Elegant. Simple. It was a space for those who craved luxury and a haven for artists to bare their souls.

Naturally, I wished Dean's gallery showed more of *his* soul, but I got my way up in our penthouse. When we had met with the interior decorator, a pint-sized beauty recommended by Adelaide, I'd put my foot down: *no* white, black, and grey majority. I wanted colour. I wanted vibrancy. Nothing crazy-bright or clashing—but the space needed to scream *us*. And it did. I had never truly felt at peace in the city until I stepped into our completed penthouse, my hand in Dean's. It was then that I had finally come home.

Unlike a number of the launches we had researched in the last few months, Dean's started on time. At nine o'clock sharp, the doors opened, and in poured the huge line of VIPs. The volume skyrocketed, rousing Lily, but as always, the kitten didn't seem to mind the chaos. She just blinked her big blue eyes up at all the people who beelined for me, eager to talk shop, fashion, and, of course, Lily.

About a half hour in, Dean pulled me away for photos at the press wall. We kept it *very* vanilla, Dean's arm around my shoulders, my waist, his hand on the small of my back. The press seemed more interested in Lily than they did us; as soon as I told them her name, they were calling for *her* instead of Dean and me—all we had to do was stand there and grin like proud parents. Lily, meanwhile, lapped up the attention like she was queen for the night, her fluffy tail flicking ever so slightly, her ears up and alert.

Things took a turn for the silly when Adelaide and her friends jumped in on our photos. Dean's little sister was roughly my height, with one half of her head buzzed, the other covered in coppery curls that rolled down to mid-back. Adelaide and her entourage were a walking ad for Chanel, Gucci, Yves Saint Laurent, and Michael Kors—and they were all beyond buzzed. Still, we got some fun pictures out of it, and I was sure magazines would print those, along with a close-up shot of Lily. Dean and I were just background noise, and we were both *totally* fine with it.

Afterward, as other guests took to the press wall, I left Dean to give interviews with a few columnists. While the gallery was full, completely stocked to the brim with happy, chatting people, there was only one person I wanted to talk to—and she was currently holding a flute of champagne to her ample chest as she perused Dean's wall of masterpieces.

"Penny!"

Looking positively gorgeous in a plum pencil skirt and a sleek white bralette, Penny whirled around, her raven locks stick-straight and swept back with a thin black headband.

"Hey gorgeous girl," she greeted, drawing me into a hug when I launched myself at her. Lily gave a sharp meow of protest, squished between us, and I eased back with a giggle, hoisting her up higher and out of our combined cleavage. Penny's gaze swept over me briefly, and she arched a brow at my collar. "Nice Cartier."

"Thanks." I beamed, touching a finger to Dean's gift. I'd found it sitting on the dining table this morning in my usual spot. "I'm so glad you could make it."

"Of course!" Penny took a quick sip of the sparkling golden liquid. "I wouldn't miss it for anything."

Given it was a work night, I was even more appreciative of Penny making an appearance. She seldom booked a night off from Elysium; in fact, I couldn't remember the last time she *hadn't* worked seven days a week. Unfortunately, me leaving the escorting business in March —all the while refusing Dean's payment at the time, though I folded when he suggested we put it toward buying this building—meant Penny and I had gone from seeing each other nearly every night to only once a week, when we could swing it. Dean and I had visited Elysium as patrons a handful of times in the last few months, but it wasn't the same. I *missed* doing scenes with Penny, even if they were all ridiculous concepts thought up by the production team.

"Love the hair, by the way," she noted, twirling a lock of my rose gold around her finger. "Is it darker?"

"I had it touched up this week," I said with a nod. After I had stopped escorting, I'd also wanted to distance myself from the innocent girl-next-door look the fetish club had cultivated for me. Even though Dean *liked* the look, he was supportive of whatever I chose to do.

"Just not bald," he'd insisted lightly as I scoured the internet for a new hairstyle. "I prefer having something to hold."

Something to hold. Right. I'd snorted back then, not bothering to look up from my phone. More like something to yank back, something to split into reins while he rode me from behind. Of course I wouldn't take that away from him: not when I liked him having something to hold, too. So, I'd kept it long, but the blonde was gone and had been for about three months. I'd had my hairdresser experiment with different shades of rose gold, something different and fun but not so out-there that Dean couldn't introduce me to his mom.

It felt right, the change. I wasn't the girl next door anymore. I wasn't the doe-eyed, pouty-lipped innocent. I was Dean's submissive—and that meant I could be whoever I wanted to be, go wherever the mood took me in the moment. Brat. Kitten. Princess. Slave. Submissive. Lover. Partner. Equal. I was all those things and more.

Besides, I had a feeling that Dean didn't miss the blonde —not from the way he'd pounced on me the second I'd breezed into our penthouse with my new hair.

"My, my, my..." A hand settled on my lower back as a faintly accented, deeply masculine voice rumbled in my ear.

"Fetching creature, you *must* tell me who designed your dress."

I checked my instinct to elbow the guy in the gut when Penny rolled her eyes and smirked. Instead, I adopted my charmed Elysium grin, then peeked over my shoulder and fluttered my lashes. "Why, Monsieur Renaldi, I believe that was *you*."

Dean had told me his fashion god friend and fellow Dom would be in attendance tonight, but I hadn't expected him to be so drop-dead gorgeous. Eyes like the Mediterranean Sea met mine unflinchingly, his smile both charming and sinful as Felix speared a large hand through his mahogany waves. He moved in beside me, his hand abandoning my lower back so it could scoop up Penny's and kiss it.

"Ah, yes, that's why it looks so familiar." He looked me up and down, much in the same way that Penny did with everyone she met, and then nodded. "A vision. A masterpiece."

I motioned down to the perfectly tailored white midi. While the fabric was rigid, it contoured to my body perfectly. "Oh, you mean the dress, right?"

"But of course."

"*Ugh.*" Penny made a gagging sound as Felix's dangerous grin softened into something so openly affectionate that it caught me off guard. My best friend, meanwhile, was too busy snarking at him to notice. Biting back a knowing smile, I busied myself with Lily's collar and pretended not to have seen a thing.

"Now, what are we drinking?" Felix tutted at Penny's champagne glass, impishly, teasingly—like a boy who craved the attention of the most elusive girl in the room. "Champagne? *Mais non*—surely we can find you something more to your rough and tumble tastes, Penelope."

My eyebrows shot up before I could stop them. *No one* called Penny by her full name—not even me. I'd always assumed she wouldn't mind, but her comfort zone was clearly somewhere within the nickname.

Before she could answer, her cheeks pinking, Felix turned his attention elsewhere—right to an approaching Dean, whom he embraced warmly.

"*Félicitations*," he said, the deep, rich timbre of his voice carrying over the crowd, over the music. From there, it was all rapid back and forth in French, too fast for me to catch— not that I was focused on picking out the words. I knew Dean spoke the language fluently, along with Greek and Italian, but had never had the pleasure of hearing him do so.

I bit my lower lip, the fire in my belly flaring again. Yeah. When we christened the office later tonight, he was *absolutely* required to whisper filthy French nothings in my ear while he had his way with me. A shiver shot down my spine just imagining it.

Penny, meanwhile, appeared nonplussed by the pair, her gaze on the nearest of Dean's paintings.

"How many of these works are yours, my friend?" Felix inquired, jumping back into English as he steered Dean into the fold. My Dom chuckled and motioned to the trio in front of us.

"Only these three."

Felix frowned. "So few? You deserve more than a wall."

"The gallery isn't for me." The goal was to eventually showcase talent when the talent otherwise wouldn't be showcased. Dean wanted to bring in art students and those who couldn't afford the price of wall space at galleries around the city. He wanted new, daring, and innovative. He wanted to *make* artists—give them a shot when no one else would.

Felix clapped him hard on the shoulder, then shot me a wink. "So humble, your sir."

My entire face burned as Felix smirked, his gaze dipping down to my collar fleetingly before darting straight to Penny.

Who still wasn't paying him any attention.

Oi.

I smiled indulgently as Dean tucked me under his arm, then kissed Lily's soft little head. Never mind. It wasn't my business. Still, when Penny glanced my way, I lifted a curious eyebrow, then pinned her with a look that said we'd be discussing a certain Frenchman later. Her eyes shot upward in a half roll, and then jumped to Dean.

"Donahue, did I hear there was an open bar at this thing?"

Dean motioned toward the sea of people. "Across the way—just opposite the DJ booth, by the elevator."

Penny swooped in and kissed my cheek, murmuring her congratulations as she wiped the lipstick off, then arched a brow at Felix. "Order me a scotch, visionary."

She shot Dean a smile before sauntering off in her black stilettos, Felix trailing after her wearing the same open affection I'd caught earlier. My eyes narrowed slightly as I watched them go. Oh, yeah. We were *definitely* having a talk sometime very soon about—this. Him. The gorgeous fashion designer positively drooling over her.

As one of the waiters drifted by us, Dean snatched two champagne flutes, then downed half of one and handed it to me. I grinned, taking a little sip myself. While I'd had no problem drinking more than I usually did when we were in the Caribbean, just the two of us, I wasn't a fan of alcohol at public functions, especially ones as important as tonight. Dean could stomach a few glasses of champagne. I, on the other hand, might end up throwing myself in with Adelaide's socialite friends and doing something I'd regret.

Like climbing onto the DJ's stage and groping at the turntables. I pressed my lips together to stifle a giggle as, over Dean's shoulder, I spied Eliza tactfully pulling the girl in the too-short black miniskirt back into the crowd.

"How are you, sweetheart?" Dean murmured, champagne in one hand, Lily's adorable little face in the other. "Are you happy?"

While coddling our kitten, Dean had his Dom stare fixed squarely on me. He asked me that often—was I happy. With him. With the move. With our dynamic. With— everything. And I had the same response each time.

"Yes, sir." I sidled in closer and tipped my head back, not caring that I looked sickeningly in love. "Are you?"

"Very," he rumbled back. Behind him, a cluster of onlookers were slowly making their way over, eyeing Dean curiously, chatting amongst themselves. He was the man of the hour—and as much as I would have liked to, I couldn't hoard him all to myself tonight. Grinning, I nodded in their direction, repositioning Lily on my arm so that Dean's bowtie was no longer within reach of idle kitten paws.

"Your fans await."

His arm smoothed around my lower back, gripping my hip possessively. "Let them wait." Dean kissed my temple and then lifted his glass. "Here's to us, sweetheart."

I nibbled my lower lip for a moment, smiling, and then clinked our glasses together. "To us..."

THE END

Have no fear! You'll be able to briefly catch up with Belle and Dean in PENNY, the second duet of the UNBOWED series, out early 2019. Beyond that, it's time for Penny and Felix's story to be told—and, I promise, you won't want to miss a single filthy word of it. Dean has his kinky fantasies, but playboy Dom Felix Renaldi is another beast entirely.

RULE #2: YOU BELONG TO YOUR SIR.

Penny

I haven't subbed for anyone in ten years—not since The Incident.

Dominating clients has always made me feel safer, even if it isn't what gets me off.

But for a million dollars, I can pretend. I can play the role of fashion god Felix Renaldi's spoiled, pampered kitten.

I'm not that wide-eyed submissive anymore. I've learned to how to protect myself, made myself hard—the Ice Queen of Elysium.

I can and will shield my heart, especially from the one man who makes it race.

Felix

I've known Penny since she was eighteen.

I've watched her blossom into the exquisite creature she is today.

A hustler who bows to no one. A princess with expensive tastes. A brat in need of a firm hand.

An escort who cannot refuse my offer. Four fashion weeks spent as my submissive. New York. Milan. London. Paris. One million dollars. One chance to show her that she can hustle and submit, speak her mind *and* kneel at my feet.

She denies it, but I know what she craves.

And I'm going to give it to her.

I'm going to make her scream.

THANKS FOR READING!

Thank you so much for reading! You are my new favourite person, and I appreciate you taking the time to give a little love to my cuties who kink. Like I said, Belle and Dean will be back for a brief visit in Penny and Felix's story, which will debut spring 2019!

If you enjoyed Belle and Dean's romance and want to support the sexy series, please consider leaving a review at the retailer of your choice, including Goodreads. Reviews help indie authors thrive. I also use reviews as a way to gauge what series to work on next. If contemporary erotic romance with a dash of kink is your thing, let me know!

Best wishes,

Liz

CONNECT WITH LIZ ON SOCIAL MEDIA:

Website

Facebook

Twitter

Goodreads

Tumblr
Pinterest
Instagram

ABOUT THE AUTHOR

Liz is a Canadian author who grew up in the Middle East. She has a degree in Bioarchaeology from Western University, and when she isn't writing about her own snarky characters, she is reading about other people's snarky characters, babying her herb garden, loitering on social media, or taking care of her many animals.

Liz dabbles in both paranormal and contemporary erotic romance. Her paranormals are usually dark and angsty, and her contemporaries are stress-free smutfests, but you'll find both riddled with feels. Most of all, she loves writing realistic characters in fantastical settings.

More from Liz Meldon:

CONTEMPORARY EROTIC ROMANCE

All In Trilogy – Sugar Daddies, Billionaires, and Menages – oh my!

    Finn (#1)

    Cole (#2)

    Skye (#3)

    All In Trilogy: Book Bundle + Bonus Content

Unbowed – standalone erotic romances featuring kink escorts the alpha men who love them

Belle: Part 1
Belle: Part 2
Penny: Part 1 (2019)
Penny: Part 2 (2019)

Unbowed Novels
Belle (#1) – September 2018

Erotic Short Shorts – an Erotic Short Story Series
Happy Hour (2016)
Holiday Hell (2017)
Bliss (2018)

PARANORMAL ROMANCE

The Hunt – a Demon Romance
Predator (#1)
Prey *(#2)*
Stalker *(#3)*
Killer *(#4)*
The Hunt: Book Bundle #1
The Hunt: Book Bundle #2
The Hunt: The Complete Edition
The Uprising
The Fall

Dark Days – a Vampire/Wolf Shifter Romance
Semester One (December 2018)
Semester Two (January 2019)

Lovers and Liars: Immortal Wars – a fantasy and paranormal romance series about the old world gods going to war

Court of the Phantom Queen (2017) – Book #1 (fantasy romance, novella)

Apollo's Priestess (2017) – Book #2 (shifter paranormal romance, novella)

To the North (TBD) – Book #3 (fantasy romance, novella)

Games We Play – a **(Vampire/Hunter) Duology**

The Fool (2015) – Prologue

The King (2016) – Book #1

The Queen (TBD) – Book #2